THE COMPLETE WRITINGS OF HENRY WADSWORTH LONGFELLOW

WITH PORTRAITS, ILLUSTRATIONS AND FACSIMILES

IN ELEVEN VOLUMES

VOLUME V

Henry Wadsworth Longfellow

POETICAL WORKS

IN SIX VOLUMES

V

CHRISTUS : A MYSTERY

WILDSIDE PRESS

www.wildsidepress.com

CONTENTS

CHRISTUS: A MYSTERY

    INTRODUCTORY NOTE 3

    INTROITUS 21

PART I. THE DIVINE TRAGEDY

    THE FIRST PASSOVER

        I. VOX CLAMANTIS 29

        II. MOUNT QUARANTANIA 33

        III. THE MARRIAGE IN CANA . . . 36

        IV. IN THE CORNFIELDS 42

        V. NAZARETH 46

        VI. THE SEA OF GALILEE 49

        VII. THE DEMONIAC OF GADARA . . 53

        VIII. TALITHA CUMI 58

        IX. THE TOWER OF MAGDALA . . 60

        X. THE HOUSE OF SIMON THE PHARISEE . 63

    THE SECOND PASSOVER

        I. BEFORE THE GATES OF MACHÆRUS . 67

        II. HEROD'S BANQUET-HALL . . . 69

        III. UNDER THE WALLS OF MACHÆRUS . 74

        IV. NICODEMUS AT NIGHT 77

        V. BLIND BARTIMEUS 81

        VI. JACOB'S WELL 85

        VII. THE COASTS OF CÆSAREA PHILIPPI . 90

        VIII. THE YOUNG RULER 97

        IX. AT BETHANY 100

        X. BORN BLIND 102

        XI. SIMON MAGUS AND HELEN OF TYRE . 107

CONTENTS

THE THIRD PASSOVER

    I. THE ENTRY INTO JERUSALEM . . 114

    II. SOLOMON'S PORCH 118

    III. LORD, IS IT I? 124

    IV. THE GARDEN OF GETHSEMANE . . 127

    V. THE PALACE OF CAIAPHAS . . . 130

    VI. PONTIUS PILATE 136

    VII. BARABBAS IN PRISON . . . 138

    VIII. ECCE HOMO 141

    IX. ACELDAMA 145

    X. THE THREE CROSSES 147

    XI. THE TWO MARYS 150

    XII. THE SEA OF GALILEE 152

EPILOGUE

    SYMBOLUM APOSTOLORUM 158

FIRST INTERLUDE

    THE ABBOT JOACHIM 160

PART II. THE GOLDEN LEGEND

    PROLOGUE

    THE SPIRE OF STRASBURG CATHEDRAL . 169

    I. THE CASTLE OF VAUTSBERG ON THE RHINE 173

    COURTYARD OF THE CASTLE . . . 186

    II. A FARM IN THE ODENWALD . . . 192

    A ROOM IN THE FARM-HOUSE . . . 201

    ELSIE'S CHAMBER 208

    THE CHAMBER OF GOTTLIEB AND URSULA . 209

    A VILLAGE CHURCH 215

    A ROOM IN THE FARM-HOUSE . . . 227

    IN THE GARDEN 228

    III. A STREET IN STRASBURG 230

    SQUARE IN FRONT OF THE CATHEDRAL . 238

    IN THE CATHEDRAL 242

CONTENTS

THE NATIVITY: A MIRACLE-PLAY

INTROITUS. 245

    I. HEAVEN 245

    II. MARY AT THE WELL 247

    III. THE ANGELS OF THE SEVEN PLANETS 248

    IV. THE WISE MEN OF THE EAST . . 251

    V. THE FLIGHT INTO EGYPT . . . 252

    VI. THE SLAUGHTER OF THE INNOCENTS . 255

    VII. JESUS AT PLAY WITH HIS SCHOOL-

        MATES 257

    VIII. THE VILLAGE SCHOOL 259

    IX. CROWNED WITH FLOWERS . . . 261

EPILOGUE 263

IV. THE ROAD TO HIRSCHAU 263

    THE CONVENT OF HIRSCHAU IN THE

      BLACK FOREST 266

    THE SCRIPTORIUM 271

    THE CLOISTERS 274

    THE CHAPEL 279

    THE REFECTORY 282

    THE NEIGHBORING NUNNERY . . . 293

V. A COVERED BRIDGE AT LUCERNE . . 301

    THE DEVIL'S BRIDGE 305

    THE SAINT GOTHARD PASS 308

    AT THE FOOT OF THE ALPS . . . 310

    THE INN AT GENOA 316

    AT SEA 319

VI. THE SCHOOL OF SALERNO 322

    THE FARM-HOUSE IN THE ODENWALD . 334

    THE CASTLE OF VAUTSBERG ON THE RHINE 340

EPILOGUE

    THE TWO RECORDING ANGELS ASCENDING 344

CONTENTS

SECOND INTERLUDE

    MARTIN LUTHER 347

PART III. THE NEW ENGLAND TRAGEDIES

    JOHN ENDICOTT

        PROLOGUE 357

        ACT I. 359

        ACT II. 372

        ACT III. 391

        ACT IV. 413

        ACT V. 432

    GILES COREY OF THE SALEM FARMS

        PROLOGUE 447

        ACT I. 449

        ACT II. 464

        ACT III. 482

        ACT IV. 499

        ACT V. 515

        FINALE 525

        SAINT JOHN 525

NOTES 529

LIST OF ILLUSTRATIONS

HENRY W. LONGFELLOW IN 1876   Frontispiece

From a painting by Ernest W. Longfellow
in the possession of the family

THE DIVINE TRAGEDY

HABAKKUK, ISAIAH, AND JONAH
         John S. Sargent   22

From the original mural painting in the
Boston Public Library

CHRIST AND NICODEMUS   *John LaFarge*   78

From the original mural painting in
Trinity Church, Boston

CHRIST AND MARY MAGDALENE
         John LaFarge   152

From the original mural painting in
St. Thomas's Church, New York City

THE GOLDEN LEGEND

"TOUCH THE GOBLET NO MORE"
         Arthur I. Keller   186

"BELIEVE NOT WHAT SHE SAYS
FOR SHE IS MAD"   *Arthur I. Keller*   334

THE NEW ENGLAND TRAGEDIES

"AND YE SHALL BE ACCURSED
FOREVERMORE"   *Fred C. Yohn*   404

"I HEAR THE INWARD CALLING
OF THE SPIRIT"
         Fred C. Yohn   430

CHRISTUS: A MYSTERY

INTRODUCTORY NOTE

THERE is no one of Mr. Longfellow's writings which may be said to have so dominated his literary life as that which is included under the title of " Christus." The study of Dante and the translation of the "Divina Commedia" subtended a wider arc in time, but from the nature of things the interpretation of a great work was subordinate to the development of a theme which was interior to the poet's thought and emotion. Yet even in point of time, that which elapsed between the first conception of " Christus " and its final accomplishment was scarcely less than that which extended from the day when Mr. Longfellow opened Dante to the end of his life, — for so long did he live in companionship with the great seer. There is an entry in his journal, under date of November 8, 1841, which indicates how intensely and how comprehensively the conception of "Christus" possessed him at the outset.

" This evening it has come into my mind to undertake a long and elaborate poem by the holy name of CHRIST; the theme of which would be the various aspects of Christendom in the Apostolic, Middle, and Modern Ages.

" And the swete smoke of the odorous incense whych came of the wholsome and fervent desyres of them that had fayth ascended up before God, out of the aungel's hande. — BALE, ' Image,' part i."

It was not till 1873 that the work as it now stands was published; and during those thirty-two years, which represent almost the whole of Mr. Longfellow's productive period, the subject of the trilogy seems never to have been long absent from his mind. The theme in its majesty was a flame by night and a pillar of cloud by day, which led his mind in all its onward movement, and he esteemed the work which he had undertaken as the really great work of his life. His religious nature was profoundly moved by it, and the degree of doubt which attended every step of his progress marked the height of the endeavor which he put forth.

There was nothing violent or eccentric in this sudden resolution. The entry in his journal, his biographer states, is the only one for that year, but his correspondence and the dates of his poems indicate clearly enough that the course of his mental and spiritual life was flowing in a direction which made this resolve a most natural and at the same time inspiring expression of his personality. He had been singing those psalms of life, triumphant, sympathetic, aspiring, which showed how strong a hold the ethical principle had of him; he had been steeping his soul in

Dante ; he had been moved by the tender ec-
clesiasticism of " The Children of the Lord's
Supper," and in recording a passage in the life
of Christ had fancied himself a monk of the
Middle Ages ; while the whole tenor of his life
and thought had shown how strong a personal
apprehension he had of the divine in humanity.

The summer following this decision Mr.
Longfellow spent at Marienberg on the Rhine,
and the frequent reminder which he had there
of mediævalism may have helped to formulate
his purpose. In his note-book he jotted down
this outline :

" Christus, a dramatic poem, in three parts :
    Part First. The Times of Christ (Hope).
    Part Second. The Middle Ages (Faith).
    Part Third. The Present (Charity)."

The words in parentheses, his biographer ex-
plains, are in pencil and were probably added
later.

The first indication of actual work upon the
subject does not appear until the end of 1849,
when he seems to have decided to take up first
the second division. He had dismissed his volume of poems, " The Seaside and the Fireside,"
" another stone rolled over the hill-top ! " and
proceeded in his diary, November 19 : " Now
I long to try a loftier strain, the sublimer Song
whose broken melodies have for so many years
breathed through my soul in the better hours

of life, and which I trust and believe will ere long unite themselves into a symphony not all unworthy the sublime theme, but furnishing 'some equivalent expression for the trouble and wrath of life, for its sorrow and its mystery.'" On December 10th, he wrote : "A bleak and dismal day. Wrote in the morning ' The Challenge of Thor ' as Prologue or ' Introitus ' to the second part of ' Christus.' " This he laid aside, taking it up again ten years later, when he proposed to write the " Saga of King Olaf." It is probable that he had in mind the opposition of northern paganism to the Christianity of sacerdotalism, and the supremacy of the latter. But the theme of the drama was constantly before him in one shape or another. In his diary, under date of January 10, 1850, he records : " In the evening, pondered and meditated upon sundry scenes of ' Christus.' In such meditation one tastes the delight of the poetic vision, without the pain of putting it into words." The scheme of his first venture had evidently been more or less determined upon, for a few weeks later he notes : " February 28. And so ends the winter and the vacation. Not quite satisfactorily to me. Yet something I have done. Some half dozen scenes or more are written of ' The Golden Legend,' which is Part Second of ' Christus ; ' and the whole is much clearer in my mind as to handling, division, and the form and pressure of the several parts." It is to be noted that already in 1839 there had crossed his mind the notion of writing a drama based upon the legend of " Der Arme Heinrich," and that he had perceived the value of Elsie. " I have a heroine," he says, " as sweet as Imogen, could I but paint her so."

In April he had begun to be thoroughly absorbed in his work and sighed over an increase of his college duties. " And so ' The Golden Legend ' waits," he regretfully says again when recording a day of interruptions. His progress from this time till the completion of his work may be gathered in a measure from successive entries in his diary.

" August 10, 1850. Wrote a few lines in ' The Golden Legend.' Something I add nearly every day. Slowly it goes on; *eppur si muove!* and that is something for this lazy weather.

" September 8. In the evening, wrote a passage on the Virgin, in ' The Golden Legend,' which is nearly finished.

" November 16. We did not go to town to-day, but enjoyed it at home. I wrote the first part of the last scene of ' The Golden Legend,' — the Scholastic at the gates of the School of Salerno.

" November 27. Worked a little on the ' Legend.'

" November 29. Wrote letters, and a few lines in the ' Legend.' I hope to finish it before the year closes, — and should certainly do so, but for my lectures.

"December 7. More snow. C. triumphant with his sled; and I with mine, namely, my poem, 'The Golden Legend,' which is drawing to a close. Ah! if I had but time to work on it!

"December 20. Finished the 'Epilogue' of 'The Golden Legend.' Only one intermediate scene and part of another remain to be done.

"January 16, 1851. Copied some parts of 'The Golden Legend.' Oh for a pair of eyes to work with!

"March 6. A soft brown mist fills the air. I have a leisure day, and shall give the first hours of it to the Monk Felix, which will find a place in 'The Golden Legend.' The poem is now fairly finished, and wants only a touch here and there. This is Part Second of 'Christus.' And the question is, shall it be published now?

"May 8. I have some proof-sheets of 'The Golden Legend' from the printers. When a thing gets into type, one first fairly sees it as it is.

"June 4. Going on slowly with stereotyping 'The Golden Legend.' It brings it out clearer to see it in print; the mazes of manuscript are obscure and perplexing. I still work a good deal upon it.

"August 7. The lazy days lag onward. I cannot write. Fields comes out to dine. I show him 'The Golden Legend,' and tell him to announce it,— which he is eager to do. For my part I have lost all enthusiasm about it. Probably it will fail.

"October 8. 'The Golden Legend' creeps slowly through the press. There are still a few pages toward the end to be retouched, and I am in no mood for it.

"November 3. I have added a new scene to ' The Golden Legend,' — the Prince and Elsie at the Castle. Not long; just a little point of light after so much gloom and shadow of death.

"December 31. In poetry this has not been a productive year with me. I have only revised ' The Golden Legend' and written one or two scenes in it and one or two lyrics. I hope that next year will see more accomplished."

When this last entry was made the book had been published and had immediately met with a hearty welcome. The author gave no intimation of the relation which the work held to a larger plan. He had taken for the core of his poem the story of " Der Arme Heinrich " as told by Hartmann von der Aue, a minnesinger of the twelfth century, to be found in Mailáth's " Altdeutsche Gedichte," published in Stuttgart, in 1809, and it was not till after the book was issued that he caught sight of Jacobus de Voragine's " Legenda Aurea." His own account of his work may be read in brief in a letter which he wrote to an English correspondent at this time. " I am glad to know," he says, " that you find something to like in ' The Golden Legend.' I have endeavored to show in it, among other things, that through the darkness and corruption of the Middle Ages ran a bright, deep stream of Faith, strong enough for all the exigencies of life and death.

In order to do this, I had to introduce some portion of this darkness and corruption as a background. I am sure you will be glad to know that the monk's sermon is not wholly of my own invention. The worst passage in it is from a sermon of Fra Gabriella Barletta, an Italian preacher of the fifteenth century. The Miracle Play is founded on the Apocryphal Gospels of James and the Infancy of Christ. Both this and the sermon show how sacred themes were handled in ' the days of long ago.' "

It is a strong illustration of the importance which Mr. Longfellow attached to " The Golden Legend " as a portion of a larger, more inclusive work, that we find him regretting, while his book was in full tide of success, that he had not taken a theme more fit to his purpose which had been chosen by another poet. " We stayed at home," he writes, April 2, 1852, " reading ' The Saint's Tragedy,' the story of St. Elizabeth of Hungary, put into dramatic form with great power. I wish I had hit upon this theme for my ' Golden Legend,' the mediæval part of my Trilogy. It is nobler and more characteristic than my obscure legend. Strange, that while I was writing a dramatic poem illustrating the Middle Ages, Kingsley should have been doing the same, and that we should have chosen precisely the same period, about 1230. His poem was published first, but I never saw it, or a review of it, till two days ago." Whether or not Mr. Longfellow would have wrought at the other theme with any more satisfaction to himself, " The Golden Legend " has taken its place as a faithful exponent of the phase of Christianity which it described. " Longfellow," says a competent authority,[1] " in his ' Golden Legend ' has entered more closely into the temper of the monk, for good and for evil, than ever yet theological writer or historian, though they may have given their life's labor to the analysis."

" Christus " was, however, pressing upon the poet's mind; the completion of the second division only made him more desirous of fulfilling the noble theme. " The Golden Legend " had been published a few weeks when he wrote in his diary one Sunday : " December 28, 1851. The weather, which has been intensely cold, suddenly changes to rain; and avalanches of snow thunder from the college-roofs all sermon-time. A grand accompaniment to Mr. Ellis, who was preaching about the old prophets, — an excellent discourse. Ah me! how many things there are to meditate upon in this great world! And all this meditation, — of what avail is it, if it does not end in some action? The great theme of my poem haunts me ever; but I cannot bring it into act."

[1] John Ruskin : *Modern Painters*, vol. v. chap. xx.

It was nearly a score of years before another number of the Trilogy was ready, though it is probable that Mr. Longfellow was in the neighborhood of "The New England Trage- dies" when he was diverted for the time by the attractive theme of "The Courtship of Miles Standish." As far back as 1839 he had thought of a drama on Cotton Mather. It is curious that he should have mentioned that and a drama on "the old poetic legend of 'Der Arme Heinrich'" in the same sentence as possible themes, a couple of years before the conception of "Christus" came to him. In the spring of 1856 he was contemplating a tragedy which should take in the Puritans and the Quakers, and preparing for it by looking over books on the two sects, "particularly," he says, "Besse's 'Sufferings of the Quakers,'— a strange record of violent persecution for merest trifles." He notes on April 2d of that year: "Wrote a scene in my new drama, 'The Old Colony,' just to break ground," and a month later: "May 1. At home all day pondering the New England Tragedy, and writing notes and bits of scenes." He was still experimenting on it in July and in November, but then he seems to have made a new start and to have begun "The Courtship of Miles Standish" as a drama, although immediately after an entry indicating this new start, he writes: "December 9. Got at the college library Bishop's 'New England Judged,' — a vindication of the Quakers. Not so good as Besse. December 10. Went to town. For the first time in my life looked in at the library of the N. E. Historical Society; and took out Norton's 'Heart of New England Rent,' — a justification of the Puritans against the Quakers." From these books he jotted down for use characteristic phrases. An interesting illustration of the manner in which the poet was wont to avail himself of the most human means for his purpose is in the record of August 17, 1857. "Go in the morning to hear a Quakeress from England, Priscilla Green, speak in the church. She spoke with a sweet voice and very clear enunciation; very deliberately, and breaking now and then into a rhythmic chant, in which the voice seemed floating up and down on wings. I was much interested, and could have listened an hour longer. It was a very great pleasure to me to hear such a musical voice."

On the 27th of August, 1857, he had finished the first rough draft of " Wenlock Christison," and later resumed his " Miles Standish " as an idyl. For a while this poem excluded the tragedy, but he took up the latter when the "Courtship" was completed and began a revision. On the 17th of August, 1858, he notes : " The morning, as usual, worm-eaten with the writing of letters. I am now going to try a scene in 'Wenlock Christison.' I write accordingly scene second of act first. Just as I finish the bells ring noon. There is a distant booming of cannon. F. comes in and says, 'The Queen's message has arrived by the Atlantic cable.'" "Dec. 13. I have been at work on 'Wenlock Christison,' moulding and shaping it."

It was ten years after this that "The New England Tragedies" emerged from the printing office. Ten copies at first were printed to guard against accident to the manuscript copy, as the author was about leaving home for a considerable absence in Europe. In October of the same year, 1868, the book was published simultaneously in Boston and London. It would seem as if this whole division of the Trilogy caused the poet great doubt, and that he held back from publication out of distrust of his work. He makes but little reference to it in his diary, recording once that he read a portion to Mr. Fields, who received it rather coldly. In this case, more emphatically than in the case of "The Golden Legend," the relation of the part to the whole was uppermost in the poet's mind. It may be that he originally intended to wait until he could write the first part before publishing the third, but finally gave out the modern portion, as before, with no intimation of its place in a larger plan. But "The New England Trage-

dies" had no such intrinsic attractiveness as
"The Golden Legend," and in absence of any
explanation of the author's ulterior design was
taken on its own ground with comparative indif-
ference. The title of "Wenlock Christison"
given to the former of the two tragedies was
changed, when the book was published, to "John
Endicott." Mr. Longfellow's biographer states:
"The third part of this Trilogy did not altogether satisfy him, and with reason, as representing the modern phase of Christianity. 'The
New England Tragedies' may not have been
originally written for this use; at least it has
the aspect of an afterthought. And his journal
mentions a projected third drama, the scene to
be laid among the Moravians of Bethlehem, by
which he hopes to be 'able to harmonize the
discord of "The New England Tragedies," and
thus give a not unfitting close to the work.'
This, however, was not written." [1]

However this may be, it is most probable
that Mr. Longfellow finally regarded the "Tragedies" as satisfying the requirements of the
Trilogy, and was thenceforth impelled by an
increased desire to complete his task by the pre-
paration of the first and most difficult number.
In the latter part of 1870 he began to make
essays in it, and early in January, 1871, he
writes in his diary: "The subject of 'The

[1] *Life of Henry Wadsworth Longfellow*, ii. 458.

Divine Tragedy' has taken entire possession of me. All day pondering upon and arranging it." On the 8th of January he records that during the past week he has written five scenes. Further entries, in their chronological order, give a glimpse of his progress in the work and his attitude toward it.

" January 13, 1871. Wrote ' Gamaliel the Scribe,' and part of the ' Porch of Solomon.' [After this each day's entry records the writing a scene, sometimes two.]

" January 27. Wrote ' The Three Crosses ' and ' The Two Maries,' and now ' The Divine Tragedy ' is finished in its first shape, and needs only revision and perhaps amplification, here and there.

" February 8. Began the second Interlude, ' Luther in the Wartburg,' to come after ' The Golden Legend.'

" February 9. Read in ' Luther's Life ' by Michelet, and his ' Table Talk.' Translated ' Ein feste Burg.'

" February 12. Began ' St. John ' to serve as prologue to the third part of ' Christus.'

" February 13. Wrote ' At Bethany ' for ' The Divine Tragedy ; ' a very short scene, but it would be no better for being longer.

" September 25. Begin the printing of the ' Tragedy.'

" October 29. Read over proofs of the Interludes and Finales, and am doubtful and perplexed.

" November 16. All the last week perplexed and busy with final correction of the ' Tragedy.' Two editions of the 'Tragedy' will be published at the same time. I never had so many doubts and hesitations about any book as about this.

"December 12. 'The Divine Tragedy' is published to-day."

"The Divine Tragedy" was published thus at the close of 1871, and in the autumn of 1872 "Christus" appeared as a complete work. It is an interesting illustration of the place which the work held in his mind that he should now incorporate in it the poem of "Blind Bartimeus," which, when he wrote it, he was disposed to refer in imagination to a monk of the Middle Ages. The design of the poet now stood revealed, and it is worth while to note the effect upon another poet who was peculiarly susceptible, through his own studies and modes of thought, of appreciating a purpose long sustained and brought to an artistic completeness. Bayard Taylor was made aware of the plan of "Christus" when "The Divine Tragedy" was published, and, with Mr. Longfellow's consent, he printed in the "New York Tribune" an interesting conspectus of the whole work, supplying the connecting links by means of the interludes and finale sent him in advance by the author. Mr. Taylor took a very strong interest in the matter, for he had an ardent desire for the supremacy of poetry. "Since Milton's 'Paradise Regained,'" he wrote to Mr. Whitelaw Reid, "and Klopstock's 'Messiah' the theme has not been handled by any competent poet; so Longfellow's work is both a daring venture and (probably) a success all the higher for the failure of others."

The first edition of " The Golden Legend " was without notes. Afterward, upon occasion of an English illustrated edition, Mr. Longfellow was urged to provide notes, and in his diary, under date of September 18, 1853, he refers to a conversation with Charles Sumner. " We talked about notes to 'The Golden Legend.' Every work of art should explain itself. All prefaces, and the like, are like labels coming out of the mouths of people in pictures. Such is my view of the matter." Nevertheless, he yielded, and prepared notes which subsequently appeared in American editions and are given at the end of this volume, but he provided none for the other dramas of the Trilogy, and they are indeed scarcely necessary, though " The New England Tragedies" permit illustration of this character.

CHRISTUS: A MYSTERY

CHRISTUS: A MYSTERY

INTROITUS

The ANGEL (*bearing the* PROPHET HABAKKUK *through the air*)

PROPHET

WHY dost thou bear me aloft
O Angel of God, on thy pinions
O'er realms and dominions?
Softly I float as a cloud
In air, for thy right hand upholds me,
Thy garment enfolds me!

ANGEL

Lo! as I passed on my way
In the harvest-field I beheld thee,
When no man compelled thee,
Bearing with thine own hands
This food to the famishing reapers,
A flock without keepers!

The fragrant sheaves of the wheat
Made the air above them sweet;
Sweeter and more divine
Was the scent of the scattered grain,
That the reaper's hand let fall
To be gathered again
By the hand of the gleaner!

21

CHRISTUS: A MYSTERY

Sweetest, divinest of all,
Was the humble deed of thine,
And the meekness of thy demeanor!

PROPHET

Angel of Light,
I cannot gainsay thee,
I can but obey thee!

ANGEL

Beautiful was it in the Lord's sight,
To behold his Prophet
Feeding those that toil,
The tillers of the soil.
But why should the reapers eat of it
And not the Prophet of Zion
In the den of the lion?
The Prophet should feed the Prophet!
Therefore I thee have uplifted,
And bear thee aloft by the hair
Of thy head, like a cloud that is drifted
Through the vast unknown of the air!

Five days hath the Prophet been lying
In Babylon, in the den
Of the lions, death-defying,
Defying hunger and thirst;
But the worst
Is the mockery of men!
Alas! how full of fear
Is the fate of Prophet and Seer!
Forevermore, forevermore,

JONAH · ISAIAH · HABAKKVK ·

INTROITUS

It shall be as it hath been heretofore;
The age in which they live
Will not forgive
The splendor of the everlasting light,
That makes their foreheads bright,
Nor the sublime
Forerunning of their time!

PROPHET

Oh tell me, for thou knowest,
Wherefore and by what grace,
Have I, who am least and lowest,
Been chosen to this place,
To this exalted part?

ANGEL

Because thou art
The Struggler; and from thy youth
Thy humble and patient life
Hath been a strife
And battle for the Truth;
Nor hast thou paused nor halted,
Nor ever in thy pride
Turned from the poor aside,
But with deed and word and pen
Hast served thy fellow-men;
Therefore art thou exalted!

PROPHET

By thine arrow's light
Thou goest onward through the night,
And by the clear

CHRISTUS: A MYSTERY

Sheen of thy glittering spear!
When will our journey end?

ANGEL

Lo, it is ended!
Yon silver gleam
Is the Euphrates' stream.
Let us descend
Into the city splendid,
Into the City of Gold!

PROPHET

Behold!
As if the stars had fallen from their places
Into the firmament below,
The streets, the gardens, and the vacant
   spaces
With light are all aglow;
And hark!
As we draw near,
What sound is it I hear
Ascending through the dark?

ANGEL

The tumultuous noise of the nations,
Their rejoicings and lamentations,
The pleadings of their prayer,
The groans of their despair,
The cry of their imprecations,
Their wrath, their love, their hate!

INTROITUS

PROPHET

Surely the world doth wait
The coming of its Redeemer !

ANGEL

Awake from thy sleep, O dreamer !
The hour is near, though late ;
Awake ! write the vision sublime,
The vision, that is for a time,
Though it tarry, wait ; it is nigh ;
In the end it will speak and not lie.

PART ONE

THE DIVINE TRAGEDY

THE FIRST PASSOVER

I

VOX CLAMANTIS

JOHN THE BAPTIST

Repent! repent! repent!
For the kingdom of God is at hand,
And all the land
Full of the knowledge of the Lord shall be
As the waters cover the sea,
And encircle the continent!

Repent! repent! repent!
For lo, the hour appointed,
The hour so long foretold
By the Prophets of old,
Of the coming of the Anointed,
The Messiah, the Paraclete,
The Desire of the Nations, is nigh!
He shall not strive nor cry,
Nor his voice be heard in the street;
Nor the bruised reed shall He break,
Nor quench the smoking flax;
And many of them that sleep
In the dust of earth shall awake,
On that great and terrible day,
And the wicked shall wail and weep,
And be blown like a smoke away,

And be melted away like wax.
Repent! repent! repent!

O Priest, and Pharisee,
Who hath warned you to flee
From the wrath that is to be?
From the coming anguish and ire?
The axe is laid at the root
Of the trees, and every tree
That bringeth not forth good fruit
Is hewn down and cast into the fire!

Ye Scribes, why come ye hither?
In the hour that is uncertain,
In the day of anguish and trouble,
He that stretcheth the heavens as a curtain
And spreadeth them out as a tent,
Shall blow upon you, and ye shall wither,
And the whirlwind shall take you away as stubble!
Repent! repent! repent!

PRIEST

Who art thou, O man of prayer!
In raiment of camel's hair,
Begirt with leathern thong,
That here in the wilderness,
With a cry as of one in distress,
Preachest unto this throng?
Art thou the Christ?

JOHN

Priest of Jerusalem,

30

In meekness and humbleness,
I deny not, I confess
I am not the Christ!

PRIEST

What shall we say unto them
That sent us here? Reveal
Thy name, and naught conceal!
Art thou Elias?

JOHN

No!

PRIEST

Art thou that Prophet, then,
Of lamentation and woe,
Who, as a symbol and sign
Of impending wrath divine
Upon unbelieving men,
Shattered the vessel of clay
In the Valley of Slaughter?

JOHN

Nay.

I am not he thou namest!

PRIEST

Who art thou, and what is the word
That here thou proclaimest?

JOHN

I am the voice of one

31

CHRISTUS: A MYSTERY

Crying in the wilderness alone:
Prepare ye the way of the Lord;
Make his paths straight
In the land that is desolate!

PRIEST

If thou be not the Christ,
Nor yet Elias, nor he
That, in sign of the things to be,
Shattered the vessel of clay
In the Valley of Slaughter,
Then declare unto us, and say
By what authority now
Baptizest thou?

JOHN

I indeed baptize you with water
Unto repentance; but He,
That cometh after me,
Is mightier than I and higher;
The latchet of whose shoes
I am not worthy to unloose;
He shall baptize you with fire,
And with the Holy Ghost!
Whose fan is in his hand;
He will purge to the uttermost
His floor, and garner his wheat,
But will burn the chaff in the brand
And fire of unquenchable heat!
Repent! repent! repent!

THE DIVINE TRAGEDY

II

MOUNT QUARANTANIA

I

LUCIFER

Not in the lightning's flash, nor in the thunder,
Not in the tempest, nor the cloudy storm,
    Will I array my form;
But part invisible these boughs asunder,
And move and murmur, as the wind upheaves
    And whispers in the leaves.

Not as a terror and a desolation,
Not in my natural shape, inspiring fear
    And dread, will I appear;
But in soft tones of sweetness and persuasion,
A sound as of the fall of mountain streams,
    Or voices heard in dreams.

He sitteth there in silence, worn and wasted
With famine, and uplifts his hollow eyes
    To the unpitying skies;
For forty days and nights he hath not tasted
Of food or drink, his parted lips are pale,
    Surely his strength must fail.

Wherefore dost thou in penitential fasting
Waste and consume the beauty of thy youth?
    Ah, if thou be in truth
The Son of the Unnamed, the Everlasting,

CHRISTUS: A MYSTERY

Command these stones beneath thy feet to be
Changed into bread for thee!

CHRISTUS

'T is written: Man shall not live by bread alone,
But by each word that from God's mouth proceed-
eth!

II

LUCIFER

Too weak, alas! too weak is the temptation
For one whose soul to nobler things aspires
Than sensual desires!
Ah, could I, by some sudden aberration,
Lead and delude to suicidal death
This Christ of Nazareth!

Unto the holy Temple on Moriah,
With its resplendent domes, and manifold
Bright pinnacles of gold,
Where they await thy coming, O Messiah!
Lo, I have brought thee! Let thy glory here
Be manifest and clear.

Reveal thyself by royal act and gesture
Descending with the bright triumphant host
Of all the highermost
Archangels, and about thee as a vesture
The shining clouds, and all thy splendors show
Unto the world below!

THE DIVINE TRAGEDY

Cast thyself down, it is the hour appointed;
And God hath given his angels charge and care
    To keep thee and upbear
Upon their hands his only Son, the Anointed,
Lest he should dash his foot against a stone
    And die, and be unknown.

CHRISTUS

'T is written : Thou shalt not tempt the Lord thy
    God!

III

LUCIFER

I cannot thus delude him to perdition !
But one temptation still remains untried,
    The trial of his pride,
The thirst of power, the fever of ambition !
Surely by these a humble peasant's son
    At last may be undone !

Above the yawning chasms and deep abysses,
Across the headlong torrents, I have brought
    Thy footsteps, swift as thought;
And from the highest of these precipices,
The Kingdoms of the world thine eyes behold,
    Like a great map unrolled.

From far-off Lebanon, with cedars crested,
To where the waters of the Asphalt Lake
    On its white pebbles break,
    And the vast desert, silent, sand-invested,

CHRISTUS: A MYSTERY

These kingdoms all are mine, and thine shall be,
    If thou wilt worship me!

CHRISTUS

Get thee behind me, Satan! thou shalt worship
The Lord thy God; Him only shalt thou serve!

ANGELS MINISTRANT

The sun goes down; the evening shadows lengthen,
The fever and the struggle of the day
    Abate and pass away;
Thine Angels Ministrant, we come to strengthen
And comfort thee, and crown thee with the palm,
    The silence and the calm.

III

THE MARRIAGE IN CANA

THE MUSICIANS

    Rise up, my love, my fair one,
    Rise up, and come away,
    For lo! the winter is past,
    The rain is over and gone,
    The flowers appear on the earth,
The time of the singing of birds is come,
And the voice of the turtle is heard in our land.

THE BRIDEGROOM

Sweetly the minstrels sing the Song of Songs!
My heart runs forward with it, and I say:

THE DIVINE TRAGEDY

Oh set me as a seal upon thine heart,
And set me as a seal upon thine arm;
For love is strong as life, and strong as death,
And cruel as the grave is jealousy!

THE MUSICIANS

I sleep, but my heart awaketh;
'T is the voice of my beloved
Who knocketh, saying: Open to me,
My sister, my love, my dove,
For my head is filled with dew,
My locks with the drops of the night!

THE BRIDE

Ah yes, I sleep, and yet my heart awaketh.
It is the voice of my beloved who knocks.

THE BRIDEGROOM

O beautiful as Rebecca at the fountain,
O beautiful as Ruth among the sheaves!
O fairest among women! O undefiled!
Thou art all fair, my love, there's no spot in
thee!

THE MUSICIANS

My beloved is white and ruddy,
The chiefest among ten thousand;
His locks are black as a raven,
His eyes are the eyes of doves,
Of doves by the rivers of water,
His lips are like unto lilies,
Dropping sweet-smelling myrrh.

CHRISTUS: A MYSTERY

ARCHITRICLINUS

Who is that youth with the dark azure eyes,
And hair, in color like unto the wine,
Parted upon his forehead, and behind
Falling in flowing locks?

PARANYMPHUS

                The Nazarene
Who preacheth to the poor in field and village
The coming of God's Kingdom.

ARCHITRICLINUS

                    How serene
His aspect is! manly yet womanly.

PARANYMPHUS

Most beautiful among the sons of men!
Oft known to weep, but never known to laugh.

ARCHITRICLINUS

And tell me, she with eyes of olive tint,
And skin as fair as wheat, and pale brown hair,
The woman at his side?

PARANYMPHUS

             His mother, Mary.

ARCHITRICLINUS

And the tall figure standing close behind them,
Clad all in white, with face and beard like ashes,
As if he were Elias, the White Witness,

THE DIVINE TRAGEDY

Come from his cave on Carmel to foretell
The end of all things?

PARANYMPHUS

That is Manahem
The Essenian, he who dwells among the palms
Near the Dead Sea.

ARCHITRICLINUS

He who foretold to Herod
He should one day be King?

PARANYMPHUS

The same.

ARCHITRICLINUS

Then why
Doth he come here to sadden with his presence
Our marriage feast, belonging to a sect
Haters of women, and that taste not wine?

THE MUSICIANS

My undefiled is but one,
The only one of her mother,
The choice of her that bare her;
The daughters saw her and blessed her;
The queens and the concubines praised her;
Saying, Lo! who is this
That looketh forth as the morning?

MANAHEM (aside)

The Ruler of the Feast is gazing at me,

39

As if he asked, why is that old man here
Among the revellers ? And thou, the Anointed !
Why art thou here ? I see as in a vision
A figure clothed in purple, crowned with thorns
I see a cross uplifted in the darkness,
And hear a cry of agony, that shall echo
Forever and forever through the world !

ARCHITRICLINUS

Give us more wine. These goblets are all empty.

MARY (*to* CHRISTUS)

They have no wine !

CHRISTUS

   O woman, what have I
To do with thee ? Mine hour is not yet come.

MARY (*to the servants*)

Whatever he shall say to you, that do.

CHRISTUS

Fill up these pots with water.

THE MUSICIANS

 Come, my beloved,
 Let us go forth into the field,
 Let us lodge in the villages ;
 Let us get up early to the vineyards,
 Let us see if the vine flourish,
 Whether the tender grape appear,
 And the pomegranates bud forth.

THE DIVINE TRAGEDY

CHRISTUS

Draw out now
And bear unto the Ruler of the Feast.

MANAHEM (*aside*)

O thou, brought up among the Essenians,
Nurtured in abstinence, taste not the wine!
It is the poison of dragons from the vineyards
Of Sodom, and the taste of death is in it!

ARCHITRICLINUS (*to the* BRIDEGROOM)

All men set forth good wine at the beginning;
And when men have well drunk, that which is worse,
But thou hast kept the good wine until now.

MANAHEM (*aside*)

The things that have been and shall be no more,
The things that are, and that hereafter shall be,
The things that might have been, and yet were not,
The fading twilight of great joys departed,
The daybreak of great truths as yet unrisen,
The intuition and the expectation
Of something, which, when come, is not the same,
But only like its forecast in men's dreams,
The longing, the delay, and the delight,
Sweeter for the delay; youth, hope, love, death,
And disappointment which is also death,
All these make up the sum of human life;
A dream within a dream, a wind at night
Howling across the desert in despair,
Seeking for something lost, it cannot find.
Fate or foreseeing, or whatever name

41

CHRISTUS: A MYSTERY

Men call it, matters not; what is to be
Hath been fore-written in the thought divine
From the beginning. None can hide from it,
But it will find him out; nor run from it,
But it o'ertaketh him! The Lord hath said it.

THE BRIDEGROOM (*to the* BRIDE, *on the balcony*)

When Abraham went with Sarah into Egypt,
The land was all illumined with her beauty;
But thou dost make the very night itself
Brighter than day! Behold, in glad procession,
Crowding the threshold of the sky above us,
The stars come forth to meet thee with their lamps;
And the soft winds, the ambassadors of flowers,
From neighboring gardens and from fields unseen,
Come laden with odors unto thee, my Queen!

THE MUSICIANS

Awake, O north-wind,
And come, thou wind of the South.
Blow, blow upon my garden,
That the spices thereof may flow out.

IV

IN THE CORNFIELDS

PHILIP

Onward through leagues of sun-illumined corn,
As if through parted seas, the pathway runs,
And crowned with sunshine as the Prince of Peace

Walks the beloved Master, leading us,
As Moses led our fathers in old times
Out of the land of bondage! We have found
Him of whom Moses and the Prophets wrote,
Jesus of Nazareth, the Son of Joseph.

NATHANAEL

Can any good come out of Nazareth?
Can this be the Messiah?

PHILIP

Come and see.

NATHANAEL

The summer sun grows hot; I am anhungered.
How cheerily the Sabbath-breaking quail
Pipes in the corn, and bids us to his Feast
Of Wheat Sheaves! How the bearded, ripening ears
Toss in the roofless temple of the air;
As if the unseen hand of some High-Priest
Waved them before Mount Tabor as an altar!
It were no harm, if we should pluck and eat.

PHILIP

How wonderful it is to walk abroad
With the Good Master! Since the miracle
He wrought at Cana, at the marriage feast,
His fame hath gone abroad through all the land,
And when we come to Nazareth, thou shalt see
How his own people will receive their Prophet,
And hail him as Messiah! See, he turns
And looks at thee.

CHRISTUS: A MYSTERY

CHRISTUS

Behold an Israelite
In whom there is no guile.

NATHANAEL

          Whence knowest thou me?

CHRISTUS

Before that Philip called thee, when thou wast
Under the fig-tree, I beheld thee.

NATHANAEL

                  Rabbi!
Thou art the Son of God, thou art the King
Of Israel!

CHRISTUS

          Because I said I saw thee
Under the fig-tree, before Philip called thee,
Believest thou? Thou shalt see greater things.
Hereafter thou shalt see the heavens unclosed,
The angels of God ascending and descending
Upon the Son of Man!

PHARISEES (*passing*)

          Hail, Rabbi!

CHRISTUS

                  Hail!

PHARISEES

Behold how thy disciples do a thing

Which is not lawful on the Sabbath-day,
And thou forbiddest them not!

CHRISTUS

                    Have ye not read
What David did when he anhungered was,
And all they that were with him? How he entered
Into the house of God, and ate the shewbread,
Which was not lawful saving for the priests?
Have ye not read, how on the Sabbath-days
The priests profane the Sabbath in the Temple,
And yet are blameless? But I say to you,
One in this place is greater than the Temple!
And had ye known the meaning of the words,
I will have mercy and not sacrifice,
The guiltless ye would not condemn. The Sabbath
Was made for man, and not man for the Sabbath.
                    Passes on with the disciples.

PHARISEES

This is, alas! some poor demoniac
Wandering about the fields, and uttering
His unintelligible blasphemies
Among the common people, who receive
As prophecies the words they comprehend not!
Deluded folk! The incomprehensible
Alone excites their wonder. There is none
So visionary, or so void of sense,
But he will find a crowd to follow him!

CHRISTUS: A MYSTERY

V

NAZARETH

CHRISTUS (*reading in the Synagogue*)
The Spirit of the Lord God is upon me.
He hath anointed me to preach good tidings
Unto the poor; to heal the broken-hearted;
To comfort those that mourn, and to throw open
The prison doors of captives, and proclaim
The Year Acceptable of the Lord, our God!
He closes the book and sits down.

A PHARISEE

Who is this youth? He hath taken the Teacher's
    seat!
Will he instruct the Elders?

A PRIEST

            Fifty years
Have I been Priest here in the Synagogue,
And never have I seen so young a man
Sit in the Teacher's seat!

CHRISTUS

            Behold, to-day
This scripture is fulfilled. One is appointed
And hath been sent to them that mourn in Zion,
To give them beauty for ashes, and the oil
Of joy for mourning! They shall build again
The old waste places; and again raise up

THE DIVINE TRAGEDY

The former desolations, and repair
The cities that are wasted ! As a bridegroom
Decketh himself with ornaments ; as a bride
Adorneth herself with jewels, so the Lord
Hath clothed me with the robe of righteousness !

A PRIEST

He speaks the Prophet's words ; but with an air
As if himself had been foreshadowed in them !

CHRISTUS

For Zion's sake I will not hold my peace,
And for Jerusalem's sake I will not rest
Until its righteousness be as a brightness,
And its salvation as a lamp that burneth !
Thou shalt be called no longer the Forsaken,
Nor any more thy land, the Desolate.
The Lord hath sworn, by his right hand hath sworn,
And by his arm of strength : I will no more
Give to thine enemies thy corn as meat ;
The sons of strangers shall not drink thy wine.
Go through, go through the gates ! Prepare a way
Unto the people ! Gather out the stones !
Lift up a standard for the people !

A PRIEST

                    Ah !

These are seditious words !

CHRISTUS

                    And they shall call them
The holy people ; the redeemed of God !

And thou, Jerusalem, shalt be called Sought out,
A city not forsaken!

A PHARISEE

Is not this
The carpenter Joseph's son? Is not his mother
Called Mary? and his brethren and his sisters
Are they not with us? Doth he make himself
To be a prophet?

CHRISTUS

No man is a prophet
In his own country, and among his kin.
In his own house no prophet is accepted.
I say to you, in the land of Israel
Were many widows in Elijah's day,
When for three years and more the heavens were shut,
And a great famine was throughout the land;
But unto no one was Elijah sent
Save to Sarepta, to a city of Sidon,
And to a woman there that was a widow.
And many lepers were there in the land
Of Israel, in the time of Eliseus
The Prophet, and yet none of them was cleansed,
Save Naaman the Syrian!

A PRIEST

Say no more!
Thou comest here into our Synagogue
And speakest to the Elders and the Priests,
As if the very mantle of Elijah
Had fallen upon thee! Art thou not ashamed?

THE DIVINE TRAGEDY

A PHARISEE

We want no prophets here! Let him be driven
From Synagogue and city! Let him go
And prophesy to the Samaritans!

AN ELDER

The world is changed. We Elders are as nothing!
We are but yesterdays, that have no part
Or portion in to-day! Dry leaves that rustle,
That make a little sound, and then are dust!

A PHARISEE

A carpenter's apprentice! a mechanic,
Whom we have seen at work here in the town
Day after day; a stripling without learning,
Shall he pretend to unfold the Word of God
To men grown old in study of the Law?

CHRISTUS *is thrust out.*

VI

THE SEA OF GALILEE

PETER *and* ANDREW *mending their nets*

PETER

Never was such a marvellous draught of fishes
Heard of in Galilee! The market-places
Both of Bethsaida and Capernaum
Are full of them! Yet we had toiled all night
And taken nothing, when the Master said:

Launch out into the deep, and cast your nets;
And doing this, we caught such multitudes
Our nets like spiders' webs were snapped asunder,
And with the draught we filled two ships so full
That they began to sink. Then I knelt down
Amazed, and said: O Lord, depart from me,
I am a sinful man. And he made answer:
Simon, fear not; henceforth thou shalt catch men!
What was the meaning of those words?

ANDREW

                              I know not.
But here is Philip, come from Nazareth.
He hath been with the Master. Tell us, Philip,
What tidings dost thou bring?

PHILIP

                          Most wonderful!
As we drew near to Nain, out of the gate
Upon a bier was carried the dead body
Of a young man, his mother's only son,
And she a widow, who with lamentation
Bewailed her loss, and the much people with her;
And when the Master saw her he was filled
With pity; and he said to her: Weep not!
And came and touched the bier, and they that bare it
Stood still; and then he said: Young man, arise!
And he that had been dead sat up, and soon
Began to speak; and he delivered him
Unto his mother. And there came a fear
On all the people, and they glorified
The Lord, and said, rejoicing: A great prophet

Is risen up among us ! and the Lord
Hath visited his people !

PETER

A great prophet ?
Ay, greater than a prophet : greater even
Than John the Baptist !

PHILIP

Yet the Nazarenes
Rejected him.

PETER

The Nazarenes are dogs !
As natural brute beasts, they growl at things
They do not understand ; and they shall perish,
Utterly perish in their own corruption.
The Nazarenes are dogs !

PHILIP

They drave him forth
Out of their Synagogue, out of their city,
And would have cast him down a precipice,
But, passing through the midst of them, he van-
      ished
Out of their hands.

PETER

Wells are they without water,
Clouds carried with a tempest, unto whom
The mist of darkness is reserved forever !

CHRISTUS: A MYSTERY

PHILIP

Behold, he cometh. There is one man with him
I am amazed to see!

ANDREW

What man is that?

PHILIP

Judas Iscariot; he that cometh last,
Girt with a leathern apron. No one knoweth
His history; but the rumor of him is
He had an unclean spirit in his youth.
It hath not left him yet.

CHRISTUS (*passing*)

Come unto me,
All ye that labor and are heavy laden,
And I will give you rest! Come unto me,
And take my yoke upon you and learn of me,
For I am meek, and I am lowly in heart,
And ye shall all find rest unto your souls!

PHILIP

Oh, there is something in that voice that reaches
The innermost recesses of my spirit!
I feel that it might say unto the blind,
Receive your sight! and straightway they would
see!
I feel that it might say unto the dead,
Arise! and they would hear it and obey!
Behold, he beckons to us!

THE DIVINE TRAGEDY

CHRISTUS (*to* PETER *and* ANDREW)
           Follow me!

PETER

Master, I will leave all and follow thee.

VII

THE DEMONIAC OF GADARA

A GADARENE

He hath escaped, hath plucked his chains asunder,
And broken his fetters ; always night and day
Is in the mountains here, and in the tombs,
Crying aloud, and cutting himself with stones,
Exceeding fierce, so that no man can tame him !

THE DEMONIAC (*from above, unseen*)

O Aschmedai ! O Aschmedai, have pity !

A GADARENE

Listen ! It is his voice ! Go warn the people
Just landing from the lake !

THE DEMONIAC

           O Aschmedai !
Thou angel of the bottomless pit, have pity !
It was enough to hurl King Solomon,
On whom be peace ! two hundred leagues away
Into the country, and to make him scullion
In the kitchen of the King of Maschkemen !

Why dost thou hurl me here among these rocks,
And cut me with these stones?

A GADARENE

                He raves and mutters
He knows not what.

THE DEMONIAC (*appearing from a tomb among the rocks*)
          The wild cock Tarnegal
Singeth to me, and bids me to the banquet,
Where all the Jews shall come; for they have slain
Behemoth the great ox, who daily cropped
A thousand hills for food, and at a draught
Drank up the river Jordan, and have slain
The huge Leviathan, and stretched his skin
Upon the high walls of Jerusalem,
And made them shine from one end of the world
Unto the other; and the fowl Barjuchne,
Whose outspread wings eclipse the sun, and make
Midnight at noon o'er all the continents!
And we shall drink the wine of Paradise
From Adam's cellars.

A GADARENE
          O thou unclean spirit!

THE DEMONIAC (*hurling down a stone*)
This is the wonderful Barjuchne's egg,
That fell out of her nest, and broke to pieces
And swept away three hundred cedar-trees,
And threescore villages! — Rabbi Eliezer,
How thou didst sin there in that seaport town

54

When thou hadst carried safe thy chest of silver
Over the seven rivers for her sake!
I too have sinned beyond the reach of pardon.
Ye hills and mountains, pray for mercy on me!
Ye stars and planets, pray for mercy on me!
Ye sun and moon, oh pray for mercy on me!

                    CHRISTUS *and his disciples pass.*

A GADARENE

There is a man here of Decapolis,
Who hath an unclean spirit; so that none
Can pass this way. He lives among the tombs
Up there upon the cliffs, and hurls down stones
On those who pass beneath.

CHRISTUS

                    Come out of him,
Thou unclean spirit!

THE DEMONIAC

             What have I to do
With thee, thou Son of God? Do not torment us.

CHRISTUS

What is thy name?

THE DEMONIAC

             Legion; for we are many.
Cain, the first murderer; and the King Belshazzar,
And Evil Merodach of Babylon,
And Admatha, the death-cloud, prince of Persia;

And Aschmedai, the angel of the pit,
And many other devils. We are Legion.
Send us not forth beyond Decapolis;
Command us not to go into the deep!
There is a herd of swine here in the pastures,
Let us go into them.

CHRISTUS

                    Come out of him,
Thou unclean spirit!

A GADARENE

                    See, how stupefied,
How motionless he stands! He cries no more;
He seems bewildered and in silence stares
As one who, walking in his sleep, awakes
And knows not where he is, and looks about him,
And at his nakedness, and is ashamed.

THE DEMONIAC

Why am I here alone among the tombs?
What have they done to me, that I am naked?
Ah, woe is me!

CHRISTUS

                    Go home unto thy friends
And tell them how great things the Lord hath
        done
For thee, and how He had compassion on thee!

A SWINEHERD (*running*)

The herds! the herds! O most unlucky day!

They were all feeding quiet in the sun,
When suddenly they started, and grew savage
As the wild boars of Tabor, and together
Rushed down a precipice into the sea!
They are all drowned!

PETER

                    Thus righteously are punished
The apostate Jews, that eat the flesh of swine,
And broth of such abominable things!

GREEKS OF GADARA

We sacrifice a sow unto Demeter
At the beginning of harvest, and another
To Dionysus at the vintage-time.
Therefore we prize our herds of swine, and count
          them
Not as unclean, but as things consecrate
To the immortal gods. O great magician,
Depart out of our coasts; let us alone,
We are afraid of thee.

PETER

                    Let us depart;
For they that sanctify and purify
Themselves in gardens, eating flesh of swine,
And the abomination, and the mouse,
Shall be consumed together, saith the Lord!

CHRISTUS: A MYSTERY

VIII

TALITHA CUMI

JAIRUS (*at the feet of* CHRISTUS)

O Master! I entreat thee! I implore thee!
My daughter lieth at the point of death;
I pray thee come and lay thy hands upon her,
And she shall live!

CHRISTUS

Who was it touched my garments?

SIMON PETER

Thou seest the multitude that throng and press
    thee,
And sayest thou, Who touched me? 'T was not I.

CHRISTUS

Some one hath touched my garments; I perceive
That virtue is gone out of me.

A WOMAN

             O Master!
Forgive me! For I said within myself,
If I so much as touch his garment's hem,
I shall be whole.

CHRISTUS

         Be of good comfort, daughter!
Thy faith hath made thee whole. Depart in peace.

THE DIVINE TRAGEDY

A MESSENGER (*from the house*)

Why troublest thou the Master? Hearest thou
    not
The flute-players, and the voices of the women
Singing their lamentation? She is dead!

THE MINSTRELS AND MOURNERS

We have girded ourselves with sackcloth!
We have covered our heads with ashes!
For our young men die, and our maidens
Swoon in the streets of the city;
And into their mother's bosom
They pour out their souls like water!

CHRISTUS (*going in*)

Give place. Why make ye this ado, and weep?
She is not dead, but sleepeth.

THE MOTHER (*from within*)

                         Cruel Death!
To take away from me this tender blossom!
To take away my dove, my lamb, my darling!

THE MINSTRELS AND MOURNERS

He hath led me and brought into darkness,
Like the dead of old in dark places!
He hath bent his bow, and hath set me
Apart as a mark for his arrow!
He hath covered himself with a cloud,
That our prayer should not pass through and
    reach him!

CHRISTUS: A MYSTERY

He stands beside her bed! He takes her hand!
Listen, he speaks to her!

CHRISTUS (*within*)

Maiden, arise!

THE CROWD

See, she obeys his voice! She stirs! She lives!
Her mother holds her folded in her arms!
O miracle of miracles! O marvel!

IX

THE TOWER OF MAGDALA

MARY MAGDALENE

Companionless, unsatisfied, forlorn,
I sit here in this lonely tower, and look
Upon the lake below me, and the hills
That swoon with heat, and see as in a vision
All my past life unroll itself before me.
The princes and the merchants come to me,
Merchants of Tyre and Princes of Damascus,
And pass, and disappear, and are no more;
But leave behind their merchandise and jewels,
Their perfumes, and their gold, and their disgust.
I loathe them, and the very memory of them
Is unto me, as thought of food to one
Cloyed with the luscious figs of Dalmanutha!
What if hereafter, in the long hereafter

THE DIVINE TRAGEDY

Of endless joy or pain, or joy in pain,
It were my punishment to be with them
Grown hideous and decrepit in their sins,
And hear them say: Thou that hast brought us
    here,
Be unto us as thou hast been of old!

I look upon this raiment that I wear,
These silks, and these embroideries, and they seem
Only as cerements wrapped about my limbs!
I look upon these rings thick set with pearls,
And emerald and amethyst and jasper,
And they are burning coals upon my flesh!
This serpent on my wrist becomes alive!
Away, thou viper! and away, ye garlands,
Whose odors bring the swift remembrance back
Of the unhallowed revels in these chambers!
But yesterday,— and yet it seems to me
Something remote, like a pathetic song
Sung long ago by minstrels in the street,—
But yesterday, as from this tower I gazed,
Over the olive and the walnut-trees
Upon the lake and the white ships, and wondered
Whither and whence they steered, and who was in
    them,
A fisher's boat drew near the landing-place
Under the oleanders, and the people
Came up from it, and passed beneath the tower,
Close under me. In front of them, as leader,
Walked one of royal aspect, clothed in white,
Who lifted up his eyes, and looked at me,
And all at once the air seemed filled and living

With a mysterious power, that streamed from him,
And overflowed me with an atmosphere
Of light and love. As one entranced I stood,
And when I woke again, lo! he was gone;
So that I said: Perhaps it is a dream.
But from that very hour the seven demons
That had their habitation in this body
Which men call beautiful, departed from me!

This morning, when the first gleam of the dawn
Made Lebanon a glory in the air,
And all below was darkness, I beheld
An angel, or a spirit glorified,
With wind-tossed garments walking on the lake.
The face I could not see, but I distinguished
The attitude and gesture, and I knew
'T was he that healed me. And the gusty wind
Brought to mine ears a voice, which seemed to
     say:
Be of good cheer! 'T is I! Be not afraid!
And from the darkness, scarcely heard, the answer:
If it be thou, bid me come unto thee
Upon the water! And the voice said: Come!
And then I heard a cry of fear: Lord, save me!
As of a drowning man. And then the voice:
Why didst thou doubt, O thou of little faith!
At this all vanished, and the wind was hushed,
And the great sun came up above the hills,
And the swift-flying vapors hid themselves
In caverns among the rocks! Oh, I must find
     him
And follow him, and be with him forever!

Thou box of alabaster, in whose walls
The souls of flowers lie pent, the precious balm
And spikenard of Arabian farms, the spirits
Of aromatic herbs, ethereal natures
Nursed by the sun and dew, not all unworthy
To bathe his consecrated feet, whose step
Makes every threshold holy that he crosses;
Let us go forth upon our pilgrimage,
Thou and I only! Let us search for him
Until we find him, and pour out our souls
Before his feet, till all that's left of us
Shall be the broken caskets that once held us!

X

THE HOUSE OF SIMON THE PHARISEE

A GUEST (*at table*)

Are ye deceived? Have any of the Rulers
Believed on him? or do they know indeed
This man to be the very Christ? Howbeit
We know whence this man is, but when the
        Christ
Shall come, none knoweth whence he is.

CHRISTUS

Whereunto shall I liken, then, the men
Of this generation? and what are they like?
They are like children sitting in the markets,
And calling unto one another, saying:
We have piped unto you, and ye have not danced;

63

We have mourned unto you, and ye have not
    wept!
This say I unto you, for John the Baptist
Came neither eating bread nor drinking wine;
Ye say he hath a devil. The Son of Man
Eating and drinking cometh, and ye say:
Behold a gluttonous man, and a wine-bibber;
Behold a friend of publicans and sinners!

A GUEST (*aside to* SIMON)

Who is that woman yonder, gliding in
So silently behind him?

SIMON

        It is Mary,
Who dwelleth in the Tower of Magdala.

THE GUEST

See, how she kneels there weeping, and her tears
Fall on his feet; and her long, golden hair
Waves to and fro and wipes them dry again.
And now she kisses them, and from a box
Of alabaster is anointing them
With precious ointment, filling all the house
With its sweet odor!

SIMON (*aside*)

        Oh, this man, forsooth,
Were he indeed a prophet, would have known
Who and what manner of woman this may be
That toucheth him! would know she is a sin-
    ner!

CHRISTUS

Simon, somewhat have I to say to thee.

SIMON

Master, say on.

CHRISTUS

     A certain creditor
Had once two debtors; and the one of them
Owed him five hundred pence; the other, fifty.
They having naught to pay withal, he frankly
Forgave them both. Now tell me which of them
Will love him most?

SIMON

       He, I suppose, to whom
He most forgave.

CHRISTUS

      Yea, thou hast rightly judged.
Seest thou this woman? When thine house I entered,
Thou gavest me no water for my feet,
But she hath washed them with her tears, and wiped
   them
With her own hair. Thou gavest me no kiss;
This woman hath not ceased, since I came in,
To kiss my feet. My head with oil didst thou
Anoint not; but this woman hath anointed
My feet with ointment. Hence I say to thee,
Her sins, which have been many, are forgiven,
For she loved much.

CHRISTUS: A MYSTERY

THE GUESTS

Oh, who, then, is this man
That pardoneth also sins without atonement?

CHRISTUS

Woman, thy faith hath saved thee! Go in peace!

THE SECOND PASSOVER

I

BEFORE THE GATES OF MACHÆRUS

MANAHEM

WELCOME, O wilderness, and welcome, night
And solitude, and ye swift-flying stars
That drift with golden sands the barren heavens,
Welcome once more! The Angels of the Wind
Hasten across the desert to receive me;
And sweeter than men's voices are to me
The voices of these solitudes; the sound
Of unseen rivulets, and the far-off cry
Of bitterns in the reeds of water-pools.
And lo! above me, like the Prophet's arrow
Shot from the eastern window, high in air
The clamorous cranes go singing through the night.
O ye mysterious pilgrims of the air,
Would I had wings that I might follow you!

I look forth from these mountains, and behold
The omnipotent and omnipresent night,
Mysterious as the future and the fate
That hangs o'er all men's lives! I see beneath me
The desert stretching to the Dead Sea shore,
And westward, faint and far away, the glimmer
Of torches on Mount Olivet, announcing
The rising of the Moon of Passover.

CHRISTUS: A MYSTERY

Like a great cross it seems on which suspended,
With head bowed down in agony, I see
A human figure! Hide, O merciful heaven,
The awful apparition from my sight!

And thou, Machærus, lifting high and black
Thy dreadful walls against the rising moon,
Haunted by demons and by apparitions,
Lilith, and Jezerhara, and Bedargon,
How grim thou showest in the uncertain light,
A palace and a prison, where King Herod
Feasts with Herodias, while the Baptist John
Fasts, and consumes his unavailing life!
And in thy courtyard grows the untithed rue,
Huge as the olives of Gethsemane,
And ancient as the terebinth of Hebron,
Coeval with the world. Would that its leaves
Medicinal could purge thee of the demons
That now possess thee, and the cunning fox
That burrows in thy walls, contriving mischief!
                    Music is heard from within.
Angels of God! Sandalphon, thou that weavest
The prayers of men into immortal garlands,
And thou, Metatron, who dost gather up
Their songs, and bear them to the gates of heaven,
Now gather up together in your hands
The prayers that fill this prison, and the songs
That echo from the ceiling of this palace,
And lay them side by side before God's feet!
                    He enters the castle.

THE DIVINE TRAGEDY

II

HEROD'S BANQUET-HALL

MANAHEM

Thou hast sent for me, O King, and I am here.

HEROD

Who art thou?

MANAHEM

Manahem, the Essenian.

HEROD

I recognize thy features, but what mean
These torn and faded garments? On thy road
Have demons crowded thee, and rubbed against
     thee,
And given thee weary knees? A cup of wine!

MANAHEM

The Essenians drink no wine.

HEROD

          What wilt thou, then?

MANAHEM

Nothing.

HEROD

    Not even a cup of water?

MANAHEM

Nothing.

Why hast thou sent for me?

HEROD

Dost thou remember
One day when I, a schoolboy in the streets
Of the great city, met thee on my way
To school, and thou didst say to me : Hereafter
Thou shalt be king?

MANAHEM

Yea, I remember it.

HEROD

Thinking thou didst not know me, I replied :
I am of humble birth; whereat, thou, smiling,
Didst smite me with thy hand, and saidst again :
Thou shalt be king; and let the friendly blows
That Manahem hath given thee on this day
Remind thee of the fickleness of fortune.

MANAHEM

What more?

HEROD

No more.

MANAHEM

Yea, for I said to thee :
It shall be well with thee if thou love justice

And clemency towards thy fellow men.
Hast thou done this, O King?

HEROD

Go, ask my people.

MANAHEM

And then, foreseeing all thy life, I added:
But these thou wilt forget; and at the end
Of life the Lord will punish thee.

HEROD

The end!
When will that come? For this I sent to thee.
How long shall I still reign? Thou dost not answer!
Speak! Shall I reign ten years?

MANAHEM

Thou shalt reign twenty,
Nay, thirty years. I cannot name the end.

HEROD

Thirty? I thank thee, good Essenian!.
This is my birthday, and a happier one
Was never mine. We hold a banquet here.
See, yonder are Herodias and her daughter.

MANAHEM (*aside*)

'T is said that devils sometimes take the shape
Of ministering angels, clothed with air,
That they may be inhabitants of earth,
And lead man to destruction. Such are these.

71

HEROD

Knowest thou John the Baptist?

MANAHEM

                    Yea, I know him;
Who knows him not?

HEROD

                    Know, then, this John the Baptist
Said that it was not lawful I should marry
My brother Philip's wife, and John the Baptist
Is here in prison. In my father's time
Matthias Margaloth was put to death
For tearing the golden eagle from its station
Above the Temple Gate, — a slighter crime
Than John is guilty of. These things are warnings
To intermeddlers not to play with eagles,
Living or dead. I think the Essenians
Are wiser, or more wary, are they not?

MANAHEM

The Essenians do not marry.

HEROD

                    Thou hast given
My words a meaning foreign to my thought.

MANAHEM

Let me go hence, O King!

HEROD

                    Stay yet a while,

And see the daughter of Herodias dance.
Cleopatra of Jerusalem, my mother,
In her best days, was not more beautiful.

Music. THE DAUGHTER OF HERODIAS *dances.*

HEROD

Oh, what was Miriam dancing with her timbrel,
Compared to this one?

MANAHEM (*aside*)

O thou Angel of Death,
Dancing at funerals among the women,
When men bear out the dead! The air is hot
And stifles me! Oh for a breath of air!
Bid me depart, O King!

HEROD

Not yet. Come hither,
Salome, thou enchantress! Ask of me
Whate'er thou wilt; and even unto the half
Of all my kingdom, I will give it thee,
As the Lord liveth!

DAUGHTER OF HERODIAS (*kneeling*)

Give me here the head
Of John the Baptist on this silver charger!

HEROD

Not that, dear child! I dare not; for the people
Regard John as a prophet.

73

CHRISTUS: A MYSTERY

DAUGHTER OF HERODIAS

Thou hast sworn it.

HEROD

For mine oath's sake, then. Send unto the prison;
Let him die quickly. Oh, accursed oath!

MANAHEM

Bid me depart, O King!

HEROD

Good Manahem,
Give me thy hand. I love the Essenians.
He's gone and hears me not! The guests are dumb,
Awaiting the pale face, the silent witness.
The lamps flare; and the curtains of the doorways
Wave to and fro as if a ghost were passing!
Strengthen my heart, red wine of Ascalon!

III

UNDER THE WALLS OF MACHÆRUS

MANAHEM (*rushing out*)

Away from this Palace of sin!
The demons, the terrible powers
Of the air, that haunt its towers
And hide in its water-spouts,
Deafen me with the din
Of their laughter and their shouts
For the crimes that are done within!

Sink back into the earth,
Or vanish into the air,
Thou castle of despair!
Let it all be but a dream
Of the things of monstrous birth,
Of the things that only seem!
White Angel of the Moon,
Onafiel! be my guide
Out of this hateful place
Of sin and death, nor hide
In yon black cloud too soon
Thy pale and tranquil face!

A trumpet is blown from the walls.

Hark! hark! It is the breath
Of the trump of doom and death,
From the battlements overhead
Like a burden of sorrow cast
On the midnight and the blast,
A wailing for the dead,
That the gusts drop and uplift!
O Herod, thy vengeance is swift!
O Herodias, thou hast been
The demon, the evil thing,
That in place of Esther the Queen,
In place of the lawful bride,
Hast lain at night by the side
Of Ahasuerus the king!

The trumpet again.

The Prophet of God is dead!
At a drunken monarch's call,
At a dancing-woman's beck,
They have severed that stubborn neck

75

And into the banquet-hall
Are bearing the ghastly head!

A body is thrown from the tower.

A torch of lurid red
Lights the window with its glow;
And a white mass as of snow
Is hurled into the abyss
Of the black precipice,
That yawns for it below!
O hand of the Most High,
O hand of Adonai!
Bury it, hide it away
From the birds and beasts of prey,
And the eyes of the homicide,
More pitiless than they,
As thou didst bury of yore
The body of him that died
On the mountain of Peor!

Even now I behold a sign,
A threatening of wrath divine,
A watery, wandering star,
Through whose streaming hair, and the white
Unfolding garments of light,
That trail behind it afar,
The constellations shine!
And the whiteness and brightness appear
Like the Angel bearing the Seer
By the hair of his head, in the might
And rush of his vehement flight.
And I listen until I hear
From fathomless depths of the sky

The voice of his prophecy
Sounding louder and more near!

Malediction! malediction!
May the lightnings of heaven fall
On palace and prison wall,
And their desolation be
As the day of fear and affliction,
As the day of anguish and ire,
With the burning and fuel of fire,
In the Valley of the Sea!

IV

NICODEMUS AT NIGHT

NICODEMUS

The streets are silent. The dark houses seem
Like sepulchres, in which the sleepers lie
Wrapped in their shrouds, and for the moment dead.
The lamps are all extinguished; only one
Burns steadily, and from the door its light
Lies like a shining gate across the street.
He waits for me. Ah, should this be at last
The long-expected Christ! I see him there
Sitting alone, deep-buried in his thought,
As if the weight of all the world were resting
Upon him, and thus bowed him down. O Rabbi,
We know thou art a Teacher come from God,
For no man can perform the miracles
Thou dost perform, except the Lord be with him.

CHRISTUS: A MYSTERY

Thou art a prophet, sent here to proclaim
The Kingdom of the Lord. Behold in me
A Ruler of the Jews, who long have waited
The coming of that kingdom. Tell me of it.

CHRISTUS

Verily, verily I say unto thee,
Except a man be born again, he cannot
Behold the Kingdom of God !

NICODEMUS

                              Be born again ?
How can a man be born when he is old ?
Say, can he enter for a second time
Into his mother's womb, and so be born ?

CHRISTUS

Verily I say unto thee, except
A man be born of water and the spirit,
He cannot enter into the Kingdom of God.
For that which of the flesh is born, is flesh;
And that which of the spirit is born, is spirit.

NICODEMUS

We Israelites from the Primeval Man
Adam Ahelion derive our bodies;
Our souls are breathings of the Holy Ghost.
No more than this we know, or need to know.

CHRISTUS

Then marvel not, that I said unto thee
Ye must be born again.

Christ and Nicodemus

THE DIVINE TRAGEDY

NICODEMUS

        The mystery
Of birth and death we cannot comprehend.

CHRISTUS

The wind bloweth where it listeth, and we hear
The sound thereof, but know not whence it cometh,
Nor whither it goeth. So is every one
Born of the spirit!

NICODEMUS (*aside*)

        How can these things be?
He seems to speak of some vague realm of shadows,
Some unsubstantial kingdom of the air!
It is not this the Jews are waiting for,
Nor can this be the Christ, the Son of David,
Who shall deliver us!

CHRISTUS

        Art thou a master
Of Israel, and knowest not these things?
We speak that we do know, and testify
That we have seen, and ye will not receive
Our witness. If I tell you earthly things,
And ye believe not, how shall ye believe,
If I should tell you of things heavenly?
And no man hath ascended up to heaven,
But He alone that first came down from heaven,
Even the Son of Man which is in heaven!

NICODEMUS (*aside*)

This is a dreamer of dreams; a visionary,

CHRISTUS: A MYSTERY

Whose brain is overtasked, until he deems
The unseen world to be a thing substantial,
And this we live in, an unreal vision !
And yet his presence fascinates and fills me
With wonder, and I feel myself exalted
Into a higher region, and become
Myself in part a dreamer of his dreams,
A seer of his visions !

CHRISTUS

And as Moses
Uplifted the serpent in the wilderness,
So must the Son of Man be lifted up ;
That whosoever shall believe in Him
Shall perish not, but have eternal life.
He that believes in Him is not condemned ;
He that believes not, is condemned already.

NICODEMUS (*aside*)

He speaketh like a Prophet of the Lord !

CHRISTUS

This is the condemnation ; that the light
Is come into the world, and men loved darkness
Rather than light, because their deeds are evil !

NICODEMUS (*aside*)

Of me he speaketh ! He reproveth me,
Because I come by night to question him !

CHRISTUS

For every one that doeth evil deeds
80

Hateth the light, nor cometh to the light,
Lest he should be reproved.

NICODEMUS (*aside*)

Alas, how truly
He readeth what is passing in my heart!

CHRISTUS

But he that doeth truth comes to the light,
So that his deeds may be made manifest,
That they are wrought in God.

NICODEMUS

Alas! alas!

V

BLIND BARTIMEUS

BARTIMEUS

Be not impatient, Chilion; it is pleasant
To sit here in the shadow of the walls
Under the palms, and hear the hum of bees,
And rumor of voices passing to and fro,
And drowsy bells of caravans on their way
To Sidon or Damascus. This is still
The City of Palms, and yet the walls thou seest
Are not the old walls, not the walls where Rahab
Hid the two spies, and let them down by cords
Out of the window, when the gates were shut,
And it was dark. Those walls were overthrown

CHRISTUS: A MYSTERY

When Joshua's army shouted, and the priests
Blew with their seven trumpets.

CHILION

When was that?

BARTIMEUS

O my sweet rose of Jericho, I know not.
Hundreds of years ago. And over there
Beyond the river, the great prophet Elijah
Was taken by a whirlwind up to heaven
In chariot of fire, with fiery horses.
That is the plain of Moab; and beyond it
Rise the blue summits of Mount Abarim,
Nebo and Pisgah and Peor, where Moses
Died, whom the Lord knew face to face, and whom
He buried in a valley, and no man
Knows of his sepulchre unto this day.

CHILION

Would thou couldst see these places, as I see them.

BARTIMEUS

I have not seen a glimmer of the light
Since thou wast born. I never saw thy face,
And yet I seem to see it; and one day
Perhaps shall see it; for there is a Prophet
In Galilee, the Messiah, the Son of David,
Who heals the blind, if I could only find him.
I hear the sound of many feet approaching,
And voices, like the murmur of a crowd!
What seest thou?

CHILION

A young man clad in white
Is coming through the gateway, and a crowd
Of people follow.

BARTIMEUS

Can it be the Prophet!
O neighbors, tell me who it is that passes?

ONE OF THE CROWD

Jesus of Nazareth.

BARTIMEUS (*crying*)

O Son of David!
Have mercy on me!

MANY OF THE CROWD

Peace, Blind Bartimeus!
Do not disturb the Master.

BARTIMEUS (*crying more vehemently*)

Son of David,
Have mercy on me!

ONE OF THE CROWD

See, the Master stops.
Be of good comfort; rise, He calleth thee!

BARTIMEUS (*casting away his cloak*)

Chilion! good neighbors! lead me on.

83

CHRISTUS: A MYSTERY

CHRISTUS

What wilt thou
That I should do to thee?

BARTIMEUS

Good Lord! my sight —
That I receive my sight!

CHRISTUS

Receive thy sight!
Thy faith hath made thee whole!

THE CROWD

He sees again!
CHRISTUS *passes on. The crowd gathers round*
BARTIMEUS.

BARTIMEUS

I see again; but sight bewilders me!
Like a remembered dream, familiar things
Come back to me. I see the tender sky
Above me, see the trees, the city walls,
And the old gateway, through whose echoing arch
I groped so many years; and you, my neighbors;
But know you by your friendly voices only.
How beautiful the world is! and how wide!
Oh, I am miles away, if I but look!
Where art thou, Chilion?

CHILION

Father, I am here.

THE DIVINE TRAGEDY

BARTIMEUS

Oh let me gaze upon thy face, dear child!
For I have only seen thee with my hands!
How beautiful thou art! I should have known thee;
Thou hast her eyes whom we shall see hereafter!
O God of Abraham! Elion! Adonai!
Who art thyself a Father, pardon me
If for a moment I have thee postponed
To the affections and the thoughts of earth,
Thee, and the adoration that I owe thee,
When by thy power alone these darkened eyes
Have been unsealed again to see thy light!

VI

JACOB'S WELL

A SAMARITAN WOMAN

The sun is hot; and the dry east-wind blowing
Fills all the air with dust. The birds are silent;
Even the little fieldfares in the corn
No longer twitter; only the grasshoppers
Sing their incessant song of sun and summer.
I wonder who those strangers were I met
Going into the city? Galileans
They seemed to me in speaking, when they asked
The short way to the market-place. Perhaps
They are fishermen from the lake; or travellers,
Looking to find the inn. And here is some one
Sitting beside the well; another stranger;
A Galilean also by his looks.

CHRISTUS: A MYSTERY

What can so many Jews be doing here
Together in Samaria ? Are they going
Up to Jerusalem to the Passover ?
Our Passover is better here at Sychem,
For here is Ebal ; here is Gerizim,
The mountain where our father Abraham
Went up to offer Isaac ; here the tomb
Of Joseph, — for they brought his bones from Egypt
And buried them in this land, and it is holy.

CHRISTUS

Give me to drink.

SAMARITAN WOMAN

How can it be that thou,
Being a Jew, askest to drink of me
Which am a woman of Samaria ?
You Jews despise us ; have no dealings with us ;
Make us a byword ; call us in derision
The silly folk of Sychar. Sir, how is it
Thou askest drink of me ?

CHRISTUS

If thou hadst known
The gift of God, and who it is that sayeth
Give me to drink, thou wouldst have asked of Him ;
He would have given thee the living water.

SAMARITAN WOMAN

Sir, thou hast naught to draw with, and the well
Is deep ! Whence hast thou living water ?
Say, art thou greater than our father Jacob,

Which gave this well to us, and drank thereof
Himself, and all his children and his cattle ?

CHRISTUS

Ah, whosoever drinketh of this water
Shall thirst again; but whosoever drinketh
The water I shall give him shall not thirst
Forevermore, for it shall be within him
A well of living water, springing up
Into life everlasting.

SAMARITAN WOMAN

Every day
I must go to and fro, in heat and cold,
And I am weary. Give me of this water,
That I may thirst not, nor come here to draw.

CHRISTUS

Go call thy husband, woman, and come hither.

SAMARITAN WOMAN

I have no husband, Sir.

CHRISTUS

Thou hast well said
I have no husband. Thou hast had five husbands;
And he whom now thou hast is not thy husband.

SAMARITAN WOMAN

Surely thou art a prophet, for thou readest
The hidden things of life ! Our fathers worshipped
Upon this mountain Gerizim; and ye say

87

The only place in which men ought to worship
Is at Jerusalem.

CHRISTUS

Believe me, woman,
The hour is coming, when ye neither shall
Upon this mount, nor at Jerusalem,
Worship the Father; for the hour is coming,
And is now come, when the true worshippers
Shall worship the Father in spirit and in truth!
The Father seeketh such to worship Him.
God is a spirit; and they that worship Him
Must worship Him in spirit and in truth.

SAMARITAN WOMAN

Master, I know that the Messiah cometh,
Which is called Christ; and He will tell us all
    things.

CHRISTUS

I that speak unto thee am He!

THE DISCIPLES (*returning*)

Behold,
The Master sitting by the well, and talking
With a Samaritan woman! With a woman
Of Sychar, the silly people, always boasting
Of their Mount Ebal, and Mount Gerizim,
Their Everlasting Mountain, which they think
Higher and holier than our Mount Moriah!
Why, once upon the Feast of the New Moon,
When our great Sanhedrim of Jerusalem

Had all its watch-fires kindled on the hills
To warn the distant villages, these people
Lighted up others to mislead the Jews,
And make a mockery of their festival!
See, she has left the Master; and is running
Back to the city!

SAMARITAN WOMAN
Oh, come see a man
Who hath told me all things that I ever did!
Say, is not this the Christ?

THE DISCIPLES
Lo, Master, here
Is food, that we have brought thee from the city.
We pray thee eat it.

CHRISTUS
I have food to eat
Ye know not of.

THE DISCIPLES (*to each other*)
Hath any man been here,
And brought Him aught to eat, while we were gone?

CHRISTUS
The food I speak of is to do the will
Of Him that sent me, and to finish his work.
Do ye not say, Lo! there are yet four months
And cometh harvest? I say unto you,
Lift up your eyes, and look upon the fields,
For they are white already unto harvest!

VII

THE COASTS OF CÆSAREA PHILIPPI

CHRISTUS (*going up the mountain*)
Who do the people say I am ?

JOHN

           Some say
That thou art John the Baptist ; some, Elias ;
And others Jeremiah.

JAMES

          Or that one
Of the old Prophets is arisen again.

CHRISTUS

But who say ye I am ?

PETER

           Thou art the Christ !
Thou art the Son of God !

CHRISTUS

           Blessed art thou,
Simon Barjona ! Flesh and blood hath not
Revealed it unto thee, but even my Father,
Which is in Heaven. And I say unto thee
That thou art Peter ; and upon this rock
I build my Church, and all the gates of Hell

Shall not prevail against it. But take heed
Ye tell to no man that I am the Christ.
For I must go up to Jerusalem,
And suffer many things, and be rejected
Of the Chief Priests, and of the Scribes and El-
      ders,
And must be crucified, and the third day
Shall rise again !

PETER

           Be it far from thee, Lord !
This shall not be !

CHRISTUS

           Get thee behind me, Satan !
Thou savorest not the things that be of God,
But those that be of men ! If any will
Come after me, let him deny himself,
And daily take his cross, and follow me.
For whosoever will save his life shall lose it,
And whosoever will lose his life shall find it.
For wherein shall a man be profited
If he shall gain the whole world, and shall lose
Himself or be a castaway?

JAMES (*after a long pause*)
               Why doth
The Master lead us up into this mountain ?

PETER

He goeth up to pray.

CHRISTUS: A MYSTERY

JOHN

     See, where He standeth
Above us on the summit of the hill!
His face shines as the sun! and all his rai-
  ment
Exceeding white as snow, so as no fuller
On earth can white them! He is not alone;
There are two with Him there; two men of
  eld,
Their white beards blowing on the mountain
  air,
Are talking with him.

JAMES

    I am sore afraid!

PETER

Who and whence are they?

JOHN

     Moses and Elias!

PETER

O Master! it is good for us to be here!
If thou wilt, let us make three tabernacles;
For thee one, and for Moses and Elias!

JOHN

Behold a bright cloud sailing in the sun!
It overshadows us. A golden mist
Now hides them from us, and envelops us

And all the mountain in a luminous shadow!
I see no more. The nearest rocks are hidden.

VOICE (*from the cloud*)

Lo! this is my beloved Son! Hear Him!

PETER

It is the voice of God. He speaketh to us,
As from the burning bush He spake to Moses!

JOHN

The cloud-wreaths roll away. The veil is lifted;
We see again. Behold! He is alone.
It was a vision that our eyes beheld,
And it hath vanished into the unseen.

CHRISTUS (*coming down from the mountain*)

I charge ye, tell the vision unto no one,
Till the Son of Man be risen from the dead!

PETER (*aside*)

Again He speaks of it! What can it mean,
This rising from the dead?

JAMES

      Why say the Scribes
Elias must first come?

CHRISTUS

     He cometh first,
Restoring all things. But I say to you,
That this Elias is already come.

They knew him not, but have done unto him
Whate'er they listed, as is written of him.

PETER (*aside*)

It is of John the Baptist he is speaking.

JAMES

As we descend, see, at the mountain's foot,
A crowd of people; coming, going, thronging
Round the disciples, that we left behind us,
Seeming impatient, that we stay so long.

PETER

It is some blind man, or some paralytic
That waits the Master's coming to be healed.

JAMES

I see a boy, who struggles and demeans him
As if an unclean spirit tormented him!

A CERTAIN MAN (*running forward*)

Lord! I beseech thee, look upon my son.
He is mine only child; a lunatic,
And sorely vexed; for oftentimes he falleth
Into the fire and oft into the water.
Wherever the dumb spirit taketh him
He teareth him. He gnasheth with his teeth,
And pines away. I spake to thy disciples
That they should cast him out, and they could not.

CHRISTUS

O faithless generation and perverse!

How long shall I be with you, and suffer you?
Bring thy son hither.

BYSTANDERS

        How the unclean spirit
Seizes the boy, and tortures him with pain!
He falleth to the ground and wallows, foaming!
He cannot live.

CHRISTUS

        How long is it ago
Since this came unto him?

THE FATHER

          Even of a child.
Oh, have compassion on us, Lord, and help us,
If thou canst help us.

CHRISTUS

         If thou canst believe.
For unto him that verily believeth,
All things are possible.

THE FATHER

         Lord, I believe!
Help thou mine unbelief!

CHRISTUS

         Dumb and deaf spirit,
Come out of him, I charge thee, and no more
Enter thou into him!

      The boy utters a loud cry of pain, and then lies still.

CHRISTUS: A MYSTERY

BYSTANDERS

How motionless
He lieth there. No life is left in him.
His eyes are like a blind man's, that see not.
The boy is dead!

OTHERS

Behold! the Master stoops,
And takes him by the hand, and lifts him up.
He is not dead.

DISCIPLES

But one word from those lips,
But one touch of that hand, and he is healed!
Ah, why could we not do it?

THE FATHER

My poor child!
Now thou art mine again. The unclean spirit
Shall never more torment thee! Look at me!
Speak unto me! Say that thou knowest me!

DISCIPLES (*to* CHRISTUS, *departing*)

Good Master, tell us, for what reason was it
We could not cast him out?

CHRISTUS

Because of your unbelief!

VIII

THE YOUNG RULER

CHRISTUS

Two men went up into the temple to pray.
The one was a self-righteous Pharisee,
The other a Publican. And the Pharisee
Stood and prayed thus within himself! O God,
I thank thee I am not as other men,
Extortioners, unjust, adulterers,
Or even as this Publican. I fast
Twice in the week, and also I give tithes
Of all that I possess! The Publican,
Standing afar off, would not lift so much
Even as his eyes to heaven, but smote his breast,
Saying: God be merciful to me a sinner!
I tell you that this man went to his house
More justified than the other. Every one
That doth exalt himself shall be abased,
And he that humbleth himself shall be exalted!

CHILDREN (*among themselves*)

Let us go nearer! He is telling stories!
Let us go listen to them.

AN OLD JEW

      Children, children!
What are ye doing here? Why do ye crowd us?
It was such little vagabonds as you,
That followed Elisha, mocking him and crying:

Go up, thou bald-head ! But the bears — the bears
Came out of the wood, and tare them !

A MOTHER

Speak not thus !
We brought them here, that He might lay his
hands
On them, and bless them.

CHRISTUS

Suffer little children
To come unto me, and forbid them not ;
Of such is the kingdom of heaven ; and their angels
Look always on my Father's face.
Takes them in his arms and blesses them.

A YOUNG RULER (*running*)

Good Master !
What good thing shall I do, that I may have
Eternal life ?

CHRISTUS

Why callest thou me good ?
There is none good but one, and that is God.
If thou wilt enter into life eternal,
Keep the commandments.

YOUNG RULER

Which of them ?

CHRISTUS

Thou shalt not

Commit adultery ; thou shalt not kill ;
Thou shalt not steal ; thou shalt not bear false witness ;
Honor thy father and thy mother ; and love
Thy neighbor as thyself.

YOUNG RULER

From my youth up
All these things have I kept. What lack I yet ?

JOHN

With what divine compassion in his eyes
The Master looks upon this eager youth,
As if He loved him !

CHRISTUS

Wouldst thou perfect be,
Sell all thou hast, and give it to the poor,
And come, take up thy cross, and follow me,
And thou shalt have thy treasure in the heavens.

JOHN

Behold, how sorrowful he turns away !

CHRISTUS

Children ! how hard it is for them that trust
In riches to enter into the kingdom of God !
'T is easier for a camel to go through
A needle's eye, than for the rich to enter
The kingdom of God !

JOHN

Ah, who then can be saved ?

CHRISTUS

With men this is indeed impossible,
But unto God all things are possible!

PETER

Behold, we have left all, and followed thee.
What shall we have therefor?

CHRISTUS

Eternal life.

IX

AT BETHANY

MARTHA *busy about household affairs.* MARY *sitting at the feet of* CHRISTUS

MARTHA

She sitteth idly at the Master's feet,
And troubles not herself with household cares.
'T is the old story. When a guest arrives
She gives up all to be with him; while I
Must be the drudge, make ready the guest-chamber,
Prepare the food, set everything in order,
And see that naught is wanting in the house.
She shows her love by words, and I by works.

MARY

O Master! when thou comest, it is always
A Sabbath in the house. I cannot work;

I must sit at thy feet; must see thee, hear thee!
I have a feeble, wayward, doubting heart,
Incapable of endurance or great thoughts,
Striving for something that it cannot reach,
Baffled and disappointed, wounded, hungry;
And only when I hear thee am I happy,
And only when I see thee am at peace!
Stronger than I, and wiser, and far better
In every manner, is my sister Martha.
Thou seest how well she orders everything
To make thee welcome; how she comes and
　　goes,
Careful and cumbered ever with much serving,
While I but welcome thee with foolish words!
Whene'er thou speakest to me, I am happy;
When thou art silent, I am satisfied.
Thy presence is enough. I ask no more.
Only to be with thee, only to see thee,
Sufficeth me. My heart is then at rest.
I wonder I am worthy of so much.

MARTHA

Lord, dost thou care not that my sister Mary
Hath left me thus to wait on thee alone?
I pray thee, bid her help me.

CHRISTUS

　　　　　　　Martha, Martha,
Careful and troubled about many things
Art thou, and yet one thing alone is needful!
Thy sister Mary hath chosen that good part,
Which never shall be taken away from her!

CHRISTUS: A MYSTERY

X

BORN BLIND

A JEW

Who is this beggar blinking in the sun?
Is it not he who used to sit and beg
By the Gate Beautiful?

ANOTHER

It is the same.

A THIRD

It is not he, but like him, for that beggar
Was blind from birth. It cannot be the same.

THE BEGGAR

Yea, I am he.

A JEW

How have thine eyes been opened?

THE BEGGAR

A man that is called Jesus made a clay
And put it on mine eyes, and said to me:
Go to Siloam's Pool and wash thyself.
I went and washed, and I received my sight.

A JEW

Where is He?

THE DIVINE TRAGEDY

I know not.

                    What is this crowd
Gathered about a beggar? What has happened?

Here is a man who hath been blind from birth,
And now he sees. He says a man called Jesus
Hath healed him.

                    As God liveth, the Nazarene!
How was this done?

                    Rabboni, he put clay
Upon mine eyes; I washed, and now I see.

When did he this?

                    Rabboni, yesterday.

The Sabbath day. This man is not of God
Because he keepeth not the Sabbath day!

How can a man that is a sinner do
Such miracles?

CHRISTUS: A MYSTERY

PHARISEES

What dost thou say of him
That hath restored thy sight?

THE BEGGAR

He is a Prophet.

A JEW

This is a wonderful story, but not true.
A beggar's fiction. He was not born blind,
And never has been blind!

OTHERS

Here are his parents.
Ask them.

PHARISEES

Is this your son?

THE PARENTS

Rabboni, yea;
We know this is our son.

PHARISEES

Was he born blind?

THE PARENTS

He was born blind.

PHARISEES

Then how doth he now see?

THE PARENTS (*aside*)

What answer shall we make? If we confess
It was the Christ, we shall be driven forth
Out of the Synagogue! We know, Rabboni,
This is our son, and that he was born blind;
But by what means he seeth, we know not,
Or who his eyes hath opened, we know not.
He is of age; ask him; we cannot say;
He shall speak for himself.

PHARISEES

Give God the praise!
We know the man that healed thee is a sinner!

THE BEGGAR

Whether He be a sinner, I know not;
One thing I know; that whereas I was blind,
I now do see.

PHARISEES

How opened he thine eyes?
What did he do?

THE BEGGAR

I have already told you.
Ye did not hear; why would ye hear again?
Will ye be his disciples?

PHARISEES

God of Moses!
Are we demoniacs, are we halt or blind,
Or palsy-stricken, or lepers, or the like,

That we should join the Synagogue of Satan,
And follow jugglers? Thou art his disciple,
But we are disciples of Moses; and we know
That God spake unto Moses; but this fellow,
We know not whence he is!

THE BEGGAR

                   Why, herein is
A marvellous thing! Ye know not whence He is,
Yet He hath opened mine eyes! We know that God
Heareth not sinners; but if any man
Doeth God's will, and is his worshipper,
Him doth He hear. Oh, since the world began
It was not heard that any man hath opened
The eyes of one that was born blind. If He
Were not of God, surely He could do nothing!

PHARISEES

Thou, who wast altogether born in sins
And in iniquities, dost thou teach us?
Away with thee out of the holy places,
Thou reprobate, thou beggar, thou blasphemer!
                   THE BEGGAR *is cast out.*

XI

SIMON MAGUS AND HELEN OF TYRE

On the house-top at Endor. Night. A lighted lantern on a table.

SIMON

Swift are the blessed Immortals to the mortal
That perseveres! So doth it stand recorded
In the divine Chaldæan Oracles
Of Zoroaster, once Ezekiel's slave,
Who in his native East betook himself
To lonely meditation, and the writing
On the dried skins of oxen the Twelve Books
Of the Avesta and the Oracles!
Therefore I persevere; and I have brought
      thee
From the great city of Tyre, where men deride
The things they comprehend not, to this plain
Of Esdraelon, in the Hebrew tongue
Called Armageddon, and this town of Endor,
Where men believe; where all the air is full
Of marvellous traditions, and the Enchantress
That summoned up the ghost of Samuel
Is still remembered. Thou hast seen the land;
Is it not fair to look on?

HELEN

           It is fair,
Yet not so fair as Tyre.

SIMON

Is not Mount Tabor
As beautiful as Carmel by the Sea?

HELEN

It is too silent and too solitary;
I miss the tumult of the streets; the sounds
Of traffic, and the going to and fro
Of people in gay attire, with cloaks of purple,
And gold and silver jewelry!

SIMON

Inventions
Of Ahriman, the spirit of the dark,
The Evil Spirit!

HELEN

I regret the gossip
Of friends and neighbors at the open door
On summer nights.

SIMON

An idle waste of time.

HELEN

The singing and the dancing, the delight
Of music and of motion. Woe is me,
To give up all these pleasures, and to lead
The life we lead!

SIMON

Thou canst not raise thyself

Up to the level of my higher thought,
And though possessing thee, I still remain
Apart from thee, and, with thee, am alone
In my high dreams.

HELEN

Happier was I in Tyre.
Oh, I remember how the gallant ships
Came sailing in, with ivory, gold, and silver,
And apes and peacocks; and the singing sailors,
And the gay captains with their silken dresses,
Smelling of aloes, myrrh, and cinnamon!

SIMON

But the dishonor, Helen! Let the ships
Of Tarshish howl for that!

HELEN

And what dishonor?
Remember Rahab, and how she became
The ancestress of the great Psalmist David;
And wherefore should not I, Helen of Tyre,
Attain like honor?

SIMON

Thou art Helen of Tyre,
And hast been Helen of Troy, and hast been Rahab,
The Queen of Sheba, and Semiramis,
And Sara of seven husbands, and Jezebel,
And other women of the like allurements;
And now thou art Minerva, the first Æon,
The Mother of Angels!

HELEN

And the concubine
Of Simon the Magician! Is it honor
For one who has been all these noble dames,
To tramp about the dirty villages
And cities of Samaria with a juggler?
A charmer of serpents?

SIMON

He who knows himself
Knows all things in himself. I have charmed thee,
Thou beautiful asp: yet am I no magician.
I am the Power of God, and the Beauty of God!
I am the Paraclete, the Comforter!

HELEN

Illusions! Thou deceiver, self-deceived!
Thou dost usurp the titles of another;
Thou art not what thou sayest.

SIMON

Am I not?
Then feel my power.

HELEN

Would I had ne'er left Tyre!
He looks at her, and she sinks into a deep sleep.

SIMON

Go, see it in thy dreams, fair unbeliever!
And leave me unto mine, if they be dreams,
That take such shapes before me, that I see them;

110

THE DIVINE TRAGEDY

These effable and ineffable impressions
Of the mysterious world, that come to me
From the elements of Fire and Earth and Water,
And the all-nourishing Ether ! It is written,
Look not on Nature, for her name is fatal !
Yet there are Principles, that make apparent
The images of unapparent things,
And the impression of vague characters
And visions most divine appear in ether.
So speak the Oracles ; then wherefore fatal ?
I take this orange-bough, with its five leaves,
Each equidistant on the upright stem ;
And I project them on a plane below,
In the circumference of a circle drawn
About a centre where the stem is planted,
And each still equidistant from the other ;
As if a thread of gossamer were drawn
Down from each leaf, and fastened with a pin.
Now if from these five points a line be traced
To each alternate point, we shall obtain
The Pentagram, or Solomon's Pentangle,
A charm against all witchcraft, and a sign,
Which on the banner of Antiochus
Drove back the fierce barbarians of the North,
Demons esteemed, and gave the Syrian King
The sacred name of Soter, or of Savior.
Thus Nature works mysteriously with man ;
And from the Eternal One, as from a centre,
All things proceed, in fire, air, earth, and water,
And all are subject to one law, which broken
Even in a single point, is broken in all ;
Demons rush in, and chaos comes again.

CHRISTUS: A MYSTERY

By this will I compel the stubborn spirits,
That guard the treasures, hid in caverns deep
On Gerizim, by Uzzi the High-Priest,
The ark and holy vessels, to reveal
Their secret unto me, and to restore
These precious things to the Samaritans.
A mist is rising from the plain below me,
And as I look, the vapors shape themselves
Into strange figures, as if unawares
My lips had breathed the Tetragrammaton,
And from their graves, o'er all the battle-fields
Of Armageddon, the long-buried captains
Had started, with their thousands, and ten thou-
      sands,
And rushed together to renew their wars,
Powerless, and weaponless, and without a sound!
Wake, Helen, from thy sleep! The air grows cold;
Let us go down.

HELEN (*awaking*)
Oh, would I were at home!

SIMON
Thou sayest that I usurp another's titles.
In youth I saw the Wise Men of the East,
Magalath and Pangalath and Saracen,
Who followed the bright star, but home returned
For fear of Herod by another way.
Oh shining worlds above me! in what deep
Recesses of your realms of mystery
Lies hidden now that star? and where are they
That brought the gifts of frankincense and myrrh?

THE DIVINE TRAGEDY

HELEN

The Nazarene still liveth.

SIMON

            We have heard
His name in many towns, but have not seen Him.
He flits before us; tarries not; is gone
When we approach, like something unsubstantial,
Made of the air, and fading into air.
He is at Nazareth, He is at Nain,
Or at the Lovely Village on the Lake,
Or sailing on its waters.

HELEN

            So say those
Who do not wish to find Him.

SIMON

            Can this be
The King of Israel, whom the Wise Men worshipped?
Or does He fear to meet me? It would seem so.
We should soon learn which of us twain usurps
The titles of the other, as thou sayest.
                    They go down.

THE THIRD PASSOVER

I

THE ENTRY INTO JERUSALEM

THE SYRO-PHŒNICIAN WOMAN *and her* DAUGHTER *on the house-top at Jerusalem.*

THE DAUGHTER (*singing*)

BLIND Bartimeus at the gates
Of Jericho in darkness waits;
He hears the crowd; — he hears a breath
Say, It is Christ of Nazareth!
And calls, in tones of agony,
'Ιησοῦ, ἐλέησόν με !

The thronging multitudes increase:
Blind Bartimeus, hold thy peace!
But still, above the noisy crowd,
The beggar's cry is shrill and loud;
Until they say, He calleth thee!
Θάρσει· ἔγειραι, φωνεῖ σε !

Then saith the Christ, as silent stands
The crowd, What wilt thou at my hands?
And he replies, Oh, give me light!
Rabbi, restore the blind man's sight!
And Jesus answers, Ὕπαγε·
'Η πίστις σου σέσωκέ σε !

114

THE DIVINE TRAGEDY

Ye that have eyes, yet cannot see,
In darkness and in misery,
Recall those mighty voices three,
'Ιησοῦ, ἐλέησόν με !
Θάρσει· ἔγειραι, ὕπαγε !
'Η πίστις σου σέσωκέ σε !

THE MOTHER

Thy faith hath saved thee ! Ah, how true that is !
For I had faith ; and when the Master came
Into the coasts of Tyre and Sidon, fleeing
From those who sought to slay Him, I went forth
And cried unto Him, saying : Have mercy on
      me,
O Lord, thou Son of David ! for my daughter
Is grievously tormented with a devil.
But He passed on, and answered not a word.
And his disciples said, beseeching Him :
Send her away ! She crieth after us !
And then the Master answered them and said :
I am not sent but unto the lost sheep
Of the House of Israel ! Then I worshipped
      Him,
Saying : Lord, help me ! And He answered me,
It is not meet to take the children's bread
And cast it unto dogs ! Truth, Lord, I said ;
And yet the dogs may eat the crumbs which fall
From off their master's table ; and He turned,
And answered me ; and said to me : O woman,
Great is thy faith ; then be it unto thee
Even as thou wilt. And from that very hour
Thou wast made whole, my darling ! my delight !

CHRISTUS: A MYSTERY

THE DAUGHTER

There came upon my dark and troubled mind
A calm, as when the tumult of the city
Suddenly ceases, and I lie and hear
The silver trumpets of the Temple blowing
Their welcome to the Sabbath. Still I wonder,
That one who was so far away from me,
And could not see me, by his thought alone
Had power to heal me. Oh that I could see Him!

THE MOTHER

Perhaps thou wilt; for I have brought thee here
To keep the holy Passover, and lay
Thine offering of thanksgiving on the altar.
Thou mayst both see and hear Him. Hark!

VOICES (*afar off*)

Hosanna!

THE DAUGHTER

A crowd comes pouring through the city gate!
O mother, look!

VOICES (*in the street*)

Hosanna to the Son
Of David!

THE DAUGHTER

A great multitude of people
Fills all the street; and riding on an ass
Comes one of noble aspect, like a king!

THE DIVINE TRAGEDY

The people spread their garments in the way,
And scatter branches of the palm-trees!

                              Blessed
Is He that cometh in the name of the Lord!
Hosanna in the highest!

OTHER VOICES

                Who is this?

VOICES

Jesus of Nazareth!

THE DAUGHTER

                Mother, it is He!

VOICES

He hath called Lazarus of Bethany
Out of his grave, and raised him from the dead!
Hosanna in the highest!

PHARISEES

                Ye perceive
That nothing we prevail. Behold, the world
Is all gone after him!

THE DAUGHTER

                What majesty,
What power is in that care-worn countenance!
What sweetness, what compassion! I no longer
Wonder that He hath healed me!

CHRISTUS: A MYSTERY

VOICES

                     Peace in heaven,
And glory in the highest!

PHARISEES

                Rabbi! Rabbi!
Rebuke thy followers!

CHRISTUS

                Should they hold their peace
The very stones beneath us would cry out!

THE DAUGHTER

All hath passed by me like a dream of wonder!
But I have seen Him, and have heard his voice,
And I am satisfied! I ask no more!

II

SOLOMON'S PORCH

GAMALIEL THE SCRIBE

When Rabban Simeon, upon whom be peace!
Taught in these Schools, he boasted that his pen
Had written no word that he could call his own,
But wholly and always had been consecrated
To the transcribing of the Law and Prophets.
He used to say, and never tired of saying,
The world itself was built upon the Law.
And ancient Hillel said, that whosoever
Gains a good name, gains something for himself,

But he who gains a knowledge of the Law
Gains everlasting life. And they spake truly.
Great is the Written Law; but greater still
The Unwritten, the Traditions of the Elders,
The lovely words of Levites, spoken first
To Moses on the Mount, and handed down
From mouth to mouth, in one unbroken sound
And sequence of divine authority,
The voice of God resounding through the ages.

The Written Law is water; the Unwritten
Is precious wine; the Written Law is salt,
The Unwritten costly spice; the Written Law
Is but the body; the Unwritten, the soul
That quickens it and makes it breathe and live.
I can remember, many years ago,
A little bright-eyed school-boy, a mere stripling,
Son of a Galilean carpenter,
From Nazareth, I think, who came one day
And sat here in the Temple with the Scribes,
Hearing us speak, and asking many questions,
And we were all astonished at his quickness.
And when his mother came, and said: Behold
Thy father and I have sought thee, sorrowing;
He looked as one astonished, and made answer,
How is it that ye sought me? Wist ye not
That I must be about my Father's business?
Often since then I see him here among us,
Or dream I see him, with his upraised face
Intent and eager, and I often wonder
Unto what manner of manhood he hath grown!
Perhaps a poor mechanic, like his father,

Lost in his little Galilean village
And toiling at his craft, to die unknown
And be no more remembered among men.

CHRISTUS (*in the outer court*)

The Scribes and Pharisees sit in Moses' seat;
All, therefore, whatsoever they command you,
Observe and do; but follow not their works;
They say and do not. They bind heavy burdens
And very grievous to be borne, and lay them
Upon men's shoulders, but they move them not
With so much as a finger!

GAMALIEL (*looking forth*)
                    Who is this
Exhorting in the outer courts so loudly?

CHRISTUS

Their works they do for to be seen of men.
They make broad their phylacteries, and enlarge
The borders of their garments, and they love
The uppermost rooms at feasts, and the chief seats
In Synagogues, and greetings in the markets,
And to be called of all men Rabbi, Rabbi!

GAMALIEL

It is that loud and turbulent Galilean,
That came here at the Feast of Dedication,
And stirred the people up to break the Law!

CHRISTUS

Woe unto you, ye Scribes and Pharisees,

Ye hypocrites! for ye shut up the kingdom
Of heaven, and neither go ye in yourselves
Nor suffer them that are entering to go in!

GAMALIEL

How eagerly the people throng and listen,
As if his ribald words were words of wisdom!

CHRISTUS

Woe unto you, ye Scribes and Pharisees,
Ye hypocrites! for ye devour the houses
Of widows, and for pretence ye make long prayers;
Therefore shall ye receive the more damnation.

GAMALIEL

This brawler is no Jew, — he is a vile
Samaritan, and hath an unclean spirit!

CHRISTUS

Woe unto you, ye Scribes and Pharisees,
Ye hypocrites! ye compass sea and land
To make one proselyte, and when he is made
Ye make him twofold more the child of hell
Than you yourselves are!

GAMALIEL

O my father's father!
Hillel of blessed memory, hear and judge!

CHRISTUS

Woe unto you, ye Scribes and Pharisees,
Ye hypocrites! for ye pay tithe of mint,

CHRISTUS: A MYSTERY

Of anise, and of cumin, and omit
The weightier matters of the law of God,
Judgment and faith and mercy ; and all these
Ye ought to have done, nor leave undone the others !

GAMALIEL

O Rabban Simeon ! how must thy bones
Stir in their grave to hear such blasphemies !

CHRISTUS

Woe unto you, ye Scribes and Pharisees,
Ye hypocrites ! for ye make clean and sweet
The outside of the cup and of the platter,
But they within are full of all excess !

GAMALIEL

Patience of God ! canst thou endure so long ?
Or art thou deaf, or gone upon a journey ?

CHRISTUS

Woe unto you, ye Scribes and Pharisees,
Ye hypocrites ! for ye are very like
To whited sepulchres, which indeed appear
Beautiful outwardly, but are within
Filled full of dead men's bones and all uncleanness !

GAMALIEL

Am I awake ? Is this Jerusalem ?
And are these Jews that throng and stare and listen ?

CHRISTUS

Woe unto you, ye Scribes and Pharisees,

Ye hypocrites ! because ye build the tombs
Of prophets, and adorn the sepulchres
Of righteous men, and say : If we had lived
When lived our fathers, we would not have been
Partakers with them in the blood of Prophets.
So ye be witnesses unto yourselves,
That ye are children of them that killed the
        Prophets !
Fill ye up then the measure of your fathers.
I send unto you Prophets and Wise Men,
And Scribes, and some ye crucify, and some
Scourge in your Synagogues, and persecute
From city to city ; that on you may come
The righteous blood that hath been shed on earth,
From the blood of righteous Abel to the blood
Of Zacharias, son of Barachias,
Ye slew between the Temple and the altar !

GAMALIEL

Oh, had I here my subtle dialectician,
My little Saul of Tarsus, the tent-maker,
Whose wit is sharper than his needle's point,
He would delight to foil this noisy wrangler !

CHRISTUS

Jerusalem ! Jerusalem ! O thou
That killest the Prophets, and that stonest them
Which are sent unto thee, how often would I
Have gathered together thy children, as a hen
Gathereth her chickens underneath her wing,
And ye would not ! Behold, your house is left
Unto you desolate !

THE PEOPLE

This is a Prophet !
This is the Christ that was to come !

GAMALIEL

Ye fools !
Think ye, shall Christ come out of Galilee ?

III

LORD, IS IT I ?

CHRISTUS

One of you shall betray me.

THE DISCIPLES

Is it I ?
Lord, is it I ?

CHRISTUS

One of the Twelve it is
That dippeth with me in this dish his hand ;
He shall betray me. Lo, the Son of Man
Goeth indeed as it is written of Him ;
But woe shall be unto that man by whom
He is betrayed ! Good were it for that man
If he had ne'er been born !

JUDAS ISCARIOT

Lord, is it I ?

CHRISTUS

Ay, thou hast said. And that thou doest, do quickly.

THE DIVINE TRAGEDY

JUDAS ISCARIOT (*going out*)
Ah, woe is me!

CHRISTUS

All ye shall be offended
Because of me this night; for it is written :
Awake, O sword against my shepherd! Smite
The shepherd, saith the Lord of hosts, and scattered
Shall be the sheep! — But after I am risen
I go before you into Galilee.

PETER

O Master! though all men shall be offended
Because of thee, yet will not I be !

CHRISTUS

Simon,
Behold how Satan hath desired to have you,
That he may sift you as one sifteth wheat!
Whither I go thou canst not follow me —
Not now; but thou shalt follow me hereafter.

PETER

Wherefore can I not follow thee ? I am ready
To go with thee to prison and to death.

CHRISTUS

Verily say I unto thee, this night,
Ere the cock crow, thou shalt deny me thrice !

PETER

Though I should die, yet will I not deny thee.

CHRISTUS: A MYSTERY

CHRISTUS

When first I sent you forth without a purse,
Or scrip, or shoes, did ye lack anything?

THE DISCIPLES

Not anything.

CHRISTUS

But he that hath a purse,
Now let him take it, and likewise his scrip;
And he that hath no sword, let him go sell
His clothes and buy one. That which hath been
    written
Must be accomplished now: He hath poured
    out
His soul even unto death; He hath been numbered
With the transgressors, and himself hath borne
The sin of many, and made intercession
For the transgressors. And here have an end
The things concerning me.

PETER

Behold, O Lord,
Behold, here are two swords!

CHRISTUS

It is enough.

THE DIVINE TRAGEDY

IV

THE GARDEN OF GETHSEMANE

CHRISTUS

My spirit is exceeding sorrowful
Even unto death ! Tarry ye here and watch.

He goes apart.

PETER

Under this ancient olive-tree, that spreads
Its broad centennial branches like a tent,
Let us lie down and rest.

JOHN

What are those torches,
That glimmer on Brook Kedron there below us ?

JAMES

It is some marriage feast ; the joyful maidens
Go out to meet the bridegroom.

PETER

I am weary.
The struggles of this day have overcome me.

They sleep.

CHRISTUS (*falling on his face*)

Father ! all things are possible to thee, —
Oh let this cup pass from me ! Nevertheless
Not as I will, but as thou wilt, be done !

127

CHRISTUS: A MYSTERY

(Returning to the Disciples)

What! could ye not watch with me for one
    hour?
Oh watch and pray, that ye may enter not
Into temptation. For the spirit indeed
Is willing, but the flesh is weak!

JOHN

                Alas!
It is for sorrow that our eyes are heavy. —
I see again the glimmer of those torches
Among the olives; they are coming hither.

JAMES

Outside the garden wall the path divides;
Surely they come not hither.
                   They sleep again.

CHRISTUS *(as before)*

             O my Father!
If this cup may not pass away from me,
Except I drink of it, thy will be done.
    (Returning to the Disciples)
Sleep on; and take your rest!

JOHN

             Beloved Master,
Alas! we know not what to answer thee!
It is for sorrow that our eyes are heavy. —
Behold, the torches now encompass us.

THE DIVINE TRAGEDY

JAMES

They do but go about the garden wall,
Seeking for some one, or for something lost.

They sleep again.

CHRISTUS (*as before*)

If this cup may not pass away from me,
Except I drink of it, thy will be done.

(*Returning to the Disciples*)

It is enough! Behold, the Son of Man
Hath been betrayed into the hands of sinners!
The hour is come. Rise up, let us be going;
For he that shall betray me is at hand.

JOHN

Ah me! See, from his forehead, in the torchlight,
Great drops of blood are falling to the ground!

PETER

What lights are these? What torches glare and glisten
Upon the swords and armor of these men?
And there among them Judas Iscariot!

He smites the servant of the High-Priest with his sword.

CHRISTUS

Put up thy sword into its sheath; for they
That take the sword shall perish with the sword.
The cup my Father hath given me to drink,
Shall I not drink it? Think'st thou that I cannot
Pray to my Father, and that He shall give me
More than twelve legions of angels presently?

JUDAS (*to* CHRISTUS, *kissing him*)

Hail, Master! hail!

CHRISTUS

     Friend, wherefore art thou come?
Whom seek ye?

CAPTAIN OF THE TEMPLE

  Jesus of Nazareth.

CHRISTUS

       I am he.
Are ye come hither as against a thief,
With swords and staves to take me? When I daily
Was with you in the Temple, ye stretched forth
No hands to take me! But this is your hour,
And this the power of darkness. If ye seek
Me only, let these others go their way.

   The Disciples depart. CHRISTUS *is bound and*
   led away. A certain young man follows Him,
   having a linen cloth cast about his body. They
   lay hold of him, and the young man flees from
   them naked.

V

THE PALACE OF CAIAPHAS

PHARISEES

What do we? Clearly something must we do,
For this man worketh many miracles.

CAIAPHAS

I am informed that he is a mechanic;

A carpenter's son; a Galilean peasant,
Keeping disreputable company.

PHARISEES

The people say that here in Bethany
He hath raised up a certain Lazarus,
Who had been dead three days.

CAIAPHAS

                      Impossible!
There is no resurrection of the dead;
This Lazarus should be taken, and put to death
As an impostor. If this Galilean
Would be content to stay in Galilee,
And preach in country towns, I should not heed
      him.
But when he comes up to Jerusalem
Riding in triumph, as I am informed,
And drives the money-changers from the Temple,
That is another matter.

PHARISEES

            If we thus
Let him alone, all will believe on him,
And then the Romans come and take away
Our place and nation.

CAIAPHAS

               Ye know nothing at all.
Simon Ben Camith, my great predecessor,
On whom be peace! would have dealt presently
With such a demagogue. I shall no less.

The man must die. Do ye consider not
It is expedient that one man should die,
Not the whole nation perish? What is death?
It differeth from sleep but in duration.
We sleep and wake again; an hour or two
Later or earlier, and it matters not,
And if we never wake it matters not;
When we are in our graves we are at peace,
Nothing can wake us or disturb us more.
There is no resurrection.

PHARISEES (*aside*)

              O most faithful
Disciple of Hircanus Maccabæus,
Will nothing but complete annihilation
Comfort and satisfy thee?

CAIAPHAS

              While ye are talking
And plotting, and contriving how to take him,
Fearing the people, and so doing naught,
I, who fear not the people, have been acting;
Have taken this Prophet, this young Nazarene,
Who by Beelzebub the Prince of devils
Casteth out devils, and doth raise the dead,
That might as well be dead, and left in peace.
Annas my father-in-law hath sent him hither.
I hear the guard. Behold your Galilean!

(CHRISTUS *is brought in, bound.*)

SERVANT (*in the vestibule*)
Why art thou up so late, my pretty damsel?

DAMSEL

Why art thou up so early, pretty man?
It is not cock-crow yet, and art thou stirring?

SERVANT

What brings thee here?

DAMSEL

What brings the rest of you?

SERVANT

Come here and warm thy hands.

DAMSEL (*to* PETER)

Art thou not also
One of this man's disciples?

PETER

I am not.

DAMSEL

Now surely thou art also one of them;
Thou art a Galilean, and thy speech
Bewrayeth thee.

PETER

Woman, I know Him not!

CAIAPHAS (*to* CHRISTUS, *in the Hall*)

Who art thou? Tell us plainly of thyself
And of thy doctrines, and of thy disciples.

CHRISTUS: A MYSTERY

CHRISTUS

Lo, I have spoken openly to the world,
I have taught ever in the Synagogue,
And in the Temple, where the Jews resort;
In secret have said nothing. Wherefore then
Askest thou me of this? Ask them that heard me
What I have said to them. Behold they know
What I have said!

OFFICER (*striking him*)

    What, fellow! answerest thou
The High-Priest so?

CHRISTUS

    If I have spoken evil,
Bear witness of the evil; but if well,
Why smitest thou me?

CAIAPHAS

    Where are the witnesses?
Let them say what they know.

THE TWO FALSE WITNESSES

     We heard Him say:
I will destroy this Temple made with hands,
And will within three days build up another
Made without hands.

SCRIBES *and* PHARISEES

    He is o'erwhelmed with shame
And cannot answer!

THE DIVINE TRAGEDY

CAIAPHAS

> Dost thou answer nothing?
What is thit thing they witness here against thee?

SCRIBES *and* PHARISEES

He holds his peace.

CAIAPHAS

> Tell us, art thou the Christ?
I do adjure thee by the living God,
Tell us, art thou indeed the Christ?

CHRISTUS

> I am.
Hereafter shall ye see the Son of Man
Sit on the right hand of the power of God,
And come in clouds of heaven!

CAIAPHAS (*rending his clothes*)

> It is enough.
He hath spoken blasphemy! What further need
Have we of witnesses? Now ye have heard
His blasphemy. What think ye? Is he guilty?

SCRIBES *and* PHARISEES

Guilty of death!

KINSMAN OF MALCHUS (*to* PETER, *in the vestibule*)

> Surely I know thy face,
Did I not see thee in the garden with him?

PETER

How couldst thou see me? I swear unto thee

CHRISTUS: A MYSTERY

I do not know this man of whom ye speak!

The cock crows.

Hark! the cock crows! That sorrowful, pale face
Seeks for me in the crowd, and looks at me,
As if He would remind me of those words:
Ere the cock crow thou shalt deny me thrice!

Goes out weeping. CHRISTUS *is blindfolded and buffeted.*

AN OFFICER (*striking him with his palm*)

Prophesy unto us, thou Christ, thou Prophet!
Who is it smote thee?

CAIAPHAS

Lead Him unto Pilate!

VI

PONTIUS PILATE

PILATE

Wholly incomprehensible to me,
Vainglorious, obstinate, and given up
To unintelligible old traditions,
And proud, and self-conceited are these Jews!
Not long ago, I marched the legions down
From Cæsarea to their winter-quarters
Here in Jerusalem, with the effigies
Of Cæsar on their ensigns, and a tumult
Arose among these Jews, because their Law
Forbids the making of all images!

They threw themselves upon the ground with
    wild
Expostulations, bared their necks, and cried
That they would sooner die than have their Law
Infringed in any manner; as if Numa
Were not as great as Moses, and the Laws
Of the Twelve Tables as their Pentateuch!

And then, again, when I desired to span
Their valley with an aqueduct, and bring
A rushing river in to wash the city
And its inhabitants, — they all rebelled
As if they had been herds of unwashed swine!
Thousands and thousands of them got together
And raised so great a clamor round my doors,
That, fearing violent outbreak, I desisted,
And left them to their wallowing in the mire.

And now here comes the reverend Sanhedrim
Of lawyers, priests, and Scribes and Pharisees,
Like old and toothless mastiffs, that can bark,
But cannot bite, howling their accusations
Against a mild enthusiast, who hath preached
I know not what new doctrine, being King
Of some vague kingdom in the other world,
That hath no more to do with Rome and Cæsar
Than I have with the patriarch Abraham!
Finding this man to be a Galilean
I sent Him straight to Herod, and I hope
That is the last of it ; but if it be not,
I still have power to pardon and release Him,
As is the custom at the Passover,

And so accommodate the matter smoothly,
Seeming to yield to them, yet saving Him;
A prudent and sagacious policy
For Roman Governors in the Provinces.

Incomprehensible, fanatic people!
Ye have a God, who seemeth like yourselves
Incomprehensible, dwelling apart,
Majestic, cloud-encompassed, clothed in darkness!
One whom ye fear, but love not; yet ye have
No Goddesses to soften your stern lives,
And make you tender unto human weakness,
While we of Rome have everywhere around us
Our amiable divinities, that haunt
The woodlands, and the waters, and frequent
Our households, with their sweet and gracious pre-
    sence!
I will go in, and while these Jews are wrangling,
Read my Ovidius on the Art of Love.

VII

BARABBAS IN PRISON

BARABBAS (*to his fellow-prisoners*)
Barabbas is my name,
Barabbas, the Son of Shame,
   Is the meaning I suppose;
I'm no better than the best,
And whether worse than the rest
   Of my fellow-men, who knows?

THE DIVINE TRAGEDY

I was once, to say it in brief,
A highwayman, a robber-chief,
  In the open light of day.
So much I am free to confess;
But all men, more or less,
  Are robbers in their way.

From my cavern in the crags,
From my lair of leaves and flags,
  I could see, like ants, below,
The camels with their load
Of merchandise, on the road
  That leadeth to Jericho.

And I struck them unaware,
As an eagle from the air
  Drops down upon bird or beast;
And I had my heart's desire
Of the merchants of Sidon and Tyre,
  And Damascus and the East.

But it is not for that I fear;
It is not for that I am here
  In these iron fetters bound;
Sedition! that is the word
That Pontius Pilate heard,
  And he liketh not the sound.

What, think ye, would he care
For a Jew slain here or there,
  Or a plundered caravan?
But Cæsar! — ah, that is a crime,

CHRISTUS: A MYSTERY

To the uttermost end of time
  Shall not be forgiven to man.

Therefore was Herod wroth
With Matthias Margaloth,
  And burned him for a show !
Therefore his wrath did smite
Judas the Gaulonite,
  And his followers, as ye know.

For that cause, and no more,
Am I here, as I said before ;
  For one unlucky night,
Jucundus, the captain of horse,
Was upon us with all his force,
  And I was caught in the fight.

I might have fled with the rest,
But my dagger was in the breast
  Of a Roman equerry ;
As we rolled there in the street,
They bound me, hands and feet ;
  And this is the end of me.

Who cares for death ? Not I !
A thousand times I would die,
  Rather than suffer wrong !
Already those women of mine
Are mixing the myrrh and the wine ;
  I shall not be with you long.

THE DIVINE TRAGEDY

VIII

ECCE HOMO

PILATE (*on the tessellated pavement in front of his palace*)
Ye have brought unto me this man, as one
Who doth pervert the people; and behold!
I have examined him, and found no fault
Touching the things whereof ye do accuse him.
No, nor yet Herod; for I sent you to him,
And nothing worthy of death he findeth in him.
Ye have a custom at the Passover,
That one condemned to death shall be released.
Whom will ye, then, that I release to you?
Jesus Barabbas, called the Son of Shame,
Or Jesus, Son of Joseph, called the Christ?

THE PEOPLE (*shouting*)

Not this man, but Barabbas!

PILATE

               What then will ye
That I should do with him that is called Christ?

THE PEOPLE

Crucify him!

PILATE

             Why, what evil hath he done?
Lo, I have found no cause of death in him;
I will chastise him, and then let him go.

THE PEOPLE (*more vehemently*)

Crucify him! crucify him!

A MESSENGER (*to* PILATE)

            Thy wife sends
This message to thee, — Have thou naught to do
With that just man; for I this day in dreams
Have suffered many things because of him.

PILATE (*aside*)

The Gods speak to us in our dreams! I tremble
At what I have to do! O Claudia,
How shall I save him? Yet one effort more,
Or he must perish!

                  Washes his hands before them.
          I am innocent
Of the blood of this just person; see ye to it!

THE PEOPLE

Let his blood be on us and on our children!

VOICES (*within the palace*)

Put on thy royal robes; put on thy crown,
And take thy sceptre! Hail, thou King of the
    Jews!

PILATE

I bring him forth to you, that ye may know
I find no fault in him. Behold the man!

         CHRISTUS *is led in, with the purple robe and
      crown of thorns.*

CHIEF PRIESTS *and* OFFICERS

Crucify him ! crucify him !

PILATE

                     Take ye him ;
I find no fault in him.

CHIEF PRIESTS

          We have a Law,
And by our Law he ought to die ; because
He made himself to be the Son of God.

PILATE (*aside*)

Ah ! there are Sons of God, and demi-gods
More than ye know, ye ignorant High-Priests !
       (*To* CHRISTUS)
Whence art thou ?

CHIEF PRIESTS

        Crucify him ! crucify him !

PILATE (*to* CHRISTUS)

Dost thou not answer me ? Dost thou not know
That I have power enough to crucify thee ?
That I have also power to set thee free ?

CHRISTUS

Thou couldest have no power at all against me
Except that it were given thee from above ;
Therefore hath he that sent me unto thee
The greater sin.

CHRISTUS: A MYSTERY

CHIEF PRIESTS

If thou let this man go,
Thou art not Cæsar's friend. For whosoever
Maketh himself a King, speaks against Cæsar.

PILATE

Ye Jews, behold your King!

CHIEF PRIESTS

       Away with him !
Crucify him !

PILATE

Shall I crucify your King?

CHIEF PRIESTS

We have no King but Cæsar!

PILATE

        Take him, then,
Take him, ye cruel and bloodthirsty Priests,
More merciless than the plebeian mob,
Who pity and spare the fainting gladiator
Blood-stained in Roman amphitheatres, —
Take him, and crucify him if ye will;
But if the immortal Gods do ever mingle
With the affairs of mortals, which I doubt not,
And hold the attribute of justice dear,
They will commission the Eumenides
To scatter you to the four winds of heaven,
Exacting tear for tear, and blood for blood.
Here, take ye this inscription, Priests, and nail it

Upon the cross, above your victim's head:
Jesus of Nazareth, King of the Jews.

CHIEF PRIESTS

Nay, we entreat! write not, the King of the Jews;
But that he said: I am the King of the Jews!

PILATE

Enough. What I have written, I have written.

IX

ACELDAMA

JUDAS ISCARIOT

Lost! lost! forever lost! I have betrayed
The innocent blood! O God! if thou art love,
Why didst thou leave me naked to the tempter?
Why didst thou not commission thy swift lightning
To strike me dead? or why did I not perish
With those by Herod slain, the innocent children
Who went with playthings in their little hands
Into the darkness of the other world,
As if to bed? Or wherefore was I born,
If thou in thy foreknowledge didst perceive
All that I am, and all that I must be?
I know I am not generous, am not gentle,
Like other men; but I have tried to be,
And I have failed. I thought by following Him
I should grow like Him; but the unclean spirit
That from my childhood up hath tortured me

Hath been too cunning and too strong for me.
Am I to blame for this? Am I to blame
Because I cannot love, and ne'er have known
The love of woman or the love of children?
It is a curse and a fatality,
A mark, that hath been set upon my forehead,
That none shall slay me, for it were a mercy
That I were dead, or never had been born.

Too late! too late! I shall not see Him more
Among the living. That sweet, patient face
Will never more rebuke me, nor those lips
Repeat the words: One of you shall betray me!
It stung me into madness. How I loved,
Yet hated Him! But in the other world!
I will be there before Him, and will wait
Until He comes, and fall down on my knees
And kiss his feet, imploring pardon, pardon!

I heard Him say: All sins shall be forgiven,
Except the sin against the Holy Ghost.
That shall not be forgiven in this world,
Nor in the world to come. Is that my sin?
Have I offended so there is no hope
Here nor hereafter? That I soon shall know.
O God, have mercy! Christ have mercy on me!
                Throws himself headlong from the cliff.

X

THE THREE CROSSES

MANAHEM, THE ESSENIAN

Three crosses in this noonday night uplifted,
Three human figures, that in mortal pain
Gleam white against the supernatural darkness;
Two thieves, that writhe in torture, and between
    them
The Suffering Messiah, the Son of Joseph,
Ay, the Messiah Triumphant, Son of David!
A crown of thorns on that dishonored head!
Those hands that healed the sick now pierced with
    nails,
Those feet that wandered homeless through the world
Now crossed and bleeding, and at rest forever!
And the three faithful Maries, overwhelmed
By this great sorrow, kneeling, praying, weeping!
O Joseph Caiaphas, thou great High-Priest,
How wilt thou answer for this deed of blood?

SCRIBES *and* ELDERS

Thou that destroyest the Temple, and dost build it
In three days, save thyself; and if thou be
The Son of God, come down now from the cross.

CHIEF PRIESTS

Others he saved, himself he cannot save!
Let Christ the King of Israel descend
That we may see and believe!

CHRISTUS: A MYSTERY

SCRIBES *and* ELDERS

In God he trusted;
Let Him deliver him, if He will have him,
And we will then believe.

CHRISTUS

Father! forgive them;
They know not what they do.

THE IMPENITENT THIEF

If thou be Christ,
Oh save thyself and us!

THE PENITENT THIEF

Remember me,
Lord, when thou comest into thine own kingdom.

CHRISTUS

This day shalt thou be with me in Paradise.

MANAHEM

Golgotha! Golgotha! Oh the pain and darkness!
Oh the uplifted cross, that shall forever
Shine through the darkness, and shall conquer pain
By the triumphant memory of this hour!

SIMON MAGUS

O Nazarene! I find thee here at last!
Thou art no more a phantom unto me!
This is the end of one who called himself
The Son of God! Such is the fate of those
Who preach new doctrines. 'T is not what he did,

But what he said, hath brought him unto this.
I will speak evil of no dignitaries.
This is my hour of triumph, Nazarene!

THE YOUNG RULER

This is the end of him who said to me :
Sell that thou hast, and give unto the poor!
This is the treasure in heaven he promised me!

CHRISTUS

Eloi, Eloi, lama sabacthani!

A SOLDIER (*preparing the hyssop*)

He calleth for Elias!

ANOTHER

Nay, let be!
See if Elias now will come to save him!

CHRISTUS

I thirst.

A SOLDIER

Give him the wormwood!

CHRISTUS (*with a loud cry, bowing his head*)

It is finished!

XI

THE TWO MARIES

MARY MAGDALENE

We have arisen early, yet the sun
O'ertakes us ere we reach the sepulchre,
To wrap the body of our blessed Lord
With our sweet spices.

MARY, MOTHER OF JAMES

           Lo, this is the garden,
And yonder is the sepulchre. But who
Shall roll away the stone for us to enter?

MARY MAGDALENE

It hath been rolled away! The sepulchre
Is open! Ah, who hath been here before us,
When we rose early, wishing to be first?

MARY, MOTHER OF JAMES

I am affrighted!

MARY MAGDALENE

           Hush! I will stoop down
And look within. There is a young man sitting
On the right side, clothed in a long white garment!
It is an angel!

THE ANGEL

           Fear not; ye are seeking
Jesus of Nazareth, which was crucified.

Why do ye seek the living among the dead?
He is no longer here; he is arisen!
Come see the place where the Lord lay! Remember
How He spake unto you in Galilee,
Saying: The Son of Man must be delivered
Into the hands of sinful men; by them
Be crucified, and the third day rise again!
But go your way, and say to his disciples,
He goeth before you into Galilee;
There shall ye see Him as He said to you.

MARY, MOTHER OF JAMES

I will go swiftly for them.

MARY MAGDALENE (*alone, weeping*)
      They have taken
My Lord away from me, and now I know not
Where they have laid Him! Who is there to tell me?
This is the gardener. Surely he must know.

CHRISTUS

Woman, why weepest thou? Whom seekest thou?

MARY MAGDALENE

They have taken my Lord away; I cannot find Him.
O Sir, if thou have borne him hence, I pray thee
Tell me where thou hast laid Him.

CHRISTUS
      Mary!

MARY MAGDALENE
      Rabboni!

XII

THE SEA OF GALILEE

NATHANAEL (*in the ship*)
All is now ended.

JOHN
Nay, He is arisen.
I ran unto the tomb, and stooping down
Looked in, and saw the linen grave-clothes lying,
Yet dared not enter.

PETER
I went in, and saw
The napkin that had been about his head,
Not lying with the other linen clothes,
But wrapped together in a separate place.

THOMAS
And I have seen Him. I have seen the print
Of nails upon his hands, and thrust my hand
Into his side. I know He is arisen;
But where are now the kingdom and the glory
He promised unto us? We have all dreamed
That we were princes, and we wake to find
We are but fishermen.

PETER
Who should have been
Fishers of men!

152

Christ and Mary Magdalene

THE DIVINE TRAGEDY

JOHN

We have come back again
To the old life, the peaceful life, among
The white towns of the Galilean lake.

PETER

They seem to me like silent sepulchres
In the gray light of morning! The old life,
Yea, the old life! for we have toiled all night
And have caught nothing.

JOHN

Do ye see a man
Standing upon the beach and beckoning?
'T is like an apparition. He hath kindled
A fire of coals, and seems to wait for us.
He calleth.

CHRISTUS (*from the shore*)
Children, have ye any meat?

PETER

Alas! We have caught nothing.

CHRISTUS

Cast the net
On the right side of the ship, and ye shall find.

PETER

How that reminds me of the days gone by,
And one who said: Launch out into the deep,
And cast your nets!

NATHANAEL

We have but let them down
And they are filled, so that we cannot draw them!

JOHN

It is the Lord!

PETER (*girding his fisher's coat about him*)

He said: When I am risen
I will go before you into Galilee!

He casts himself into the lake.

JOHN

There is no fear in love; for perfect love
Casteth out fear. Now then, if ye are men,
Put forth your strength; we are not far from shore;
The net is heavy, but breaks not. All is safe.

PETER (*on the shore*)

Dear Lord! I heard thy voice and could not wait.
Let me behold thy face, and kiss thy feet!
Thou art not dead, thou livest! Again I see thee.
Pardon, dear Lord! I am a sinful man;
I have denied thee thrice. Have mercy on me!

THE OTHERS (*coming to land*)

Dear Lord! stay with us! cheer us! comfort us!
Lo! we again have found thee! Leave us not!

CHRISTUS

Bring hither of the fish that ye have caught,
And come and eat!

154

JOHN

Behold ! He breaketh bread
As He was wont. From his own blessed hands
Again we take it.

CHRISTUS

Simon, son of Jonas,
Lovest thou me, more than these others ?

PETER

Yea,
More, Lord, than all men ; even more than these.
Thou knowest that I love thee.

CHRISTUS

Feed my lambs.

THOMAS (*aside*)

How more than we do ? He remaineth ever
Self-confident and boastful as before.
Nothing will cure him.

CHRISTUS

Simon, son of Jonas,
Lovest thou me ?

PETER

· Yea, dearest Lord, I love thee.
Thou knowest that I love thee.

CHRISTUS

Feed my sheep.

THOMAS (*aside*)

Again, the selfsame question, and the answer
Repeated with more vehemence. Can the Master
Doubt if we love Him?

CHRISTUS

Simon, son of Jonas,
Lovest thou me?

PETER (*grieved*)

Dear Lord! thou knowest all things-
Thou knowest that I love thee.

CHRISTUS

Feed my sheep.
When thou wast young thou girdedst thyself, and
walkedst
Whither thou wouldst; but when thou shalt be
old,
Thou shalt stretch forth thy hands, and other men
Shall gird and carry thee whither thou wouldst
not.
Follow thou me!

JOHN (*aside*)

It is a prophecy
Of what death he shall die.

PETER (*pointing to* JOHN)

Tell me, O Lord,
And what shall this man do?

156

THE DIVINE TRAGEDY

CHRISTUS

                    And if I will
He tarry till I come, what is it to thee?
Follow thou me!

PETER

Yea, I will follow thee, dear Lord and Master!
Will follow thee through fasting and temptation,
Through all thine agony and bloody sweat,
Thy cross and passion, even unto death!

CHRISTUS: A MYSTERY

EPILOGUE

PETER

I BELIEVE in God the Father Almighty;

JOHN

Maker of Heaven and Earth;

JAMES

And in Jesus Christ his only Son, our Lord;

.ANDREW

Who was conceived by the Holy Ghost, born of the
Virgin Mary;

PHILIP

Suffered under Pontius Pilate, was crucified, dead and
buried;

THOMAS

And the third day He rose again from the dead;

BARTHOLOMEW

He ascended into Heaven, and sitteth on the right
hand of God, the Father Almighty;

MATTHEW

From thence He shall come to judge the quick and
the dead.

THE DIVINE TRAGEDY

JAMES, THE SON OF ALPHEUS

I believe in the Holy Ghost; the holy Catholic
Church;

SIMON ZELOTES

The communion of Saints ; the forgiveness of sins ;

JUDE

The resurrection of the body ;

MATTHIAS

And the Life Everlasting.

FIRST INTERLUDE

THE ABBOT JOACHIM

A room in the Convent of Flora in Calabria. Night.

JOACHIM

THE wind is rising; it seizes and shakes
The doors and window-blinds, and makes
Mysterious moanings in the halls;
The convent-chimneys seem almost
The trumpets of some heavenly host,
Setting its watch upon our walls!
Where it listeth, there it bloweth;
We hear the sound, but no man knoweth
Whence it cometh or whither it goeth,
And thus it is with the Holy Ghost.
O breath of God! O my delight
In many a vigil of the night,
Like the great voice in Patmos heard
By John, the Evangelist of the Word,
I hear thee behind me saying: Write
In a book the things that thou hast seen,
The things that are, and that have been,
And the things that shall hereafter be!

This convent, on the rocky crest
Of the Calabrian hills, to me
A Patmos is wherein I rest;

THE ABBOT JOACHIM

While round about me like a sea
The white mists roll, and overflow
The world that lies unseen below
In darkness and in mystery.
Here in the Spirit, in the vast
Embrace of God's encircling arm,
Am I uplifted from all harm;
The world seems something far away,
Something belonging to the Past,
A hostelry, a peasant's farm,
That lodged me for a night or day,
In which I care not to remain,
Nor having left, to see again.

Thus, in the hollow of God's hand
I dwelt on sacred Tabor's height
When as a simple acolyte
I journeyed to the Holy Land,
A pilgrim for my Master's sake,
And saw the Galilean Lake,
And walked through many a village street
That once had echoed to his feet.
There first I heard the great command,
The voice behind me saying: Write!
And suddenly my soul became
Illumined by a flash of flame,
That left imprinted on my thought
The image I in vain had sought,
And which forever shall remain;
As sometimes from these windows high,
Gazing at midnight on the sky
Black with a storm of wind and rain,

CHRISTUS: A MYSTERY

I have beheld a sudden glare
Of lightning lay the landscape bare,
With tower and town and hill and plain
Distinct, and burnt into my brain,
Never to be effaced again!

And I have written. These volumes three,
The Apocalypse, the Harmony
Of the Sacred Scriptures, new and old,
And the Psalter with Ten Strings, enfold
Within their pages, all and each,
The Eternal Gospel that I teach.
Well I remember the Kingdom of Heaven
Hath been likened to a little leaven
Hidden in two measures of meal,
Until it leavened the whole mass;
So likewise will it come to pass
With the doctrine that I here conceal.

Open and manifest to me
The truth appears, and must be told;
All sacred mysteries are threefold;
Three Persons in the Trinity,
Three ages of Humanity,
And Holy Scriptures likewise three,
Of Fear, of Wisdom, and of Love;
For Wisdom that begins in Fear
Endeth in Love; the atmosphere
In which the soul delights to be,
And finds that perfect liberty,
Which cometh only from above.

THE ABBOT JOACHIM

In the first Age, the early prime
And dawn of all historic time,
The Father reigned; and face to face
He spake with the primeval race.
Bright Angels, on his errands sent,
Sat with the patriarch in his tent;
His prophets thundered in the street;
His lightnings flashed, his hail-storms beat;
In earthquake and in flood and flame,
In tempest and in cloud He came!
The fear of God is in his Book;
The pages of the Pentateuch
Are full of the terror of his name.

Then reigned the Son; his Covenant
Was peace on earth, good-will to man;
With Him the reign of Law began.
He was the Wisdom and the Word,
And sent his Angels Ministrant,
Unterrified and undeterred
To rescue souls forlorn and lost,
The troubled, tempted, tempest-tost,
To heal, to comfort, and to teach.
The fiery tongues of Pentecost
His symbols were, that they should preach
In every form of human speech,
From continent to continent.
He is the Light Divine, whose rays
Across the thousand years unspent
Shine through the darkness of our days,
And touch with their celestial fires

Our churches and our convent spires.
His Book is the New Testament.

These Ages now are of the Past;
And the Third Age begins at last.
The coming of the Holy Ghost,
The reign of Grace, the reign of Love
Brightens the mountain-tops above,
And the dark outline of the coast.
Already the whole land is white
With convent walls, as if by night
A snow had fallen on hill and height!
Already from the streets and marts
Of town and traffic, and low cares,
Men climb the consecrated stairs
With weary feet, and bleeding hearts;
And leave the world, and its delights,
Its passions, struggles, and despairs,
For contemplation and for prayers
In cloister-cells of cœnobites.

Eternal benedictions rest
Upon thy name, Saint Benedict!
Founder of convents in the West,
Who built on Mount Cassino's crest
In the Land of Labor, thine eagle's nest!
May I be found not derelict
In aught of faith or godly fear,
If I have written, in many a page,
The Gospel of the coming age,
The Eternal Gospel men shall hear.
Oh may I live resembling thee,

THE ABBOT JOACHIM

And die at last as thou hast died;
So that hereafter men may see,
Within the choir, a form of air,
Standing with arms outstretched in prayer,
As one that hath been crucified!

My work is finished; I am strong
In faith and hope and charity;
For I have written the things I see,
The things that have been and shall be,
Conscious of right, nor fearing wrong;
Because I am in love with Love,
And the sole thing I hate is Hate;
For Hate is death; and Love is life,
A peace, a splendor from above;
And Hate, a never-ending strife,
A smoke, a blackness from the abyss
Where unclean serpents coil and hiss!
Love is the Holy Ghost within;
Hate the unpardonable sin!
Who preaches otherwise than this,
Betrays his Master with a kiss!

PART TWO

THE GOLDEN LEGEND

PROLOGUE

THE SPIRE OF STRASBURG CATHEDRAL

Night and storm. LUCIFER, *with the Powers of the Air,*
trying to tear down the Cross.

LUCIFER

HASTEN ! hasten !
O ye spirits !
From its station drag the ponderous
Cross of iron, that to mock us
Is uplifted high in air !

VOICES

Oh, we cannot !
For around it
All the Saints and Guardian Angels
Throng in legions to protect it ;
They defeat us everywhere !

THE BELLS

Laudo Deum verum !
Plebem voco !
Congrego clerum !

LUCIFER

Lower ! lower !
Hover downward !

CHRISTUS: A MYSTERY

Seize the loud, vociferous bells, and
Clashing, clanging, to the pavement
Hurl them from their windy tower!

VOICES

All thy thunders
Here are harmless!
For these bells have been anointed,
And baptized with holy water!
They defy our utmost power.

THE BELLS

Defunctos ploro!
Pestem fugo!
Festa decoro!

LUCIFER

Shake the casements!
Break the painted
Panes, that flame with gold and crimson;
Scatter them like leaves of Autumn,
Swept away before the blast!

VOICES

Oh, we cannot!
The Archangel
Michael flames from every window,
With the sword of fire that drove us
Headlong, out of heaven, aghast!

THE BELLS

Funera plango!

THE GOLDEN LEGEND

> Fulgura frango!
> Sabbata pango!

Aim your lightnings
At the oaken,
Massive, iron-studded portals!
Sack the house of God, and scatter
Wide the ashes of the dead!

VOICES

Oh, we cannot!
The Apostles
And the Martyrs, wrapped in mantles,
Stand as warders at the entrance,
Stand as sentinels o'erhead!

THE BELLS

> Excito lentos!
> Dissipo ventos!
> Paco cruentos!

LUCIFER

Baffled! baffled!
Inefficient,
Craven spirits! leave this labor
Unto Time, the great Destroyer!
Come away, ere night is gone!

VOICES

Onward! onward!
With the night-wind,

171

CHRISTUS: A MYSTERY

Over field and farm and forest,
Lonely homestead, darksome hamlet,
Blighting all we breathe upon !
> *They sweep away. Organ and Gregorian Chant.*

CHOIR

Nocte surgentes
Vigilemus omnes !

I

THE CASTLE OF VAUTSBERG ON THE RHINE

A chamber in a tower. PRINCE HENRY, *sitting alone, ill
and restless. Midnight.*

PRINCE HENRY

I cannot sleep! my fervid brain
Calls up the vanished Past again,
And throws its misty splendors deep
Into the pallid realms of sleep!
A breath from that far-distant shore
Comes freshening ever more and more,
And wafts o'er intervening seas
Sweet odors from the Hesperides!
A wind, that through the corridor
Just stirs the curtain, and no more,
And, touching the æolian strings,
Faints with the burden that it brings!
Come back! ye friendships long departed!
That like o'erflowing streamlets started,
And now are dwindled, one by one,
To stony channels in the sun!
Come back! ye friends, whose lives are ended,
Come back, with all that light attended,
Which seemed to darken and decay
When ye arose and went away!

They come, the shapes of joy and woe,
The airy crowds of long ago,

CHRISTUS: A MYSTERY

The dreams and fancies known of yore,
That have been, and shall be no more.
They change the cloisters of the night
Into a garden of delight;
They make the dark and dreary hours
Open and blossom into flowers!
I would not sleep! I love to be
Again in their fair company;
But ere my lips can bid them stay,
They pass and vanish quite away!
Alas! our memories may retrace
Each circumstance of time and place,
Season and scene come back again,
And outward things unchanged remain;
The rest we cannot reinstate;
Ourselves we cannot re-create,
Nor set our souls to the same key
Of the remembered harmony!

Rest! rest! Oh, give me rest and peace!
The thought of life that ne'er shall cease
Has something in it like despair,
A weight I am too weak to bear!
Sweeter to this afflicted breast
The thought of never-ending rest!
Sweeter the undisturbed and deep
Tranquillity of endless sleep!
          A flash of lightning, out of which LUCIFER *appears,*
          in the garb of a travelling Physician.

LUCIFER

All hail, Prince Henry!

THE GOLDEN LEGEND

PRINCE HENRY (*starting*)
                    Who is it speaks?
Who and what are you?

LUCIFER
                    One who seeks
A moment's audience with the Prince.

PRINCE HENRY
When came you in?

LUCIFER
                    A moment since.
I found your study door unlocked,
And thought you answered when I knocked.

PRINCE HENRY
I did not hear you.

LUCIFER
                    You heard the thunder;
It was loud enough to waken the dead.
And it is not a matter of special wonder
That, when God is walking overhead,
You should not hear my feeble tread.

PRINCE HENRY
What may your wish or purpose be?

LUCIFER
Nothing or everything, as it pleases
175

CHRISTUS: A MYSTERY

Your Highness. You behold in me
Only a travelling Physician;
One of the few who have a mission
To cure incurable diseases,
Or those that are called so.

PRINCE HENRY

                                 Can you bring
The dead to life?

LUCIFER

                       Yes; very nearly.
And, what is a wiser and better thing,
Can keep the living from ever needing
Such an unnatural, strange proceeding,
By showing conclusively and clearly
That death is a stupid blunder merely,
And not a necessity of our lives.
My being here is accidental;
The storm, that against your casement drives,
In the little village below waylaid me.
And there I heard, with a secret delight,
Of your maladies physical and mental,
Which neither astonished nor dismayed me.
And I hastened hither, though late in the night,
To proffer my aid!

PRINCE HENRY (ironically)

                    For this you came!
Ah, how can I ever hope to requite
This honor from one so erudite?

176

THE GOLDEN LEGEND

LUCIFER

The honor is mine, or will be when
I have cured your disease.

PRINCE HENRY

But not till then.

LUCIFER

What is your illness?

PRINCE HENRY

It has no name.
A smouldering, dull, perpetual flame,
As in a kiln, burns in my veins,
Sending up vapors to the head;
My heart has become a dull lagoon,
Which a kind of leprosy drinks and drains;
I am accounted as one who is dead,
And, indeed, I think that I shall be soon.

LUCIFER

And has Gordonius the Divine,
In his famous Lily of Medicine, —
I see the book lies open before you, —
No remedy potent enough to restore you?

PRINCE HENRY

None whatever!

LUCIFER

The dead are dead,
And their oracles dumb, when questioned

Of the new diseases that human life
Evolves in its progress, rank and rife.
Consult the dead upon things that were,
But the living only on things that are.
Have you done this, by the appliance
And aid of doctors?

PRINCE HENRY

      Ay, whole schools
Of doctors, with their learned rules;
But the case is quite beyond their science.
Even the doctors of Salern
Send me back word they can discern
No cure for a malady like this,
Save one which in its nature is
Impossible, and cannot be!

LUCIFER

That sounds oracular!

PRINCE HENRY

      Unendurable!

LUCIFER

What is their remedy?

PRINCE HENRY

      You shall see;
Writ in this scroll is the mystery.

LUCIFER (*reading*)

" Not to be cured, yet not incurable!

The only remedy that remains
Is the blood that flows from a maiden's veins,
Who of her own free will shall die,
And give her life as the price of yours!"

That is the strangest of all cures,
And one, I think, you will never try;
The prescription you may well put by,
As something impossible to find
Before the world itself shall end!
And yet who knows? One cannot say
That into some maiden's brain that kind
Of madness will not find its way.
Meanwhile permit me to recommend,
As the matter admits of no delay,
My wonderful Catholicon,
Of very subtile and magical powers!

PRINCE HENRY

Purge with your nostrums and drugs infernal
The spouts and gargoyles of these towers,
Not me! My faith is utterly gone
In every power but the Power Supernal!
Pray tell me, of what school are you?

LUCIFER

Both of the Old and of the New!
The school of Hermes Trismegistus,
Who uttered his oracles sublime
Before the Olympiads, in the dew
Of the early dusk and dawn of Time,
The reign of dateless old Hephæstus!

CHRISTUS: A MYSTERY

As northward, from its Nubian springs,
The Nile, forever new and old,
Among the living and the dead,
Its mighty, mystic stream has rolled;
So, starting from its fountain-head
Under the lotus-leaves of Isis,
From the dead demigods of eld,
Through long, unbroken lines of kings
Its course the sacred art has held,
Unchecked, unchanged by man's devices.
This art the Arabian Geber taught,
And in alembics, finely wrought,
Distilling herbs and flowers, discovered
The secret that so long had hovered
Upon the misty verge of Truth,
The Elixir of Perpetual Youth,
Called Alcohol, in the Arab speech!
Like him, this wondrous lore I teach!

PRINCE HENRY

What! an adept?

LUCIFER

Nor less, nor more!

PRINCE HENRY

I am a reader of your books,
A lover of that mystic lore!
With such a piercing glance it looks
Into great Nature's open eye,
And sees within it trembling lie

Line 20. I am a reader of such books,

THE GOLDEN LEGEND

The portrait of the Deity!
And yet, alas! with all my pains,
The secret and the mystery
Have baffled and eluded me,
Unseen the grand result remains!

LUCIFER (*showing a flask*)

Behold it here! this little flask
Contains the wonderful quintessence,
The perfect flower and efflorescence,
Of all the knowledge man can ask!
Hold it up thus against the light!

PRINCE HENRY

How limpid, pure, and crystalline,
How quick, and tremulous, and bright
The little wavelets dance and shine,
As were it the Water of Life in sooth!

LUCIFER

It is! It assuages every pain,
Cures all disease, and gives again
To age the swift delights of youth.
Inhale its fragrance.

PRINCE HENRY

It is sweet.
A thousand different odors meet
And mingle in its rare perfume,
Such as the winds of summer waft
At open windows through a room!

CHRISTUS: A MYSTERY

LUCIFER

Will you not taste it?

PRINCE HENRY

Will one draught
Suffice?

LUCIFER

If not, you can drink more.

PRINCE HENRY

Into this crystal goblet pour
So much as safely I may drink.

LUCIFER (*pouring*)

Let not the quantity alarm you;
You may drink all; it will not harm you.

PRINCE HENRY

I am as one who on the brink
Of a dark river stands and sees
The waters flow, the landscape dim
Around him waver, wheel, and swim,
And, ere he plunges, stops to think
Into what whirlpools he may sink;
One moment pauses, and no more,
Then madly plunges from the shore!
Headlong into the mysteries
Of life and death I boldly leap,
Nor fear the fateful current's sweep,

Line 15. Headlong into the dark mysteries

THE GOLDEN LEGEND

Nor what in ambush lurks below!
For death is better than disease!
An ANGEL *with an æolian harp hovers in the air.*

ANGEL

Woe! woe! eternal woe!
Not only the whispered prayer
Of love,
But the imprecations of hate,
Reverberate
For ever and ever through the air
Above!
This fearful curse
Shakes the great universe!

LUCIFER (disappearing)

Drink! drink!
And thy soul shall sink
Down into the dark abyss,
Into the infinite abyss,
From which no plummet nor rope
Ever drew up the silver sand of hope!

PRINCE HENRY (drinking)

It is like a draught of fire!
Through every vein
I feel again
The fever of youth, the soft desire;
A rapture that is almost pain
Throbs in my heart and fills my brain!
O joy! O joy! I feel
The band of steel

183

CHRISTUS: A MYSTERY

That so long and heavily has pressed
Upon my breast
Uplifted, and the malediction
Of my affliction
Is taken from me, and my weary breast
At length finds rest.

THE ANGEL

It is but the rest of the fire, from which the air has
      been taken !
It is but the rest of the sand, when the hour-glass is
      not shaken !
It is but the rest of the tide between the ebb and the
      flow !
It is but the rest of the wind between the flaws that
      blow !
With fiendish laughter,
Hereafter,
This false physician
Will mock thee in thy perdition.

PRINCE HENRY

Speak ! speak !
Who says that I am ill ?
I am not ill ! I am not weak !
The trance, the swoon, the dream, is o'er !
I feel the chill of death no more !
At length,
I stand renewed in all my strength !
Beneath me I can feel
The great earth stagger and reel,
As if the feet of a descending God

Upon its surface trod,
And like a pebble it rolled beneath his heel!
This, O brave physician! this
Is thy great Palingenesis!   *Drinks again.*

THE ANGEL

Touch the goblet no more!
It will make thy heart sore
To its very core!
Its perfume is the breath
Of the Angel of Death,
And the light that within it lies
Is the flash of his evil eyes.
Beware! Oh, beware!
For sickness, sorrow, and care
All are there!

PRINCE HENRY (*sinking back*)

O thou voice within my breast!
Why entreat me, why upbraid me,
When the steadfast tongues of truth
And the flattering hopes of youth
Have all deceived me and betrayed me?
Give me, give me rest, oh rest!
Golden visions wave and hover,
Golden vapors, water streaming,
Landscapes moving, changing, gleaming!
I am like a happy lover
Who illumines life with dreaming!
Brave physician! Rare physician!
Well hast thou fulfilled thy mission!
                    His head falls on his book.

185

CHRISTUS: A MYSTERY

THE ANGEL (*receding*)

Alas! alas!
Like a vapor the golden vision
Shall fade and pass,
And thou wilt find in thy heart again
Only the blight of pain,
And bitter, bitter, bitter contrition!

COURTYARD OF THE CASTLE

HUBERT *standing by the gateway.*

HUBERT

How sad the grand old castle looks
O'erhead, the unmolested rooks
Upon the turret's windy top
Sit, talking of the farmer's crop;
Here in the courtyard springs the grass,
So few are now the feet that pass;
The stately peacocks, bolder grown,
Come hopping down the steps of stone,
As if the castle were their own;
And I, the poor old seneschal,
Haunt, like a ghost, the banquet-hall.
Alas! the merry guests no more
Crowd through the hospitable door;
No eyes with youth and passion shine,
No cheeks glow redder than the wine;
No song, no laugh, no jovial din
Of drinking wassail to the pin;
But all is silent, sad, and drear,
And now the only sounds I hear

Touch the goblet no more

Are the hoarse rooks upon the walls,
And horses stamping in their stalls!

A horn sounds.

What ho! that merry, sudden blast
Reminds me of the days long past!
And, as of old resounding, grate
The heavy hinges of the gate,
And, clattering loud, with iron clank,
Down goes the sounding bridge of plank,
As if it were in haste to greet
The pressure of a traveller's feet!

Enter WALTER *the Minnesinger.*

WALTER

How now, my friend! This looks quite lonely!
No banner flying from the walls,
No pages and no seneschals,
No warders, and one porter only!
Is it you, Hubert?

HUBERT

Ah! Master Walter!

WALTER

Alas! how forms and faces alter!
I did not know you. You look older!
Your hair has grown much grayer and thinner,
And you stoop a little in the shoulder!

HUBERT

Alack! I am a poor old sinner,

187

And, like these towers, begin to moulder;
And you have been absent many a year!

WALTER

How is the Prince?

HUBERT

          He is not here;
He has been ill: and now has fled.

WALTER

Speak it out frankly: say he's dead!
Is it not so?

HUBERT

         No; if you please,
A strange, mysterious disease
Fell on him with a sudden blight.
Whole hours together he would stand
Upon the terrace, in a dream,
Resting his head upon his hand,
Best pleased when he was most alone,
Like Saint John Nepomuck in stone,
Looking down into a stream.
In the Round Tower, night after night,
He sat and bleared his eyes with books;
Until one morning we found him there
Stretched on the floor, as if in a swoon
He had fallen from his chair.
We hardly recognized his sweet looks!

WALTER

Poor Prince!

THE GOLDEN LEGEND

HUBERT

     I think he might have mended;
And he did mend; but very soon
The priests came flocking in, like rooks,
With all their crosiers and their crooks,
And so at last the matter ended.

WALTER

How did it end?

HUBERT

     Why, in Saint Rochus
They made him stand, and wait his doom;
And, as if he were condemned to the tomb,
Began to mutter their hocus-pocus.
First, the Mass for the Dead they chanted,
Then three times laid upon his head
A shovelful of churchyard clay,
Saying to him, as he stood undaunted,
" This is a sign that thou art dead,
So in thy heart be penitent! "
And forth from the chapel door he went
Into disgrace and banishment,
Clothed in a cloak of hodden gray,
And bearing a wallet, and a bell,
Whose sound should be a perpetual knell
To keep all travellers away.

WALTER

Oh, horrible fate! Outcast, rejected,
As one with pestilence infected!

189

CHRISTUS: A MYSTERY

HUBERT

Then was the family tomb unsealed,
And broken helmet, sword, and shield,
Buried together, in common wreck,
As is the custom, when the last
Of any princely house has passed,
And thrice, as with a trumpet-blast,
A herald shouted down the stair
The words of warning and despair,
" O Hoheneck ! O Hoheneck ! "

WALTER

Still in my soul that cry goes on, —
Forever gone ! forever gone !
Ah, what a cruel sense of loss,
Like a black shadow, would fall across
The hearts of all, if he should die !
His gracious presence upon earth
Was as a fire upon a hearth ;
As pleasant songs, at morning sung,
The words that dropped from his sweet tongue
Strengthened our hearts ; or, heard at night,
Made all our slumbers soft and light.
Where is he ?

HUBERT

In the Odenwald.
Some of his tenants, unappalled
By fear of death, or priestly word, —
A holy family, that make
Each meal a Supper of the Lord, —
Have him beneath their watch and ward,

For love of him, and Jesus' sake !
Pray you come in. For why should I
With out-door hospitality
My prince's friend thus entertain ?

WALTER

I would a moment here remain.
But you, good Hubert, go before,
Fill me a goblet of May-drink,
As aromatic as the May
From which it steals the breath away,
And which he loved so well of yore;
It is of him that I would think.
You shall attend me, when I call,
In the ancestral banquet-hall.
Unseen companions, guests of air,
You cannot wait on, will be there;
They taste not food, they drink not wine,
But their soft eyes look into mine,
And their lips speak to me, and all
The vast and shadowy banquet-hall
Is full of looks and words divine!
                (*Leaning over the parapet*)
The day is done; and slowly from the scene
The stooping sun up-gathers his spent shafts,
And puts them back into his golden quiver !
Below me in the valley, deep and green
As goblets are, from which in thirsty draughts
We drink its wine, the swift and mantling river
Flows on triumphant through these lovely regions,
Etched with the shadows of its sombre margent,
And soft, reflected clouds of gold and argent !

191

Yes, there it flows, forever, broad and still,
As when the vanguard of the Roman legions
First saw it from the top of yonder hill!
How beautiful it is! Fresh fields of wheat,
Vineyard, and town, and tower with fluttering flag,
The consecrated chapel on the crag,
And the white hamlet gathered round its base,
Like Mary sitting at her Saviour's feet,
And looking up at his beloved face!
O friend! O best of friends! Thy absence more
Than the impending night darkens the landscape o'er!

II

A FARM IN THE ODENWALD

A garden; morning; PRINCE HENRY *seated, with a book.*
ELSIE, *at a distance, gathering flowers.*

PRINCE HENRY (*reading*)

One morning, all alone,
Out of his convent of gray stone,
Into the forest older, darker, grayer,
His lips moving as if in prayer,
His head sunken upon his breast
As in a dream of rest,
Walked the Monk Felix. All about
The broad, sweet sunshine lay without,
Filling the summer air;
And within the woodlands as he trod,
The dusk was like the Truce of God

Line 22. The twilight was like the Truce of God

THE GOLDEN LEGEND

With worldly woe and care ;
Under him lay the golden moss ;
And above him the boughs of hoary trees
Waved, and made the sign of the cross,
And whispered their Benedicites ;
And from the ground
Rose an odor sweet and fragrant
Of the wild-flowers and the vagrant
Vines that wandered,
Seeking the sunshine, round and round.

These he heeded not, but pondered
On the volume in his hand,
Wherein amazed he read :
" A thousand years in thy sight
Are but as yesterday when it is past,
And as a watch in the night ! "
And with his eyes downcast
In humility he said :
" I believe, O Lord,
What is written in thy Word,
But alas ! I do not understand ! "

And lo ! he heard
The sudden singing of a bird,
A snow-white bird, that from a cloud

Line 3. And above him the boughs of hemlock-trees
Lines 12–17. A volume of Saint Augustine,
           Wherein he read of the unseen
           Splendors of God's great town
           In the unknown land,
           And, with his eyes cast down
Line 20. What herein I have read,

193

CHRISTUS: A MYSTERY

Dropped down,
And among the branches brown
Sat singing,
So sweet, and clear, and loud,
It seemed a thousand harp-strings ringing.
And the Monk Felix closed his book,
And long, long,
With rapturous look,
He listened to the song,
And hardly breathed or stirred,
Until he saw, as in a vision,
The land Elysian,
And in the heavenly city heard
Angelic feet
Fall on the golden flagging of the street.
And he would fain
Have caught the wondrous bird,
But strove in vain ;
For it flew away, away,
Far over hill and dell,
And instead of its sweet singing
He heard the convent bell
Suddenly in the silence ringing
For the service of noonday.
And he retraced
His pathway homeward sadly and in haste.

In the convent there was a change !
He looked for each well-known face,
But the faces were new and strange;
New figures sat in the oaken stalls,
New voices chanted in the choir;

Yet the place was the same place,
The same dusky walls
Of cold, gray stone,
The same cloisters and belfry and spire.

A stranger and alone
Among that brotherhood
The Monk Felix stood.
" Forty years," said a Friar,
" Have I been Prior
Of this convent in the wood,
But for that space
Never have I beheld thy face ! "

The heart of the Monk Felix fell :
And he answered, with submissive tone,
" This morning, after the hour ot Prime,
I left my cell,
And wandered forth alone,
Listening all the time
To the melodious singing
Of a beautiful white bird,
Until I heard
The bells of the convent ringing
Noon from their noisy towers.
It was as if I dreamed ;
For what to me had seemed
Moments only, had been hours ! "

" Years ! " said a voice close by.
It was an aged monk who spoke,
From a bench of oak

Fastened against the wall; —
He was the oldest monk of all.
For a whole century
Had he been there,
Serving God in prayer,
The meekest and humblest of his creatures.
He remembered well the features
Of Felix, and he said,
Speaking distinct and slow :
" One hundred years ago,
When I was a novice in this place,
There was here a monk, full of God's grace,
Who bore the name
Of Felix, and this man must be the same."

And straightway
They brought forth to the light of day
A volume old and brown,
A huge tome, bound
In brass and wild-boar's hide,
Wherein were written down
The names of all who had died
In the convent, since it was edified.
And there they found,
Just as the old monk said,
That on a certain day and date,
One hundred years before,
Had gone forth from the convent gate
The Monk Felix, and never more
Had entered that sacred door.
He had been counted among the dead !
And they knew, at last,

That, such had been the power
Of that celestial and immortal song,
A hundred years had passed,
And had not seemed so long
As a single hour!

ELSIE *comes in with flowers*

ELSIE

Here are flowers for you,
But they are not all for you.
Some of them are for the Virgin
And for Saint Cecilia.

PRINCE HENRY

As thou standest there,
Thou seemest to me like the angel
That brought the immortal roses
To Saint Cecilia's bridal chamber.

ELSIE

But these will fade.

PRINCE HENRY

Themselves will fade,
But not their memory,
And memory has the power
To re-create them from the dust.
They remind me, too,
Of martyred Dorothea,
Who from celestial gardens sent
Flowers as her witnesses
To him who scoffed and doubted.

197

CHRISTUS: A MYSTERY

Do you know the story
Of Christ and the Sultan's daughter?
That is the prettiest legend of them all.

PRINCE HENRY

Then tell it to me.
But first come hither.
Lay the flowers down beside me,
And put both thy hands in mine.
Now tell me the story.

ELSIE

Early in the morning
The Sultan's daughter
Walked in her father's garden,
Gathering the bright flowers,
All full of dew.

PRINCE HENRY

Just as thou hast been doing
This morning, dearest Elsie.

ELSIE

And as she gathered them
She wondered more and more
Who was the Master of the Flowers,
And made them grow
Out of the cold, dark earth.
" In my heart," she said,
" I love him ; and for him

198

Would leave my father's palace,
To labor in his garden."

PRINCE HENRY

Dear, innocent child!
How sweetly thou recallest
The long-forgotten legend,
That in my early childhood
My mother told me!
Upon my brain
It reappears once more,
As a birth-mark on the forehead
When a hand suddenly
Is laid upon it, and removed!

ELSIE

And at midnight,
As she lay upon her bed,
She heard a voice
Call to her from the garden,
And, looking forth from her window,
She saw a beautiful youth
Standing among the flowers.
It was the Lord Jesus;
And she went down to Him,
And opened the door for Him;
And He said to her, " O maiden!
Thou hast thought of me with love,
And for thy sake
Out of my Father's kingdom
Have I come hither:
I am the Master of the Flowers.

CHRISTUS: A MYSTERY

My garden is in Paradise,
And if thou wilt go with me,
Thy bridal garland
Shall be of bright red flowers."
And then He took from his finger
A golden ring,
And asked the Sultan's daughter
If she would be his bride.
And when she answered Him with love,
His wounds began to bleed,
And she said to him,
" O Love ! how red thy heart is,
And thy hands are full of roses."
" For thy sake," answered He,
" For thy sake is my heart so red,
For thee I bring these roses ;
I gathered them at the cross
Whereon I died for thee !
Come, for my Father calls.
Thou art my elected bride !"
And the Sultan's daughter
Followed Him to his Father's garden.

PRINCE HENRY

Wouldst thou have done so, Elsie ?

ELSIE

Yes, very gladly.

PRINCE HENRY

Then the Celestial Bridegroom
Will come for thee also.

Upon thy forehead He will place,
Not his crown of thorns,
But a crown of roses.
In thy bridal chamber,
Like Saint Cecilia,
Thou shalt hear sweet music,
And breathe the fragrance
Of flowers immortal!
Go now and place these flowers
Before her picture.

A ROOM IN THE FARM-HOUSE

Twilight. URSULA *spinning.* GOTTLIEB *asleep in his chair.*

URSULA

Darker and darker! Hardly a glimmer
Of light comes in at the window-pane;
Or is it my eyes are growing dimmer?
I cannot disentangle this skein,
Nor wind it rightly upon the reel.
Elsie!

GOTTLIEB (*starting*)

The stopping of thy wheel
Has awakened me out of a pleasant dream.
I thought I was sitting beside a stream,
And heard the grinding of a mill,
When suddenly the wheels stood still,
And a voice cried " Elsie " in my ear!
It startled me, it seemed so near.

CHRISTUS: A MYSTERY

URSULA

I was calling her : I want a light.
I cannot see to spin my flax.
Bring the lamp, Elsie. Dost thou hear?

ELSIE (*within*)

In a moment!

GOTTLIEB

    Where are Bertha and Max?

URSULA

They are sitting with Elsie at the door.
She is telling them stories of the wood,
And the Wolf, and little Red Ridinghood.

GOTTLIEB

And where is the Prince?

URSULA

             In his room overhead;
I heard him walking across the floor,
As he always does, with a heavy tread.

ELSIE *comes in with a lamp.* MAX *and* BERTHA *follow her ; and
they all sing the Evening Song on the lighting of the lamps.*

EVENING SONG

    O gladsome light
    Of the Father Immortal,
    And of the celestial
    Sacred and blessed
    Jesus, our Saviour!

THE GOLDEN LEGEND

Now to the sunset
Again hast thou brought us ;
And, seeing the evening
Twilight, we bless thee,
Praise thee, adore thee !

Father omnipotent !
Son, the Life-giver !
Spirit, the Comforter !
Worthy at all times
Of worship and wonder !

PRINCE HENRY (*at the door*)

Amen !

URSULA

Who was it said Amen ?

ELSIE

It was the Prince : he stood at the door,
And listened a moment, as we chanted
The evening song. He is gone again.
I have often seen him there before.

URSULA

Poor Prince !

GOTTLIEB

I thought the house was haunted !
Poor Prince, alas ! and yet as mild
And patient as the gentlest child !

203

CHRISTUS: A MYSTERY

MAX

I love him because he is so good,
And makes me such fine bows and arrows,
To shoot at the robins and the sparrows,
And the red squirrels in the wood !

BERTHA

I love him, too !

GOTTLIEB

       Ah, yes ! we all
Love him, from the bottom of our hearts;
He gave us the farm, the house, and the grange,
He gave us the horses and the carts,
And the great oxen in the stall,
The vineyard, and the forest range !
We have nothing to give him but our love !

BERTHA

Did he give us the beautiful stork above
On' the chimney-top, with its large, round nest ?

GOTTLIEB

No, not the stork; by God in heaven,
As a blessing, the dear white stork was given,
But the Prince has given us all the rest.
God bless him, and make him well again.

ELSIE

Would I could do something for his sake,
Something to cure his sorrow and pain !

GOTTLIEB

That no one can; neither thou nor I,
Nor any one else.

ELSIE

And must he die?

URSULA

Yes; if the dear God does not take
Pity upon him, in his distress,
And work a miracle!

GOTTLIEB

Or unless
Some maiden, of her own accord,
Offers her life for that of her lord,
And is willing to die in his stead.

ELSIE

I will!

URSULA

Prithee, thou foolish child, be still!
Thou shouldst not say what thou dost not mean!

ELSIE

I mean it truly!

MAX

O father! this morning,
Down by the mill, in the ravine,
Hans killed a wolf, the very same

That in the night to the sheepfold came,
And ate up my lamb, that was left outside.

GOTTLIEB

I am glad he is dead. It will be a warning
To the wolves in the forest, far and wide.

MAX

And I am going to have his hide!

BERTHA

I wonder if this is the wolf that ate
Little Red Ridinghood!

URSULA

Oh, no!
That wolf was killed a long while ago.
Come, children, it is growing late.

MAX

Ah, how I wish I were a man,
As stout as Hans is, and as strong!
I would do nothing else, the whole day long,
But just kill wolves.

GOTTLIEB

Then go to bed,
And grow as fast as a little boy can.
Bertha is half asleep already.
See how she nods her heavy head,
And her sleepy feet are so unsteady
She will hardly be able to creep up stairs.

THE GOLDEN LEGEND

URSULA

Good night, my children. Here's the light.
And do not forget to say your prayers
Before you sleep.

GOTTLIEB

Good night!

MAX *and* BERTHA

Good night!
They go out with ELSIE.

URSULA (*spinning*)

She is a strange and wayward child,
That Elsie of ours. She looks so old,
And thoughts and fancies weird and wild
Seem of late to have taken hold
Of her heart, that was once so docile and mild!

GOTTLIEB

She is like all girls.

URSULA

Ah no, forsooth!
Unlike all I have ever seen.
For she has visions and strange dreams,
And in all her words and ways, she seems
Much older than she is in truth.
Who would think her but fifteen?
And there has been of late such a change!

Line 14. Who would think her but fourteen?

207

CHRISTUS: A MYSTERY

My heart is heavy with fear and doubt
That she may not live till the year is out.
She is so strange, — so strange, — so strange!

GOTTLIEB

I am not troubled with any such fear;
She will live and thrive for many a year.

ELSIE'S CHAMBER

Night. ELSIE *praying.*

ELSIE

My Redeemer and my Lord,
I beseech thee, I entreat thee,
Guide me in each act and word,
That hereafter I may meet thee,
Watching, waiting, hoping, yearning,
With my lamp well trimmed and burning!

Interceding
With these bleeding
Wounds upon thy hands and side,
For all who have lived and erred
Thou hast suffered, thou hast died,
Scourged, and mocked, and crucified,
And in the grave hast thou been buried!

If my feeble prayer can reach thee,
O my Saviour, I beseech thee,
Even as thou hast died for me,
More sincerely

Let me follow where thou leadest,
Let me, bleeding as thou bleedest,
Die, if dying I may give
Life to one who asks to live,
And more nearly,
Dying thus, resemble thee! '

THE CHAMBER OF GOTTLIEB AND URSULA

Midnight. ELSIE *standing by their bedside, weeping.*

GOTTLIEB

The wind is roaring; the rushing rain
Is loud upon roof and window-pane,
As if the Wild Huntsman of Rodenstein,
Boding evil to me and mine,
Were abroad to-night with his ghostly train!
In the brief lulls of the tempest wild,
The dogs howl in the yard; and hark!
Some one is sobbing in the dark,
Here in the chamber!

ELSIE

It is I.

URSULA

Elsie! what ails thee, my poor child?

ELSIE

I am disturbed and much distressed,
In thinking our dear Prince must die;
I cannot close mine eyes, nor rest.

CHRISTUS: A MYSTERY

GOTTLIEB

What wouldst thou ? In the Power Divine
His healing lies, not in our own;
It is in the hand of God alone.

ELSIE

Nay, He has put it into mine,
And into my heart!

GOTTLIEB

       Thy words are wild!

URSULA

What dost thou mean ? my child! my child!

ELSIE

That for our dear Prince Henry's sake
I will myself the offering make,
And give my life to purchase his.

URSULA

Am I still dreaming, or awake?
Thou speakest carelessly of death,
And yet thou knowest not what it is.

ELSIE

'T is the cessation of our breath.
Silent and motionless we lie;
And no one knoweth more than this.
I saw our little Gertrude die;
She left off breathing, and no more
I smoothed the pillow beneath her head.

She was more beautiful than before.
Like violets faded were her eyes;
By this we knew that she was dead.
Through the open window looked the skies
Into the chamber where she lay,
And the wind was like the sound of wings,
As if angels came to bear her away.
Ah! when I saw and felt these things,
I found it difficult to stay;
I longed to die, as she had died,
And go forth with her, side by side.
The Saints are dead, the Martyrs dead,
And Mary, and our Lord; and I
Would follow in humility
The way by them illumined!

URSULA

My child! my child! thou must not die!

ELSIE

Why should I live? Do I not know
The life of woman is full of woe?
Toiling on and on and on,
With breaking heart, and tearful eyes,
And silent lips, and in the soul
The secret longings that arise,
Which this world never satisfies!
Some more, some less, but of the whole
Not one quite happy, no, not one!

URSULA

It is the malediction of Eve!

CHRISTUS: A MYSTERY

ELSIE

In place of it, let me receive
The benediction of Mary, then.

GOTTLIEB

Ah, woe is me! Ah, woe is me!
Most wretched am I among men!

URSULA

Alas! that I should live to see
Thy death, beloved, and to stand
Above thy grave! Ah, woe the day!

ELSIE

Thou wilt not see it. I shall lie
Beneath the flowers of another land,
For at Salerno, far away
Over the mountains, over the sea,
It is appointed me to die!
And it will seem no more to thee
Than if at the village on market-day
I should a little longer stay
Than I am wont.

URSULA

      Even as thou sayest!
And how my heart beats, when thou stayest!
I cannot rest until my sight
Is satisfied with seeing thee.
What, then, if thou wert dead?

THE GOLDEN LEGEND

GOTTLIEB

       Ah me!
Of our old eyes thou art the light!
The joy of our old hearts art thou!
And wilt thou die?

URSULA

     Not now! not now!

ELSIE

Christ died for me, and shall not I
Be willing for my Prince to die?
You both are silent; you cannot speak.
This said I at our Saviour's feast
After confession, to the priest,
And even he made no reply.
Does he not warn us all to seek
The happier, better land on high,
Where flowers immortal never wither;
And could he forbid me to go thither?

GOTTLIEB

In God's own time, my heart's delight!
When He shall call thee, not before!

ELSIE

I heard Him call. When Christ ascended
Triumphantly, from star to star,
He left the gates of heaven ajar.
I had a vision in the night,
And saw Him standing at the door
Of his Father's mansion, vast and splendid,

And beckoning to me from afar.
I cannot stay !

GOTTLIEB

     She speaks almost
As if it were the Holy Ghost
Spake through her lips, and in her stead !
What if this were of God ?

URSULA

          Ah, then
Gainsay it dare we not.

GOTTLIEB

     Amen !
Elsie ! the words that thou hast said
Are strange and new for us to hear,
And fill our hearts with doubt and fear.
Whether it be a dark temptation
Of the Evil One, or God's inspiration,
We in our blindness cannot say.
We must think upon it, and pray ;
For evil and good it both resembles.
If it be of God, his will be done !
May He guard us from the Evil One !
How hot thy hand is ! how it trembles !
Go to thy bed, and try to sleep.

URSULA

Kiss me. Good night ; and do not weep !
          ELSIE *goes out.*

Ah, what an awful thing is this!
I almost shuddered at her kiss,
As if a ghost had touched my cheek,
I am so childish and so weak!
As soon as I see the earliest gray
Of morning glimmer in the east,
I will go over to the priest,
And hear what the good man has to say!

A VILLAGE CHURCH

A woman kneeling at the confessional.

THE PARISH PRIEST (*from within*)

Go, sin no more! Thy penance o'er,
A new and better life begin!
God maketh thee forever free
From the dominion of thy sin!
Go, sin no more! He will restore
The peace that filled thy heart before,
And pardon thine iniquity!
> *The woman goes out. The Priest comes forth, and
> walks slowly up and down the church.*

O blessed Lord! how much I need
Thy light to guide me on my way!
So many hands, that, without heed,
Still touch thy wounds, and make them bleed!
So many feet, that, day by day,
Still wander from thy fold astray!
Unless thou fill me with thy light,
I cannot lead thy flock aright;
Nor, without thy support, can bear

CHRISTUS: A MYSTERY

The burden of so great a care,
But am myself a castaway !

A pause.

The day is drawing to its close;
And what good deeds, since first it rose,
Have I presented, Lord, to thee,
As offerings of my ministry ?
What wrong repressed, what right maintained,
What struggle passed, what victory gained,
What good attempted and attained ?
Feeble, at best, is my endeavor !
I see, but cannot reach, the height
That lies forever in the light,
And yet forever and forever,
When seeming just within my grasp,
I feel my feeble hands unclasp,
And sink discouraged into night !
For thine own purpose, thou hast sent
The strife and the discouragement !

A pause.

Why stayest thou, Prince of Hoheneck ?
Why keep me pacing to and fro
Amid these aisles of sacred gloom,
Counting my footsteps as I go,
And marking with each step a tomb ?
Why should the world for thee make room,
And wait thy leisure and thy beck ?
Thou comest in the hope to hear
Some word of comfort and of cheer.
What can I say ? I cannot give
The counsel to do this and live;
But rather, firmly to deny

The tempter, though his power be strong,
And, inaccessible to wrong,
Still like a martyr live and die!

A pause.

The evening air grows dusk and brown;
I must go forth into the town,
To visit beds of pain and death,
Of restless limbs, and quivering breath,
And sorrowing hearts, and patient eyes
That see, through tears, the sun go down,
But never more shall see it rise.
The poor in body and estate,
The sick and the disconsolate,
Must not on man's convenience wait.

Goes out.

Enter LUCIFER, *as a Priest.*

LUCIFER (*with a genuflexion, mocking*)

This is the Black Pater-noster.
God was my foster,
He fostered me
Under the book of the Palm-tree!
Saint Michael was my dame.
He was born at Bethlehem,
He was made of flesh and blood.
God send me my right food,
My right food, and shelter too,
That I may to yon kirk go,
To read upon yon sweet book
Which the mighty God of heaven shook.

Line 1. The tempter though his power is strong,

CHRISTUS: A MYSTERY

Open, open, hell's gates!
Shut, shut, heaven's gates!
All the devils in the air
The stronger be, that hear the Black Prayer!

Looking round the church.

What a darksome and dismal place!
I wonder that any man has the face
To call such a hole the House of the Lord,
And the Gate of Heaven, — yet such is the word.
Ceiling, and walls, and windows old,
Covered with cobwebs, blackened with mould;
Dust on the pulpit, dust on the stairs,
Dust on the benches, and stalls, and chairs!
The pulpit, from which such ponderous sermons
Have fallen down on the brains of the Ger-
  mans,
With about as much real edification
As if a great Bible, bound in lead,
Had fallen, and struck them on the head;
And I ought to remember that sensation!
Here stands the holy-water stoup!
Holy-water it may be to many,
But to me, the veriest Liquor Gehennæ!
It smells like a filthy fast-day soup!
Near it stands the box for the poor;
With its iron padlock, safe and sure.
I and the priest of the parish know
Whither all these charities go;
Therefore, to keep up the institution,
I will add my little contribution!

He puts in money.

Underneath this mouldering tomb,

THE GOLDEN LEGEND

With statue of stone, and scutcheon of brass,
Slumbers a great lord of the village.
All his life was riot and pillage,
But at length, to escape the threatened doom
Of the everlasting, penal fire,
He died in the dress of a mendicant friar,
And bartered his wealth for a daily mass.
But all that afterwards came to pass,
And whether he finds it dull or pleasant,
Is kept a secret for the present,
At his own particular desire.

And here, in a corner of the wall,
Shadowy, silent, apart from all,
With its awful portal open wide,
And its latticed windows on either side,
And its step well worn by the bended knees
Of one or two pious centuries,
Stands the village confessional!
Within it, as an honored guest,
I will sit me down awhile and rest!
                    Seats himself in the confessional.
Here sits the priest; and faint and low,
Like the sighing of an evening breeze,
Comes through these painted lattices
The ceaseless sound of human woe;
Here, while her bosom aches and throbs
With deep and agonizing sobs,
That half are passion, half contrition,
The luckless daughter of perdition
Slowly confesses her secret shame!
The time, the place, the lover's name!

219

CHRISTUS: A MYSTERY

Here the grim murderer, with a groan,
From his bruised conscience rolls the stone,
Thinking that thus he can atone
For ravages of sword and flame!

Indeed, I marvel, and marvel greatly,
How a priest can sit here so sedately,
Reading, the whole year out and in,
Naught but the catalogue of sin,
And still keep any faith whatever
In human virtue! Never! never!

I cannot repeat a thousandth part
Of the horrors and crimes and sins and woes
That arise, when with palpitating throes
The graveyard in the human heart
Gives up its dead, at the voice of the priest,
As if he were an archangel, at least.
It makes a peculiar atmosphere,
This odor of earthly passions and crimes,
Such as I like to breathe, at times,
And such as often brings me here
In the hottest and most pestilential season.
To-day, I come for another reason;
To foster and ripen an evil thought
In a heart that is almost to madness wrought,
And to make a murderer out of a prince,
A sleight of hand I learned long since!
He comes. In the twilight he will not see
The difference between his priest and me!
In the same net was the mother caught!

PRINCE HENRY (*entering and kneeling at the confessional*)
Remorseful, penitent, and lowly,
I come to crave, O Father holy,
Thy benediction on my head.

LUCIFER

The benediction shall be said
After confession, not before!
'T is a God-speed to the parting guest,
Who stands already at the door,
Sandalled with holiness, and dressed
In garments pure from earthly stain.
Meanwhile, hast thou searched well thy breast?
Does the same madness fill thy brain?
Or have thy passion and unrest
Vanished forever from thy mind?

PRINCE HENRY

By the same madness still made blind,
By the same passion still possessed,
I come again to the house of prayer,
A man afflicted and distressed!
As in a cloudy atmosphere,
Through unseen sluices of the air,
A sudden and impetuous wind
Strikes the great forest white with fear,
And every branch, and bough, and spray
Points all its quivering leaves one way,
And meadows of grass, and fields of grain,
And the clouds above, and the slanting rain,
And smoke from chimneys of the town,

CHRISTUS: A MYSTERY

Yield themselves to it, and bow down,
So does this dreadful purpose press
Onward, with irresistible stress,
And all my thoughts and faculties,
Struck level by the strength of this,
From their true inclination turn,
And all stream forward to Salern !

LUCIFER

Alas ! we are but eddies of dust,
Uplifted by the blast, and whirled
Along the highway of the world
A moment only, then to fall
Back to a common level all,
At the subsiding of the gust !

PRINCE HENRY

O holy Father ! pardon in me
The oscillation of a mind
Unsteadfast, and that cannot find
Its centre of rest and harmony !
For evermore before mine eyes
This ghastly phantom flits and flies,
And as a madman through a crowd,
With frantic gestures and wild cries,
It hurries onward, and aloud
Repeats its awful prophecies !
Weakness is wretchedness ! To be strong
Is to be happy ! I am weak,
And cannot find the good I seek,
Because I feel and fear the wrong !

THE GOLDEN LEGEND

Be not alarmed! The Church is kind,
And in her mercy and her meekness
She meets half-way her children's weakness,
Writes their transgressions in the dust!
Though in the Decalogue we find
The mandate written, "Thou shalt not kill!"
Yet there are cases when we must.
In war, for instance, or from scathe
To guard and keep the one true Faith!
We must look at the Decalogue in the light
Of an ancient statute, that was meant
For a mild and general application,
To be understood with the reservation,
That, in certain instances, the Right
Must yield to the Expedient!
Thou art a Prince. If thou shouldst die,
What hearts and hopes would prostrate lie!
What noble deeds, what fair renown,
Into the grave with thee go down!
What acts of valor and courtesy
Remain undone, and die with thee!
Thou art the last of all thy race!
With thee a noble name expires,
And vanishes from the earth's face
The glorious memory of thy sires!
She is a peasant. In her veins
Flows common and plebeian blood;
It is such as daily and hourly stains
The dust and the turf of battle plains,
By vassals shed, in a crimson flood,
Without reserve, and without reward,

CHRISTUS: A MYSTERY

At the slightest summons of their lord!
But thine is precious; the fore-appointed
Blood of kings, of God's anointed!
Moreover, what has the world in store
For one like her, but tears and toil?
Daughter of sorrow, serf of the soil,
A peasant's child and a peasant's wife,
And her soul within her sick and sore
With the roughness and barrenness of life!
I marvel not at the heart's recoil
From a fate like this, in one so tender,
Nor at its eagerness to surrender
All the wretchedness, want, and woe
That await it in this world below,
For the unutterable splendor
Of the world of rest beyond the skies.
So the Church sanctions the sacrifice:
Therefore inhale this healing balm,
And breathe this fresh life into thine;
Accept the comfort and the calm
She offers, as a gift divine;
Let her fall down and anoint thy feet
With the ointment costly and most sweet
Of her young blood, and thou shalt live.

PRINCE HENRY

And will the righteous Heaven forgive?
No action, whether foul or fair,
Is ever done, but it leaves somewhere
A record, written by fingers ghostly,
As a blessing or a curse, and mostly
In the greater weakness or greater strength

Of the acts which follow it, till at length
The wrongs of ages are redressed,
And the justice of God made manifest !

LUCIFER

In ancient records it is stated
That, whenever an evil deed is done,
Another devil is created
To scourge and torment the offending one !
But evil is only good perverted,
And Lucifer, the bearer of Light,
But an angel fallen and deserted,
Thrust from his Father's house with a curse
Into the black and endless night.

PRINCE HENRY

If justice rules the universe,
From the good actions of good men
Angels of light should be begotten,
And thus the balance restored again.

LUCIFER

Yes ; if the world were not so rotten,
And so given over to the Devil !

PRINCE HENRY

But this deed, is it good or evil ?
Have I thine absolution free
To do it, and without restriction ?

LUCIFER

Ay ; and from whatsoever sin

Lieth around it and within,
From all crimes in which it may involve thee,
I now release thee and absolve thee!

PRINCE HENRY

Give me thy holy benediction.

LUCIFER (*stretching forth his hand and muttering*)
Maledictione perpetua
Maledicat vos
Pater eternus!

THE ANGEL (*with the æolian harp*)
Take heed! take heed!
Noble art thou in thy birth,
By the good and the great of earth
Hast thou been taught!
Be noble in every thought
And in every deed!
Let not the illusion of thy senses
Betray thee to deadly offences.
Be strong! be good! be pure!
The right only shall endure,
All things else are but false pretences.
I entreat thee, I implore,
Listen no more
To the suggestions of an evil spirit,
That even now is there,
Making the foul seem fair,
And selfishness itself a virtue and a merit!

THE GOLDEN LEGEND

A ROOM IN THE FARM-HOUSE

GOTTLIEB

It is decided ! For many days,
And nights as many, we have had
A nameless terror in our breast,
Making us timid, and afraid
Of God, and his mysterious ways !
We have been sorrowful and sad ;
Much have we suffered, much have prayed
That He would lead us as is best,
And show us what his will required.
It is decided ; and we give
Our child, O Prince, that you may live !

URSULA

It is of God. He has inspired
This purpose in her ; and through pain,
Out of a world of sin and woe,
He takes her to Himself again.
The mother's heart resists no longer ;
With the Angel of the Lord in vain
It wrestled, for he was the stronger.

GOTTLIEB

As Abraham offered long ago
His son unto the Lord, and even
The Everlasting Father in heaven
Gave his, as a lamb unto the slaughter,
So do I offer up my 'daughter !

URSULA *hides her face.*

227

CHRISTUS: A MYSTERY

ELSIE

My life is little,
Only a cup of water,
But pure and limpid.
Take it, O my Prince!
Let it refresh you,
Let it restore you.
It is given willingly,
It is given freely;
May God bless the gift!

PRINCE HENRY

And the giver!

GOTTLIEB

Amen!

PRINCE HENRY

I accept it!

GOTTLIEB

Where are the children?

URSULA

They are already asleep.

GOTTLIEB

What if they were dead?

IN THE GARDEN

ELSIE

I have one thing to ask of you.

THE GOLDEN LEGEND

What is it?

It is already granted.

Promise me,
When we are gone from here, and on our way
Are journeying to Salerno, you will not,
By word or deed, endeavor to dissuade me
And turn me from my purpose ; but remember
That as a pilgrim to the Holy City
Walks unmolested, and with thoughts of pardon
Occupied wholly, so would I approach
The gates of Heaven, in this great jubilee,
With my petition, putting off from me
All thoughts of earth, as shoes from off my feet.
Promise me this.

Thy words fall from thy lips
Like roses from the lips of Angelo : and angels
Might stoop to pick them up !

Will you not promise ?

If ever we depart upon this journey,
So long to one or both of us, I promise.

Shall we not go, then ? Have you lifted me
Into the air, only to hurl me back

Wounded upon the ground? and offered me
The waters of eternal life, to bid me
Drink the polluted puddles of this world?

PRINCE HENRY

O Elsie! what a lesson thou dost teach me!
The life which is, and that which is to come,
Suspended hang in such nice equipoise
A breath disturbs the balance; and that scale
In which we throw our hearts preponderates,
And the other, like an empty one, flies up,
And is accounted vanity and air!
To me the thought of death is terrible,
Having such hold on life. To thee it is not
So much even as the lifting of a latch;
Only a step into the open air
Out of a tent already luminous
With light that shines through its transparent walls!
O pure in heart! from thy sweet dust shall grow
Lilies, upon whose petals will be written
" Ave Maria " in characters of gold!

III

A STREET IN STRASBURG

Night. PRINCE HENRY *wandering alone, wrapped in a cloak.*

PRINCE HENRY

Still is the night. The sound of feet
Has died away from the empty street,
And like an artisan, bending down

THE GOLDEN LEGEND

His head on his anvil, the dark town
Sleeps, with a slumber deep and sweet.
Sleepless and restless, I alone,
In the dusk and damp of these walls of stone,
Wander and weep in my remorse!

CRIER OF THE DEAD (*ringing a bell*)

Wake! wake!
All ye that sleep!
Pray for the Dead!
Pray for the Dead!

PRINCE HENRY

Hark! with what accents loud and hoarse
This warder on the walls of death
Sends forth the challenge of his breath!
I see the dead that sleep in the grave!
They rise up and their garments wave,
Dimly and spectral, as they rise,
With the light of another world in their eyes!

CRIER OF THE DEAD

Wake! wake!
All ye that sleep!
Pray for the Dead!
Pray for the Dead!

PRINCE HENRY

Why for the dead, who are at rest?
Pray for the living, in whose breast
The struggle between right and wrong
Is raging terrible and strong,

231

CHRISTUS: A MYSTERY

As when good angels war with devils!
This is the Master of the Revels,
Who, at Life's flowing feast, proposes
The health of absent friends, and pledges,
Not in bright goblets crowned with roses,
And tinkling as we touch their edges,
But with his dismal, tinkling bell,
That mocks and mimics their funeral knell!

CRIER OF THE DEAD

Wake! wake!
All ye that sleep!
Pray for the Dead!
Pray for the Dead!

PRINCE HENRY

Wake not, beloved! be thy sleep
Silent as night is, and as deep!
There walks a sentinel at thy gate
Whose heart is heavy and desolate,
And the heavings of whose bosom number
The respirations of thy slumber,
As if some strange, mysterious fate
Had linked two hearts in one, and mine
Went madly wheeling about thine,
Only with wider and wilder sweep!

CRIER OF THE DEAD (*at a distance*)

Wake! wake!
All ye that sleep!
Pray for the Dead!
Pray for the Dead!

232

THE GOLDEN LEGEND

Lo! with what depth of blackness thrown
Against the clouds, far up the skies
The walls of the cathedral rise,
Like a mysterious grove of stone,
With fitful lights and shadows blending,
As from behind, the moon, ascending,
Lights its dim aisles and paths unknown!
The wind is rising; but the boughs
Rise not and fall not with the wind,
That through their foliage sobs and soughs;
Only the cloudy rack behind,
Drifting onward, wild and ragged,
Gives to each spire and buttress jagged
A seeming motion undefined.
Below on the square, an armed knight,
Still as a statue and as white,
Sits on his steed, and the moonbeams quiver
Upon the points of his armor bright
As on the ripples of a river.
He lifts the visor from his cheek,
And beckons, and makes as he would speak.

WALTER (*the Minnesinger*)

Friend! can you tell me where alight
Thuringia's horsemen for the night?
For I have lingered in the rear,
And wander vainly up and down.

PRINCE HENRY

I am a stranger in the town,
As thou art; but the voice I hear

233

Is not a stranger to mine ear.
Thou art Walter of the Vogelweid!

WALTER

Thou hast guessed rightly; and thy name
Is Henry of Hoheneck!

PRINCE HENRY

Ay, the same.

WALTER (*embracing him*)

Come closer, closer to my side!
What brings thee hither? What potent charm
Has drawn thee from thy German farm
Into the old Alsatian city?

PRINCE HENRY

A tale of wonder and of pity!
A wretched man, almost by stealth
Dragging my body to Salern,
In the vain hope and search for health,
And destined never to return.
Already thou hast heard the rest.
But what brings thee, thus armed and dight
In the equipments of a knight?

WALTER

Dost thou not see upon my breast
The cross of the Crusaders shine?
My pathway leads to Palestine.

THE GOLDEN LEGEND

PRINCE HENRY

Ah, would that way were also mine!
O noble poet! thou whose heart
Is like a nest of singing-birds
Rocked on the topmost bough of life,
Wilt thou, too, from our sky depart,
And in the clangor of the strife
Mingle the music of thy words?

WALTER

My hopes are high, my heart is proud,
And like a trumpet long and loud,
Thither my thoughts all clang and ring!
My life is in my hand, and lo!
I grasp and bend it as a bow,
And shoot forth from its trembling string
An arrow, that shall be, perchance,
Like the arrow of the Israelite king
Shot from the window toward the east,
That of the Lord's deliverance!

PRINCE HENRY

My life, alas! is what thou seest!
O enviable fate! to be
Strong, beautiful, and armed like thee
With lyre and sword, with song and steel;
A hand to smite, a heart to feel!
Thy heart, thy hand, thy lyre, thy sword,
Thou givest all unto thy Lord;
While I, so mean and abject grown,
Am thinking of myself alone.

235

CHRISTUS: A MYSTERY

WALTER

Be patient: Time will reinstate
Thy health and fortunes.

PRINCE HENRY

      'T is too late!
I cannot strive against my fate!

WALTER

Come with me; for my steed is weary;
Our journey has been long and dreary,
And, dreaming of his stall, he dints
With his impatient hoofs the flints.

PRINCE HENRY (*aside*)

I am ashamed, in my disgrace,
To look into that noble face!
To-morrow, Walter, let it be.

WALTER

To-morrow, at the dawn of day,
I shall again be on my way.
Come with me to the hostelry,
For I have many things to say.
Our journey into Italy
Perchance together we may make;
Wilt thou not do it for my sake?

PRINCE HENRY

A sick man's pace would but impede
Thine eager and impatient speed.

THE GOLDEN LEGEND

Besides, my pathway leads me round
To Hirschau, in the forest's bound,
Where I assemble man and steed,
And all things for my journey's need.

They go out.

LUCIFER (*flying over the city*)
Sleep, sleep, O city ! till the light
Wake you to sin and crime again,
Whilst on your dreams, like dismal rain,
I scatter downward through the night
My maledictions dark and deep.
I have more martyrs in your walls
Than God has ; and they cannot sleep ;
They are my bondsmen and my thralls ;
Their wretched lives are full of pain,
Wild agonies of nerve and brain ;
And every heart-beat, every breath,
Is a convulsion worse than death !
Sleep, sleep, O city ! though within
The circuit of your walls there be
No habitation free from sin,
And all its nameless misery ;
The aching heart, the aching head,
Grief for the living and the dead,
And foul corruption of the time,
Disease, distress, and want, and woe,
And crimes, and passions that may grow
Until they ripen into crime !

Line 18. The circuit of your walls there lies
Line 20. And all its nameless miseries ;

237

CHRISTUS: A MYSTERY

SQUARE IN FRONT OF THE CATHEDRAL

Easter Sunday. FRIAR CUTHBERT *preaching to the crowd from a pulpit in the open air.* PRINCE HENRY *and* ELSIE *crossing the square.*

PRINCE HENRY

This is the day, when from the dead
Our Lord arose; and everywhere,
Out of their darkness and despair,
Triumphant over fears and foes,
The hearts of his disciples rose,
When to the women, standing near,
The Angel in shining vesture said,
" The Lord is risen; he is not here ! "
And, mindful that the day is come,
On all the hearths in Christendom
The fires are quenched, to be again
Rekindled from the sun, that high
Is dancing in the cloudless sky.
The churches are all decked with flowers,
The salutations among men
Are but the Angel's words divine,
" Christ is arisen ! " and the bells
Catch the glad murmur, as it swells,
And chant together in their towers.
All hearts are glad; and free from care
The faces of the people shine.
See what a crowd is in the square,
Gayly and gallantly arrayed !

THE GOLDEN LEGEND

ELSIE

Let us go back; I am afraid!

PRINCE HENRY

Nay, let us mount the church-steps here,
Under the doorway's sacred shadow;
We can see all things, and be freer
From the crowd that madly heaves and presses!

ELSIE

What a gay pageant! what bright dresses!
It looks like a flower-besprinkled meadow.
What is that yonder on the square?

PRINCE HENRY

A pulpit in the open air,
And a Friar, who is preaching to the crowd
In a voice so deep and clear and loud,
That, if we listen, and give heed,
His lowest words will reach the ear.

FRIAR CUTHBERT (*gesticulating and cracking a postilion's
whip*)

What ho! good people! do you not hear?
Dashing along at the top of his speed,
Booted and spurred, on his jaded steed,
A courier comes with words of cheer.
Courier! what is the news, I pray?
" Christ is arisen!" Whence come you? " From
court."
Then I do not believe it; you say it in sport.

Cracks his whip again.

239

CHRISTUS: A MYSTERY

Ah, here comes another, riding this way;
We soon shall know what he has to say.
Courier ! what are the tidings to-day ?
" Christ is arisen ! " Whence come you ? " From
    town."
Then I do not believe it; away with you, clown.
                Cracks his whip more violently.
And here comes a third, who is spurring amain;
What news do you bring, with your loose-hanging
    rein,
Your spurs wet with blood, and your bridle with
    foam ?
" Christ is arisen ! " Whence come you ? " From
    Rome."
Ah, now I believe. He is risen, indeed.
Ride on with the news, at the top of your speed !
            Great applause among the crowd.
To come back to my text ! When the news was first
    spread
That Christ was arisen indeed from the dead,
Very great was the joy of the angels in heaven;
And as great the dispute as to who should carry
The tidings thereof to the Virgin Mary,
Pierced to the heart with sorrows seven.
Old Father Adam was first to propose,
As being the author of all our woes;
But he was refused, for fear, said they,
He would stop to eat apples on the way !
Abel came next, but petitioned in vain,
Because he might meet with his brother Cain !
Noah, too, was refused, lest his weakness for wine
Should delay him at every tavern-sign;

240

THE GOLDEN LEGEND

And John the Baptist could not get a vote,
On account of his old-fashioned camel's-hair coat;
And the Penitent Thief, who died on the cross,
Was reminded that all his bones were broken!
Till at last, when each in turn had spoken,
The company being still at loss,
The Angel, who rolled away the stone,
Was sent to the sepulchre, all alone,
And filled with glory that gloomy prison,
And said to the Virgin, " The Lord is arisen!"

The Cathedral bells ring.

But hark! the bells are beginning to chime;
And I feel that I am growing hoarse.
I will put an end to my discourse,
And leave the rest for some other time.
For the bells themselves are the best of preachers;
Their brazen lips are learned teachers,
From their pulpits of stone, in the upper air,
Sounding aloft, without crack or flaw,
Shriller than trumpets under the Law,
Now a sermon and now a prayer.
The clangorous hammer is the tongue,
This way, that way, beaten and swung,
That from mouth of brass, as from Mouth of Gold,
May be taught the Testaments, New and Old.
And above it the great cross-beam of wood
Representeth the Holy Rood,
Upon which, like the bell, our hopes are hung.
And the wheel wherewith it is swayed and rung
Is the mind of man, that round and round
Sways, and maketh the tongue to sound!
And the rope, with its twisted cordage three,

241

CHRISTUS: A MYSTERY

Denoteth the Scriptural Trinity
Of Morals, and Symbols, and History;
And the upward and downward motion show
That we touch upon matters high and low;
And the constant change and transmutation
Of action and of contemplation,
Downward, the Scripture brought from on high,
Upward, exalted again to the sky;
Downward, the literal interpretation,
Upward, the Vision and Mystery!

And now, my hearers, to make an end,
I have only one word more to say;
In the church, in honor of Easter day
Will be represented a Miracle Play;
And I hope you will all have the grace to attend.
Christ bring us at last to his felicity!
Pax vobiscum! et Benedicite!

IN THE CATHEDRAL

CHANT
Kyrie Eleison!
Christe Eleison!

ELSIE
I am at home here in my Father's house!
These paintings of the Saints upon the walls
Have all familiar and benignant faces.

PRINCE HENRY
The portraits of the family of God!
Thine own hereafter shall be placed among them.

THE GOLDEN LEGEND

How very grand it is and wonderful!
Never have I beheld a church so splendid!
Such columns, and such arches, and such windows,
So many tombs and statues in the chapels,
And under them so many confessionals.
They must be for the rich. I should not like
To tell my sins in such a church as this.
Who built it?

PRINCE HENRY

      A great master of his craft,
Erwin von Steinbach; but not he alone,
For many generations labored with him.
Children that came to see these Saints in stone,
As day by day out of the blocks they rose,
Grew old and died, and still the work went on,
And on, and on, and is not yet completed.
The generation that succeeds our own
Perhaps may finish it. The architect
Built his great heart into these sculptured stones,
And with him toiled his children, and their lives
Were builded, with his own, into the walls,
As offerings unto God. You see that statue
Fixing its joyous, but deep-wrinkled eyes
Upon the Pillar of the Angels yonder.
That is the image of the master, carved
By the fair hand of his own child, Sabina.

ELSIE

How beautiful is the column that he looks at!

243

CHRISTUS: A MYSTERY

PRINCE HENRY

That, too, she sculptured. At the base of it
Stand the Evangelists ; above their heads
Four Angels blowing upon marble trumpets,
And over them the blessed Christ, surrounded
By his attendant ministers, upholding
The instruments of his passion.

ELSIE

                O my Lord!
Would I could leave behind me upon earth
Some monument to thy glory, such as this!

PRINCE HENRY

A greater monument than this thou leavest
In thine own life, all purity and love!
See, too, the Rose, above the western portal
Resplendent with a thousand gorgeous colors,
The perfect flower of Gothic loveliness!

ELSIE

And, in the gallery, the long line of statues,
Christ with his twelve Apostles watching us!
> *A* BISHOP *in armor, booted and spurred, passes
> with his train.*

PRINCE HENRY

But come away ; we have not time to look.
The crowd already fills the church, and yonder
Upon a stage, a herald with a trumpet,
Clad like the Angel Gabriel, proclaims
The Mystery that will now be represented.

THE GOLDEN LEGEND

THE NATIVITY: A MIRACLE-PLAY

INTROITUS

PRÆCO

Come, good people, all and each,
Come and listen to our speech!
In your presence here I stand,
With a trumpet in my hand,
To announce the Easter Play,
Which we represent to-day!
First of all we shall rehearse,
In our action and our verse,
The Nativity of our Lord,
As written in the old record
Of the Protevangelion,
So that he who reads may run!

Blows his trumpet.

I. HEAVEN

MERCY (*at the feet of God*)

Have pity, Lord! be not afraid
To save mankind, whom thou hast made,
Nor let the souls that were betrayed
   Perish eternally!

JUSTICE

It cannot be, it must not be!
When in the garden placed by thee,
The fruit of the forbidden tree
   He ate, and he must die!

245

CHRISTUS: A MYSTERY

MERCY

Have pity, Lord! let penitence
Atone for disobedience,
Nor let the fruit of man's offence
  Be endless misery!

JUSTICE

What penitence proportionate
Can e'er be felt for sin so great?
Of the forbidden fruit he ate,
  And damned must he be!

GOD

He shall be saved, if that within
The bounds of earth one free from sin
Be found, who for his kith and kin
  Will suffer martyrdom.

THE FOUR VIRTUES

Lord! we have searched the world around,
From centre to the utmost bound,
But no such mortal can be found;
  Despairing, back we come.

WISDOM

No mortal, but a God made man,
Can ever carry out this plan,
Achieving what none other can,
  Salvation unto all!

GOD

Go, then, O my beloved Son!

It can by thee alone be done;
By thee the victory shall be won
   O'er Satan and the Fall!

Here the ANGEL GABRIEL *shall leave Paradise and*
   fly towards the earth; the jaws of Hell open
   below, and the Devils walk about, making a
   great noise.

II. MARY AT THE WELL

MARY

Along the garden walk, and thence
Through the wicket in the garden fence,
   I steal with quiet pace,
My pitcher at the well to fill,
That lies so deep and cool and still
   In this sequestered place.

These sycamores keep guard around;
I see no face, I hear no sound,
   Save bubblings of the spring,
And my companions, who, within,
The threads of gold and scarlet spin,
   And at their labor sing.

THE ANGEL GABRIEL

Hail, Virgin Mary, full of grace!

(*Here* MARY *looketh around her, trembling, and then saith:*)

MARY

Who is it speaketh in this place,
   With such a gentle voice?

CHRISTUS: A MYSTERY

GABRIEL

The Lord of heaven is with thee now!
Blessed among all women thou,
   Who art his holy choice!

MARY (*setting down the pitcher*)

What can this mean? No one is near,
And yet, such sacred words I hear,
   I almost fear to stay.

(*Here the* ANGEL, *appearing to her, shall say:*)

GABRIEL

Fear not, O Mary! but believe!
For thou, a Virgin, shalt conceive
   A child this very day.

Fear not, O Mary! from the sky
The majesty of the Most High
   Shall overshadow thee!

MARY

Behold the handmaid of the Lord!
According to thy holy word,
   So be it unto me!
Here the Devils shall again make a great noise,
under the stage.

III. THE ANGELS OF THE SEVEN PLANETS (*bearing the*
           Star of Bethlehem)

THE ANGELS

The Angels of the Planets Seven,

THE GOLDEN LEGEND

Across the shining fields of heaven
  The natal star we bring !
Dropping our sevenfold virtues down
As priceless jewels in the crown
  Of Christ, our new-born King.

RAPHAEL

I am the Angel of the Sun,
Whose flaming wheels began to run
  When God's almighty breath
Said to the darkness and the Night,
Let there be light ! and there was light !
  I bring the gift of Faith !

ONAFIEL

I am the Angel of the Moon,
Darkened to be rekindled soon
  Beneath the azure cope !
Nearest to earth, it is my ray
That best illumes the midnight way ;
  I bring the gift of Hope !

ANAEL

The Angel of the Star of Love,
The Evening Star, that shines above
  The place where lovers be,
Above all happy hearths and homes,
On roofs of thatch, or golden domes,
  I give him Charity !

ZOBIACHEL

The Planet Jupiter is mine !

CHRISTUS: A MYSTERY

The mightiest star of all that shine,
  Except the sun alone!
He is the High Priest of the Dove,
And sends, from his great throne above,
  Justice, that shall atone!

MICHAEL

The Planet Mercury, whose place
Is nearest to the sun in space,
  Is my allotted sphere!
And with celestial ardor swift
I bear upon my hands the gift
  Of heavenly Prudence here!

URIEL

I am the Minister of Mars,
The strongest star among the stars!
  My songs of power prelude
The march and battle of man's life,
And for the suffering and the strife,
  I give him Fortitude!

ORIFEL

The Angel of the uttermost
Of all the shining, heavenly host,
  From the far-off expanse
Of the Saturnian, endless space
I bring the last, the crowning grace,
  The gift of Temperance!

*A sudden light shines from the windows of the
stable in the village below.*

THE GOLDEN LEGEND

IV. THE WISE MEN OF THE EAST

The stable of the Inn. The VIRGIN *and* CHILD. *Three Gypsy Kings,* GASPAR, MELCHIOR, *and* BELSHAZZAR, *shall come in.*

GASPAR

Hail to thee, Jesus of Nazareth !
Though in a manger thou draw breath,
Thou art greater than Life and Death,
    Greater than Joy or Woe !
This cross upon the line of life
Portendeth struggle, toil, and strife,
And through a region with peril rife
    In darkness shalt thou go !

MELCHIOR

Hail to thee, King of Jerusalem !
Though humbly born in Bethlehem,
A sceptre and a diadem
    Await thy brow and hand !
The sceptre is a simple reed,
The crown will make thy temples bleed,
And in thine hour of greatest need,
    Abashed thy subjects stand !

BELSHAZZAR

Hail to thee, Christ of Christendom !
O'er all the earth thy kingdom come !
From distant Trebizond to Rome
    Thy name shall men adore !
Peace and good-will among all men,

CHRISTUS: A MYSTERY

The Virgin has returned again,
Returned the old Saturnian reign
And Golden Age once more.

THE CHILD CHRIST

Jesus, the Son of God, am I,
Born here to suffer and to die
According to the prophecy,
That other men may live!

THE VIRGIN

And now these clothes, that wrapped Him, take
And keep them precious, for his sake;
Our benediction thus we make,
Naught else have we to give.
She gives them swaddling-clothes, and they depart.

V. THE FLIGHT INTO EGYPT

Here JOSEPH *shall come in, leading an ass, on which are seated* MARY *and the* CHILD.

MARY

Here will we rest us, under these
O'erhanging branches of the trees,
Where robins chant their Litanies
And canticles of joy.

JOSEPH

My saddle-girths have given way
With trudging through the heat to-day;

To you I think it is but play
  To ride and hold the boy.

MARY

Hark ! how the robins shout and sing,
As if to hail their infant King !
I will alight at yonder spring
  To wash his little coat.

JOSEPH

And I will hobble well the ass,
Lest, being loose upon the grass,
He should escape ; for, by the mass,
  He 's nimble as a goat.
    Here MARY *shall alight and go to the spring.*

MARY

O Joseph ! I am much afraid,
For men are sleeping in the shade ;
I fear that we shall be waylaid,
  And robbed and beaten sore !
*Here a band of robbers shall be seen sleeping, two
  of whom shall rise and come forward.*

DUMACHUS

Cock's soul ! deliver up your gold !

JOSEPH

I pray you, Sirs, let go your hold !
You see that I am weak and old,
  Of wealth I have no store.

Line 17. [Not in first edition.]

253

CHRISTUS: A MYSTERY

DUMACHUS

Give up your money!

TITUS

      Prithee cease.
Let these people go in peace.

DUMACHUS

First let them pay for their release,
 And then go on their way.

TITUS

These forty groats I give in fee,
If thou wilt only silent be.

MARY

May God be merciful to thee
 Upon the Judgment Day!

JESUS

When thirty years shall have gone by,
I at Jerusalem shall die,
By Jewish hands exalted high
 On the accursed tree,
Then on my right and my left side,
These thieves shall both be crucified,
And Titus thenceforth shall abide
 In paradise with me.

*Here a great rumor of trumpets and horses, like
the noise of a king with his army, and the robbers shall take flight.*

Line 6. Let these good people go in peace!

VI. THE SLAUGHTER OF THE INNOCENTS

KING HEROD

Potz-tausend! Himmel-sacrament!
Filled am I with great wonderment
   At this unwelcome news!
Am I not Herod? Who shall dare
My crown to take, my sceptre bear,
   As king among the Jews?

*Here he shall stride up and down and flourish his
sword.*

What ho! I fain would drink a can
Of the strong wine of Canaan!
   The wine of Helbon bring
I purchased at the Fair of Tyre,
As red as blood, as hot as fire,
   And fit for any king!

             He quaffs great goblets of wine.

Now at the window will I stand,
While in the street the armed band
   The little children slay;
The babe just born in Bethlehem
Will surely slaughtered be with them,
   Nor live another day!

*Here a voice of lamentation shall be heard in the
street.*

RACHEL

O wicked king! O cruel speed!
To do this most unrighteous deed!
   My children all are slain!

CHRISTUS: A MYSTERY

HEROD

Ho seneschal! another cup!
With wine of Sorek fill it up!
   I would a bumper drain!

RAHAB

May maledictions fall and blast
Thyself and lineage, to the last
   Of all thy kith and kin!

HEROD

Another goblet! quick! and stir
Pomegranate juice and drops of myrrh
   And calamus therein!

SOLDIERS *(in the street)*

Give up thy child into our hands!
It is King Herod who commands
   That he should thus be slain!

THE NURSE MEDUSA

O monstrous men! What have ye done!
It is King Herod's only son
   That ye have cleft in twain!

HEROD

Ah, luckless day! What words of fear
Are these that smite upon my ear
   With such a doleful sound!
What torments rack my heart and head!

Would I were dead! would I were dead,
   And buried in the ground!
He falls down and writhes as though eaten by
  worms. Hell opens, and SATAN *and* ASTAROTH
  come forth, and drag him down.

VII. JESUS AT PLAY WITH HIS SCHOOLMATES

JESUS

The shower is over. Let us play,
And make some sparrows out of clay,
   Down by the river's side.

JUDAS

See, how the stream has overflowed
Its banks, and o'er the meadow road
   Is spreading far and wide!
They draw water out of the river by channels, and
  form little pools. JESUS *makes twelve sparrows*
  of clay, and the other boys do the same.

JESUS

Look! look how prettily I make
These little sparrows by the lake
   Bend down their necks and drink!
Now will I make them sing and soar
So far, they shall return no more
   Unto this river's brink.

JUDAS

That canst thou not! They are but clay,
They cannot sing, nor fly away
   Above the meadow lands!

257

CHRISTUS: A MYSTERY

JESUS

Fly, fly! ye sparrows! you are free!
And while you live, remember me,
　　Who made you with my hands.
Here JESUS *shall clap his hands, and the sparrows*
　shall fly away, chirruping.

JUDAS

Thou art a sorcerer, I know;
Oft has my mother told me so,
　　I will not play with thee!
　　　　He strikes JESUS *in the right side.*

JESUS

Ah, Judas! thou hast smote my side,
And when I shall be crucified,
　　There shall I pierced be!

(*Here* JOSEPH *shall come in, and say :*)

JOSEPH

Ye wicked boys! why do ye play,
And break the holy Sabbath day?
What, think ye, will your mothers say
　　To see you in such plight!
In such a sweat and such a heat,
With all that mud upon your feet!
There 's not a beggar in the street
　　Makes such a sorry sight!

THE GOLDEN LEGEND

VIII. THE VILLAGE SCHOOL

The RABBI BEN ISRAEL, *sitting on a high stool, with a long beard, and a rod in his hand.*

RABBI

I am the Rabbi Ben Israel,
Throughout this village known full well,
And, as my scholars all will tell,
   Learned in things divine;
The Cabala and Talmud hoar
Than all the prophets prize I more,
For water is all Bible lore,
   But Mishna is strong wine.

My fame extends from West to East,
And always, at the Purim feast,
I am as drunk as any beast
   That wallows in his sty;
The wine it so elateth me,
That I no difference can see
Between " Accursed Haman be ! "
   And " Blessed be Mordecai ! "

Come hither, Judas Iscariot;
Say, if thy lesson thou hast got
From the Rabbinical Book or not.
   Why howl the dogs at night?

JUDAS

In the Rabbinical Book, it saith
The dogs howl, when with icy breath

Great Sammael, the Angel of Death,
  Takes through the town his flight!

RABBI

Well, boy! now say, if thou art wise,
When the Angel of Death, who is full of eyes,
Comes where a sick man dying lies,
  What doth he to the wight?

JUDAS

He stands beside him, dark and tall,
Holding a sword, from which doth fall
Into his mouth a drop of gall,
  And so he turneth white.

RABBI

And now, my Judas, say to me
What the great Voices Four may be,
That quite across the world do flee,
  And are not heard by men?

JUDAS

The Voice of the Sun in heaven's dome,
The Voice of the Murmuring of Rome,
The Voice of a Soul that goeth home,
  And the Angel of the Rain!

RABBI

Right are thine answers every one!
Now little Jesus, the carpenter's son,
Let us see how thy task is done;
  Canst thou thy letters say?

THE GOLDEN LEGEND

JESUS

Aleph.

RABBI

What next? Do not stop yet!
Go on with all the alphabet.
Come, Aleph, Beth; dost thou forget?
Cock's soul! thou 'dst rather play!

JESUS

What Aleph means I fain would know,
Before I any farther go!

RABBI

Oh, by Saint Peter! wouldst thou so?
Come hither, boy, to me.
As surely as the letter Jod
Once cried aloud, and spake to God,
So surely shalt thou feel this rod,
And punished shalt thou be!

Here RABBI BEN ISRAEL *shall lift up his rod to
strike* JESUS, *and his right arm shall be para-
lyzed.*

IX. CROWNED WITH FLOWERS

JESUS, *sitting among his playmates crowned with flowers as
their King.*

BOYS

We spread our garments on the ground!
With fragrant flowers thy head is crowned,
While like a guard we stand around,
And hail thee as our King!

261

CHRISTUS: A MYSTERY

Thou art the new King of the Jews!
Nor let the passers-by refuse
To bring that homage which men use
    To majesty to bring.

(Here a traveller shall go by, and the boys shall lay hold of
his garments and say:)

BOYS

Come hither! and all reverence pay
Unto our monarch, crowned to-day!
Then go rejoicing on your way,
    In all prosperity!

TRAVELLER

Hail to the King of Bethlehem,
Who weareth in his diadem
The yellow crocus for the gem
    Of his authority!
    He passes by; and others come in, bearing on a lit-
    ter a sick child.

BOYS

Set down the litter and draw near!
The King of Bethlehem is here!
What ails the child, who seems to fear
    That we shall do him harm?

THE BEARERS

He climbed up to the robin's nest,
And out there darted, from his rest,
A serpent with a crimson crest,
    And stung him in the arm.

262

THE GOLDEN LEGEND

JESUS

Bring him to me, and let me feel
The wounded place; my touch can heal
The sting of serpents, and can steal
    The poison from the bite!
    He touches the wound, and the boy begins to cry.
Cease to lament! I can foresee
That thou hereafter known shalt be,
Among the men who follow me,
    As Simon the Canaanite!

EPILOGUE

In the after part of the day
Will be represented another play,
Of the Passion of our Blessed Lord,
Beginning directly after Nones!
At the close of which we shall accord,
By way of benison and reward,
The sight of a holy Martyr's bones!

IV

THE ROAD TO HIRSCHAU

PRINCE HENRY *and* ELSIE *with their attendants on horse-*
back.

ELSIE

Onward and onward the highway runs to the distant
    city, impatiently bearing
Tidings of human joy and disaster, of love and of
    hate, of doing and daring!

CHRISTUS: A MYSTERY

This life of ours is a wild æolian harp of many a
    joyous strain,
But under them all there runs a loud perpetual wail,
    as of souls in pain.

ELSIE

Faith alone can interpret life, and the heart that aches
    and bleeds with the stigma
Of pain, alone bears the likeness of Christ, and can
    comprehend its dark enigma.

PRINCE HENRY

Man is selfish, and seeketh pleasure with little care
    of what may betide,
Else why am I travelling here beside thee, a demon
    that rides by an angel's side?

ELSIE

All the hedges are white with dust, and the great dog
    under the creaking wain
Hangs his head in the lazy heat, while onward the
    horses toil and strain.

PRINCE HENRY

Now they stop at the wayside inn, and the wagoner
    laughs with the landlord's daughter,
While out of the dripping trough the horses distend
    their leathern sides with water.

ELSIE

All through life there are wayside inns, where man
    may refresh his soul with love;

Even the lowest may quench his thirst at rivulets fed
    by springs from above.

PRINCE HENRY

Yonder, where rises the cross of stone, our journey
    along the highway ends,
And over the fields, by a bridle path, down into the
    broad green valley descends.

ELSIE

I am not sorry to leave behind the beaten road with
    its dust and heat ;
The air will be sweeter far, and the turf will be
    softer under our horses' feet.
                 They turn down a green lane.

ELSIE

Sweet is the air with the budding haws, and the valley
    stretching for miles below
Is white with blossoming cherry-trees, as if just cov-
    ered with lightest snow.

PRINCE HENRY

Over our heads a white cascade is gleaming against
    the distant hill ;
We cannot hear it, nor see it move, but it hangs like
    a banner when winds are still.

ELSIE

Damp and cool is this deep ravine, and cool the
    sound of the brook by our side !
What is this castle that rises above us, and lords it
    over a land so wide ?

265

CHRISTUS: A MYSTERY

PRINCE HENRY

It is the home of the Counts of Calva; well have I
    known these scenes of old,
Well I remember each tower and turret, remember
    the brooklet, the wood, and the wold.

ELSIE

Hark! from the little village below us the bells of
    the church are ringing for rain!
Priests and peasants in long procession come forth
    and kneel on the arid plain.

PRINCE HENRY

They have not long to wait, for I see in the south
    uprising a little cloud,
That before the sun shall be set will cover the sky
    above us as with a shroud.   *They pass on.*

THE CONVENT OF HIRSCHAU IN THE BLACK FOREST

The Convent cellar.   FRIAR CLAUS *comes in with a light and
a basket of empty flagons.*

FRIAR CLAUS

I always enter this sacred place
With a thoughtful, solemn, and reverent pace,
Pausing long enough on each stair
To breathe an ejaculatory prayer,
And a benediction on the vines
That produce these various sorts of wines!
For my part, I am well content
That we have got through with the tedious Lent!

THE GOLDEN LEGEND

Fasting is all very well for those
Who have to contend with invisible foes;
But I am quite sure it does not agree
With a quiet, peaceable man like me,
Who am not of that nervous and meagre kind,
That are always distressed in body and mind!
And at times it really does me good
To come down among this brotherhood,
Dwelling forever underground,
Silent, contemplative, round and sound;
Each one old, and brown with mould,
But filled to the lips with the ardor of youth,
With the latent power and love of truth,
And with virtues fervent and manifold.

I have heard it said, that at Easter-tide
When buds are swelling on every side,
And the sap begins to move in the vine,
Then in all cellars, far and wide,
The oldest as well as the newest wine
Begins to stir itself, and ferment,
With a kind of revolt and discontent
At being so long in darkness pent,
And fain would burst from its sombre tun
To bask on the hillside in the sun;
As in the bosom of us poor friars,
The tumult of half-subdued desires
For the world that we have left behind
Disturbs at times all peace of mind!
And now that we have lived through Lent,
My duty it is, as often before,

Line 18. Then in all the cellars, far and wide,

CHRISTUS: A MYSTERY

To open awhile the prison-door,
And give these restless spirits vent.

Now here is a cask that stands alone,
And has stood a hundred years or more,
Its beard of cobwebs, long and hoar,
Trailing and sweeping along the floor,
Like Barbarossa, who sits in his cave,
Taciturn, sombre, sedate, and grave,
Till his beard has grown through the table of stone!
It is of the quick and not of the dead!
In its veins the blood is hot and red,
And a heart still beats in those ribs of oak
That time may have tamed, but has not broke!
It comes from Bacharach on the Rhine,
Is one of the three best kinds of wine,
And costs some hundred florins the ohm;
But that I do not consider dear,
When I remember that every year
Four butts are sent to the Pope of Rome.
And whenever a goblet thereof I drain,
The old rhyme keeps running in my brain:

> At Bacharach on the Rhine,
> At Hochheim on the Main,
> And at Würzburg on the Stein,
> Grow the three best kinds of wine!

They are all good wines, and better far
Than those of the Neckar, or those of the Ahr.
In particular, Würzburg well may boast
Of its blessed wine of the Holy Ghost,

Which of all wines I like the most.
This I shall draw for the Abbot's drinking,
Who seems to be much of my way of thinking.

Fills a flagon.

Ah! how the streamlet laughs and sings!
What a delicious fragrance springs
From the deep flagon, while it fills,
As of hyacinths and daffodils!
Between this cask and the Abbot's lips
Many have been the sips and slips;
Many have been the draughts of wine,
On their way to his, that have stopped at mine;
And many a time my soul has hankered
For a deep draught out of his silver tankard,
When it should have been busy with other affairs,
Less with its longings and more with its prayers.
But now there is no such awkward condition,
No danger of death and eternal perdition;
So here 's to the Abbot and Brothers all,
Who dwell in this convent of Peter and Paul!

He drinks.

O cordial delicious! O soother of pain!
It flashes like sunshine into my brain!
A benison rest on the Bishop who sends
Such a fudder of wine as this to his friends!
And now a flagon for such as may ask
A draught from the noble Bacharach cask,
And I will be gone, though I know full well
The cellar 's a cheerfuller place than the cell.
Behold where he stands, all sound and good,
Brown and old in his oaken hood;
Silent he seems externally

CHRISTUS: A MYSTERY

As any Carthusian monk may be;
But within, what a spirit of deep unrest!
What a seething and simmering in his breast!
As if the heaving of his great heart
Would burst his belt of oak apart!
Let me unloose this button of wood,
And quiet a little his turbulent mood.

Sets it running.

See! how its currents gleam and shine,
As if they had caught the purple hues
Of autumn sunsets on the Rhine,
Descending and mingling with the dews;
Or as if the grapes were stained with the blood
Of the innocent boy, who, some years back,
Was taken and crucified by the Jews,
In that ancient town of Bacharach;
Perdition upon those infidel Jews,
In that ancient town of Bacharach!
The beautiful town, that gives us wine
With the fragrant odor of Muscadine!
I should deem it wrong to let this pass
Without first touching my lips to the glass,
For here in the midst of the current I stand
Like the stone Pfalz in the midst of the river,
Taking toll upon either hand,
And much more grateful to the giver.

He drinks.

Here, now, is a very inferior kind,
Such as in any town you may find,
Such as one might imagine would suit
The rascal who drank wine out of a boot.
And, after all, it was not a crime,

For he won thereby Dorf Hüffelsheim.
A jolly old toper! who at a pull
Could drink a postilion's jack-boot full,
And ask with a laugh, when that was done,
If the fellow had left the other one!
This wine is as good as we can afford
To the friars, who sit at the lower board,
And cannot distinguish bad from good,
And are far better off than if they could,
Being rather the rude disciples of beer
Than of anything more refined and dear!

Fills the flagon and departs.

THE SCRIPTORIUM

FRIAR PACIFICUS *transcribing and illuminating.*

FRIAR PACIFICUS

It is growing dark! Yet one line more,
And then my work for to-day is o'er.
I come again to the name of the Lord!
Ere I that awful name record,
That is spoken so lightly among men,
Let me pause awhile, and wash my pen;
Pure from blemish and blot must it be
When it writes that word of mystery!

Thus have I labored on and on,
Nearly through the Gospel of John.
Can it be that from the lips
Of this same gentle Evangelist,
That Christ himself perhaps has kissed,

271

CHRISTUS: A MYSTERY

Came the dread Apocalypse!
It has a very awful look,
As it stands there at the end of the book,
Like the sun in an eclipse.
Ah me! when I think of that vision divine,
Think of writing it, line by line,
I stand in awe of the terrible curse,
Like the trump of doom, in the closing verse!
God forgive me! if ever I
Take aught from the book of that Prophecy,
Lest my part too should be taken away
From the Book of Life on the Judgment Day.
This is well written, though I say it!
I should not be afraid to display it
In open day, on the selfsame shelf
With the writings of Saint Thecla herself,
Or of Theodosius, who of old
Wrote the Gospels in letters of gold!
That goodly folio standing yonder,
Without a single blot or blunder,
Would not bear away the palm from mine,
If we should compare them line for line.

There, now, is an initial letter!
Saint Ulric himself never made a better!
Finished down to the leaf and the snail,
Down to the eyes on the peacock's tail!
And now, as I turn the volume over,
And see what lies between cover and cover,
What treasures of art these pages hold,
All ablaze with crimson and gold,
God forgive me! I seem to feel

A certain satisfaction steal
Into my heart, and into my brain,
As if my talent had not lain
Wrapped in a napkin, and all in vain.
Yes, I might almost say to the Lord,
Here is a copy of thy Word,
Written out with much toil and pain;
Take it, O Lord, and let it be
As something I have done for thee!

He looks from the window.

How sweet the air is! How fair the scene!
I wish I had as lovely a green
To paint my landscapes and my leaves!
How the swallows twitter under the eaves!
There, now, there is one in her nest;
I can just catch a glimpse of her head and breast,
And will sketch her thus, in her quiet nook,
For the margin of my Gospel book.

He makes a sketch.

I can see no more. Through the valley yonder
A shower is passing; I hear the thunder
Mutter its curses in the air,
The Devil's own and only prayer!
The dusty road is brown with rain,
And, speeding on with might and main,
Hitherward rides a gallant train.
They do not parley, they cannot wait,
But hurry in at the convent gate.
What a fair lady! and beside her
What a handsome, graceful, noble rider!
Now she gives him her hand to alight;
They will beg a shelter for the night.

CHRISTUS: A MYSTERY

I will go down to the corridor,
And try to see that face once more;
It will do for the face of some beautiful Saint,
Or for one of the Maries I shall paint.

Goes out.

THE CLOISTERS

The ABBOT ERNESTUS *pacing to and fro.*

ABBOT

Slowly, slowly up the wall
Steals the sunshine, steals the shade;
Evening damps begin to fall,
Evening shadows are displayed.
Round me, o'er me, everywhere,
All the sky is grand with clouds,
And athwart the evening air
Wheel the swallows home in crowds.
Shafts of sunshine from the west
Paint the dusky windows red;
Darker shadows, deeper rest,
Underneath and overhead.
Darker, darker, and more wan,
In my breast the shadows fall;
Upward steals the life of man,
As the sunshine from the wall.
From the wall into the sky,
From the roof along the spire;
Ah, the souls of those that die
Are but sunbeams lifted higher.

THE GOLDEN LEGEND

Enter PRINCE HENRY.

PRINCE HENRY

Christ is arisen!

ABBOT

Amen! He is arisen!
His peace be with you!

PRINCE HENRY

Here it reigns forever!
The peace of God, that passeth understanding,
Reigns in these cloisters and these corridors.
Are you Ernestus, Abbot of the convent?

ABBOT

I am.

PRINCE HENRY

And I Prince Henry of Hoheneck,
Who crave your hospitality to-night.

ABBOT

You are thrice welcome to our humble walls.
You do us honor; and we shall requite it,
I fear, but poorly, entertaining you
With Paschal eggs, and our poor convent wine,
The remnants of our Easter holidays.

PRINCE HENRY

How fares it with the holy monks of Hirschau?
Are all things well with them?

275

CHRISTUS: A MYSTERY

ABBOT

All things are well.

PRINCE HENRY

A noble convent! I have known it long
By the report of travellers. I now see
Their commendations lag behind the truth.
You lie here in the valley of the Nagold
As in a nest: and the still river, gliding
Along its bed, is like an admonition
How all things pass. Your lands are rich and ample,
And your revenues large. God's benediction
Rests on your convent.

ABBOT

By our charities
We strive to merit it. Our Lord and Master,
When He departed, left us in his will,
As our best legacy on earth, the poor!
These we have always with us; had we not,
Our hearts would grow as hard as are these stones.

PRINCE HENRY

If I remember right, the Counts of Calva
Founded your convent.

ABBOT

Even as you say.

PRINCE HENRY

And, if I err not, it is very old.

THE GOLDEN LEGEND

ABBOT

Within these cloisters lie already buried
Twelve holy Abbots. Underneath the flags
On which we stand, the Abbot William lies,
Of blessed memory.

PRINCE HENRY

        And whose tomb is that,
Which bears the brass escutcheon?

ABBOT

            A benefactor's.
Conrad, a Count of Calva, he who stood
Godfather to our bells.

PRINCE HENRY

         Your monks are learned
And holy men, I trust.

ABBOT

        There are among them
Learned and holy men. Yet in this age
We need another Hildebrand, to shake
And purify us like a mighty wind.
The world is wicked, and sometimes I wonder
God does not lose his patience with it wholly,
And shatter it like glass! Even here, at times,
Within these walls, where all should be at peace,
I have my trials. Time has laid his hand
Upon my heart, gently, not smiting it,
But as a harper lays his open palm
Upon his harp, to deaden its vibrations.

CHRISTUS: A MYSTERY

Ashes are on my head, and on my lips
Sackcloth, and in my breast a heaviness
And weariness of life, that makes me ready
To say to the dead Abbots under us,
" Make room for me ! " Only I see the dusk
Of evening twilight coming, and have not
Completed half my task ; and so at times
The thought of my shortcomings in this life
Falls like a shadow on the life to come.

PRINCE HENRY

We must all die, and not the old alone ;
The young have no exemption from that doom.

ABBOT

Ah, yes ! the young may die, but the old must !
That is the difference.

PRINCE HENRY

              I have heard much laud
Of your transcribers. Your Scriptorium
Is famous among all ; your manuscripts
Praised for their beauty and their excellence.

ABBOT

That is indeed our boast. If you desire it,
You shall behold these treasures. And meanwhile
Shall the Refectorarius bestow
Your horses and attendants for the night.
            They go in. The Vesper-bell rings.

THE GOLDEN LEGEND

Vespers ; after which the monks retire, a chorister leading an old monk who is blind.

PRINCE HENRY

They are all gone, save one who lingers,
Absorbed in deep and silent prayer.
As if his heart could find no rest,
At times he beats his heaving breast
With clenched and convulsive fingers,
Then lifts them trembling in the air.
A chorister, with golden hair,
Guides hitherward his heavy pace.
Can it be so ? Or does my sight
Deceive me in the uncertain light ?
Ah, no ! I recognize that face,
Though Time has touched it in his flight,
And changed the auburn hair to white.
It is Count Hugo of the Rhine,
The deadliest foe of all our race,
And hateful unto me and mine !

THE BLIND MONK

Who is it that doth stand so near
His whispered words I almost hear ?

PRINCE HENRY

I am Prince Henry of Hoheneck,
And you, Count Hugo of the Rhine !
I know you, and I see the scar,

The brand upon your forehead, shine
And redden like a baleful star!

THE BLIND MONK

Count Hugo once, but now the wreck
Of what I was. O Hoheneck!
The passionate will, the pride, the wrath
That bore me headlong on my path,
Stumbled and staggered into fear,
And failed me in my mad career,
As a tired steed some evil-doer,
Alone upon a desolate moor,
Bewildered, lost, deserted, blind,
And hearing loud and close behind
The o'ertaking steps of his pursuer.
Then suddenly from the dark there came
A voice that called me by my name,
And said to me, " Kneel down and pray! "
And so my terror passed away,
Passed utterly away forever.
Contrition, penitence, remorse,
Came on me, with o'erwhelming force;
A hope, a longing, an endeavor,
By days of penance and nights of prayer,
To frustrate and defeat despair!
Calm, deep, and still is now my heart,
With tranquil waters overflowed;
A lake whose unseen fountains start,
Where once the hot volcano glowed.
And you, O Prince of Hoheneck!
Have known me in that earlier time,
A man of violence and crime,

Whose passions brooked no curb nor check.
Behold me now, in gentler mood,
One of this holy brotherhood.
Give me your hand; here let me kneel;
Make your reproaches sharp as steel;
Spurn me, and smite me on each cheek;
No violence can harm the meek,
There is no wound Christ cannot heal!
Yes; lift your princely hand, and take
Revenge, if 't is revenge you seek;
Then pardon me, for Jesus' sake!

PRINCE HENRY

Arise, Count Hugo! let there be
No further strife nor enmity
Between us twain; we both have erred!
Too rash in act, too wroth in word,
From the beginning have we stood
In fierce, defiant attitude,
Each thoughtless of the other's right,
And each reliant on his might.
But now our souls are more subdued;
The hand of God, and not in vain,
Has touched us with the fire of pain.
Let us kneel down and side by side
Pray, till our souls are purified,
And pardon will not be denied!

They kneel.

CHRISTUS: A MYSTERY

THE REFECTORY

Gaudiolum of Monks at midnight. LUCIFER *disguised as a Friar.*

FRIAR PAUL (*sings*)
Ave! color vini clari,
Dulcis potus, non amari,
Tua nos inebriari
    Digneris potentia!

FRIAR CUTHBERT
Not so much noise, my worthy frères,
You 'll disturb the Abbot at his prayers.

FRIAR PAUL (*sings*)
O! quam placens in colore!
O! quam fragrans in odore!
O! quam sapidum in ore!
    Dulce linguae vinculum!

FRIAR CUTHBERT
I should think your tongue had broken its chain!

FRIAR PAUL (*sings*)
Felix venter quem intrabis!
Felix guttur quod rigabis!
Felix os quod tu lavabis!
    Et beata labia!

FRIAR CUTHBERT
Peace! I say, peace!

Will you never cease!
You will rouse up the Abbot, I tell you again!

FRIAR JOHN

No danger! to-night he will let us alone,
As I happen to know he has guests of his own.

FRIAR CUTHBERT

Who are they?

FRIAR JOHN

   A German Prince and his train,
Who arrived here just before the rain.
There is with him a damsel fair to see,
As slender and graceful as a reed!
When she alighted from her steed,
It seemed like a blossom blown from a tree.

FRIAR CUTHBERT [1]

None of your pale-faced girls for me!
None of your damsels of high degree!

FRIAR JOHN

Come, old fellow, drink down to your peg!
But do not drink any further, I beg!

FRIAR PAUL (*sings*)

  In the days of gold,
  The days of old,
  Crosier of wood
  And bishop of gold!

[1] For the reading of this portion of the scene in the first edition, see
post, page 542.

CHRISTUS: A MYSTERY

FRIAR CUTHBERT

What an infernal racket and riot!
Can you not drink your wine in quiet?
Why fill the convent with such scandals,
As if we were so many drunken Vandals?

FRIAR PAUL (*continues*)

Now we have changed
That law so good
To crosier of gold
And bishop of wood!

FRIAR CUTHBERT

Well, then, since you are in the mood
To give your noisy humors vent,
Sing and howl to your heart's content!

CHORUS OF MONKS

Funde vinum, funde!
Tanquam sint fluminis undae,
Nec quaeras unde,
Sed fundas semper abunde!

FRIAR JOHN

What is the name of yonder friar,
With an eye that glows like a coal of fire,
And such a black mass of tangled hair?

FRIAR PAUL

He who is sitting there,
With a rollicking,
Devil may care,

Free and easy look and air,
As if he were used to such feasting and frolicking?

FRIAR JOHN

The same.

FRIAR PAUL

He's a stranger. You had better ask his name,
And where he is going, and whence he came.

FRIAR JOHN

Hallo! Sir Friar!

FRIAR PAUL

You must raise your voice a little higher,
He does not seem to hear what you say.
Now, try again! He is looking this way.

FRIAR JOHN

Hallo! Sir Friar!
We wish to inquire
Whence you came, and where you are going,
And anything else that is worth the knowing.
So be so good as to open your head.

LUCIFER

I am a Frenchman born and bred,
Going on a pilgrimage to Rome.
My home
Is the convent of Saint Gildas de Rhuys,
Of which, very like, you never have heard.

MONKS

Never a word!

CHRISTUS: A MYSTERY

You must know, then, it is in the diocese
Called the Diocese of Vannes,
In the Province of Brittany.
From the gray rocks of Morbihan
It overlooks the angry sea;
The very seashore where,
In his great despair,
Abbot Abelard walked to and fro,
Filling the night with woe,
And wailing aloud to the merciless seas
The name of his sweet Héloïse,
Whilst overhead
The convent windows gleamed as red
As the fiery eyes of the monks within,
Who with jovial din
Gave themselves up to all kinds of sin!
Ha! that is a convent! that is an abbey!
Over the doors,
None of your death-heads carved in wood,
None of your Saints looking pious and good,
None of your Patriarchs old and shabby!
But the heads and tusks of boars,
And the cells
Hung all round with the fells
Of the fallow-deer.
And then what cheer!
What jolly, fat friars,
Sitting round the great, roaring fires,
Roaring louder than they,
With their strong wines,
And their concubines,

And never a bell,
With its swagger and swell,
Calling you up with a start of affright
In the dead of night,
To send you grumbling down dark stairs,
To mumble your prayers;
But the cheery crow
Of cocks in the yard below,
After daybreak, an hour or so,
And the barking of deep-mouthed hounds,
These are the sounds
That, instead of bells, salute the ear.
And then all day
Up and away
Through the forest, hunting the deer!
Ah, my friends! I 'm afraid that here
You are a little too pious, a little too tame,
And the more is the shame.
'T is the greatest folly
Not to be jolly;
That 's what I think!
Come, drink, drink,
Drink, and die game!

MONKS

And your Abbot What 's-his-name?

LUCIFER

Abelard!

MONKS

Did he drink hard?

287

LUCIFER

Oh, no! Not he!
He was a dry old fellow,
Without juice enough to get thoroughly mellow.
There he stood,
Lowering at us in sullen mood,
As if he had come into Brittany
Just to reform our brotherhood!

A roar of laughter.

But you see
It never would do!
For some of us knew a thing or two,
In the Abbey of Saint Gildas de Rhuys!
For instance, the great ado
With old Fulbert's niece,
The young and lovely Héloïse.

FRIAR JOHN

Stop there, if you please,
Till we drink to the fair Héloïse.

ALL (*drinking and shouting*)

Héloïse! Héloïse!

The Chapel-bell tolls.

LUCIFER (*starting*)

What is that bell for? Are you such asses
As to keep up the fashion of midnight masses?

FRIAR CUTHBERT

It is only a poor, unfortunate brother,
Who is gifted with most miraculous powers

Of getting up at all sorts of hours,
And, by way of penance and Christian meekness,
Of creeping silently out of his cell
To take a pull at that hideous bell;
So that all the monks who are lying awake
May murmur some kind of prayer for his sake,
And adapted to his peculiar weakness!

FRIAR JOHN

From frailty and fall —

ALL

Good Lord, deliver us all!

FRIAR CUTHBERT

And before the bell for matins sounds,
He takes his lantern, and goes the rounds,
Flashing it into our sleepy eyes,
Merely to say it is time to arise.
But enough of that. Go on, if you please,
With your story about Saint Gildas de Rhuys.

LUCIFER

Well, it finally came to pass
That, half in fun and half in malice,
One Sunday at Mass
We put some poison into the chalice;
But, either by accident or design,
Peter Abelard kept away
From the chapel that day,
And a poor, young friar, who in his stead
Drank the sacramental wine,

Fell on the steps of the altar, dead!
But look! do you see at the window there
That face, with a look of grief and despair,
That ghastly face, as of one in pain?

MONKS

Who? where?

LUCIFER

As I spoke, it vanished away again.

FRIAR CUTHBERT

It is that nefarious
Siebald the Refectorarius.
That fellow is always playing the scout,
Creeping and peeping and prowling about;
And then he regales
The Abbot with scandalous tales.

LUCIFER

A spy in the convent? One of the brothers
Telling scandalous tales of the others?
Out upon him, the lazy loon!
I would put a stop to that pretty soon,
In a way he should rue it.

MONKS

How shall we do it?

LUCIFER

Do you, Brother Paul,
Creep under the window, close to the wall,

And open it suddenly when I call.
Then seize the villain by the hair,
And hold him there,
And punish him soundly, once for all.

FRIAR CUTHBERT

As Saint Dunstan of old,
We are told,
Once caught the Devil by the nose!

LUCIFER

Ha! ha! that story is very clever,
But has no foundation whatsoever.
Quick! for I see his face again
Glaring in at the window-pane;
Now! now! and do not spare your blows.
> FRIAR PAUL *opens the window suddenly, and seizes*
> SIEBALD. *They beat him.*

FRIAR SIEBALD

Help! help! are you going to slay me?

FRIAR PAUL

That will teach you again to betray me!

FRIAR SIEBALD

Mercy! mercy!

FRIAR PAUL (*shouting and beating*)

Rumpas bellorum lorum
Vim confer amorum

CHRISTUS: A MYSTERY

Morum verorum rorum
Tu plena polorum!

LUCIFER

Who stands in the doorway yonder,
Stretching out his trembling hand,
Just as Abelard used to stand,
The flash of his keen, black eyes
Forerunning the thunder?

THE MONKS (*in confusion*)

The Abbot! the Abbot!

FRIAR CUTHBERT

                And what is the wonder!
He seems to have taken you by surprise.

FRIAR FRANCIS

Hide the great flagon
From the eyes of the dragon!

FRIAR CUTHBERT

Pull the brown hood over your face!
This will bring us into disgrace!

ABBOT

What mean this revel and carouse?
Is this a tavern and drinking-house?
Are you Christian monks, or heathen devils,
To pollute this convent with your revels?
Were Peter Damian still upon earth,
To be shocked by such ungodly mirth,

He would write your names, with pen of gall,
In his Book of Gomorrah, one and all !
Away, you drunkards ! to your cells,
And pray till you hear the matin-bells ;
You, Brother Francis, and you, Brother Paul !
And as a penance mark each prayer
With the scourge upon your shoulders bare ;
Nothing atones for such a sin
But the blood that follows the discipline.
And you, Brother Cuthbert, come with me
Alone into the sacristy ;
You, who should be a guide to your brothers,
And are ten times worse than all the others,
For you I 've a draught that has long been brewing,
You shall do a penance worth the doing !
Away to your prayers, then, one and all !
I wonder the very convent wall
Does not crumble and crush you in its fall !

THE NEIGHBORING NUNNERY

The ABBESS IRMINGARD *sitting with* ELSIE *in the
moon-light.*

IRMINGARD

The night is silent, the wind is still,
The moon is looking from yonder hill
Down upon convent, and grove, and garden ;
The clouds have passed away from her face,
Leaving behind them no sorrowful trace,
Only the tender and quiet grace
Of one whose heart has been healed with pardon !

And such am I. My soul within
Was dark with passion and soiled with sin.
But now its wounds are healed again;
Gone are the anguish, the terror, and pain;
For across that desolate land of woe,
O'er whose burning sands I was forced to go,
A wind from heaven began to blow;
And all my being trembled and shook,
As the leaves of the tree, or the grass of the field,
And I was healed, as the sick are healed,
When fanned by the leaves of the Holy Book!

As thou sittest in the moonlight there,
Its glory flooding thy golden hair,
And the only darkness that which lies
In the haunted chambers of thine eyes,
I feel my soul drawn unto thee,
Strangely, and strongly, and more and more,
As to one I have known and loved before;
For every soul is akin to me
That dwells in the land of mystery!

I am the Lady Irmingard,
Born of a noble race and name!
Many a wandering Suabian bard,
Whose life was dreary, and bleak, and hard,
Has found through me the way to fame.
Brief and bright were those days, and the night
Which followed was full of a lurid light.
Love, that of every woman's heart
Will have the whole, and not a part,
That is to her, in Nature's plan,

THE GOLDEN LEGEND

More than ambition is to man,
Her light, her life, her very breath,
With no alternative but death,
Found me a maiden soft and young,
Just from the convent's cloistered school,
And seated on my lowly stool,
Attentive while the minstrels sung.

Gallant, graceful, gentle, tall,
Fairest, noblest, best of all,
Was Walter of the Vogelweid;
And, whatsoever may betide,
Still I think of him with pride!
His song was of the summer-time,
The very birds sang in his rhyme;
The sunshine, the delicious air,
The fragrance of the flowers, were there;
And I grew restless as I heard,
Restless and buoyant as a bird,
Down soft, aërial currents sailing,
O'er blossomed orchards, and fields in bloom,
And through the momentary gloom
Of shadows o'er the landscape trailing,
Yielding and borne I knew not where,
But feeling resistance unavailing.

And thus, unnoticed and apart,
And more by accident than choice,
I listened to that single voice
Until the chambers of my heart
Were filled with it by night and day.
One night, — it was a night in May, —

CHRISTUS: A MYSTERY

Within the garden, unawares,
Under the blossoms in the gloom,
I heard it utter my own name
With protestations and wild prayers;
And it rang through me, and became
Like the archangel's trump of doom,
Which the soul hears, and must obey;
And mine arose as from a tomb.
My former life now seemed to me
Such as hereafter death may be,
When in the great Eternity
We shall awake and find it day.

It was a dream, and would not stay;
A dream, that in a single night
Faded and vanished out of sight.
My father's anger followed fast
This passion, as a freshening blast
Seeks out and fans the fire, whose rage
It may increase, but not assuage.
And he exclaimed: " No wandering bard
Shall win thy hand, O Irmingard!
For which Prince Henry of Hoheneck
By messenger and letter sues."
Gently, but firmly, I replied:
" Henry of Hoheneck I discard!
Never the hand of Irmingard
Shall lie in his as the hand of a bride!"
This said I, Walter, for thy sake;
This said I, for I could not choose.
After a pause, my father spake
In that cold and deliberate tone

Which turns the hearer into stone,
And seems itself the act to be
That follows with such dread certainty :
" This or the cloister and the veil ! "
No other words than these he said,
But they were like a funeral wail ;
My life was ended, my heart was dead.

That night from the castle-gate went down,
With silent, slow, and stealthy pace,
Two shadows, mounted on shadowy steeds,
Taking the narrow path that leads
Into the forest dense and brown.
In the leafy darkness of the place,
One could not distinguish form nor face,
Only a bulk without a shape,
A darker shadow in the shade ;
One scarce could say it moved or stayed.
Thus it was we made our escape !
A foaming brook, with many a bound,
Followed us like a playful hound ;
Then leaped before us, and in the hollow
Paused, and waited for us to follow,
And seemed impatient, and afraid
That our tardy flight should be betrayed
By the sound our horses' hoof-beats made.
And when we reached the plain below,
We paused a moment and drew rein
To look back at the castle again ;
And we saw the windows all aglow
With lights, that were passing to and fro ;
Our hearts with terror ceased to beat ;

CHRISTUS: A MYSTERY

The brook crept silent to our feet;
We knew what most we feared to know.
Then suddenly horns began to blow;
And we heard a shout, and a heavy tramp,
And our horses snorted in the damp
Night air of the meadows green and wide,
And in a moment, side by side,
So close, they must have seemed but one,
The shadows across the moonlight run,
And another came, and swept behind,
Like the shadow of clouds before the wind!

How I remember that breathless flight
Across the moors, in the summer night!
How under our feet the long, white road
Backward like a river flowed,
Sweeping with it fences and hedges,
Whilst farther away, and overhead,
Paler than I, with fear and dread,
The moon fled with us, as we fled
Along the forest's jagged edges!

All this I can remember well;
But of what afterwards befell
I nothing further can recall
Than a blind, desperate, headlong fall;
The rest is a blank and darkness all.
When I awoke out of this swoon,
The sun was shining, not the moon,
Making a cross upon the wall
With the bars of my windows narrow and
     tall;

THE GOLDEN LEGEND

And I prayed to it, as I had been wont to
    pray,
From early childhood, day by day,
Each morning, as in bed I lay !
I was lying again in my own room !
And I thanked God, in my fever and pain,
That those shadows on the midnight plain
Were gone, and could not come again !
I struggled no longer with my doom !

This happened many years ago.
I left my father's home to come
Like Catherine to her martyrdom,
For blindly I esteemed it so.
And when I heard the convent door
Behind me close, to ope no more,
I felt it smite me like a blow.
Through all my limbs a shudder ran,
And on my bruised spirit fell
The dampness of my narrow cell
As night air on a wounded man,
Giving intolerable pain.

But now a better life began.
I felt the agony decrease
By slow degrees, then wholly cease,
Ending in perfect rest and peace !
It was not apathy, nor dulness,
That weighed and pressed upon my brain,
But the same passion I had given
To earth before, now turned to heaven
With all its overflowing fulness.

CHRISTUS: A MYSTERY

Alas! the world is full of peril!
The path that runs through the fairest meads,
On the sunniest side of the valley, leads
Into a region bleak and sterile!
Alike in the high-born and the lowly,
The will is feeble, and passion strong.
We cannot sever right from wrong;
Some falsehood mingles with all truth;
Nor is it strange the heart of youth
Should waver and comprehend but slowly
The things that are holy and unholy!
But in this sacred, calm retreat,
We are all well and safely shielded
From winds that blow, and waves that beat,
From the cold, and rain, and blighting heat,
To which the strongest hearts have yielded.
Here we stand as the Virgins Seven,
For our celestial bridegroom yearning;
Our hearts are lamps forever burning,
With a steady and unwavering flame,
Pointing upward, forever the same,
Steadily upward toward the heaven!

The moon is hidden behind a cloud;
A sudden darkness fills the room,
And thy deep eyes, amid the gloom,
Shine like jewels in a shroud.
On the leaves is a sound of falling rain;
A bird, awakened in its nest,
Gives a faint twitter of unrest,
Then smooths its plumes and sleeps again.

Line 12. But in this sacred and calm retreat,

300

No other sounds than these I hear;
The hour of midnight must be near.
Thou art o'erspent with the day's fatigue
Of riding many a dusty league;
Sink, then, gently to thy slumber;
Me so many cares encumber,
So many ghosts, and forms of fright,
Have started from their graves to-night,
They have driven sleep from mine eyes away :
I will go down to the chapel and pray.

V

A COVERED BRIDGE AT LUCERNE

PRINCE HENRY

God's blessing on the architects who build
The bridges o'er swift rivers and abysses
Before impassable to human feet,
No less than on the builders of cathedrals,
Whose massive walls are bridges thrown across
The dark and terrible abyss of Death.
Well has the name of Pontifex been given
Unto the Church's head, as the chief builder
And architect of the invisible bridge
That leads from earth to heaven.

ELSIE

         How dark it grows!
What are these paintings on the walls around us?

CHRISTUS: A MYSTERY

PRINCE HENRY

The Dance Macaber!

ELSIE

What?

PRINCE HENRY

The Dance of Death!
All that go to and fro must look upon it,
Mindful of what they shall be, while beneath,
Among the wooden piles, the turbulent river
Rushes, impetuous as the river of life,
With dimpling eddies, ever green and bright,
Save where the shadow of this bridge falls on it.

ELSIE

Oh yes! I see it now!

PRINCE HENRY

The grim musician
Leads all men through the mazes of that dance,
To different sounds in different measures moving;
Sometimes he plays a lute, sometimes a drum,
To tempt or terrify.

ELSIE

What is this picture?

PRINCE HENRY

It is a young man singing to a nun,
Who kneels at her devotions, but in kneeling

302

Turns round to look at him; and Death, mean-
    while,
Is putting out the candles on the altar!

ELSIE

Ah, what a pity 't is that she should listen
Unto such songs, when in her orisons
She might have heard in heaven the angels singing!

PRINCE HENRY

Here he has stolen a jester's cap and bells,
And dances with the Queen.

ELSIE

                    A foolish jest!

PRINCE HENRY

And here the heart of the new-wedded wife,
Coming from church with her beloved lord,
He startles with the rattle of his drum.

ELSIE

Ah, that is sad! And yet perhaps 't is best
That she should die, with all the sunshine on her,
And all the benedictions of the morning,
Before this affluence of golden light
Shall fade into a cold and clouded gray,
Then into darkness!

PRINCE HENRY

            Under it is written,
" Nothing but death shall separate thee and me! "

ELSIE

And what is this, that follows close upon it?

PRINCE HENRY

Death, playing on a dulcimer. Behind him,
A poor old woman, with a rosary,
Follows the sound, and seems to wish her feet
Were swifter to o'ertake him. Underneath,
The inscription reads, " Better is Death than Life."

ELSIE

Better is Death than Life! Ah, yes! to thousands
Death plays upon a dulcimer, and sings
That song of consolation, till the air
Rings with it, and they cannot choose but follow
Whither he leads. And not the old alone,
But the young also hear it, and are still.

PRINCE HENRY

Yes, in their sadder moments. 'T is the sound
Of their own hearts they hear, half full of tears,
Which are like crystal cups, half filled with
    water,
Responding to the pressure of a finger
With music sweet and low and melancholy.
Let us go forward, and no longer stay
In this great picture-gallery of Death!
I hate it! ay, the very thought of it!

ELSIE

Why is it hateful to you?

304

THE GOLDEN LEGEND

PRINCE HENRY

For the reason
That life, and all that speaks of life, is lovely,
And death, and all that speaks of death, is hateful.

ELSIE

The grave itself is but a covered bridge,
Leading from light to light, through a brief darkness!

PRINCE HENRY (*emerging from the bridge*)

I breathe again more freely! Ah, how pleasant
To come once more into the light of day,
Out of that shadow of death! To hear again
The hoof-beats of our horses on firm ground,
And not upon those hollow planks, resounding
With a sepulchral echo, like the clods
On coffins in a churchyard! Yonder lies
The Lake of the Four Forest-Towns, apparelled
In light, and lingering, like a village maiden,
Hid in the bosom of her native mountains,
Then pouring all her life into another's,
Changing her name and being! Overhead,
Shaking his cloudy tresses loose in air,
Rises Pilatus, with his windy pines.

They pass on.

THE DEVIL'S BRIDGE

PRINCE HENRY *and* ELSIE (*crossing with attendants*)

GUIDE

This bridge is called the Devil's Bridge.

305

With a single arch, from ridge to ridge,
It leaps across the terrible chasm
Yawning beneath us, black and deep,
As if, in some convulsive spasm,
The summits of the hills had cracked,
And made a road for the cataract
That raves and rages down the steep!

LUCIFER (*under the bridge*)

Ha! ha!

GUIDE

Never any bridge but this
Could stand across the wild abyss;
All the rest, of wood or stone,
By the Devil's hand were overthrown.
He toppled crags from the precipice,
And whatsoe'er was built by day
In the night was swept away;
None could stand but this alone.

LUCIFER (*under the bridge*)

Ha! ha!

GUIDE

I showed you in the valley a boulder
Marked with the imprint of his shoulder;
As he was bearing it up this way,
A peasant, passing, cried, "Herr, Jé!"
And the Devil dropped it in his fright,
And vanished suddenly out of sight!

THE GOLDEN LEGEND

LUCIFER (*under the bridge*)

Ha! ha!

GUIDE

Abbot Giraldus of Einsiedel,
For pilgrims on their way to Rome,
Built this at last, with a single arch,
Under which, on its endless march
Runs the river, white with foam,
Like a thread through the eye of a needle.
And the Devil promised to let it stand,
Under compact and condition
That the first living thing which crossed
Should be surrendered into his hand,
And be beyond redemption lost.

LUCIFER (*under the bridge*)

Ha! ha! perdition!

GUIDE

At length, the bridge being all completed,
The Abbot, standing at its head,
Threw across it a loaf of bread,
Which a hungry dog sprang after,
And the rocks reëchoed with the peals of laughter
To see the Devil thus defeated!

They pass on.

LUCIFER (*under the bridge*)

Ha! ha! defeated!
For journeys and for crimes like this
I let the bridge stand o'er the abyss!

307

CHRISTUS: A MYSTERY

THE ST. GOTHARD PASS

PRINCE HENRY

This is the highest point. Two ways the rivers
Leap down to different seas, and as they roll
Grow deep and still, and their majestic presence
Becomes a benefaction to the towns
They visit, wandering silently among them,
Like patriarchs old among their shining tents.

ELSIE

How bleak and bare it is! Nothing but mosses
Grow on these rocks.

PRINCE HENRY

            Yet are they not forgotten;
Beneficent Nature sends the mists to feed them.

ELSIE

See yonder little cloud, that, borne aloft
So tenderly by the wind, floats fast away
Over the snowy peaks! It seems to me
The body of Saint Catherine, borne by angels!

PRINCE HENRY

Thou art Saint Catherine, and invisible angels
Bear thee across these chasms and precipices,
Lest thou shouldst dash thy feet against a stone!

ELSIE

Would I were borne unto my grave, as she was,

THE GOLDEN LEGEND

Upon angelic shoulders! Even now
I seem uplifted by them, light as air!
What sound is that?

PRINCE HENRY

The tumbling avalanches!

ELSIE

How awful, yet how beautiful!

PRINCE HENRY

These are
The voices of the mountains! Thus they ope
Their snowy lips, and speak unto each other,
In the primeval language, lost to man.

ELSIE

What land is this that spreads itself beneath us

PRINCE HENRY

Italy! Italy!

ELSIE

Land of the Madonna!
How beautiful it is! It seems a garden
Of Paradise!

PRINCE HENRY

Nay, of Gethsemane
To thee and me, of passion and of prayer!
Yet once of Paradise. Long years ago
I wandered as a youth among its bowers,

CHRISTUS: A MYSTERY

And never from my heart has faded quite
Its memory, that, like a summer sunset,
Encircles with a ring of purple light
All the horizon of my youth.

GUIDE

                    O friends!
The days are short, the way before us long;
We must not linger, if we think to reach
The inn at Belinzona before vespers!

They pass on.

AT THE FOOT OF THE ALPS

A halt under the trees at noon.

PRINCE HENRY

Here let us pause a moment in the trembling
Shadow and sunshine of the roadside trees,
And, our tired horses in a group assembling,
Inhale long draughts of this delicious breeze.
Our fleeter steeds have distanced our attendants;
They lag behind us with a slower pace;
We will await them under the green pendants
Of the great willows in this shady place.
Ho, Barbarossa! how thy mottled haunches
Sweat with this canter over hill and glade!
Stand still, and let these overhanging branches
Fan thy hot sides and comfort thee with shade!

ELSIE

What a delightful landscape spreads before us,

Marked with a whitewashed cottage here and there!
And, in luxuriant garlands drooping o'er us,
Blossoms of grape-vines scent the sunny air.

PRINCE HENRY

Hark! what sweet sounds are those, whose accents
    holy
Fill the warm noon with music sad and sweet!

ELSIE

It is a band of pilgrims, moving slowly
On their long journey, with uncovered feet.

PILGRIMS (*chanting the Hymn of Saint Hildebert*)

Me receptet Sion illa,
Sion David, urbs tranquilla,
Cujus faber auctor lucis,
Cujus portae lignum crucis,
Cujus claves lingua Petri,
Cujus cives semper laeti,
Cujus muri lapis vivus,
Cujus custos Rex festivus!

LUCIFER (*as a Friar in the procession*)

Here am I, too, in the pious band,
In the garb of a barefooted Carmelite dressed!
The soles of my feet are as hard and tanned
As the conscience of old Pope Hildebrand,
The Holy Satan, who made the wives
Of the bishops lead such shameful lives.
All day long I beat my breast,
And chant with a most particular zest

311

CHRISTUS: A MYSTERY

The Latin hymns, which I understand
Quite as well, I think, as the rest.
And at night such lodging in barns and sheds,
Such a hurly-burly in country inns,
Such a clatter of tongues in empty heads,
Such a helter-skelter of prayers and sins !
Of all the contrivances of the time
For sowing broadcast the seeds of crime,
There is none so pleasing to me and mine
As a pilgrimage to some far-off shrine !

PRINCE HENRY

If from the outward man we judge the inner,
And cleanliness is godliness, I fear
A hopeless reprobate, a hardened sinner,
Must be that Carmelite now passing near.

LUCIFER

There is my German Prince again,
Thus far on his journey to Salern,
And the lovesick girl, whose heated brain
Is sowing the cloud to reap the rain ;
But it 's a long road that has no turn !
Let them quietly hold their way,
I have also a part in the play.
But first I must act to my heart's content
This mummery and this merriment,
And drive this motley flock of sheep
Into the fold, where drink and sleep
The jolly old friars of Benevent.
Of a truth, it often provokes me to laugh
To see these beggars hobble along,

Lamed and maimed, and fed upon chaff,
Chanting their wonderful piff and paff,
And, to make up for not understanding the song,
Singing it fiercely, and wild, and strong!
Were it not for my magic garters and staff,
And the goblets of goodly wine I quaff,
And the mischief I make in the idle throng,
I should not continue the business long.

PILGRIMS (*chanting*)

In hâc urbe, lux solennis,
Ver aeternum, pax perennis;
In hâc odor implens caelos,
In hâc semper festum melos!

PRINCE HENRY

Do you observe that monk among the train,
Who pours from his great throat the roaring bass,
As a cathedral spout pours out the rain,
And this way turns his rubicund, round face?

ELSIE

It is the same who, on the Strasburg Square,
Preached to the people in the open air.

PRINCE HENRY

And he has crossed o'er mountain, field, and fell,
On that good steed, that seems to bear him well,
The hackney of the Friars of Orders Gray,
His own stout legs! He, too, was in the play,
Both as King Herod and Ben Israel.
Good morrow, Friar!

313

CHRISTUS: A MYSTERY

FRIAR CUTHBERT

Good morrow, noble Sir !

PRINCE HENRY

I speak in German, for, unless I err,
You are a German.

FRIAR CUTHBERT

I cannot gainsay you.
But by what instinct, or what secret sign,
Meeting me here, do you straightway divine
That northward of the Alps my country lies ?

PRINCE HENRY

Your accent, like Saint Peter's, would betray you,
Did not your yellow beard and your blue eyes.
Moreover, we have seen your face before,
And heard you preach at the Cathedral door
On Easter Sunday, in the Strasburg Square.
We were among the crowd that gathered there,
And saw you play the Rabbi with great skill,
As if, by leaning o'er so many years
To walk with little children, your own will
Had caught a childish attitude from theirs,
A kind of stooping in its form and gait,
And could no longer stand erect and straight.
Whence come you now ?

FRIAR CUTHBERT

From the old monastery
Of Hirschau, in the forest ; being sent
Upon a pilgrimage to Benevent,

To see the image of the Virgin Mary,
That moves its holy eyes, and sometimes speaks,
And lets the piteous tears run down its cheeks,
To touch the hearts of the impenitent.

PRINCE HENRY

Oh, had I faith, as in the days gone by,
That knew no doubt, and feared no mystery!

LUCIFER (*at a distance*)

Ho, Cuthbert! Friar Cuthbert!

FRIAR CUTHBERT

                           Farewell, Prince!
I cannot stay to argue and convince.

PRINCE HENRY

This is indeed the blessed Mary's land,
Virgin and Mother of our dear Redeemer!
All hearts are touched and softened at her name,
Alike the bandit, with the bloody hand,
The priest, the prince, the scholar, and the peasant,
The man of deeds, the visionary dreamer,
Pay homage to her as one ever present!
And even as children, who have much offended
A too indulgent father, in great shame,
Penitent, and yet not daring unattended
To go into his presence, at the gate
Speak with their sister, and confiding wait
Till she goes in before and intercedes;
So men, repenting of their evil deeds,
And yet not venturing rashly to draw near

With their requests an angry father's ear,
Offer to her their prayers and their confession,
And she for them in heaven makes intercession.
And if our Faith had given us nothing more
Than this example of all womanhood,
So mild, so merciful, so strong, so good,
So patient, peaceful, loyal, loving, pure,
This were enough to prove it higher and truer
Than all the creeds the world had known before.

PILGRIMS (*chanting afar off*)

Urbs coelestis, urbs beata,
Supra petram collocata,
Urbs in portu satis tuto
De longinquo te saluto,
Te saluto, te suspiro,
Te affecto, te requiro!

THE INN AT GENOA

A terrace overlooking the sea. Night.

PRINCE HENRY

It is the sea, it is the sea,
In all its vague immensity,
Fading and darkening in the distance!
Silent, majestical, and slow,
The white ships haunt it to and fro,
With all their ghostly sails unfurled,
As phantoms from another world
Haunt the dim confines of existence!
But ah! how few can comprehend

Their signals, or to what good end
From land to land they come and go!
Upon a sea more vast and dark
The spirits of the dead embark,
All voyaging to unknown coasts.
We wave our farewells from the shore,
And they depart, and come no more,
Or come as phantoms and as ghosts.

Above the darksome sea of death
Looms the great life that is to be,
A land of cloud and mystery,
A dim mirage, with shapes of men
Long dead, and passed beyond our ken.
Awe-struck we gaze, and hold our breath
Till the fair pageant vanisheth,
Leaving us in perplexity,
And doubtful whether it has been
A vision of the world unseen,
Or a bright image of our own
Against the sky in vapors thrown.

LUCIFER (*singing from the sea*)

Thou didst not make it, thou canst not mend it,
But thou hast the power to end it!
The sea is silent, the sea is discreet,
Deep it lies at thy very feet;
There is no confessor like unto Death!
Thou canst not see him, but he is near;
Thou needest not whisper above thy breath,
And he will hear;
He will answer the questions,

The vague surmises and suggestions,
That fill thy soul with doubt and fear!

PRINCE HENRY

The fisherman, who lies afloat,
With shadowy sail, in yonder boat,
Is singing softly to the Night!
But do I comprehend aright
The meaning of the words he sung
So sweetly in his native tongue?
Ah, yes! the sea is still and deep.
All things within its bosom sleep!
A single step, and all is o'er;
A plunge, a bubble, and no more;
And thou, dear Elsie, wilt be free
From martyrdom and agony.

ELSIE (*coming from her chamber upon the terrace*)
The night is calm and cloudless,
And still as still can be,
And the stars come forth to listen
To the music of the sea.
They gather, and gather, and gather,
Until they crowd the sky,
And listen, in breathless silence,
To the solemn litany.
It begins in rocky caverns,
As a voice that chants alone
To the pedals of the organ
In monotonous undertone;
And anon from shelving beaches,
And shallow sands beyond,

THE GOLDEN LEGEND

In snow-white robes uprising
The ghostly choirs respond.
And sadly and unceasing
The mournful voice sings on,
And the snow-white choirs still answer
Christe eleison !

Angel of God ! thy finer sense perceives
Celestial and perpetual harmonies !
Thy purer soul, that trembles and believes,
Hears the archangel's trumpet in the breeze,
And where the forest rolls, or ocean heaves,
Cecilia's organ sounding in the seas,
And tongues of prophets speaking in the leaves.
But I hear discord only and despair,
And whispers as of demons in the air !

AT SEA

IL PADRONE

The wind upon our quarter lies,
And on before the freshening gale,
That fills the snow-white lateen sail,
Swiftly our light felucca flies.
Around, the billows burst and foam ;
They lift her o'er the sunken rock,
They beat her sides with many a shock,
And then upon their flowing dome
They poise her, like a weathercock !
Between us and the western skies
The hills of Corsica arise ;

CHRISTUS: A MYSTERY

Eastward, in yonder long blue line,
The summits of the Apennine,
And southward, and still far away,
Salerno, on its sunny bay.
You cannot see it, where it lies.

PRINCE HENRY

Ah, would that never more mine eyes
Might see its towers by night or day!

ELSIE

Behind us, dark and awfully,
There comes a cloud out of the sea,
That bears the form of a hunted deer,
With hide of brown, and hoofs of black,
And antlers laid upon its back,
And fleeing fast and wild with fear,
As if the hounds were on its track!

PRINCE HENRY

Lo! while we gaze, it breaks and falls
In shapeless masses, like the walls
Of a burnt city. Broad and red
The fires of the descending sun
Glare through the windows, and o'erhead,
Athwart the vapors, dense and dun,
Long shafts of silvery light arise,
Like rafters that support the skies!

ELSIE

See! from its summit the lurid levin
Flashes downward without warning,

THE GOLDEN LEGEND

As Lucifer, son of the morning,
Fell from the battlements of heaven!

IL PADRONE

I must entreat you, friends, below!
The angry storm begins to blow,
For the weather changes with the moon.
All this morning, until noon,
We had baffling winds, and sudden flaws
Struck the sea with their cat's-paws.
Only a little hour ago
I was whistling to Saint Antonio
For a capful of wind to fill our sail,
And instead of a breeze he has sent a gale.
Last night I saw Saint Elmo's stars,
With their glimmering lanterns all at play
On the tops of the masts and the tips of the spars,
And I knew we should have foul weather to-day.
Cheerily, my hearties! yo heave ho!
Brail up the mainsail, and let her go
As the winds will and Saint Antonio!

Do you see that Livornese felucca,
That vessel to the windward yonder,
Running with her gunwale under?
I was looking when the wind o'ertook her.
She had all sail set, and the only wonder
Is that at once the strength of the blast
Did not carry away her mast.
She is a galley of the Gran Duca,
That, through the fear of the Algerines,
Convoys those lazy brigantines,

Laden with wine and oil from Lucca.
Now all is ready, high and low;
Blow, blow, good Saint Antonio!

Ha! that is the first dash of the rain,
With a sprinkle of spray above the rails.
Just enough to moisten our sails,
And make them ready for the strain.
See how she leaps, as the blasts o'ertake her,
And speeds away with a bone in her mouth!
Now keep her head toward the south,
And there is no danger of bank or breaker.
With the breeze behind us, on we go;
Not too much, good Saint Antonio!

VI

THE SCHOOL OF SALERNO

*A travelling Scholastic affixing his Theses to the gate of
the College*

SCHOLASTIC

There, that is my gauntlet, my banner, my shield,
Hung up as a challenge to all the field!
One hundred and twenty-five propositions,
Which I will maintain with the sword of the tongue
Against all disputants, old and young.
Let us see if doctors or dialecticians
Will dare to dispute my definitions,
Or attack any one of my learned theses.

Here stand I ; the end shall be as God pleases.
I think I have proved, by profound researches,
The error of all those doctrines so vicious
Of the old Areopagite Dionysius,
That are making such terrible work in the churches,
By Michael the Stammerer sent from the East,
And done into Latin by that Scottish beast,
Johannes Duns Scotus, who dares to maintain,
In the face of the truth, the error infernal,
That the universe is and must be eternal ;
At first laying down, as a fact fundamental,
That nothing with God can be accidental ;
Then asserting that God before the creation
Could not have existed, because it is plain
That, had He existed, He would have created ;
Which is begging the question that should be debated,
And moveth me less to anger than laughter.
All Nature, he holds, is a respiration
Of the Spirit of God, who, in breathing, hereafter
Will inhale it into his bosom again,
So that nothing but God alone will remain.
And therein he contradicteth himself ;
For he opens the whole discussion by stating,
That God can only exist in creating.
That question I think I have laid on the shelf !

> *He goes out. Two Doctors come in disputing, and
> followed by pupils.*

DOCTOR SERAFINO

I, with the Doctor Seraphic, maintain,
That a word which is only conceived in the brain

Line 8. Erigena Johannes, who dares to maintain,

323

CHRISTUS: A MYSTERY

Is a type of eternal Generation;
The spoken word is the Incarnation.

DOCTOR CHERUBINO

What do I care for the Doctor Seraphic,
With all his wordy chaffer and traffic?

DOCTOR SERAFINO

You make but a paltry show of resistance;
Universals have no real existence!

DOCTOR CHERUBINO

Your words are but idle and empty chatter;
Ideas are eternally joined to matter!

DOCTOR SERAFINO

May the Lord have mercy on your position,
You wretched, wrangling culler of herbs!

DOCTOR CHERUBINO

May He send your soul to eternal perdition,
For your Treatise on the Irregular Verbs!
They rush out fighting. Two Scholars come in.

FIRST SCHOLAR

Monte Cassino, then, is your College.
What think you of ours here at Salern?

SECOND SCHOLAR

To tell the truth, I arrived so lately,
I hardly yet have had time to discern.
So much, at least, I am bound to acknowledge:

THE GOLDEN LEGEND

The air seems healthy, the buildings stately,
And on the whole I like it greatly.

FIRST SCHOLAR

Yes, the air is sweet ; the Calabrian hills
Send us down puffs of mountain air ;
And in summer-time the sea-breeze fills
With its coolness cloister, and court, and square.
Then at every season of the year
There are crowds of guests and travellers here ;
Pilgrims, and mendicant friars, and traders
From the Levant, with figs and wine,
And bands of wounded and sick Crusaders,
Coming back from Palestine.

SECOND SCHOLAR

And what are the studies you pursue ?
What is the course you here go through ?

FIRST SCHOLAR

The first three years of the college course
Are given to Logic alone, as the source
Of all that is noble, and wise, and true.

SECOND SCHOLAR

That seems rather strange, I must confess,
In a Medical School ; yet, nevertheless,
You doubtless have reasons for that.

FIRST SCHOLAR

Oh yes !

For none but a clever dialectician

Can hope to become a great physician;
That has been settled long ago.
Logic makes an important part
Of the mystery of the healing art;
For without it how could you hope to show
That nobody knows so much as you know?
After this there are five years more
Devoted wholly to medicine,
With lectures on chirurgical lore,
And dissections of the bodies of swine,
As likest the human form divine.

SECOND SCHOLAR

What are the books now most in vogue?

FIRST SCHOLAR

Quite an extensive catalogue;
Mostly, however, books of our own;
As Gariopontus' Passionarius,
And the writings of Matthew Platearius;
And a volume universally known
As the Regimen of the School of Salern,
For Robert of Normandy written in terse
And very elegant Latin verse.
Each of these writings has its turn.
And when at length we have finished these,
Then comes the struggle for degrees,
With all the oldest and ablest critics;
The public thesis and disputation,
Question, and answer, and explanation
Of a passage out of Hippocrates,
Or Aristotle's Analytics.

THE GOLDEN LEGEND

There the triumphant Magister stands!
A book is solemnly placed in his hands,
On which he swears to follow the rule
And ancient forms of the good old School;
To report if any confectionarius
Mingles his drugs with matters various,
And to visit his patients twice a day,
And once in the night, if they live in town,
And if they are poor, to take no pay.
Having faithfully promised these,
His head is crowned with a laurel crown;
A kiss on his cheek, a ring on his hand,
The Magister Artium et Physices
Goes forth from the school like a lord of the land.
And now, as we have the whole morning before us,
Let us go in, if you make no objection,
And listen awhile to a learned prelection
On Marcus Aurelius Cassiodorus.   *They go in.*

Enter LUCIFER *as a Doctor.*

LUCIFER

This is the great School of Salern!
A land of wrangling and of quarrels,
Of brains that seethe, and hearts that burn,
Where every emulous scholar hears,
In every breath that comes to his ears,
The rustling of another's laurels!
The air of the place is called salubrious;
The neighborhood of Vesuvius lends it
An odor volcanic, that rather mends it,
And the buildings have an aspect lugubrious,

327

That inspires a feeling of awe and terror
Into the heart of the beholder,
And befits such an ancient homestead of error,
Where the old falsehoods moulder and smoulder,
And yearly by many hundred hands
Are carried away, in the zeal of youth,
And sown like tares in the field of truth,
To blossom and ripen in other lands.

What have we here, affixed to the gate?
The challenge of some scholastic wight,
Who wishes to hold a public debate
On sundry questions wrong or right!
Ah, now this is my great delight!
For I have often observed of late
That such discussions end in a fight.
Let us see what the learned wag maintains
With such a prodigal waste of brains.   *Reads.*
" Whether angels in moving from place to place
Pass through the intermediate space.
Whether God himself is the author of evil,
Or whether that is the work of the Devil.
When, where, and wherefore Lucifer fell,
And whether he now is chained in hell."
I think I can answer that question well!
So long as the boastful human mind
Consents in such mills as this to grind,
I sit very firmly upon my throne!
Of a truth it almost makes me laugh,
To see men leaving the golden grain
To gather in piles the pitiful chaff
That old Peter Lombard thrashed with his brain,

To have it caught up and tossed again
On the horns of the Dumb Ox of Cologne!

But my guests approach! there is in the air
A fragrance, like that of the Beautiful Garden
Of Paradise, in the days that were!
An odor of innocence and of prayer,
And of love, and faith that never fails,
Such as the fresh young heart exhales
Before it begins to wither and harden!
I cannot breathe such an atmosphere!
My soul is filled with a nameless fear,
That, after all my trouble and pain,
After all my restless endeavor,
The youngest, fairest soul of the twain,
The most ethereal, most divine,
Will escape from my hands for ever and ever.
But the other is already mine!
Let him live to corrupt his race,
Breathing among them, with every breath,
Weakness, selfishness, and the base
And pusillanimous fear of death.
I know his nature, and I know
That of all who in my ministry
Wander the great earth to and fro,
And on my errands come and go,
The safest and subtlest are such as he.

Enter PRINCE HENRY *and* ELSIE, *with attendants.*

PRINCE HENRY

Can you direct us to Friar Angelo?

329

CHRISTUS: A MYSTERY

LUCIFER

He stands before you.

PRINCE HENRY

Then you know our purpose.
I am Prince Henry of Hoheneck, and this
The maiden that I spake of in my letters.

LUCIFER

It is a very grave and solemn business!
We must not be precipitate. Does she
Without compulsion, of her own free will,
Consent to this?

PRINCE HENRY

Against all opposition,
Against all prayers, entreaties, protestations.
She will not be persuaded.

LUCIFER

That is strange!
Have you thought well of it?

ELSIE

I come not here
To argue, but to die. Your business is not
To question, but to kill me. I am ready.
I am impatient to be gone from here
Ere any thoughts of earth disturb again
The spirit of tranquillity within me.

THE GOLDEN LEGEND

PRINCE HENRY

Would I had not come here ! Would I were dead,
And thou wert in thy cottage in the forest,
And hadst not known me ! Why have I done this ?
Let me go back and die.

ELSIE

    It cannot be ;
Not if these cold, flat stones on which we tread
Were coulters heated white, and yonder gateway
Flamed like a furnace with a sevenfold heat.
I must fulfil my purpose.

PRINCE HENRY

    I forbid it !
Not one step further. For I only meant
To put thus far thy courage to the proof.
It is enough. I, too, have strength to die,
For thou hast taught me !

ELSIE

    O my Prince ! remember
Your promises. Let me fulfil my errand.
You do not look on life and death as I do.
There are two angels, that attend unseen
Each one of us, and in great books record
Our good and evil deeds. He who writes down
The good ones, after every action closes
His volume, and ascends with it to God.
The other keeps his dreadful day-book open
Till sunset, that we may repent ; which doing,
The record of the action fades away,

And leaves a line of white across the page.
Now if my act be good, as I believe,
It cannot be recalled. It is already
Sealed up in heaven, as a good deed accomplished.
The rest is yours. Why wait you? I am ready.

(To her attendants.)

Weep not, my friends! rather rejoice with me!
I shall not feel the pain, but shall be gone,
And you will have another friend in heaven.
Then start not at the creaking of the door
Through which I pass. I see what lies beyond it.

(To PRINCE HENRY.*)*

And you, O Prince! bear back my benison
Unto my father's house, and all within it.
This morning in the church I prayed for them,
After confession, after absolution,
When my whole soul was white, I prayed for
    them.
God will take care of them, they need me not.
And in your life let my remembrance linger,
As something not to trouble and disturb it,
But to complete it, adding life to life.
And if at times beside the evening fire
You see my face among the other faces,
Let it not be regarded as a ghost
That haunts your house, but as a guest that loves
    you.
Nay, even as one of your own family,
Without whose presence there were something
    wanting.
I have no more to say. Let us go in.

Line 2. Now if my act be good, as I believe it,

332

THE GOLDEN LEGEND

Friar Angelo! I charge you on your life,
Believe not what she says, for she is mad,
And comes here not to die, but to be healed.

ELSIE

Alas! Prince Henry!

LUCIFER

            Come with me; this way.

*ELSIE goes in with LUCIFER, who thrusts PRINCE
HENRY back and closes the door.*

PRINCE HENRY

Gone! and the light of all my life gone with her!
A sudden darkness falls upon the world!
Oh, what a vile and abject thing am I,
That purchase length of days at such a cost!
Not by her death alone, but by the death
Of all that's good and true and noble in me!
All manhood, excellence, and self-respect,
All love, and faith, and hope, and heart are dead!
All my divine nobility of nature
By this one act is forfeited forever.
I am a Prince in nothing but in name!
         (*To the attendants.*)
Why did you let this horrible deed be done?
Why did you not lay hold on her, and keep her
From self-destruction? Angelo! murderer!
        Struggles at the door, but cannot open it.

ELSIE (*within*)

Farewell, dear Prince! farewell!

333

CHRISTUS: A MYSTERY

PRINCE HENRY

Unbar the door!

LUCIFER

It is too late!

PRINCE HENRY

It shall not be too late!
They burst the door open and rush in.

THE FARM-HOUSE IN THE ODENWALD

URSULA *spinning. A summer afternoon. A table spread.*

URSULA

I have marked it well, — it must be true, —
Death never takes one alone, but two!
Whenever he enters in at a door,
Under roof of gold or roof of thatch,
He always leaves it upon the latch,
And comes again ere the year is o'er.
Never one of a household only!
Perhaps it is a mercy of God,
Lest the dead there under the sod,
In the land of strangers, should be lonely!
Ah me! I think I am lonelier here!
It is hard to go, — but harder to stay!
Were it not for the children, I should pray
That Death would take me within the year!
And Gottlieb! — he is at work all day,
In the sunny field, or the forest murk,

Heading. THE COTTAGE IN THE ODENWALD.

Believe not what she says, for she is mad

But I know that his thoughts are far away,
I know that his heart is not in his work!
And when he comes home to me at night
He is not cheery, but sits and sighs,
And I see the great tears in his eyes,
And try to be cheerful for his sake.
Only the children's hearts are light,
Mine is weary, and ready to break.
God help us! I hope we have done right;
We thought we were acting for the best!

Looking through the open door.

Who is it coming under the trees?
A man, in the Prince's livery dressed!
He looks about him with doubtful face,
As if uncertain of the place.
He stops at the beehives; — now he sees
The garden gate; — he is going past!
Can he be afraid of the bees?
No; he is coming in at last!
He fills my heart with strange alarm!

Enter a Forester.

FORESTER

Is this the tenant Gottlieb's farm?

URSULA

This is his farm, and I his wife.
Pray sit. What may your business be!

FORESTER

News from the Prince!

CHRISTUS: A MYSTERY

URSULA

     Of death or life?

FORESTER

You put your questions eagerly!

URSULA

Answer me, then! How is the Prince?

FORESTER

I left him only two hours since,
Homeward returning down the river,
As strong and well as if God, the Giver,
Had given him back his youth again.

URSULA (*despairing*)

Then Elsie, my poor child, is dead!

FORESTER

That, my good woman, I have not said.
Don't cross the bridge till you come to it,
Is a proverb old, and of excellent wit.

URSULA

Keep me no longer in this pain!

FORESTER

It is true your daughter is no more; —
That is, the peasant she was before.

URSULA

Alas! I am simple and lowly bred,
I am poor, distracted, and forlorn.

And it is not well that you of the court
Should mock me thus, and make a sport
Of a joyless mother whose child is dead,
For you, too, were of mother born!

FORESTER

Your daughter lives, and the Prince is well!
You will learn ere long how it all befell.
Her heart for a moment never failed;
But when they reached Salerno's gate,
The Prince's nobler self prevailed,
And saved her for a noble fate.
And he was healed, in his despair,
By the touch of Saint Matthew's sacred bones;
Though I think the long ride in the open air,
That pilgrimage over stocks and stones,
In the miracle must come in for a share!

URSULA

Virgin! who lovest the poor and lowly,
If the loud cry of a mother's heart
Can ever ascend to where thou art,
Into thy blessed hands and holy
Receive my prayer of praise and thanksgiving!
Let the hands that bore our Saviour bear it
Into the awful presence of God;
For thy feet with holiness are shod,
And if thou bearest it He will hear it.
Our child who was dead again is living!

FORESTER

I did not tell you she was dead;

CHRISTUS: A MYSTERY

If you thought so 't was no fault of mine;
At this very moment, while I speak,
They are sailing homeward down the Rhine,
In a splendid barge, with golden prow,
And decked with banners white and red
As the colors on your daughter's cheek.
They call her the Lady Alicia now;
For the Prince in Salerno made a vow
That Elsie only would he wed.

URSULA

Jesu Maria! what a change!
All seems to me so weird and strange!

FORESTER

I saw her standing on the deck,
Beneath an awning cool and shady;
Her cap of velvet could not hold
The tresses of her hair of gold,
That flowed and floated like the stream,
And fell in masses down her neck.
As fair and lovely did she seem
As in a story or a dream
Some beautiful and foreign lady.
And the Prince looked so grand and proud,
And waved his hand thus to the crowd
That gazed and shouted from the shore,
All down the river, long and loud.

URSULA

We shall behold our child once more;
She is not dead! She is not dead!

THE GOLDEN LEGEND

God, listening, must have overheard
The prayers, that, without sound or word,
Our hearts in secrecy have said!
Oh, bring me to her; for mine eyes
Are hungry to behold her face;
My very soul within me cries;
My very hands seem to caress her,
To see her, gaze at her, and bless her;
Dear Elsie, child of God and grace!

Goes out toward the garden.

FORESTER

There goes the good woman out of her head;
And Gottlieb's supper is waiting here;
A very capacious flagon of beer,
And a very portentous loaf of bread.
One would say his grief did not much oppress
    him.
Here's to the health of the Prince, God bless
    him!

He drinks.

Ha! it buzzes and stings like a hornet!
And what a scene there, through the door!
The forest behind and the garden before,
And midway an old man of threescore,
With a wife and children that caress him.
Let me try still further to cheer and adorn it
With a merry, echoing blast of my cornet!

Goes out, blowing his horn.

CHRISTUS: A MYSTERY

THE CASTLE OF VAUTSBERG ON THE RHINE

*Prince Henry and Elsie standing on the terrace at evening.
The sound of bells heard from a distance*

PRINCE HENRY

We are alone. The wedding guests
Ride down the hill, with plumes and cloaks,
And the descending dark invests
The Niederwald, and all the nests
Among its hoar and haunted oaks.

ELSIE

What bells are those, that ring so slow,
So mellow, musical, and low?

PRINCE HENRY

They are the bells of Geisenheim,
That with their melancholy chime
Ring out the curfew of the sun.

ELSIE

Listen, beloved.

PRINCE HENRY

          They are done!
Dear Elsie! many years ago
Those same soft bells at eventide
Rang in the ears of Charlemagne,
As, seated by Fastrada's side
At Ingelheim, in all his pride
He heard their sound with secret pain.

340

THE GOLDEN LEGEND

ELSIE

Their voices only speak to me
Of peace and deep tranquillity,
And endless confidence in thee!

PRINCE HENRY

Thou knowest the story of her ring,
How, when the court went back to Aix,
Fastrada died; and how the king
Sat watching by her night and day,
Till into one of the blue lakes,
Which water that delicious land,
They cast the ring, drawn from her hand:
And the great monarch sat serene
And sad beside the fated shore,
Nor left the land forevermore.

ELSIE

That was true love.

PRINCE HENRY

                    For him the queen
Ne'er did what thou hast done for me.

ELSIE

Wilt thou as fond and faithful be?
Wilt thou so love me after death?

PRINCE HENRY

In life's delight, in death's dismay,
In storm and sunshine, night and day,

Line 9. That water that delicious land,

341

CHRISTUS: A MYSTERY

In health, in sickness, in decay,
Here and hereafter, I am thine!
Thou hast Fastrada's ring. Beneath
The calm, blue waters of thine eyes,
Deep in thy steadfast soul it lies,
And, undisturbed by this world's breath,
With magic light its jewels shine!
This golden ring, which thou hast worn
Upon thy finger since the morn,
Is but a symbol and a semblance,
An outward fashion, a remembrance,
Of what thou wearest within unseen,
O my Fastrada, O my queen!
Behold! the hill-tops all aglow
With purple and with amethyst;
While the whole valley deep below
Is filled, and seems to overflow,
With a fast-rising tide of mist.
The evening air grows damp and chill;
Let us go in.

ELSIE

   Ah, not so soon.
See yonder fire! It is the moon
Slow rising o'er the eastern hill.
It glimmers on the forest tips,
And through the dewy foliage drips
In little rivulets of light,
And makes the heart in love with night.

PRINCE HENRY

Oft on this terrace, when the day

342

Was closing, have I stood and gazed,
And seen the landscape fade away,
And the white vapors rise and drown
Hamlet and vineyard, tower and town,
While far above the hill-tops blazed.
But then another hand than thine
Was gently held and clasped in mine;
Another head upon my breast
Was laid, as thine is now, at rest.
Why dost thou lift those tender eyes
With so much sorrow and surprise?
A minstrel's, not a maiden's hand,
Was that which in my own was pressed.
A manly form usurped thy place,
A beautiful, but bearded face,
That now is in the Holy Land,
Yet in my memory from afar
Is shining on us like a star.
But linger not. For while I speak,
A sheeted spectre white and tall,
The cold mist climbs the castle wall,
And lays his hand upon thy cheek!

They go in.

EPILOGUE

THE TWO RECORDING ANGELS ASCENDING

THE ANGEL OF GOOD DEEDS (*with closed book*)
God sent his messenger the rain,
And said unto the mountain brook,
" Rise up, and from thy caverns look
And leap, with naked, snow-white feet,
From the cool hills into the heat
Of the broad, arid plain."

God sent his messenger of faith,
And whispered in the maiden's heart,
" Rise up, and look from where thou art,
And scatter with unselfish hands
Thy freshness on the barren sands
And solitudes of Death."

O beauty of holiness,
Of self-forgetfulness, of lowliness!
O power of meekness,
Whose very gentleness and weakness
Are like the yielding, but irresistible air!
Upon the pages
Of the sealed volume that I bear,
The deed divine
Is written in characters of gold,
That never shall grow old,

THE GOLDEN LEGEND

But through all ages
Burn and shine,
With soft effulgence!
O God! it is thy indulgence
That fills the world with the bliss
Of a good deed like this!

THE ANGEL OF EVIL DEEDS (*with open book*)

Not yet, not yet
Is the red sun wholly set,
But evermore recedes,
While open still I bear
The Book of Evil Deeds,
To let the breathings of the upper air
Visit its pages and erase
The records from its face!
Fainter and fainter as I gaze
In the broad blaze
The glimmering landscape shines,
And below me the black river
Is hidden by wreaths of vapor!
Fainter and fainter the black lines
Begin to quiver
Along the whitening surface of the paper;
Shade after shade
The terrible words grow faint and fade,
And in their place
Runs a white space!

Down goes the sun!
But the soul of one,
Who by repentance

CHRISTUS: A MYSTERY

Hath escaped the dreadful sentence,
Shines bright below me as I look.
It is the end !
With closed Book
To God do I ascend.
Lo ! over the mountain steeps
A dark, gigantic shadow sweeps
Beneath my feet ;
A blackness inwardly brightening
With sullen heat,
As a storm-cloud lurid with lightning.
And a cry of lamentation,
Repeated and again repeated,
Deep and loud
As the reverberation
Of cloud answering unto cloud,
Swells and rolls away in the distance,
As if the sheeted
Lightning retreated,
Baffled and thwarted by the wind's resistance.

It is Lucifer,
The son of mystery ;
And since God suffers him to be,
He, too, is God's minister,
And labors for some good
By us not understood !

Line 1. Has escaped the dreadful sentence,

SECOND INTERLUDE

MARTIN LUTHER

A chamber in the Wartburg. Morning. MARTIN LUTHER
writing.

MARTIN LUTHER

OUR God, a Tower of Strength is He,
A goodly wall and weapon ;
From all our need He helps us free,
That now to us doth happen.
    The old evil foe
    Doth in earnest grow,
    In grim armor dight,
    Much guile and great might ;
On earth there is none like him.

Oh yes ; a tower of strength indeed,
A present help in all our need,
A sword and buckler is our God.
Innocent men have walked unshod
O'er burning ploughshares, and have trod
Unharmed on serpents in their path,
And laughed to scorn the Devil's wrath !

Safe in this Wartburg tower I stand
Where God hath led me by the hand,
And look down, with a heart at ease,
Over the pleasant neighborhoods,
Over the vast Thuringian Woods,

CHRISTUS: A MYSTERY

With flash of river, and gloom of trees,
With castles crowning the dizzy heights,
And farms and pastoral delights,
And the morning pouring everywhere
Its golden glory on the air.
Safe, yes, safe am I here at last,
Safe from the overwhelming blast
Of the mouths of Hell, that followed me fast,
And the howling demons of despair
That hunted me like a beast to his lair.

Of our own might we nothing can ;
We soon are unprotected ;
There fighteth for us the right Man,
Whom God himself elected.
Who is He ; ye exclaim ?
Christus is his name,
Lord of Sabaoth,
Very God in troth ;
The field He holds forever.

Nothing can vex the Devil more
Than the name of Him whom we adore.
Therefore doth it delight me best
To stand in the choir among the rest,
With the great organ trumpeting
Through its metallic tubes, and sing :
Et verbum caro factum est !
These words the Devil cannot endure,
For he knoweth their meaning well !
Him they trouble and repel,
Us they comfort and allure,
And happy it were, if our delight

Were as great as his affright!
Yea, music is the Prophets' art;
Among the gifts that God hath sent,
One of the most magnificent!
It calms the agitated heart;
Temptations, evil thoughts, and all
The passions that disturb the soul,
Are quelled by its divine control,
As the Evil Spirit fled from Saul,
And his distemper was allayed,
When David took his harp and played.

This world may full of Devils be,
All ready to devour us;
Yet not so sore afraid are we,
They shall not overpower us.
This World's Prince, howe'er
Fierce he may appear,
He can harm us not,
He is doomed, God wot!
One little word can slay him!

Incredible it seems to some
And to myself a mystery,
That such weak flesh and blood as we,
Armed with no other shield or sword,
Or other weapon than the Word,
Should combat and should overcome,
A spirit powerful as he!
He summons forth the Pope of Rome
With all his diabolic crew,
His shorn and shaven retinue
Of priests and children of the dark;

CHRISTUS: A MYSTERY

Kill ! kill ! they cry, the Heresiarch,
Who rouseth up all Christendom
Against us ; and at one fell blow
Seeks the whole Church to overthrow !
Not yet ; my hour is not yet come.

Yesterday in an idle mood,
Hunting with others in the wood,
I did not pass the hours in vain,
For in the very heart of all
The joyous tumult raised around,
Shouting of men, and baying of hound,
And the bugle's blithe and cheery call,
And echoes answering back again,
From crags of the distant mountain chain, —
In the very heart of this, I found
A mystery of grief and pain.
It was an image of the power
Of Satan, hunting the world about,
With his nets and traps and well-trained dogs,
His bishops and priests and theologues,
And all the rest of the rabble rout,
Seeking whom he may devour !
Enough have I had of hunting hares,
Enough of these hours of idle mirth,
Enough of nets and traps and gins !
The only hunting of any worth
Is where I can pierce with javelins
The cunning foxes and wolves and bears,
The whole iniquitous troop of beasts,
The Roman Pope and the Roman priests
That sorely infest and afflict the earth !

MARTIN LUTHER

Ye nuns, ye singing birds of the air!
The fowler hath caught you in his snare,
And keeps you safe in his gilded cage,
Singing the song that never tires,
To lure down others from their nests;
How ye flutter and beat your breasts,
Warm and soft with young desires
Against the cruel, pitiless wires,
Reclaiming your lost heritage!
Behold! a hand unbars the door,
Ye shall be captives held no more.

> The Word they shall perforce let stand,
> And little thanks they merit!
> For He is with us in the land,
> With gifts of his own Spirit!
> > Though they take our life,
> > Goods, honors, child and wife,
> > Let these pass away,
> > Little gain have they;
> The Kingdom still remaineth!

Yea, it remaineth forevermore,
However Satan may rage and roar,
Though often he whispers in my ears:
What if thy doctrines false should be?
And wrings from me a bitter sweat.
Then I put him to flight with jeers,
Saying: Saint Satan! pray for me;
If thou thinkest I am not saved yet!

And my mortal foes that lie in wait
In every avenue and gate!

CHRISTUS: A MYSTERY

As to that odious monk John Tetzel,
Hawking about his hollow wares
Like a huckster at village fairs,
And those mischievous fellows, Wetzel,
Campanus, Carlstadt, Martin Cellarius,
And all the busy, multifarious
Heretics, and disciples of Arius,
Half-learned, dunce-bold, dry and hard,
They are not worthy of my regard,
Poor and humble as I am.

But ah! Erasmus of Rotterdam,
He is the vilest miscreant
That ever walked this world below!
A Momus, making his mock and mow,
At Papist and at Protestant,
Sneering at Saint John and Saint Paul,
At God and Man, at one and all;
And yet as hollow and false and drear,
As a cracked pitcher to the ear,
And ever growing worse and worse!
Whenever I pray, I pray for a curse
On Erasmus, the Insincere!

Philip Melancthon! thou alone
Faithful among the faithless known,
Thee I hail, and only thee!
Behold the record of us three!
  Res et verba Philippus,
  Res sine verbis Lutherus;
  Erasmus verba sine re!

MARTIN LUTHER

My Philip, prayest thou for me?
Lifted above all earthly care,
From these high regions of the air,
Among the birds that day and night
Upon the branches of tall trees
Sing their lauds and litanies.
Praising God with all their might,
My Philip, unto thee I write.

My Philip! thou who knowest best
All that is passing in this breast;
The spiritual agonies,
The inward deaths, the inward hell,
And the divine new births as well,
That surely follow after these,
As after winter follows spring;
My Philip, in the night-time sing
This song of the Lord I send to thee;
And I will sing it for thy sake,
Until our answering voices make
A glorious antiphony,
And choral chant of victory!

PART THREE

THE NEW ENGLAND TRAGEDIES

JOHN ENDICOTT

DRAMATIS PERSONÆ

JOHN ENDICOTT . . .	*Governor.*
JOHN ENDICOTT . . .	*His son.*
RICHARD BELLINGHAM .	*Deputy Governor.*
JOHN NORTON	*Minister of the Gospel.*
EDWARD BUTTER . . .	*Treasurer.*
WALTER MERRY . . .	*Tithing-man.*
NICHOLAS UPSALL . . .	*An old citizen.*
SAMUEL COLE	*Landlord of the Three Mariners.*

SIMON KEMPTHORN ⎫
RALPH GOLDSMITH ⎭ . . *Sea-Captains.*

WENLOCK CHRISTISON ⎫
EDITH, *his daughter* ⎬ *Quakers.*
EDWARD WHARTON ⎭

Assistants, Halberdiers, Marshal, etc.

The Scene is in Boston in the year 1665.

PROLOGUE

TO-NIGHT we strive to read, as we may best,
This city, like an ancient palimpsest;
And bring to light, upon the blotted page,
The mournful record of an earlier age,
That, pale and half effaced, lies hidden away
Beneath the fresher writing of to-day.
Rise, then, O buried city that hast been;
Rise up, rebuilded in the painted scene,
And let our curious eyes behold once more
The pointed gable and the pent-house door,
The Meeting-house with leaden-latticed panes,
The narrow thoroughfares, the crooked lanes!

Rise, too, ye shapes and shadows of the Past,
Rise from your long-forgotten graves at last;
Let us behold your faces, let us hear
The words ye uttered in those days of fear!
Revisit your familiar haunts again, —
The scenes of triumph, and the scenes of pain,
And leave the footprints of your bleeding feet
Once more upon the pavement of the street!

Nor let the Historian blame the Poet here,
If he perchance misdate the day or year,
And group events together, by his art,
That in the Chronicles lie far apart;

Line 7. Rise, then, O buried city that has been;

357

CHRISTUS : A MYSTERY

For as the double stars, though sundered far,
Seem to the naked eye a single star,
So facts of history, at a distance seen,
Into one common point of light convene.

" Why touch upon such themes ? " perhaps some
      friend
May ask, incredulous ; " and to what good end ?
Why drag again into the light of day
The errors of an age long passed away ? "
I answer : " For the lesson that they teach :
The tolerance of opinion and of speech.
Hope, Faith, and Charity remain, — these three ;
And greatest of them all is Charity."

Let us remember, if these words be true,
That unto all men Charity is due ;
Give what we ask ; and pity, while we blame,
Lest we become copartners in the shame,
Lest we condemn, and yet ourselves partake,
And persecute the dead for conscience' sake.

Therefore it is the author seeks and strives
To represent the dead as in their lives,
And lets at times his characters unfold
Their thoughts in their own language, strong and
      bold ;
He only asks of you to do the like ;
To hear him first, and, if you will, then strike.

ACT I

SCENE I. — *Sunday afternoon. The interior of the Meeting-house. On the pulpit, an hour-glass; below, a box for contributions. JOHN NORTON in the pulpit. GOVERNOR ENDICOTT in a canopied seat, attended by four halberdiers. The congregation singing.*

> The Lord descended from above,
>   And bowed the heavens high;
> And underneath his feet He cast
>   The darkness of the sky.
>
> On Cherubim and Seraphim
>   Right royally He rode,
> And on the wings of mighty winds
>   Came flying all abroad.

NORTON (*rising and turning the hour-glass on the pulpit*)

I heard a great voice from the temple saying
Unto the Seven Angels, Go your ways;
Pour out the vials of the wrath of God
Upon the earth. And the First Angel went
And poured his vial on the earth; and straight
There fell a noisome and a grievous sore
On them which had the birth-mark of the Beast,
And them which worshipped and adored his image.
On us hath fallen this grievous pestilence.
There is a sense of terror in the air;
And apparitions of things horrible

359

Are seen by many. From the sky above us
The stars fall; and beneath us the earth quakes!
The sound of drums at midnight from afar,
The sound of horsemen riding to and fro,
As if the gates of the invisible world
Were opened, and the dead came forth to warn us, —
All these are omens of some dire disaster
Impending over us, and soon to fall.
Moreover, in the language of the Prophet,
Death is again come up into our windows,
To cut off little children from without,
And young men from the streets. And in the midst
Of all these supernatural threats and warnings
Doth Heresy uplift its horrid head;
A vision of Sin more awful and appalling
Than any phantasm, ghost, or apparition,
As arguing and portending some enlargement
Of the mysterious Power of Darkness!

EDITH *barefooted, and clad in sackcloth, with her hair hanging loose upon her shoulders, walks slowly up the aisle, followed by* WHARTON *and other Quakers. The congregation
starts up in confusion.*

EDITH (*to* NORTON, *raising her hand*)
                                        Peace!

NORTON

Anathema maranatha! The Lord cometh!

EDITH

Yea, verily He cometh, and shall judge

Line 3. The sound of drums at midnight in the air,

THE NEW ENGLAND TRAGEDIES

The shepherds of Israel who do feed themselves,
And leave their flocks to eat what they have trodden
Beneath their feet.

NORTON

Be silent, babbling woman!
Saint Paul commands all women to keep silence
Within the churches.

EDITH

Yet the women prayed
And prophesied at Corinth in his day;
And, among those on whom the fiery tongues
Of Pentecost descended, some were women!

NORTON

The Elders of the Churches, by our law,
Alone have power to open the doors of speech
And silence in the Assembly. I command you!

EDITH

The law of God is greater than your laws!
Ye build your church with blood, your town with
crime;
The heads thereof give judgment for reward;
The priests thereof teach only for their hire;
Your laws condemn the innocent to death;
And against this I bear my testimony!

NORTON

What testimony?

EDITH

That of the Holy Spirit,
Which, as your Calvin says, surpasseth reason.

NORTON

The laborer is worthy of his hire.

EDITH

Yet our great Master did not teach for hire,
And the Apostles without purse or scrip
Went forth to do his work. Behold this box
Beneath thy pulpit. Is it for the poor?
Thou canst not answer. It is for the Priest;
And against this I bear my testimony.

NORTON

Away with all these Heretics and Quakers!
Quakers, forsooth! Because a quaking fell
On Daniel, at beholding of the Vision,
Must ye needs shake and quake? Because Isaiah
Went stripped and barefoot, must ye wail and howl?
Must ye go stripped and naked? must ye make
A wailing like the dragons, and a mourning
As of the owls? Ye verify the adage
That Satan is God's ape! Away with them!

> *Tumult. The Quakers are driven out with violence,*
> EDITH *following slowly. The congregation re-*
> *tires in confusion.*

Thus freely do the Reprobates commit
Such measure of iniquity as fits them
For the intended measure of God's wrath,
And even in violating God's commands

362

Are they fulfilling the divine decree!
The will of man is but an instrument
Disposed and predetermined to its action
According unto the decree of God,
Being as much subordinate thereto
As is the axe unto the hewer's hand!

> *He descends from the pulpit, and joins* GOVERNOR
> ENDICOTT, *who comes forward to meet him.*

The omens and the wonders of the time,
Famine, and fire, and shipwreck, and disease,
The blast of corn, the death of our young men,
Our sufferings in all precious, pleasant things,
Are manifestations of the wrath divine,
Signs of God's controversy with New England.
These emissaries of the Evil One,
These servants and ambassadors of Satan,
Are but commissioned executioners
Of God's vindictive and deserved displeasure.
We must receive them as the Roman Bishop
Once received Attila, saying, I rejoice
You have come safe, whom I esteem to be
The scourge of God, sent to chastise his people.
This very heresy, perchance, may serve
The purposes of God to some good end.
With you I leave it ; but do not neglect
The holy tactics of the civil sword.

ENDICOTT

And what more can be done ?

NORTON

The hand that cut

CHRISTUS: A MYSTERY

The Red Cross from the colors of the king
Can cut the red heart from this heresy.
Fear not. All blasphemies immediate
And heresies turbulent must be suppressed
By civil power.

ENDICOTT

But in what way suppressed?

NORTON

The Book of Deuteronomy declares
That if thy son, thy daughter, or thy wife,
Ay, or the friend which is as thine own soul,
Entice thee secretly, and say to thee,
Let us serve other gods, then shall thine eye
Not pity him, but thou shalt surely kill him,
And thine own hand shall be the first upon him
To slay him.

ENDICOTT

Four already have been slain;
And others banished upon pain of death.
But they come back again to meet their doom,
Bringing the linen for their winding-sheets.
We must not go too far. In truth, I shrink
From shedding of more blood. The people murmur
At our severity.

NORTON

Then let them murmur!
Truth is relentless; justice never wavers;
The greatest firmness is the greatest mercy;

THE NEW ENGLAND TRAGEDIES

The noble order of the Magistracy
Cometh immediately from God, and yet
This noble order of the Magistracy
Is by these Heretics despised and outraged.

ENDICOTT

To-night they sleep in prison. If they die,
They cannot say that we have caused their death.
We do but guard the passage, with the sword
Pointed towards them; if they dash upon it,
Their blood will be on their own heads, not ours.

NORTON

Enough. I ask no more. My predecessor
Coped only with the milder heresies
Of Antinomians and of Anabaptists.
He was not born to wrestle with these fiends.
Chrysostom in his pulpit; Augustine
In disputation; Timothy in his house!
The lantern of Saint Botolph's ceased to burn
When from the portals of that church he came
To be a burning and a shining light
Here in the wilderness. And, as he lay
On his death-bed, he saw me in a vision
Ride on a snow-white horse into this town.
His vision was prophetic; thus I came,
A terror to the impenitent, and Death
On the pale horse of the Apocalypse
To all the accursed race of Heretics!

Exeunt.

SCENE II. — *A street. On one side,* NICHOLAS UPSALL'S *house ; on the other,* WALTER MERRY'S, *with a flock of pigeons on the roof.* UPSALL *seated in the porch of his house.*

UPSALL

O day of rest! How beautiful, how fair,
How welcome to the weary and the old!
Day of the Lord! and truce to earthly cares!
Day of the Lord, as all our days should be!
Ah, why will man by his austerities
Shut out the blessed sunshine and the light,
And make of thee a dungeon of despair!

WALTER MERRY (*entering and looking round him*)

All silent as a graveyard! No one stirring;
No footfall in the street, no sound of voices!
By righteous punishment and perseverance,
And perseverance in that punishment,
At last I 've brought this contumacious town
To strict observance of the Sabbath day.
Those wanton gospellers, the pigeons yonder,
Are now the only Sabbath-breakers left.
I cannot put them down. As if to taunt me,
They gather every Sabbath afternoon
In noisy congregation on my roof,
Billing and cooing. Whir! take that, ye Quakers.

Throws a stone at the pigeons. Sees UPSALL.

Ah! Master Nicholas!

UPSALL

                Good afternoon,
Dear neighbor Walter.

THE NEW ENGLAND TRAGEDIES

MERRY

Master Nicholas,
You have to-day withdrawn yourself from meeting.

UPSALL

Yea, I have chosen rather to worship God
Sitting in silence here at my own door.

MERRY

Worship the Devil! You this day have broken
Three of our strictest laws. First, by abstaining
From public worship. Secondly, by walking
Profanely on the Sabbath.

UPSALL

Not one step.
I have been sitting still here, seeing the pigeons
Feed in the street and fly about the roofs.

MERRY

You have been in the street with other intent
Than going to and from the Meeting-house.
And, thirdly, you are harboring Quakers here.
I am amazed!

UPSALL

Men sometimes, it is said,
Entertain angels unawares.

MERRY

Nice angels!

367

CHRISTUS: A MYSTERY

Angels in broad-brimmed hats and russet cloaks,
The color of the Devil's nutting-bag! They came
Into the Meeting-house this afternoon
More in the shape of devils than of angels.
The women screamed and fainted; and the boys
Made such an uproar in the gallery
I could not keep them quiet.

UPSALL

Neighbor Walter,
Your persecution is of no avail.

MERRY

'T is prosecution, as the Governor says,
Not persecution.

UPSALL

Well, your prosecution;
Your hangings do no good.

MERRY

The reason is,
We do not hang enough. But, mark my words,
We'll scour them; yea, I warrant ye, we'll scour
them!
And now go in and entertain your angels,
And don't be seen here in the street again
Till after sundown! — There they are again!

Exit UPSALL. MERRY *throws another stone at the*
pigeons, and then goes into his house.

SCENE III. — *A room in* UPSALL'S *house. Night.* EDITH,
WHARTON, *and other Quakers seated at a table.* UPSALL
seated near them. Several books on the table.

WHARTON

William and Marmaduke, our martyred brothers,
Sleep in untimely graves, if aught untimely
Can find place in the providence of God,
Where nothing comes too early or too late.
I saw their noble death. They to the scaffold
Walked hand in hand. Two hundred armed men
And many horsemen guarded them, for fear
Of rescue by the crowd, whose hearts were stirred.

EDITH

O holy martyrs !

WHARTON

       When they tried to speak,
Their voices by the roll of drums were drowned.
When they were dead they still looked fresh and
    fair,
The terror of death was not upon their faces.
Our sister Mary, likewise, the meek woman,
Has passed through martyrdom to her reward ;
Exclaiming, as they led her to her death,
" These many days I 've been in Paradise."
And, when she died, Priest Wilson threw the hang-
    man
His handkerchief, to cover the pale face
He dared not look upon.

CHRISTUS: A MYSTERY

EDITH

As persecuted,
Yet not forsaken; as unknown, yet known;
As dying, and behold we are alive;
As sorrowful, and yet rejoicing alway;
As having nothing, yet possessing all!

WHARTON

And Leddra, too, is dead. But from his prison,
The day before his death, he sent these words
Unto the little flock of Christ: "Whatever
May come upon the followers of the Light, —
Distress, affliction, famine, nakedness,
Or perils in the city or the sea,
Or persecution, or even death itself, —
I am persuaded that God's armor of Light,
As it is loved and lived in, will preserve you.
Yea, death itself; through which you will find en-
        trance
Into the pleasant pastures of the fold,
Where you shall feed forever as the herds
That roam at large in the low valleys of Achor.
And as the flowing of the ocean fills
Each creek and branch thereof, and then retires,
Leaving behind a sweet and wholesome savor;
So doth the virtue and the life of God
Flow evermore into the hearts of those
Whom He hath made partakers of his nature;
And, when it but withdraws itself a little,
Leaves a sweet savor after it, that many
Can say they are made clean by every word
That He hath spoken to them in their silence."

EDITH (*rising, and breaking into a kind of chant*)

Truly we do but grope here in the dark,
Near the partition-wall of Life and Death,
At every moment dreading or desiring
To lay our hands upon the unseen door!
Let us, then, labor for an inward stillness, —
An inward stillness and an inward healing;
That perfect silence where the lips and heart
Are still, and we no longer entertain
Our own imperfect thoughts and vain opinions,
But God alone speaks in us, and we wait
In singleness of heart, that we may know
His will, and in the silence of our spirits,
That we may do His will, and do that only!

> *A long pause, interrupted by the sound of a drum
> approaching; then shouts in the street, and a loud
> knocking at the door.*

MARSHAL

Within there! Open the door!

MERRY

Will no one answer?

MARSHAL

In the King's name! Within there!

MERRY

Open the door!

UPSALL (*from the window*)

It is not barred. Come in. Nothing prevents you.

The poor man's door is ever on the latch.
He needs no bolt nor bar to shut out thieves;
He fears no enemies, and has no friends
Importunate enough to need a key.

Enter JOHN ENDICOTT, *the* MARSHAL, MERRY, *and a crowd.*
Seeing the Quakers silent and unmoved, they pause, awe-
struck. ENDICOTT *opposite* EDITH.

MARSHAL

In the King's name do I arrest you all !
Away with them to prison. Master Upsall,
You are again discovered harboring here
These ranters and disturbers of the peace.
You know the law.

UPSALL

    I know it, and am ready
To suffer yet again its penalties.

EDITH (*to* ENDICOTT)

" Why dost thou persecute me, Saul of Tarsus ? "

ACT II

SCENE I. — JOHN ENDICOTT's *room. Early morning.*

JOHN ENDICOTT

" Why dost thou persecute me, Saul of Tarsus ? "
All night these words were ringing in mine ears !

Line 4. Importunate enough to turn the key upon them.

A sorrowful sweet face; a look that pierced me
With meek reproach; a voice of resignation
That had a life of suffering in its tone;
And that was all! And yet I could not sleep,
Or, when I slept, I dreamed that awful dream!
I stood beneath the elm-tree on the Common
On which the Quakers have been hanged, and heard
A voice, not hers, that cried amid the darkness,
"This is Aceldama, the field of blood!
I will have mercy, and not sacrifice!"
    (*Opens the window, and looks out.*)
The sun is up already; and my heart
Sickens and sinks within me when I think
How many tragedies will be enacted
Before his setting. As the earth rolls round,
It seems to me a huge Ixion's wheel,
Upon whose whirling spokes we are bound fast,
And must go with it! Ah, how bright the sun
Strikes on the sea and on the masts of vessels,
That are uplifted in the morning air,
Like crosses of some peaceable crusade!
It makes me long to sail for lands unknown,
No matter whither! Under me, in shadow,
Gloomy and narrow lies the little town,
Still sleeping, but to wake and toil awhile,
Then sleep again. How dismal looks the prison,
How grim and sombre in the sunless street, —
The prison where she sleeps, or wakes and waits
For what I dare not think of, — death, perhaps!
A word that has been said may be unsaid:
It is but air. But when a deed is done
It cannot be undone, nor can our thoughts

Reach out to all the mischiefs that may follow.
'T is time for morning prayers. I will go down.
My father, though severe, is kind and just;
And when his heart is tender with devotion, —
When from his lips have fallen the words, " Forgive us
As we forgive," — then will I intercede
For these poor people, and perhaps may save them.

Exit.

SCENE II. — *Dock Square. On one side, the tavern of the Three Mariners. In the background, a quaint building with gables; and, beyond it, wharves and shipping.* CAPTAIN KEMPTHORN *and others seated at a table before the door.* SAMUEL COLE *standing near them.*

KEMPTHORN

Come, drink about ! Remember Parson Melham,
And bless the man who first invented flip !

They drink.

COLE

Pray, Master Kempthorn, where were you last night ?

KEMPTHORN

On board the Swallow, Simon Kempthorn, master,
Up for Barbadoes, and the Windward Islands.

COLE

The town was in a tumult.

KEMPTHORN

And for what ?

THE NEW ENGLAND TRAGEDIES

COLE

Your Quakers were arrested.

KEMPTHORN

How my Quakers?

COLE

Those you brought in your vessel from Barbadoes.
They made an uproar in the Meeting-house
Yesterday, and they 're now in prison for it.
I owe you little thanks for bringing them
To the Three Mariners.

KEMPTHORN

They have not harmed you.
I tell you, Goodman Cole, that Quaker girl
Is precious as a sea-bream's eye. I tell you
It was a lucky day when first she set
Her little foot upon the Swallow's deck,
Bringing good luck, fair winds, and pleasant weather.

COLE

I am a law-abiding citizen;
I have a seat in the new Meeting-house,
A cow-right on the Common; and, besides,
Am corporal in the Great Artillery.
I rid me of the vagabonds at once.

KEMPTHORN

Why should you not have Quakers at your tavern
If you have fiddlers?

COLE

Never! never! never!
If you want fiddling you must go elsewhere,
To the Green Dragon and the Admiral Vernon,
And other such disreputable places.
But the Three Mariners is an orderly house,
Most orderly, quiet, and respectable.
Lord Leigh said he could be as quiet here
As at the Governor's. And have I not
King Charles's Twelve Good Rules, all framed and
        glazed,
Hanging in my best parlor?

KEMPTHORN

Here 's a health
To good King Charles. Will you not drink the King?
Then drink confusion to old Parson Palmer.

COLE

And who is Parson Palmer? I don't know him.

KEMPTHORN

He had his cellar underneath his pulpit,
And so preached o'er his liquor, just as you do.
                                        A drum within.

COLE

Here comes the Marshal.

MERRY (*within*)

Make room for the Marshal.
376

THE NEW ENGLAND TRAGEDIES

How pompous and imposing he appears!
His great buff doublet bellying like a mainsail,
And all his streamers fluttering in the wind.
What holds he in his hand?

COLE

A Proclamation.

Enter the MARSHAL, *with a proclamation; and* MERRY, *with
a halberd. They are preceded by a drummer, and followed
by the hangman, with an armful of books, and a crowd of
people, among whom are* UPSALL *and* JOHN ENDICOTT. *A
pile is made of the books.*

MERRY

Silence, the drum! Good citizens, attend
To the new laws enacted by the Court.

MARSHAL (*reads*)

" Whereas a cursed sect of Heretics
Has lately risen, commonly called Quakers,
Who take upon themselves to be commissioned
Immediately of God, and furthermore
Infallibly assisted by the Spirit
To write and utter blasphemous opinions,
Despising Government and the order of God
In Church and Commonwealth, and speaking evil
Of Dignities, reproaching and reviling
The Magistrates and Ministers, and seeking
To turn the people from their faith, and thus
Gain proselytes to their pernicious ways; —
This Court, considering the premises,

And to prevent like mischief as is wrought
By their means in our land, doth hereby order,
That whatsoever master or commander
Of any ship, bark, pink, or catch shall bring
To any roadstead, harbor, creek, or cove
Within this Jurisdiction any Quakers,
Or other blasphemous Heretics, shall pay
Unto the Treasurer of the Commonwealth
One hundred pounds, and for default thereof
Be put in prison, and continue there
Till the said sum be satisfied and paid."

COLE

Now, Simon Kempthorn, what say you to that?

KEMPTHORN

I pray you, Cole, lend me a hundred pounds!

MARSHAL (*reads*)

" If any one within this Jurisdiction
Shall henceforth entertain, or shall conceal
Quakers, or other blasphemous Heretics,
Knowing them so to be, every such person
Shall forfeit to the country forty shillings
For each hour's entertainment or concealment,
And shall be sent to prison, as aforesaid,
Until the forfeiture be wholly paid."
                                    Murmurs in the crowd.

KEMPTHORN

Now, Goodman Cole, I think your turn has come!

378

COLE

Knowing them so to be!

KEMPTHORN

.At forty shillings
The hour, your fine will be some forty pounds!

COLE

Knowing them so to be! That is the law.

MARSHAL (*reads*)

" And it is further ordered and enacted,
If any Quaker or Quakers shall presume
To come henceforth into this Jurisdiction,
Every male Quaker for the first offence
Shall have one ear cut off; and shall be kept
At labor in the Workhouse, till such time
As he be sent away at his own charge.
And for the repetition of the offence
Shall have his other ear cut off, and then
Be branded in the palm of his right hand.
And every woman Quaker shall be whipt
Severely in three towns; and every Quaker,
Or he or she, that shall for a third time
Herein again offend, shall have their tongues
Bored through with a hot iron, and shall be
Sentenced to Banishment on pain of Death."
                              Loud murmurs.

(*The voice of* CHRISTISON *in the crowd*)

O patience of the Lord! How long, how long,
Ere thou avenge the blood of Thine Elect?

CHRISTUS: A MYSTERY

MERRY

Silence, there, silence! Do not break the peace!

MARSHAL (*reads*)

" Every inhabitant of this Jurisdiction
Who shall defend the horrible opinions
Of Quakers, by denying due respect
To equals and superiors, and withdrawing
From Church Assemblies, and thereby approving
The abusive and destructive practices
Of this accursed sect, in opposition
To all the orthodox received opinions
Of godly men, shall be forthwith committed
Unto close prison for one month; and then
Refusing to retract and to reform
The opinions as aforesaid, he shall be
Sentenced to Banishment on pain of Death.
By the Court. Edward Rawson, Secretary."
Now, hangman, do your duty. Burn those books.
> *Loud murmurs in the crowd. The pile of books is
> lighted.*

UPSALL

I testify against these cruel laws!
Forerunners are they of some judgment on us;
And, in the love and tenderness I bear
Unto this town and people, I beseech you,
O Magistrates, take heed, lest ye be found
As fighters against God!

JOHN ENDICOTT (*taking* UPSALL'S *hand*)

Upsall, I thank you

For speaking words such as some younger man,
I, or another, should have said before you.
Such laws as these are cruel and oppressive;
A blot on this fair town, and a disgrace
To any Christian people.

MERRY (*aside, listening behind them*)
       Here 's sedition!
I never thought that any good would come
Of this young popinjay, with his long hair
And his great boots, fit only for the Russians
Or barbarous Indians, as his father says!

THE VOICE

Woe to the bloody town! And rightfully
Men call it the Lost Town! The blood of Abel
Cries from the ground, and at the final judgment
The Lord will say, " Cain, Cain! where is thy
  brother ? "

MERRY

Silence there in the crowd!

UPSALL (*aside*)
      'T is Christison!

THE VOICE

O foolish people, ye that think to burn
And to consume the truth of God, I tell you
That every flame is a loud tongue of fire
To publish it abroad to all the world
Louder than tongues of men!

KEMPTHORN (*springing to his feet*)
                  Well said, my hearty.
There 's a brave fellow ! There 's a man of pluck !
A man who 's not afraid to say his say,
Though a whole town 's against him. Rain, rain,
    rain,
Bones of Saint Botolph, and put out this fire !
       The drum beats. Exeunt all but MERRY, KEMP-
       THORN, *and* COLE.

MERRY

And now that matter 's ended, Goodman Cole,
Fetch me a mug of ale, your strongest ale.

KEMPTHORN (*sitting down*)

And me another mug of flip ; and put
Two gills of brandy in it.
                     Exit COLE.

MERRY

            No ; no more.
Not a drop more, I say. You 've had enough.

KEMPTHORN

And who are you, sir ?

MERRY

           I 'm a Tithing-man,
And Merry is my name.

KEMPTHORN

           A merry name !

I like it; and I 'll drink your merry health
Till all is blue.

MERRY

And then you will be clapped
Into the stocks, with the red letter D
Hung round about your neck for drunkenness.
You 're a free-drinker, — yes, and a free-thinker!

KEMPTHORN

And you are Andrew Merry, or Merry Andrew.

MERRY

My name is Walter Merry, and not Andrew.

KEMPTHORN

Andrew or Walter, you 're a merry fellow;
I 'll swear to that.

MERRY

No swearing, let me tell you.
The other day one Shorthose had his tongue
Put into a cleft stick for profane swearing.
                    COLE *brings the ale.*

KEMPTHORN

Well, where 's my flip? As sure as my name 's
    Kempthorn —

MERRY

Is your name Kempthorn?

KEMPTHORN

That's the name I go by.

MERRY

What, Captain Simon Kempthorn of the Swallow?

KEMPTHORN

No other.

MERRY (*touching him on the shoulder*)

Then you're wanted. I arrest you
In the King's name.

KEMPTHORN

And where's your warrant?

MERRY (*unfolding a paper, and reading*)

Here.

Listen to me. " Hereby you are required,
In the King's name, to apprehend the body
Of Simon Kempthorn, mariner, and him
Safely to bring before me, there to answer
All such objections as are laid to him,
Touching the Quakers." Signed, John Endicott.

KEMPTHORN

Has it the Governor's seal?

MERRY

Ay, here it is.

KEMPTHORN

Death's head and cross-bones. That's a pirate's flag!

384

MERRY

Beware how you revile the Magistrates;
You may be whipped for that.

KEMPTHORN

Then mum 's the word.
Exeunt MERRY *and* KEMPTHORN.

COLE

There 's mischief brewing! Sure, there 's mischief
brewing!
I feel like Master Josselyn when he found
The hornet's nest, and thought it some strange
fruit,
Until the seeds came out, and then he dropped it.
Exit.

SCENE III. — *A room in the Governor's house.* *Enter* GOV-
ERNOR ENDICOTT *and* MERRY.

ENDICOTT

My son, you say?

MERRY

Your Worship's eldest son.

ENDICOTT

Speaking against the laws?

MERRY

Ay, worshipful sir.

385

CHRISTUS: A MYSTERY

ENDICOTT

And in the public market-place?

MERRY

                   I saw him
With my own eyes, heard him with my own ears.

ENDICOTT

Impossible!

MERRY

            He stood there in the crowd
With Nicholas Upsall, when the laws were read
To-day against the Quakers, and I heard him
Denounce and vilipend them as unjust,
And cruel, wicked, and abominable.

ENDICOTT

Ungrateful son! O God! thou layest upon me
A burden heavier than I can bear!
Surely the power of Satan must be great
Upon the earth, if even the elect
Are thus deceived and fall away from grace!

MERRY

Worshipful sir! I meant no harm —

ENDICOTT

                    'T is well.
You 've done your duty, though you 've done it
      roughly,
And every word you 've uttered since you came
Has stabbed me to the heart!

MERRY

I do beseech
Your Worship's pardon !

ENDICOTT

He whom I have nurtured
And brought up in the reverence of the Lord !
The child of all my hopes and my affections !
He upon whom I leaned as a sure staff
For my old age ! It is God's chastisement
For leaning upon any arm but His !

MERRY

Your Worship ! —

ENDICOTT

And this comes from holding parley
With the delusions and deceits of Satan.
At once, forever, must they be crushed out,
Or all the land will reek with heresy !
Pray, have you any children ?

MERRY

No, not any.

ENDICOTT

Thank God for that. He has delivered you
From a great care. Enough ; my private griefs
Too long have kept me from the public service.

Exit MERRY. ENDICOTT *seats himself at the table
and arranges his papers.*

387

The hour has come; and I am eager now
To sit in judgment on these Heretics.

A knock.

Come in. Who is it? (*Not looking up.*)

JOHN ENDICOTT

It is I.

ENDICOTT (*restraining himself*)

Sit down!

JOHN ENDICOTT (*sitting down*)

I come to intercede for these poor people
Who are in prison, and await their trial.

ENDICOTT

It is of them I wish to speak with you.
I have been angry with you, but 't is passed.
For when I hear your footsteps come or go,
See in your features your dead mother's face,
And in your voice detect some tone of hers,
All anger vanishes, and I remember
The days that are no more, and come no more,
When as a child you sat upon my knee,
And prattled of your playthings, and the games
You played among the pear-trees in the orchard!

JOHN ENDICOTT

Oh, let the memory of my noble mother
Plead with you to be mild and merciful!
For mercy more becomes a Magistrate
Than the vindictive wrath which men call justice!

388

THE NEW ENGLAND TRAGEDIES

ENDICOTT

The sin of heresy is a deadly sin.
'T is like the falling of the snow, whose crystals
The traveller plays with, thoughtless of his danger,
Until he sees the air so full of light
That it is dark; and blindly staggering onward,
Lost, and bewildered, he sits down to rest;
There falls a pleasant drowsiness upon him,
And what he thinks is sleep, alas! is death.

JOHN ENDICOTT

And yet who is there that has never doubted?
And doubting and believing, has not said,
"Lord, I believe; help thou my unbelief"?

ENDICOTT

In the same way we trifle with our doubts,
Whose shining shapes are like the stars descending;
Until at last, bewildered and dismayed,
Blinded by that which seemed to give us light,
We sink to sleep, and find that it is death,
(Rising)
Death to the soul through all eternity!
Alas that I should see you growing up
To man's estate, and in the admonition
And nurture of the Law, to find you now
Pleading for Heretics!

JOHN ENDICOTT *(rising)*

         In the sight of God,
Perhaps all men are Heretics. Who dares
To say that he alone has found the truth?

We cannot always feel and think and act
As those who go before us. Had you done so,
You would not now be here.

ENDICOTT

                    Have you forgotten
The doom of Heretics, and the fate of those
Who aid and comfort them? Have you forgotten
That in the market-place this very day
You trampled on the laws? What right have you,
An inexperienced and untravelled youth,
To sit in judgment here upon the acts
Of older men and wiser than yourself,
Thus stirring up sedition in the streets,
And making me a byword and a jest?

JOHN ENDICOTT

Words of an inexperienced youth like me
Were powerless if the acts of older men
Went not before them. 'T is these laws themselves
Stir up sedition, not my judgment of them.

ENDICOTT

Take heed, lest I be called, as Brutus was,
To be the judge of my own son! Begone!
When you are tired of feeding upon husks,
Return again to duty and submission,
But not till then.

JOHN ENDICOTT
I hear and I obey!

Exit.

390

ENDICOTT

Oh happy, happy they who have no children!
He's gone! I hear the hall door shut behind him.
It sends a dismal echo through my heart,
As if forever it had closed between us,
And I should look upon his face no more!
Oh, this will drag me down into my grave, —
To that eternal resting-place wherein
Man lieth down, and riseth not again!
Till the heavens be no more he shall not wake,
Nor be roused from his sleep ; for Thou dost change
His countenance, and sendest him away!

Exit.

ACT III

Scene I. — *The Court of Assistants.* Endicott, Bellingham, Atherton, *and other magistrates.* Kempthorn,
Merry, *and constables. Afterwards* Wharton, Edith,
and Christison.

ENDICOTT

Call Captain Simon Kempthorn.

MERRY

Simon Kempthorn,
Come to the bar!

Kempthorn *comes forward.*

ENDICOTT

You are accused of bringing

391

CHRISTUS: A MYSTERY

Into this Jurisdiction, from Barbadoes,
Some persons of that sort and sect of people
Known by the name of Quakers, and maintaining
Most dangerous and heretical opinions;
Purposely coming here to propagate
Their heresies and errors; bringing with them
And spreading sundry books here, which contain
Their doctrines most corrupt and blasphemous,
And contrary to the truth professed among us.
What say you to this charge?

KEMPTHORN

      I do acknowledge,
Among the passengers on board the Swallow
Were certain persons saying Thee and Thou.
They seemed a harmless people, mostways silent,
Particularly when they said their prayers.

ENDICOTT

Harmless and silent as the pestilence!
You'd better have brought the fever or the plague
Among us in your ship! Therefore, this Court,
For preservation of the Peace and Truth,
Hereby commands you speedily to transport,
Or cause to be transported speedily,
The aforesaid persons hence unto Barbadoes,
From whence they came; you paying all the charges
Of their imprisonment.

KEMPTHORN

    Worshipful sir,

No ship e'er prospered that has carried Quakers
Against their will! I knew a vessel once—

ENDICOTT

And for the more effectual performance
Hereof you are to give security
In bonds amounting to one hundred pounds.
On your refusal, you will be committed
To prison till you do it.

KEMPTHORN

           But you see
I cannot do it. The law, sir, of Barbadoes
Forbids the landing Quakers on the island.

ENDICOTT

Then you will be committed. Who comes next?

MERRY

There is another charge against the Captain.

ENDICOTT

What is it?

MERRY

           Profane swearing, please your Worship.
He cursed and swore from Dock Square to the Court-
house.

ENDICOTT

Then let him stand in the pillory for one hour.
              Exit KEMPTHORN *with constable.*
Who's next?

CHRISTUS: A MYSTERY

MERRY

The Quakers.

ENDICOTT

Call them.

MERRY

Edward Wharton,
Come to the bar!

WHARTON

Yea, even to the bench.

ENDICOTT

Take off your hat.

WHARTON

My hat offendeth not.
If it offendeth any, let him take it;
For I shall not resist.

ENDICOTT

Take off his hat.
Let him be fined ten shillings for contempt.

MERRY *takes off* WHARTON'S *hat.*

WHARTON

What evil have I done?

ENDICOTT

Your hair's too long;
And in not putting off your hat to us

394

You 've disobeyed and broken that commandment
Which sayeth " Honor thy father and thy mother."

WHARTON

John Endicott, thou art become too proud ;
And lovest him who putteth off the hat,
And honoreth thee by bowing of the body,
And sayeth " Worshipful sir ! " 'T is time for thee
To give such follies over, for thou mayest
Be drawing very near unto thy grave.

ENDICOTT

Now, sirrah, leave your canting. Take the oath.

WHARTON

Nay, sirrah me no sirrahs !

ENDICOTT

     Will you swear ?

WHARTON

Nay, I will not.

ENDICOTT

    You made a great disturbance
And uproar yesterday in the Meeting-house,
Having your hat on.

WHARTON

     I made no disturbance ;
For peacefully I stood, like other people.
I spake no words ; moved against none my hand ;

But by the hair they haled me out, and dashed
Their books into my face.

ENDICOTT

You, Edward Wharton,
On pain of death, depart this Jurisdiction
Within ten days. Such is your sentence. Go.

WHARTON

John Endicott, it had been well for thee
If this day's doings thou hadst left undone.
But, banish me as far as thou hast power,
Beyond the guard and presence of my God
Thou canst not banish me!

ENDICOTT

Depart the Court;
We have no time to listen to your babble.
Who 's next?

Exit WHARTON.

MERRY

This woman, for the same offence.

EDITH comes forward.

ENDICOTT

What is your name?

EDITH

'T is to the world unknown,
But written in the Book of Life.

ENDICOTT

Take heed
It be not written in the Book of Death!
What is it?

EDITH

Edith Christison.

ENDICOTT (*with eagerness*)

The daughter
Of Wenlock Christison?

EDITH

I am his daughter.

ENDICOTT

Your father hath given us trouble many times.
A bold man and a violent, who sets
At naught the authority of our Church and State,
And is in banishment on pain of death.
Where are you living?

EDITH

In the Lord.

ENDICOTT

Make answer
Without evasion. Where?

EDITH

My outward being
Is in Barbadoes.

ENDICOTT

Then why come you here?

EDITH

I come upon an errand of the Lord.

ENDICOTT

'T is not the business of the Lord you 're doing;
It is the Devil's. Will you take the oath?
Give her the Book.

MERRY *offers the book.*

EDITH

You offer me this Book
To swear on; and it saith, " Swear not at all,
Neither by heaven, because it is God's Throne,
Nor by the earth, because it is his footstool!"
I dare not swear.

ENDICOTT

You dare not? Yet you Quakers
Deny this Book of Holy Writ, the Bible,
To be the Word of God.

EDITH (*reverentially*)

Christ is the Word,
The everlasting oath of God. I dare not.

ENDICOTT

You own yourself a Quaker, — do you not?

THE NEW ENGLAND TRAGEDIES

EDITH

I own that in derision and reproach
I am so called.

ENDICOTT

Then you deny the Scripture
To be the rule of life.

EDITH

Yea, I believe
The Inner Light, and not the Written Word,
To be the rule of life.

ENDICOTT

And you deny
That the Lord's Day is holy.

EDITH

Every day
Is the Lord's Day. It runs through all our lives,
As through the pages of the Holy Bible,
" Thus saith the Lord."

ENDICOTT

You are accused of making
An horrible disturbance, and affrighting
The people in the Meeting-house on Sunday.
What answer make you ?

EDITH

I do not deny

CHRISTUS: A MYSTERY

That I was present in your Steeple-house
On the First Day ; but I made no disturbance.

ENDICOTT

Why came you there ?

EDITH

     Because the Lord commanded.
His word was in my heart, a burning fire
Shut up within me and consuming me,
And I was very weary with forbearing ;
I could not stay.

ENDICOTT

    'T was not the Lord that sent you ;
As an incarnate devil did you come !

EDITH

On the First Day, when, seated in my chamber,
I heard the bells toll, calling you together,
The sound struck at my life, as once at his,
The holy man, our Founder, when he heard
The far-off bells toll in the Vale of Beavor.
It sounded like a market bell to call
The folk together, that the Priest might set
His wares to sale. And the Lord said within me,
" Thou must go cry aloud against that Idol,
And all the worshippers thereof." I went
Barefooted, clad in sackcloth, and I stood
And listened at the threshold ; and I heard
The praying and the singing and the preaching,
Which were but outward forms, and without power.

400

Then rose a cry within me, and my heart
Was filled with admonitions and reproofs.
Remembering how the Prophets and Apostles
Denounced the covetous hirelings and diviners,
I entered in, and spake the words the Lord
Commanded me to speak. I could no less.

ENDICOTT

Are you a Prophetess?

EDITH

              Is it not written,
" Upon my handmaidens will I pour out
My spirit, and they shall prophesy " ?

ENDICOTT

                   Enough ;
For out of your own mouth are you condemned!
Need we hear further?

THE JUDGES

            We are satisfied.

ENDICOTT

It is sufficient. Edith Christison,
The sentence of the Court is, that you be
Scourged in three towns, with forty stripes save one,
Then banished upon pain of death !

EDITH

                Your sentence
Is truly no more terrible to me

Than had you blown a feather into the air,
And, as it fell upon me, you had said,
" Take heed it hurt thee not ! " God's will be
    done !

WENLOCK CHRISTISON (*unseen in the crowd*)

Woe to the city of blood ! The stone shall cry
Out of the wall ; the beam from out the timber
Shall answer it ! Woe unto him that buildeth
A town with blood, and stablisheth a city
By his iniquity !

ENDICOTT

        Who is it makes
Such outcry here ?

CHRISTISON (*coming forward*)

        I, Wenlock Christison !

ENDICOTT

Banished on pain of death, why come you here ?

CHRISTISON

I come to warn you that you shed no more
The blood of innocent men ! It cries aloud
For vengeance to the Lord !

ENDICOTT

            Your life is forfeit
Unto the law ; and you shall surely die,
And shall not live.

THE NEW ENGLAND TRAGEDIES

CHRISTISON

Like unto Eleazer,
Maintaining the excellence of ancient years
And the honor of his gray head, I stand before you;
Like him disdaining all hypocrisy,
Lest, through desire to live a little longer,
I get a stain to my old age and name!

ENDICOTT

Being in banishment, on pain of death,
You come now in among us in rebellion.

CHRISTISON

I come not in among you in rebellion,
But in obedience to the Lord of Heaven.
Not in contempt to any Magistrate,
But only in the love I bear your souls,
As ye shall know hereafter, when all men
Give an account of deeds done in the body!
God's righteous judgments ye cannot escape.

ONE OF THE JUDGES

Those who have gone before you said the same,
And yet no judgment of the Lord hath fallen
Upon us.

CHRISTISON

He but waiteth till the measure
Of your iniquities shall be filled up,
And ye have run your race. Then will his wrath
Descend upon you to the uttermost!
For thy part, Humphrey Atherton, it hangs

Over thy head already. It shall come
Suddenly, as a thief doth in the night,
And in the hour when least thou thinkest of it!

ENDICOTT

We have a law, and by that law you die.

CHRISTISON

I, a free man of England and freeborn,
Appeal unto the laws of mine own nation!

ENDICOTT

There's no appeal to England from this Court!
What! do you think our statutes are but paper?
Are but dead leaves that rustle in the wind?
Or litter to be trampled under foot?
What say ye, Judges of the Court, — what say ye?
Shall this man suffer death? Speak your opinions.

ONE OF THE JUDGES

I am a mortal man, and die I must,
And that erelong; and I must then appear
Before the awful judgment-seat of Christ,
To give account of deeds done in the body.
My greatest glory on that day will be,
That I have given my vote against this man.

CHRISTISON

If, Thomas Danforth, thou hast nothing more
To glory in upon that dreadful day
Than blood of innocent people, then thy glory
Will be turned into shame! The Lord hath said it!

And ye shall be accursed forevermore

ANOTHER JUDGE

I cannot give consent, while other men
Who have been banished upon pain of death
Are now in their own houses here among us.

ENDICOTT

Ye that will not consent, make record of it.
I thank my God that I am not afraid
To give my judgment. Wenlock Christison,
You must be taken back from hence to prison,
Thence to the place of public execution,
There to be hanged till you be dead — dead
    — dead !

CHRISTISON

If ye have power to take my life from me, —
Which I do question, — God hath power to raise
The principle of life in other men,
And send them here among you. There shall be
No peace unto the wicked, saith my God.
Listen, ye Magistrates, for the Lord hath said it !
The day ye put his servitors to death,
That day the Day of your own Visitation,
The Day of Wrath, shall pass above your heads,
And ye shall be accursed forevermore !
      (*To* EDITH, *embracing her*)
Cheer up, dear heart ! they have not power to
    harm us.
        Exeunt CHRISTISON *and* EDITH *guarded. The
        Scene closes.*

CHRISTUS: A MYSTERY

SCENE II.— *A street.* *Enter* JOHN ENDICOTT *and* UPSALL.

JOHN ENDICOTT

Scourged in three towns! and yet the busy people
Go up and down the streets on their affairs
Of business or of pleasure, as if nothing
Had.happened to disturb them or their thoughts!
When bloody tragedies like this are acted,
The pulses of a nation should stand still;
The town should be in mourning, and the people
Speak only in low whispers to each other.

UPSALL

I know this people; and that underneath
A cold outside there burns a secret fire
That will find vent, and will not be put out,
Till every remnant of these barbarous laws
Shall be to ashes burned, and blown away.

JOHN ENDICOTT

Scourged in three towns! It is incredible
Such things can be! I feel the blood within me
Fast mounting in rebellion, since in vain
Have I implored compassion of my father!

UPSALL

You know your father only as a father;
I know him better as a Magistrate.
He is a man both loving and severe;
A tender heart; a will inflexible.

None ever loved him more than I have loved him.
He is an upright man and a just man
In all things save the treatment of the Quakers.

JOHN ENDICOTT

Yet I have found him cruel and unjust
Even as a father. He has driven me forth
Into the street; has shut his door upon me,
With words of bitterness. I am as homeless
As these poor Quakers are.

UPSALL

         Then come with me.
You shall be welcome for your father's sake,
And the old friendship that has been between us.
He will relent erelong. A father's anger
Is like a sword without a handle, piercing
Both ways alike, and wounding him that wields it
No less than him that it is pointed at.

                    Exeunt.

SCENE III. — *The prison. Night.* EDITH *reading the Bible
by a lamp.*

EDITH

" Blessed are ye when men shall persecute you,
And shall revile you, and shall say against you
All manner of evil falsely for my sake!
Rejoice, and be exceeding glad, for great
Is your reward in heaven. For so the prophets,
Which were before you, have been persecuted."

CHRISTUS: A MYSTERY

Enter JOHN ENDICOTT.

JOHN ENDICOTT

Edith !

EDITH

Who is it speaketh ?

JOHN ENDICOTT

          Saul of Tarsus ;
As thou didst call me once.

EDITH (*coming forward*)

          Yea, I remember.
Thou art the Governor's son.

JOHN ENDICOTT

          I am ashamed
Thou shouldst remember me.

EDITH

          Why comest thou
Into this dark guest-chamber in the night ?
What seekest thou ?

JOHN ENDICOTT

Forgiveness !

EDITH

          I forgive
All who have injured me. What hast thou done ?

JOHN ENDICOTT

I have betrayed thee, thinking that in this
I did God service. Now, in deep contrition,
I come to rescue thee.

EDITH

From what?

JOHN ENDICOTT

From prison.

EDITH

I am safe here within these gloomy walls.

JOHN ENDICOTT

From scourging in the streets, and in three towns!

EDITH

Remembering who was scourged for me, I shrink not
Nor shudder at the forty stripes save one.

JOHN ENDICOTT

Perhaps from death itself!

EDITH

I fear not death,
Knowing who died for me.

JOHN ENDICOTT (*aside*)

Surely some divine
Ambassador is speaking through those lips
And looking through those eyes! I cannot answer!

CHRISTUS: A MYSTERY

EDITH

If all these prison doors stood opened wide
I would not cross the threshold, — not one step.
There are invisible bars I cannot break ;
There are invisible doors that shut me in,
And keep me ever steadfast to my purpose.

JOHN ENDICOTT

Thou hast the patience and the faith of Saints !

EDITH

Thy Priest hath been with me this day to save
    me,
Not only from the death that comes to all,
But from the second death !

JOHN ENDICOTT

              The Pharisee !
My heart revolts against him and his creed !
Alas ! the coat that was without a seam
Is rent asunder by contending sects ;
Each bears away a portion of the garment,
Blindly believing that he has the whole !

EDITH

When Death, the Healer, shall have touched our
    eyes
With moist clay of the grave, then shall we see
The truth as we have never yet beheld it.
But he that overcometh shall not be
Hurt of the second death. Has he forgotten
The many mansions in our father's house ?

THE NEW ENGLAND TRAGEDIES

There is no pity in his iron heart!
The hands that now bear stamped upon their palms
The burning sign of Heresy, hereafter
Shall be uplifted against such accusers,
And then the imprinted letter and its meaning
Will not be Heresy, but Holiness!

EDITH

Remember, thou condemnest thine own father!

JOHN ENDICOTT

I have no father! He has cast me off.
I am as homeless as the wind that moans
And wanders through the streets. Oh, come with
    me!
Do not delay. Thy God shall be my God,
And where thou goest I will go.

EDITH

                I cannot.
Yet will I not deny it, nor conceal it;
From the first moment I beheld thy face
I felt a tenderness in my soul towards thee.
My mind has since been inward to the Lord,
Waiting his word. It has not yet been spoken.

JOHN ENDICOTT

I cannot wait. Trust me. Oh, come with me!

EDITH

In the next room, my father, an old man,

Sitteth imprisoned and condemned to death,
Willing to prove his faith by martyrdom;
And thinkest thou his daughter would do less?

JOHN ENDICOTT

Oh, life is sweet, and death is terrible!

EDITH

I have too long walked hand in hand with death
To shudder at that pale familiar face.
But leave me now. I wish to be alone.

JOHN ENDICOTT

Not yet. Oh, let me stay.

EDITH

Urge me no more.

JOHN ENDICOTT

Alas! good-night. I will not say good-by!

EDITH

Put this temptation underneath thy feet.
To him that overcometh shall be given
The white stone with the new name written on it,
That no man knows save him that doth receive it,
And I will give thee a new name, and call thee
Paul of Damascus and not Saul of Tarsus.

Exit ENDICOTT. EDITH *sits down again to read the
Bible.*

ACT IV

SCENE I. — *King Street, in front of the town-house.* KEMP-
THORN *in the pillory.* MERRY *and a crowd of lookers-on.*

KEMPTHORN (*sings*)
The world is full of care,
    Much like unto a bubble ;
Women and care, and care and women,
    And women and care and trouble.   ·

Good Master Merry, may I say confound ?

MERRY
Ay, that you may.

KEMPTHORN
            Well, then, with your permission,
Confound the Pillory !

MERRY
            That 's the very thing
The joiner said who made the Shrewsbury stocks.
He said, Confound the stocks, because they put him
Into his own. He was the first man in them.

KEMPTHORN
For swearing, was it ?

MERRY
            No, it was for charging ;

He charged the town too much; and so the town,
To make things square, set him in his own stocks,
And fined him five pound sterling, — just enough
To settle his own bill.

KEMPTHORN

         And served him right;
But, Master Merry, is it not eight bells?

MERRY

Not quite.

KEMPTHORN

        For, do you see? I'm getting tired
Of being perched aloft here in this cro' nest
Like the first mate of a whaler, or a Middy
Mast-headed, looking out for land! Sail ho!
Here comes a heavy-laden merchantman
With the lee clews eased off, and running free
Before the wind. A solid man of Boston.
A comfortable man, with dividends,
And the first salmon, and the first green peas.
                A gentleman passes.
He does not even turn his head to look.
He's gone without a word. Here comes another,
A different kind of craft on a taut bow-line, —
Deacon Giles Firmin the apothecary,
A pious and a ponderous citizen,
Looking as rubicund and round and splendid
As the great bottle in his own shop window!
            DEACON FIRMIN *passes.*
And here's my host of the Three Mariners,

My creditor and trusty taverner,
My corporal in the Great Artillery!
He's not a man to pass me without speaking.

      COLE *looks away and passes.*

Don't yaw so; keep your luff, old hypocrite!
Respectable, ah yes, respectable,
You, with your seat in the new Meeting-house,
Your cow-right on the Common! But who's this?
I did not know the Mary Ann was in!
And yet this is my old friend, Captain Goldsmith,
As sure as I stand in the bilboes here.
Why, Ralph, my boy!

   Enter RALPH GOLDSMITH.

    GOLDSMITH

      Why, Simon, is it you?
Set in the bilboes?

    KEMPTHORN

      Chock-a-block, you see,
And without chafing-gear.

    GOLDSMITH

      And what's it for?

    KEMPTHORN

Ask that starbowline with the boat-hook there,
That handsome man.

    MERRY (*bowing*)
     For swearing.

     415

KEMPTHORN

In this town
They put sea-captains in the stocks for swearing,
And Quakers for not swearing. So look out.

GOLDSMITH

I pray you set him free; he meant no harm;
'T is an old habit he picked up afloat.

MERRY

Well, as your time is out, you may come down.
The law allows you now to go at large
Like Elder Oliver's horse upon the Common.

KEMPTHORN

Now, hearties, bear a hand! Let go and haul.
          KEMPTHORN *is set free, and comes forward, shaking*
          GOLDSMITH'S *hand.*

KEMPTHORN

Give me your hand, Ralph. Ah, how good it feels!
The hand of an old friend.

GOLDSMITH

God bless you, Simon!

KEMPTHORN

Now let us make a straight wake for the tavern
Of the Three Mariners, Samuel Cole commander;
Where we can take our ease, and see the shipping,
And talk about old times.

GOLDSMITH

First I must pay
My duty to the Governor, and take him
His letters and despatches. Come with me.

KEMPTHORN

I 'd rather not. I saw him yesterday.

GOLDSMITH

Then wait for me at the Three Nuns and Comb.

KEMPTHORN

I thank you. That 's too near to the town pump.
I will go with you to the Governor's,
And wait outside there, sailing off and on ;
If I am wanted, you can hoist a signal.

MERRY

Shall I go with you and point out the way ?

GOLDSMITH

Oh no, I thank you. I am not a stranger
Here in your crooked little town.

MERRY

How now, sir ?

Do you abuse our town ?

Exit.

GOLDSMITH

Oh, no offence.

417

CHRISTUS: A MYSTERY

KEMPTHORN

Ralph, I am under bonds for a hundred pound.

GOLDSMITH

Hard lines. What for?

KEMPTHORN

        To take some Quakers back
I brought here from Barbadoes in the Swallow.
And how to do it I don't clearly see,
For one of them is banished, and another
Is sentenced to be hanged! What shall I do?

GOLDSMITH

Just slip your hawser on some cloudy night;
Sheer off, and pay it with the topsail, Simon!

                            Exeunt.

SCENE II. — *Street in front of the prison. In the background
a gateway and several flights of steps leading up terraces
to the Governor's house. A pump on one side of the street.*
JOHN ENDICOTT, MERRY, UPSALL, *and others. A drum
beats.*

JOHN ENDICOTT

Oh shame, shame, shame!

MERRY

        Yes, it would be a shame
But for the damnable sin of Heresy!

JOHN ENDICOTT

A woman scourged and dragged about our streets!

THE NEW ENGLAND TRAGEDIES

MERRY

Well, Roxbury and Dorchester must take
Their share of shame. She will be whipped in each!
Three towns, and Forty Stripes save one; that makes
Thirteen in each.

JOHN ENDICOTT

           And are we Jews or Christians?
See where she comes, amid a gaping crowd!
And she a child. Oh, pitiful! pitiful!
There 's blood upon her clothes, her hands, her feet!

> *Enter* MARSHAL *and a drummer,* EDITH, *stripped to
> the waist, followed by the hangman with a
> scourge, and a noisy crowd.*

EDITH

Here let me rest one moment. I am tired.
Will some one give me water?

MERRY

           At his peril.

UPSALL

Alas! that I should live to see this day!

A WOMAN

Did I forsake my father and my mother
And come here to New England to see this?

EDITH

I am athirst. Will no one give me water?

CHRISTUS: A MYSTERY

JOHN ENDICOTT (*making his way through the crowd with water*)

In the Lord's name!

EDITH (*drinking*)

In his name I receive it!
Sweet as the water of Samaria's well
This water tastes. I thank thee. Is it thou?
I was afraid thou hadst deserted me.

JOHN ENDICOTT

Never will I desert thee, nor deny thee.
Be comforted.

MERRY

O Master Endicott,
Be careful what you say.

JOHN ENDICOTT

Peace, idle babbler!

MERRY

You 'll rue these words!

JOHN ENDICOTT

Art thou not better now?

EDITH

They 've struck me as with roses.

JOHN ENDICOTT

Ah, these wounds!
These bloody garments!

420

THE NEW ENGLAND TRAGEDIES

EDITH

It is granted me
To seal my testimony with my blood.

JOHN ENDICOTT

O blood-red seal of man's vindictive wrath!
O roses of the garden of the Lord!
I, of the household of Iscariot,
I have betrayed in thee my Lord and Master!

WENLOCK CHRISTISON *appears above, at the window of
the prison, stretching out his hands through the bars.*

CHRISTISON

Be of good courage, O my child! my child!
Blessed art thou when men shall persecute thee!
Fear not their faces, saith the Lord, fear not,
For I am with thee to deliver thee.

A CITIZEN

Who is it crying from the prison yonder?

MERRY

It is old Wenlock Christison.

CHRISTISON

Remember
Him who was scourged, and mocked, and crucified!
I see his messengers attending thee.
Be steadfast, oh, be steadfast to the end!

EDITH (*with exultation*)

I cannot reach thee with these arms, O father!

But closely in my soul do I embrace thee
And hold thee. In thy dungeon and thy death
I will be with thee, and will comfort thee!

MARSHAL

Come, put an end to this. Let the drum beat.
The drum beats. Exeunt all but JOHN ENDICOTT,
UPSALL, *and* MERRY.

CHRISTISON

Dear child, farewell! Never shall I behold
Thy face again with these bleared eyes of flesh;
And never wast thou fairer, lovelier, dearer
Than now, when scourged and bleeding, and insulted
For the truth's sake. O pitiless, pitiless town!
The wrath of God hangs over thee; and the day
Is near at hand when thou shalt be abandoned
To desolation and the breeding of nettles.
The bittern and the cormorant shall lodge
Upon thine upper lintels, and their voice
Sing in thy windows. Yea, thus saith the Lord!

JOHN ENDICOTT

Awake! awake! ye sleepers, ere too late,
And wipe these bloody statutes from your books!
Exit.

MERRY

Take heed; the walls have ears!

UPSALL

At last, the heart
Of every honest man must speak or break!

Enter GOVERNOR ENDICOTT *with his halberdiers.*

ENDICOTT

What is this stir and tumult in the street?

MERRY

Worshipful sir, the whipping of a girl,
And her old father howling from the prison.

ENDICOTT (*to his halberdiers*)

Go on.

CHRISTISON

Antiochus! Antiochus!
O thou that slayest the Maccabees! The Lord
Shall smite thee with incurable disease,
And no man shall endure to carry thee!

MERRY

Peace, old blasphemer!

CHRISTISON

I both feel and see
The presence and the waft of death go forth
Against thee, and already thou dost look
Like one that's dead!

MERRY (*pointing*)

And there is your own son,
Worshipful sir, abetting the sedition.

ENDICOTT

Arrest him. Do not spare him.

MERRY (*aside*)
> His own child!
There is some special providence takes care
That none shall be too happy in this world!
His own first-born.

ENDICOTT
> O Absalom, my son!
> *Exeunt; the Governor with his halberdiers as-*
> *cending the steps of his house.*

SCENE III. — *The Governor's private room. Papers upon the*
table. ENDICOTT *and* BELLINGHAM.

ENDICOTT

There is a ship from England has come in,
Bringing despatches and much news from home.
His Majesty was at the Abbey crowned;
And when the coronation was complete
There passed a mighty tempest o'er the city,
Portentous with great thunderings and lightnings.

BELLINGHAM

After his father's, if I well remember,
There was an earthquake, that foreboded evil.

ENDICOTT

Ten of the Regicides have been put to death!
The bodies of Cromwell, Ireton, and Bradshaw
Have been dragged from their graves, and publicly
Hanged in their shrouds at Tyburn.

THE NEW ENGLAND TRAGEDIES

BELLINGHAM

Horrible!

ENDICOTT

Thus the old tyranny revives again!
Its arm is long enough to reach us here,
As you will see. For, more insulting still
Than flaunting in our faces dead men's shrouds,
Here is the King's Mandamus, taking from us,
From this day forth, all power to punish Quakers.

BELLINGHAM

That takes from us all power; we are but puppets,
And can no longer execute our laws.

ENDICOTT

His Majesty begins with pleasant words,
" Trusty and well-beloved, we greet you well; "
Then with a ruthless hand he strips from me
All that which makes me what I am; as if
From some old general in the field, grown gray
In service, scarred with many wounds,
Just at the hour of victory, he should strip
His badge of office and his well-gained honors,
And thrust him back into the ranks again.

Opens the Mandamus, and hands it to BELLINGHAM ;
and, while he is reading, ENDICOTT *walks up
and down the room.*

Here, read it for yourself; you see his words
Are pleasant words — considerate — not reproach-
ful —
Nothing could be more gentle — or more royal;

But then the meaning underneath the words,
Mark that. He says all people known as Quakers
Among us, now condemned to suffer death
Or any corporal punishment whatever,
Who are imprisoned, or may be obnoxious
To the like condemnation, shall be sent
Forthwith to England, to be dealt with there
In such wise as shall be agreeable
Unto the English law and their demerits.
Is it not so ?

BELLINGHAM (*returning the paper*)
Ay, so the paper says.

ENDICOTT

It means we shall no longer rule the Province ;
It means farewell to law and liberty,
Authority, respect for Magistrates,
The peace and welfare of the Commonwealth.
If all the knaves upon this continent
Can make appeal to England, and so thwart
The ends of truth and justice by delay,
Our power is gone forever. We are nothing
But ciphers, valueless save when we follow
Some unit ; and our unit is the King !
'T is he that gives us value.

BELLINGHAM
I confess
Such seems to be the meaning of this paper,
But being the King's Mandamus, signed and sealed,
We must obey, or we are in rebellion.

ENDICOTT

I tell you, Richard Bellingham, — I tell you,
That this is the beginning of a struggle
Of which no mortal can foresee the end.
I shall not live to fight the battle for you,
I am a man disgraced in every way ;
This order takes from me my self-respect
And the respect of others. 'T is my doom,
Yes, my death-warrant, but must be obeyed !
Take it, and see that it is executed
So far as this, that all be set at large ;
But see that none of them be sent to England
To bear false witness, and to spread reports
That might be prejudicial to ourselves.

Exit BELLINGHAM.

There 's a dull pain keeps knocking at my heart,
Dolefully saying, " Set thy house in order,
For thou shalt surely die, and shalt not live ! "
For me the shadow on the dial-plate
Goeth not back, but on into the dark !

Exit.

SCENE IV. — *The street. A crowd, reading a placard on the
door of the Meeting-house.* NICHOLAS UPSALL *among them.
Enter* JOHN NORTON.

NORTON

What is this gathering here ?

UPSALL

One William Brand,
An old man like ourselves, and weak in body,

Has been so cruelly tortured in his prison,
The people are excited, and they threaten
To tear the prison down.

NORTON

What has been done?

UPSALL

He has been put in irons, with his neck
And heels tied close together, and so left
From five in the morning until nine at night.

NORTON

What more was done?

UPSALL

He has been kept five days
In prison without food, and cruelly beaten,
So that his limbs were cold, his senses stopped.

NORTON

What more?

UPSALL

And is this not enough?

NORTON

Now hear me.
This William Brand of yours has tried to beat
Our Gospel Ordinances black and blue;
And, if he has been beaten in like manner,
It is but justice, and I will appear

In his behalf that did so. I suppose
That he refused to work.

UPSALL

He was too weak.
How could an old man work, when he was starving?

NORTON

And what is this placard?

UPSALL

The Magistrates,
To appease the people and prevent a tumult,
Have put up these placards throughout the town,
Declaring that the jailer shall be dealt with
Impartially and sternly by the Court.

NORTON (*tearing down the placard*)

Down with this weak and cowardly concession,
This flag of truce with Satan and with Sin!
I fling it in his face! I trample it
Under my feet! It is his cunning craft,
The masterpiece of his diplomacy,
To cry and plead for boundless toleration.
But toleration is the first-born child
Of all abominations and deceits.
There is no room in Christ's triumphant army
For tolerationists. And if an Angel
Preach any other gospel unto you
Than that ye have received, God's malediction
Descend upon him! Let him be accursed!

Exit.

429

CHRISTUS: A MYSTERY

Now, go thy ways, John Norton! go thy ways,
Thou Orthodox Evangelist, as men call thee!
But even now there cometh out of England,
Like an o'ertaking and accusing conscience,
An outraged man, to call thee to account
For the unrighteous murder of his son!   *Exit.*

SCENE V. — *The Wilderness. Enter* EDITH.

EDITH

How beautiful are these autumnal woods!
The wilderness doth blossom like the rose,
And change into a garden of the Lord!
How silent everywhere! Alone and lost
Here in the forest, there comes over me
An inward awfulness. I recall the words
Of the Apostle Paul: " In journeyings often,
Often in perils in the wilderness,
In weariness, in painfulness, in watchings,
In hunger and thirst, in cold and nakedness;"
And I forget my weariness and pain,
My watchings, and my hunger and my thirst.
The Lord hath said that He will seek his flock
In cloudy and dark days, and they shall dwell
Securely in the wilderness, and sleep
Safe in the woods! Whichever way I turn,
I come back with my face towards the town.
Dimly I see it, and the sea beyond it.
O cruel town! I know what waits me there,
And yet I must go back; for ever louder

I hear the inward calling of the spirit

I hear the inward calling of the Spirit,
And must obey the voice. O woods, that wear
Your golden crown of martyrdom, blood-stained,
From you I learn a lesson of submission,
And am obedient even unto death,
If God so wills it.   *Exit.*

JOHN ENDICOTT (*within*)
Edith! Edith! Edith!
                                                 He enters.

It is in vain! I call, she answers not;
I follow, but I find no trace of her!
Blood! blood! The leaves above me and around
        me
Are red with blood! The pathways of the forest,
The clouds that canopy the setting sun,
And even the little river in the meadows
Are stained with it! Where'er I look, I see it!
Away, thou horrible vision! Leave me! leave
        me!
Alas! yon winding stream, that gropes its way
Through mist and shadow, doubling on itself,
At length will find, by the unerring law
Of nature, what it seeks. O soul of man,
Groping through mist and shadow, and recoiling
Back on thyself, are, too, thy devious ways
Subject to law? and when thou seemest to wander
The farthest from thy goal, art thou still drawing
Nearer and nearer to it, till at length
Thou findest, like the river, what thou seekest?
                                                 Exit.

431

ACT V

SCENE I. — *Daybreak. Street in front of* UPSALL'S *house.
A light in the window. Enter* JOHN ENDICOTT.

JOHN ENDICOTT

O silent, sombre, and deserted streets,
To me ye 're peopled with a sad procession,
And echo only to the voice of sorrow !
O houses full of peacefulness and sleep,
Far better were it to awake no more
Than wake to look upon such scenes again !
There is a light in Master Upsall's window.
The good man is already risen, for sleep
Deserts the couches of the old.

Knocks at UPSALL'S *door.*

UPSALL (*at the window*)
                                   Who 's there ?

JOHN ENDICOTT

Am I so changed you do not know my voice ?

UPSALL

I know you. Have you heard what things have happened ?

JOHN ENDICOTT

I have heard nothing.

THE NEW ENGLAND TRAGEDIES

UPSALL

Stay; I will come down.

JOHN ENDICOTT

I am afraid some dreadful news awaits me!
I do not dare to ask, yet am impatient
To know the worst. Oh, I am very weary
With waiting and with watching and pursuing!

Enter UPSALL.

UPSALL

Thank God, you have come back! I 've much to tell
    you.
Where have you been?

JOHN ENDICOTT

You know that I was seized,
Fined, and released again. You know that Edith,
After her scourging in three towns, was banished
Into the wilderness, into the land
That is not sown; and there I followed her,
But found her not. Where is she?

UPSALL

She is here.

JOHN ENDICOTT

Oh, do not speak that word, for it means death!

UPSALL

No, it means life. She sleeps in yonder chamber.

Listen to me. When news of Leddra's death
Reached England, Edward Burroughs, having boldly
Got access to the presence of the King,
Told him there was a vein of innocent blood
Opened in his dominions here, which threatened
To overrun them all. The King replied,
" But I will stop that vein ! " and he forthwith
Sent his Mandamus to our Magistrates,
That they proceed no further in this business.
So all are pardoned, and all set at large.

JOHN ENDICOTT

Thank God ! This is a victory for truth !
Our thoughts are free. They cannot be shut up
In prison walls, nor put to death on scaffolds !

UPSALL

Come in ; the morning air blows sharp and cold
Through the damp streets.

JOHN ENDICOTT

        It is the dawn of day
That chases the old darkness from our sky,
And fills the land with liberty and light.

              Exeunt.

SCENE II. — *The parlor of the Three Mariners. Enter*
KEMPTHORN.

KEMPTHORN

A dull life this, — a dull life anyway !
Ready for sea ; the cargo all aboard,

Cleared for Barbadoes, and a fair wind blowing
From nor'-nor'-west; and I, an idle lubber,
Laid neck and heels by that confounded bond!
I said to Ralph, says I, " What 's to be done ? "
Says he : " Just slip your hawser in the night;
Sheer off, and pay it with the topsail, Simon."
But that won't do ; because, you see, the owners
Somehow or other are mixed up with it.
Here are King Charles's Twelve Good Rules, that
    Cole
Thinks as important as the Rule of Three.
       (*Reads*)
" Make no comparisons ; make no long meals."
Those are good rules and golden for a landlord
To hang in his best parlor, framed and glazed!
" Maintain no ill opinions ; urge no healths."
I drink the King's, whatever he may say,
And, as to ill opinions, that depends.
Now of Ralph Goldsmith I 've a good opinion,
And of the bilboes I 've an ill opinion ;
And both of these opinions I 'll maintain
As long as there 's a shot left in the locker.

    Enter EDWARD BUTTER *with an ear-trumpet.*

BUTTER

Good morning, Captain Kempthorn.

KEMPTHORN

                Sir, to you.
You 've the advantage of me. I don't know you.
What may I call your name ?

BUTTER

That's not your name?

KEMPTHORN

Yes, that's my name. What's yours?

BUTTER

My name is Butter.
I am the treasurer of the Commonwealth.

KEMPTHORN

Will you be seated?

BUTTER

What say? Who's conceited?

KEMPTHORN

Will you sit down?

BUTTER

Oh, thank you.

KEMPTHORN

Spread yourself
Upon this chair, sweet Butter.

BUTTER (*sitting down*)

A fine morning.

KEMPTHORN

Nothing's the matter with it that I know of.
I have seen better, and I have seen worse.
The wind's nor'west. That's fair for them that sail.

436

BUTTER

You need not speak so loud; I understand you.
You sail to-day.

KEMPTHORN

No, I don't sail to-day.
So, be it fair or foul, it matters not.
Say, will you smoke? There's choice tobacco here.

BUTTER

No, thank you. It's against the law to smoke.

KEMPTHORN

Then, will you drink? There's good ale at this inn.

BUTTER

No, thank you. It's against the law to drink.

KEMPTHORN

Well, almost everything's against the law
In this good town. Give a wide berth to one thing,
You're sure to fetch up soon on something else.

BUTTER

And so you sail to-day for dear Old England.
I am not one of those who think a sup
Of this New England air is better worth
Than a whole draught of our Old England's ale.

KEMPTHORN

Nor I. Give me the ale and keep the air.
But, as I said, I do not sail to-day.

CHRISTUS: A MYSTERY

BUTTER

Ah yes; you sail to-day.

KEMPTHORN

                I 'm under bonds
To take some Quakers back to the Barbadoes;
And one of them is banished, and another
Is sentenced to be hanged.

BUTTER

                        No, all are pardoned,
All are set free, by order of the Court;
But some of them would fain return to England.
You must not take them. Upon that condition
Your bond is cancelled.

KEMPTHORN

                    Ah, the wind has shifted!
I pray you, do you speak officially?

BUTTER

I always speak officially. To prove it,
Here is the bond.

*   Rising and giving a paper.*

KEMPTHORN

                And here 's my hand upon it.
And, look you, when I say I 'll do a thing
The thing is done. Am I now free to go?

BUTTER

What say?

438

KEMPTHORN

I say, confound the tedious man
With his strange speaking-trumpet! Can I go?

BUTTER

You're free to go, by order of the Court.
Your servant, sir.   *Exit.*

KEMPTHORN (*shouting from the window*)
                    Swallow, ahoy! Hallo!
If ever a man was happy to leave Boston,
That man is Simon Kempthorn of the Swallow!

Reënter BUTTER.

BUTTER

Pray, did you call?

KEMPTHORN

                    Call? Yes, I hailed the Swallow.

BUTTER

That's not my name. My name is Edward Butter.
You need not speak so loud.

KEMPTHORN (*shaking hands*)
                    Good-by! Good-by!

BUTTER

Your servant, sir.

KEMPTHORN

                    And yours a thousand times!
                                        Exeunt.

CHRISTUS: A MYSTERY

Scene III. — Governor Endicott's *private room. An open window.* Endicott *seated in an arm-chair.* Bellingham *standing near.*

ENDICOTT

O lost, O loved ! wilt thou return no more ?
O loved and lost, and loved the more when lost !
How many men are dragged into their graves
By their rebellious children ! I now feel
The agony of a father's breaking heart
In David's cry, " O Absalom, my son ! "

BELLINGHAM

Can you not turn your thoughts a little while
To public matters ? There are papers here
That need attention.

ENDICOTT

      Trouble me no more !
My business now is with another world.
Ah, Richard Bellingham ! I greatly fear
That in my righteous zeal I have been led
To doing many things which, left undone,
My mind would now be easier. Did I dream it,
Or has some person told me, that John Norton
Is dead ?

BELLINGHAM

      You have not dreamed it. He is dead,
And gone to his reward. It was no dream.

440

THE NEW ENGLAND TRAGEDIES

ENDICOTT

Then it was very sudden; for I saw him
Standing where you now stand, not long ago.

BELLINGHAM

By his own fireside, in the afternoon,
A faintness and a giddiness came o'er him;
And, leaning on the chimney-piece, he cried,
" The hand of God is on me!" and fell dead.

ENDICOTT

And did not some one say, or have I dreamed it,
That Humphrey Atherton is dead?

BELLINGHAM

       Alas!
He too is gone, and by a death as sudden.
Returning home one evening, at the place
Where usually the Quakers have been scourged,
His horse took fright, and threw him to the ground,
So that his brains were dashed about the street.

ENDICOTT

I am not superstitious, Bellingham,
And yet I tremble lest it may have been
A judgment on him.

BELLINGHAM

     So the people think.
They say his horse saw standing in the way
The ghost of William Leddra, and was frightened.
And furthermore, brave Richard Davenport,

The captain of the Castle, in the storm
Has been struck dead by lightning.

ENDICOTT

Speak no more.
For as I listen to your voice it seems
As if the Seven Thunders uttered their voices,
And the dead bodies lay about the streets
Of the disconsolate city! Bellingham,
I did not put those wretched men to death.
I did but guard the passage with the sword
Pointed towards them, and they rushed upon it!
Yet now I would that I had taken no part
In all that bloody work.

BELLINGHAM

The guilt of it
Be on their heads, not ours.

ENDICOTT

Are all set free?

BELLINGHAM

All are at large.

ENDICOTT

And none have been sent back
To England to malign us with the King?

BELLINGHAM

The ship that brought them sails this very hour,
But carries no one back.

A distant cannon.

THE NEW ENGLAND TRAGEDIES

ENDICOTT

What is that gun?

BELLINGHAM

Her parting signal. Through the window there,
Look, you can see her sails, above the roofs,
Dropping below the Castle, outward bound.

ENDICOTT

O white, white, white! Would that my soul had
    wings
As spotless as those shining sails to fly with!
Now lay this cushion straight. I thank you. Hark!
I thought I heard the hall door open and shut!
I thought I heard the footsteps of my boy!

BELLINGHAM

It was the wind. There 's no one in the passage.

ENDICOTT

O Absalom, my son! I feel the world
Sinking beneath me, sinking, sinking, sinking!
Death knocks! I go to meet him! Welcome, Death!
     Rises, and sinks back dead; his head falling aside
     upon his shoulder.

BELLINGHAM

O ghastly sight! Like one who has been hanged!
Endicott! Endicott! He makes no answer!
     (*Raises* ENDICOTT's *head*)
He breathes no more! How bright this signet-ring
Glitters upon his hand, where he has worn it

CHRISTUS: A MYSTERY

Through such long years of trouble, as if Death
Had given him this memento of affection,
And whispered in his ear, " Remember me ! "
How placid and how quiet is his face,
Now that the struggle and the strife are ended !
Only the acrid spirit of the times
Corroded this true steel. Oh, rest in peace,
Courageous heart ! Forever rest in peace !

GILES COREY
OF THE SALEM FARMS

DRAMATIS PERSONÆ

GILES COREY	Farmer.
JOHN HATHORNE	Magistrate.
COTTON MATHER	Minister of the Gospel.
JONATHAN WALCOT	A youth.
RICHARD GARDNER	Sea-Captain.
JOHN GLOYD	Corey's hired man.
MARTHA	Wife of Giles Corey.
TITUBA	An Indian Woman.
MARY WALCOT	One of the Afflicted.

The Scene is in Salem in the year 1692.

PROLOGUE

DELUSIONS of the days that once have been,
Witchcraft and wonders of the world unseen,
Phantoms of air, and necromantic arts
That crushed the weak and awed the stoutest hearts, —
These are our theme to-night; and vaguely here,
Through the dim mists that crowd the atmosphere,
We draw the outlines of weird figures cast
In shadow on the background of the Past.

Who would believe that in the quiet town
Of Salem, and amid the woods that crown
The neighboring hillsides, and the sunny farms
That fold it safe in their paternal arms, —
Who would believe that in those peaceful streets,
Where the great elms shut out the summer heats,
Where quiet reigns, and breathes through brain and
      breast
The benediction of unbroken rest, —
Who would believe such deeds could find a place
As these whose tragic history we retrace?

'T was but a village then: the goodman ploughed
His ample acres under sun or cloud;
The goodwife at her doorstep sat and spun,
And gossiped with her neighbors in the sun;
The only men of dignity and state
Were then the Minister and the Magistrate,

CHRISTUS: A MYSTERY

Who ruled their little realm with iron rod,
Less in the love than in the fear of God;
And who believed devoutly in the Powers
Of Darkness, working in this world of ours,
In spells of Witchcraft, incantations dread,
And shrouded apparitions of the dead.

Upon this simple folk " with fire and flame,"
Saith the old Chronicle, " the Devil came;
Scattering his firebrands and his poisonous darts,
To set on fire of Hell all tongues and hearts!
And 't is no wonder; for, with all his host,
There most he rages where he hateth most,
And is most hated; so on us he brings
All these stupendous and portentous things! "

Something of this our scene to-night will show;
And ye who listen to the Tale of Woe,
Be not too swift in casting the first stone,
Nor think New England bears the guilt alone.
This sudden burst of wickedness and crime
Was but the common madness of the time,
When in all lands, that lie within the sound
Of Sabbath bells, a Witch was burned or drowned.

ACT I

SCENE I. — *The woods near Salem Village. Enter* TITUBA,
with a basket of herbs.

TITUBA

Here's monk's-hood, that breeds fever in the blood;
And deadly nightshade, that makes men see ghosts;
And henbane, that will shake them with convulsions;
And meadow-saffron and black hellebore,
That rack the nerves, and puff the skin with dropsy;
And bitter-sweet, and briony, and eye-bright,
That cause eruptions, nosebleed, rheumatisms;
I know them, and the places where they hide
In field and meadow; and I know their secrets,
And gather them because they give me power
Over all men and women. Armed with these,
I, Tituba, an Indian and a slave,
Am stronger than the captain with his sword,
Am richer than the merchant with his money,
Am wiser than the scholar with his books,
Mightier than Ministers and Magistrates,
With all the fear and reverence that attend them!
For I can fill their bones with aches and pains,
Can make them cough with asthma, shake with palsy,
Can make their daughters see and talk with ghosts,
Or fall into delirium and convulsions.
I have the Evil Eye, the Evil Hand;
A touch from me, and they are weak with pain,

A look from me, and they consume and die.
The death of cattle and the blight of corn,
The shipwreck, the tornado, and the fire, —
These are my doings, and they know it not.
Thus I work vengeance on mine enemies,
Who, while they call me slave, are slaves to me!

Exit TITUBA.

Enter MATHER, *booted and spurred, with a riding-whip in his
hand.*

MATHER

Methinks that I have come by paths unknown
Into the land and atmosphere of Witches;
For, meditating as I journeyed on,
Lo! I have lost my way! If I remember
Rightly, it is Scribonius the learned
That tells the story of a man who, praying
For one that was possessed by Evil Spirits,
Was struck by Evil Spirits in the face;
I, journeying to circumvent the Witches,
Surely by Witches have been led astray.
I am persuaded there are few affairs
In which the Devil doth not interfere.
We cannot undertake a journey even,
But Satan will be there to meddle with it
By hindering or by furthering. He hath led me
Into this thicket, struck me in the face
With branches of the trees, and so entangled
The fetlocks of my horse with vines and brambles,
That I must needs dismount, and search on foot
For the lost pathway leading to the village.

450

(*Reënter* TITUBA)

What shape is this? What monstrous apparition,
Exceeding fierce, that none may pass that way?
Tell me, good woman, if you are a woman —

TITUBA

I am a woman, but I am not good.
I am a Witch!

MATHER

        Then tell me, Witch and woman,
For you must know the pathways through this wood,
Where lieth Salem Village?

TITUBA

           Reverend sir,
The village is near by. I 'm going there
With these few herbs. I 'll lead you. Follow me.

MATHER

First say, who are you? I am loath to follow
A stranger in this wilderness, for fear
Of being misled, and left in some morass.
Who are you?

TITUBA

       I am Tituba the Witch,
Wife of John Indian.

MATHER

       You are Tituba?

I know you then. You have renounced the Devil,
And have become a penitent confessor.
The Lord be praised! Go on, I 'll follow you.
Wait only till I fetch my horse, that stands
Tethered among the trees, not far from here.

TITUBA

Let me get up behind you, reverend sir.

MATHER

The Lord forbid! What would the people think,
If they should see the Reverend Cotton Mather
Ride into Salem with a Witch behind him?
The Lord forbid!

TITUBA

                I do not need a horse!
I can ride through the air upon a stick,
Above the tree-tops and above the houses,
And no one see me, no one overtake me!

                                    Exeunt.

SCENE II. — *A room at* JUSTICE HATHORNE'S. *A clock in
the corner. Enter* HATHORNE *and* MATHER.

HATHORNE

You are welcome, reverend sir, thrice welcome here
Beneath my humble roof.

MATHER

                I thank your Worship.

THE NEW ENGLAND TRAGEDIES

HATHORNE

Pray you be seated. You must be fatigued
With your long ride through unfrequented woods.

They sit down.

MATHER

You know the purport of my visit here, —
To be advised by you, and counsel with you,
And with the Reverend Clergy of the village,
Touching these witchcrafts that so much afflict you ;
And see with mine own eyes the wonders told
Of spectres and the shadows of the dead,
That come back from their graves to speak with men.

HATHORNE

Some men there are, I have known such, who think
That the two worlds — the seen and the unseen,
The world of matter and the world of spirit —
Are like the hemispheres upon our maps,
And touch each other only at a point.
But these two worlds are not divided thus,
Save for the purposes of common speech.
They form one globe, in which the parted seas
All flow together and are intermingled,
While the great continents remain distinct.

MATHER

I doubt it not. The spiritual world
Lies all about us, and its avenues
Are open to the unseen feet of phantoms
That come and go, and we perceive them not,

Save by their influence, or when at times
A most mysterious Providence permits them
To manifest themselves to mortal eyes.

HATHORNE

You, who are always welcome here among us,
Are doubly welcome now. We need your wisdom,
Your learning in these things, to be our guide.
The Devil hath come down in wrath upon us,
And ravages the land with all his hosts.

MATHER

The Unclean Spirit said, " My name is Legion ! "
Multitudes in the Valley of Destruction !
But when our fervent, well-directed prayers,
Which are the great artillery of Heaven,
Are brought into the field, I see them scattered
And driven like Autumn leaves before the wind.

HATHORNE

You, as a Minister of God, can meet them
With spiritual weapons ; but, alas !
I, as a Magistrate, must combat them
With weapons from the armory of the flesh.

MATHER

These wonders of the world invisible, —
These spectral shapes that haunt our habitations, —
The multiplied and manifold afflictions
With which the aged and the dying saints
Have their death prefaced and their age imbittered, —
Are but prophetic trumpets that proclaim

The Second Coming of our Lord on earth.
The evening wolves will be much more abroad,
When we are near the evening of the world.

HATHORNE

When you shall see, as I have hourly seen,
The sorceries and the witchcrafts that torment us,
See children tortured by invisible spirits,
And wasted and consumed by powers unseen,
You will confess the half has not been told you.

MATHER

It must be so. The death-pangs of the Devil
Will make him more a Devil than before;
And Nebuchadnezzar's furnace will be heated
Seven times more hot before its putting out.

HATHORNE

Advise me, reverend sir. I look to you
For counsel and for guidance in this matter.
What further shall we do?

MATHER

           Remember this,
That as a sparrow falls not to the ground
Without the will of God, so not a Devil
Can come down from the air without his leave.
We must inquire.

HATHORNE

           Dear sir, we have inquired;

Sifted the matter thoroughly through and through,
And then resifted it.

MATHER

If God permits
These Evil Spirits from the unseen regions
To visit us with surprising informations,
We must inquire what cause there is for this,
But not receive the testimony borne
By spectres as conclusive proof of guilt
In the accused.

HATHORNE

Upon such evidence
We do not rest our case. The ways are many
In which the guilty do betray themselves.

MATHER

Be careful. Carry the knife with such exactness,
That on one side no innocent blood be shed
By too excessive zeal, and, on the other
No shelter given to any work of darkness.

HATHORNE

For one, I do not fear excess of zeal.
What do we gain by parleying with the Devil?
You reason, but you hesitate to act!
Ah, reverend sir! believe me, in such cases
The only safety is in acting promptly.
'T is not the part of wisdom to delay
In things where not to do is still to do
A deed more fatal than the deed we shrink from.

You are a man of books and meditation,
But I am one who acts.

MATHER

            God give us wisdom
In the directing of this thorny business,
And guide us, lest New England should become
Of an unsavory and sulphurous odor
In the opinion of the world abroad !

                  The clock strikes.

I never hear the striking of a clock
Without a warning and an admonition
That time is on the wing, and we must quicken
Our tardy pace in journeying Heavenward,
As Israel did in journeying Canaan-ward !

                  They rise.

HATHORNE

Then let us make all haste ; and I will show you
In what disguises and what fearful shapes
The Unclean Spirits haunt this neighborhood,
And you will pardon my excess of zeal.

MATHER

Ah, poor New England ! He who hurricanoed
The house of Job is making now on thee
One last assault, more deadly and more snarled
With unintelligible circumstances
Than any thou hast hitherto encountered !

                  Exeunt.

457

CHRISTUS: A MYSTERY

SCENE III. -— *A room in* WALCOT's *house.* MARY WALCOT
seated in an arm-chair. TITUBA *with a mirror.*

MARY

Tell me another story, Tituba.
A drowsiness is stealing over me
Which is not sleep; for, though I close mine eyes,
I am awake, and in another world.
Dim faces of the dead and of the absent
Come floating up before me, — floating, fading,
And disappearing.

TITUBA

   Look into this glass.
What see you?

MARY

    Nothing but a golden vapor.
Yes, something more. An island, with the sea
Breaking all round it, like a blooming hedge.
What land is this?

TITUBA

   It is San Salvador,
Where Tituba was born. What see you now?

MARY

A man all black and fierce.

TITUBA

    That is my father.
He was an Obi man, and taught me magic, —

Taught me the use of herbs and images.
What is he doing?

                    MARY

                    Holding in his hand
A waxen figure. He is melting it
Slowly before a fire.

                    TITUBA

                    And now what see you?

                    MARY

A woman lying on a bed of leaves,
Wasted and worn away. Ah, she is dying!

                    TITUBA

That is the way the Obi men destroy
The people they dislike! That is the way
Some one is wasting and consuming you.

                    MARY

You terrify me, Tituba! Oh, save me
From those who make me pine and waste away!
Who are they? Tell me.

                    TITUBA

                    That I do not know,
But you will see them. They will come to you.

                    MARY

No, do not let them come! I cannot bear it!
I am too weak to bear it! I am dying.
                    Falls into a trance.

CHRISTUS: A MYSTERY

TITUBA

Hark! there is some one coming.

Enter HATHORNE, MATHER, *and* WALCOT.

WALCOT

                              There she lies,
Wasted and worn by devilish incantations!
O my poor sister!

MATHER

                    Is she always thus?

WALCOT

Nay, she is sometimes tortured by convulsions.

MATHER

Poor child! How thin she is! How wan and wasted!

HATHORNE

Observe her. She is troubled in her sleep.

MATHER

Some fearful vision haunts her.

HATHORNE

                        You now see
With your own eyes, and touch with your own hands,
The mysteries of this Witchcraft.

MATHER

                        One would need

The hands of Briareus and the eyes of Argus
To see and touch them all.

HATHORNE

You now have entered
The realm of ghosts and phantoms, — the vast realm
Of the unknown and the invisible,
Through whose wide-open gates there blows a wind
From the dark valley of the shadow of Death,
That freezes us with horror.

MARY (*starting*)

Take her hence!
Take her away from me. I see her there!
She 's coming to torment me!

WALCOT (*taking her hand*)

O my sister!
What frightens you? She neither hears nor sees me.
She 's in a trance.

MARY

Do you not see her there?

TITUBA

My child, who is it?

MARY

Ah, I do not know.
I cannot see her face.

TITUBA

How is she clad?

MARY

She wears a crimson bodice. In her hand
She holds an image, and is pinching it
Between her fingers. Ah, she tortures me!
I see her face now. It is Goodwife Bishop!
Why does she torture me? I never harmed her!
And now she strikes me with an iron rod!
Oh, I am beaten!

MATHER

       This is wonderful!
I can see nothing! Is this apparition
Visibly there, and yet we cannot see it?

HATHORNE

It is. The spectre is invisible
Unto our grosser senses, but she sees it.

MARY

Look! look! there is another clad in gray!
She holds a spindle in her hand, and threatens
To stab me with it! It is Goodwife Corey!
Keep her away! Now she is coming at me!
O mercy! mercy!

WALCOT (*thrusting with his sword*)

       There is nothing there!

MATHER (*to* HATHORNE)

Do you see anything?

HATHORNE

       The laws that govern

The spiritual world prevent our seeing
Things palpable and visible to her.
These spectres are to us as if they were not.
Mark her; she wakes.

TITUBA *touches her, and she awakes.*

MARY

Who are these gentlemen?

WALCOT

They are our friends. Dear Mary, are you better?

MARY

Weak, very weak.
(*Taking a spindle from her lap, and holding it up*)
How came this spindle here?

TITUBA

You wrenched it from the hand of Goodwife Corey
When she rushed at you.

HATHORNE

Mark that, reverend sir!

MATHER

It is most marvellous, most inexplicable!

TITUBA (*picking up a bit of gray cloth from the floor*)
And here, too, is a bit of her gray dress,
That the sword cut away.

MATHER

Beholding this,

463

It were indeed by far more credulous
To be incredulous than to believe.
None but a Sadducee, who doubts of all
Pertaining to the spiritual world,
Could doubt such manifest and damning proofs!

HATHORNE

Are you convinced?

MATHER (*to* MARY)

   Dear child, be comforted!
Only by prayer and fasting can you drive
These Unclean Spirits from you. An old man
Gives you his blessing. God be with you, Mary!

ACT II

SCENE I. — GILES COREY'S *farm. Morning. Enter* COREY,
with a horseshoe and a hammer.

COREY

The Lord hath prospered me. The rising sun
Shines on my Hundred Acres and my woods
As if he loved them! On a morn like this
I can forgive mine enemies, and thank God
For all his goodness unto me and mine.
My orchard groans with russets and pear-mains;
My ripening corn shines golden in the sun;
My barns are crammed with hay, my cattle
   thrive;
The birds sing blithely on the trees around me!

And blither than the birds my heart within me.
But Satan still goes up and down the earth;
And to protect this house from his assaults,
And keep the powers of darkness from my door,
This horseshoe will I nail upon the threshold.

Nails down the horseshoe.

There, ye night-hags and witches that torment
The neighborhood, ye shall not enter here! —
What is the matter in the field? — John Gloyd!
The cattle are all running to the woods! —
John Gloyd! Where is the man?

(*Enter* JOHN GLOYD)

Look there!

What ails the cattle? Are they all bewitched?
They run like mad.

GLOYD

They have been overlooked.

COREY

The Evil Eye is on them sure enough.
Call all the men. Be quick. Go after them!

Exit GLOYD *and enter* MARTHA.

MARTHA

What is amiss?

COREY

The cattle are bewitched.
They are broken loose and making for the woods.

MARTHA

Why will you harbor such delusions, Giles?

Bewitched ? Well, then it was John Gloyd bewitched
    them ;
I saw him even now take down the bars
And turn them loose ! They 're only frolicsome.

COREY

The rascal !

MARTHA

    I was standing in the road,
Talking with Goodwife Proctor, and I saw him.

COREY

With Proctor's wife ? And what says Goodwife
    Proctor ?

MARTHA

Sad things indeed ; the saddest you can hear
Of Bridget Bishop. She 's cried out upon !

COREY

Poor soul ! I 've known her forty year or more.
She was the widow Wasselby ; and then
She married Oliver, and Bishop next.
She 's had three husbands. I remember well
My games of shovel-board at Bishop's tavern
In the old merry days, and she so gay
With her red paragon bodice and her ribbons !
Ah, Bridget Bishop always was a Witch !

MARTHA

They 'll little help her now, — her cap and ribbons,

466

And her red paragon bodice, and her plumes,
With which she flaunted in the Meeting-house!
When next she goes there, it will be for trial.

COREY

When will that be?

MARTHA

This very day at ten.

COREY

Then get you ready. We will go and see it.
Come; you shall ride behind me on the pillion.

MARTHA

Not I. You know I do not like such things.
I wonder you should. I do not believe
In Witches nor in Witchcraft.

COREY

Well, I do.
There's a strange fascination in it all,
That draws me on and on, I know not why.

MARTHA

What do we know of spirits good or ill,
Or of their power to help us or to harm us?

COREY

Surely what's in the Bible must be true.
Did not an Evil Spirit come on Saul?
Did not the Witch of Endor bring the ghost
Of Samuel from his grave? The Bible says so.

467

CHRISTUS: A MYSTERY

MARTHA

That happened very long ago.

COREY

                                        With God

There is no long ago.

MARTHA

                        There is with us.

COREY

And Mary Magdalene had seven devils,
And he who dwelt among the tombs a legion!

MARTHA

God's power is infinite. I do not doubt it.
If in His providence He once permitted
Such things to be among the Israelites,
It does not follow He permits them now,
And among us who are not Israelites.
But we will not dispute about it, Giles.
Go to the village, if you think it best,
And leave me here; I'll go about my work.

                                Exit into the house.

COREY

And I will go and saddle the gray mare.
The last word always. That is woman's nature.
If an old man will marry a young wife,
He must make up his mind to many things.
It's putting new cloth into an old garment,

When the strain comes, it is the old gives way.

Goes to the door.

O Martha! I forgot to tell you something.
I 've had a letter from a friend of mine,
A certain Richard Gardner of Nantucket,
Master and owner of a whaling-vessel;
He writes that he is coming down to see us.
I hope you 'll like him.

MARTHA

I will do my best.

COREY

That 's a good woman. Now I will be gone.
I 've not seen Gardner for this twenty year;
But there is something of the sea about him, —
Something so open, generous, large, and strong,
It makes me love him better than a brother.

Exit.

MARTHA *comes to the door.*

MARTHA

Oh these old friends and cronies of my husband,
These captains from Nantucket and the Cape,
That come and turn my house into a tavern
With their carousing! Still, there 's something frank
In these seafaring men that makes me like them.
Why, here 's a horseshoe nailed upon the doorstep!
Giles has done this to keep away the Witches.
I hope this Richard Gardner will bring with him
A gale of good sound common-sense, to blow
The fog of these delusions from his brain!

COREY (*within*)

Ho! Martha! Martha!

(*Enter* COREY)

Have you seen my saddle?

MARTHA

I saw it yesterday.

COREY

Where did you see it?

MARTHA

On a gray mare, that somebody was riding
Along the village road.

COREY

Who was it? Tell me.

MARTHA

Some one who should have stayed at home.

COREY (*restraining himself*)

I see!

Don't vex me, Martha. Tell me where it is.

MARTHA

I've hidden it away.

COREY

Go fetch it me.

470

MARTHA

Go find it.

COREY

No. I 'll ride down to the village
Bare-back; and when the people stare and say,
" Giles Corey, where 's your saddle ? " I will answer,
" A Witch has stolen it." How shall you like that ?

MARTHA

I shall not like it.

COREY

Then go fetch the saddle.
Exit MARTHA.
If an old man will marry a young wife,
Why then — why then — why then — he must spell
Baker!

Enter MARTHA *with the saddle, which she throws down.*

MARTHA

There! There 's the saddle.

COREY

Take it up.

MARTHA

I won't.

COREY

Then let it lie there. I 'll ride to the village,
And say you are a Witch!

MARTHA

No, not that, Giles.

She takes up the saddle.

COREY

Now come with me, and saddle the gray mare
With your own hands; and you shall see me
     ride
Along the village road as is becoming
Giles Corey of the Salem Farms, your hus-
     band!

Exeunt.

SCENE II. — *The Green in front of the Meeting-house in Salem Village. People coming and going. Enter* GILES COREY.

COREY

A melancholy end! Who would have thought
That Bridget Bishop e'er would come to this?
Accused, convicted, and condemned to death
For Witchcraft! And so good a woman too!

A FARMER

Good morrow, neighbor Corey.

COREY (*not hearing him*)

                              Who is safe?
How do I know but under my own roof
I too may harbor Witches, and some Devil
Be plotting and contriving against me?

FARMER

He does not hear. Good morrow, neighbor Corey!

COREY

Good morrow.

FARMER

Have you seen John Proctor lately?

COREY

No, I have not.

FARMER

Then do not see him, Corey.

COREY

Why should I not?

FARMER

Because he's angry with you.
So keep out of his way. Avoid a quarrel.

COREY

Why does he seek to fix a quarrel on me?

FARMER

He says you burned his house.

COREY

I burn his house?
If he says that, John Proctor is a liar!
The night his house was burned I was in bed,
And I can prove it! Why, we are old friends!
He could not say that of me.

FARMER

He did say it.

I heard him say it.

.

COREY

Then he shall unsay it.

FARMER

He said you did it out of spite to him
For taking part against you in the quarrel
You had with your John Gloyd about his wages.
He says you murdered Goodell; that you trampled
Upon his body till he breathed no more.
And so beware of him; that's my advice!

Exit.

COREY

By Heaven! this is too much! I'll seek him
    out,
And make him eat his words, or strangle him.
I'll not be slandered at a time like this,
When every word is made an accusation,
When every whisper kills, and every man
Walks with a halter round his neck!
    (*Enter* GLOYD *in haste*)

What now?

GLOYD

I came to look for you. The cattle —

COREY

Well,

What of them? Have you found them?

GLOYD

They are dead.
I followed them through the woods, across the mead-
    ows;
Then they all leaped into the Ipswich River,
And swam across, but could not climb the bank,
And so were drowned.

COREY

You are to blame for this;
For you took down the bars, and let them loose.

GLOYD

That I deny. They broke the fences down.
You know they were bewitched.

COREY

Ah, my poor cattle!
The Evil Eye was on them; that is true.
Day of disaster! Most unlucky day!
Why did I leave my ploughing and my reaping
To plough and reap this Sodom and Gomorrah?
Oh, I could drown myself for sheer vexation!

Exit.

GLOYD

He's going for his cattle. He won't find them.
By this time they have drifted out to sea.
They will not break his fences any more,
Though they may break his heart. And what care I?

Exit.

SCENE III. — COREY'S *kitchen. A table with supper.* MARTHA
knitting.

MARTHA

He 's come at last. I hear him in the passage.
Something has gone amiss with him to-day;
I know it by his step, and by the sound
The door made as he shut it. He is angry.

Enter COREY *with his riding-whip. As he speaks he takes off
his hat and gloves, and throws them down violently.*

COREY

I say if Satan ever entered man
He 's in John Proctor!

MARTHA

                            Giles, what is the matter?
You frighten me.

COREY

                    I say if any man
Can have a Devil in him, then that man
Is Proctor, — is John Proctor, and no other!

MARTHA

Why, what has he been doing?

COREY

                            Everything!
What do you think I heard there in the village?

MARTHA

I 'm sure I cannot guess. What did you hear?

COREY

He says I burned his house!

MARTHA

                    Does he say that?

COREY

He says I burned his house. I was in bed
And fast asleep that night; and I can prove it.

MARTHA

If he says that, I think the Father of Lies
Is surely in the man.

COREY

                    He does say that,
And that I did it to wreak vengeance on him
For taking sides against me in the quarrel
I had with that John Gloyd about his wages.
And God knows that I never bore him malice
For that, as I have told him twenty times!

MARTHA

It is John Gloyd has stirred him up to this.
I do not like that Gloyd. I think him crafty,
Not to be trusted, sullen, and untruthful.
Come, have your supper. You are tired and hungry.

COREY

I 'm angry, and not hungry.

CHRISTUS: A MYSTERY

MARTHA

      Do eat something.
You 'll be the better for it.

COREY (*sitting down*)
      I 'm not hungry.

MARTHA

Let not the sun go down upon your wrath.

COREY

It has gone down upon it, and will rise
To-morrow, and go down again upon it.
They have trumped up against me the old story
Of causing Goodell's death by trampling on him.

MARTHA

Oh, that is false. I know it to be false.

COREY

He has been dead these fourteen years or more.
Why can't they let him rest ? Why must they drag him
Out of his grave to give me a bad name ?
I did not kill him. In his bed he died,
As most men die, because his hour had come.
I have wronged no man. Why should Proctor say
Such things about me ? I will not forgive him
Till he confesses he has slandered me.
Then, I 've more trouble. All my cattle gone.

MARTHA

They will come back again.

COREY

Not in this world.
Did I not tell you they were overlooked?
They ran down through the woods, into the meadows,
And tried to swim the river, and were drowned.
It is a heavy loss.

MARTHA

I 'm sorry for it.

COREY

All my dear oxen dead. I loved them, Martha,
Next to yourself. I liked to look at them,
And watch the breath come out of their wide nostrils,
And see their patient eyes. Somehow I thought
It gave me strength only to look at them.
And how they strained their necks against the yoke
If I but spoke, or touched them with the goad!
They were my friends; and when Gloyd came and
    told me
They were all drowned, I could have drowned my-
    self
From sheer vexation; and I said as much
To Gloyd and others.

MARTHA

Do not trust John Gloyd
With anything you would not have repeated.

COREY

As I came through the woods this afternoon,
Impatient at my loss, and much perplexed

With all that I had heard there in the village,
The yellow leaves lit up the trees about me
Like an enchanted palace, and I wished
I knew enough of magic or of Witchcraft
To change them into gold. Then suddenly
A tree shook down some crimson leaves upon me,
Like drops of blood, and in the path before me
Stood Tituba the Indian, the old crone.

MARTHA

Were you not frightened ?

COREY

        No, I do not think
I know the meaning of that word. Why frightened ?
I am not one of those who think the Lord
Is waiting till He catches them some day
In the back yard alone ! What should I fear ?
She started from the bushes by the path,
And had a basket full of herbs and roots
For some witch-broth or other, — the old hag !

MARTHA

She has been here to-day.

COREY

        With hand outstretched
She said : " Giles Corey, will you sign the Book ? "
" Avaunt ! " I cried : " Get thee behind me, Satan ! "
At which she laughed and left me. But a voice
Was whispering in my ear continually :

" Self-murder is no crime. The life of man
Is his, to keep it or to throw away ! "

MARTHA

'T was a temptation of the Evil One !
Giles, Giles ! why will you harbor these dark
    thoughts ?

COREY (*rising*)

I am too tired to talk. I 'll go to bed.

MARTHA

First tell me something about Bridget Bishop.
How did she look ? You saw her ? You were there ?

COREY

I 'll tell you that to-morrow, not to-night.
I 'll go to bed.

MARTHA

First let us pray together.

COREY

I cannot pray to-night.

MARTHA

Say the Lord's Prayer,
And that will comfort you.

COREY

I cannot say,

" As we forgive those that have sinned against us,"
When I do not forgive them.

MARTHA (*kneeling on the hearth*)
God forgive you!

COREY

I will not make believe! I say, to-night
There 's something thwarts me when I wish to pray,
And thrusts into my mind, instead of prayers,
Hate and revenge, and things that are not prayers.
Something of my old self, — my old, bad life, —
And the old Adam in me, rises up,
And will not let me pray. I am afraid
The Devil hinders me. You know I say
Just what I think, and nothing more nor less,
And, when I pray, my heart is in my prayer.
I cannot say one thing and mean another.
If I can't pray, I will not make believe!
Exit COREY. MARTHA *continues kneeling.*

ACT III

SCENE I. — GILES COREY'S *kitchen. Morning.* COREY *and*
MARTHA *sitting at the breakfast-table.*

COREY (*rising*)
Well, now I 've told you all I saw and heard
Of Bridget Bishop; and I must be gone.

MARTHA

Don't go into the village, Giles, to-day.
Last night you came back tired and out of humor.

COREY

Say, angry; say, right angry. I was never
In a more devilish temper in my life.
All things went wrong with me.

MARTHA

                    You were much vexed;
So don't go to the village.

COREY (*going*)

                  No, I won't.
I won't go near it. We are going to mow
The Ipswich meadows for the aftermath,
The crop of sedge and rowens.

MARTHA

                     Stay a moment.
I want to tell you what I dreamed last night.
Do you believe in dreams?

COREY

                Why, yes and no.
When they come true, then I believe in them;
When they come false, I don't believe in them.
But let me hear. What did you dream about?

MARTHA

I dreamed that you and I were both in prison;

That we had fetters on our hands and feet;
That we were taken before the Magistrates,
And tried for Witchcraft, and condemned to death!
I wished to pray; they would not let me pray;
You tried to comfort me, and they forbade it.
But the most dreadful thing in all my dream
Was that they made you testify against me!
And then there came a kind of mist between us;
I could not see you; and I woke in terror.
I never was more thankful in my life
Than when I found you sleeping at my side!

COREY (*with tenderness*)

It was our talk last night that made you dream.
I'm sorry for it. I'll control myself
Another time, and keep my temper down!
I do not like such dreams. — Remember, Martha,
I'm going to mow the Ipswich River meadows;
If Gardner comes, you'll tell him where to find me.

Exit.

MARTHA

So this delusion grows from bad to worse.
First, a forsaken and forlorn old woman,
Ragged and wretched, and without a friend;
Then something higher. Now it's Bridget Bishop;
God only knows whose turn it will be next!
The Magistrates are blind, the people mad!
If they would only seize the Afflicted Children,
And put them in the Workhouse, where they should
    be,
There'd be an end of all this wickedness.

Exit.

SCENE II. — *A street in Salem Village. Enter* MATHER *and* HATHORNE.

MATHER

Yet one thing troubles me.

HATHORNE

And what is that?

MATHER

May not the Devil take the outward shape
Of innocent persons? Are we not in danger,
Perhaps, of punishing some who are not guilty?

HATHORNE

As I have said, we do not trust alone
To spectral evidence.

MATHER

And then again,
If any shall be put to death for Witchcraft,
We do but kill the body, not the soul.
The Unclean Spirits that possessed them once
Live still, to enter into other bodies.
What have we gained? Surely, there's nothing
    gained.

HATHORNE

Doth not the Scripture say, "Thou shalt not suffer
A Witch to live?"

485

CHRISTUS: A MYSTERY

MATHER

The Scripture sayeth it,
But speaketh to the Jews ; and we are Christians.
What say the laws of England ?

HATHORNE

They make Witchcraft
Felony without the benefit of Clergy.
Witches are burned in England. You have read —
For you read all things, not a book escapes you —
The famous Demonology of King James ?

MATHER

A curious volume. I remember also
The plot of the Two Hundred, with one Fian,
The Registrar of the Devil, at their head,
To drown his Majesty on his return
From Denmark ; how they sailed in sieves or rid-
	dles
Unto North Berwick Kirk in Lothian,
And, landing there, danced hand in hand, and sang,
" Goodwife, go ye before ! goodwife, go ye !
If ye 'll not go before, goodwife, let me ! "
While Geilis Duncan played the Witches' Reel
Upon a jews-harp.

HATHORNE

Then you know full well
The English law, and that in England Witches,
When lawfully convicted and attainted,
Are put to death.

THE NEW ENGLAND TRAGEDIES

MATHER

When lawfully convicted;
That is the point.

HATHORNE

You heard the evidence
Produced before us yesterday at the trial
Of Bridget Bishop.

MATHER

One of the Afflicted,
I know, bore witness to the apparition
Of ghosts unto the spectre of this Bishop,
Saying, " You murdered us! " of the truth whereof
There was in matter of fact too much suspicion.

HATHORNE

And when she cast her eyes on the Afflicted,
They were struck down; and this in such a manner
There could be no collusion in the business.
And when the accused but laid her hand upon them,
As they lay in their swoons, they straight revived,
Although they stirred not when the others touched
them.

MATHER

What most convinced me of the woman's guilt
Was finding hidden in her cellar wall
Those poppets made of rags, with headless pins
Stuck into them point outwards, and whereof
She could not give a reasonable account.

HATHORNE

When you shall read the testimony given
Before the Court in all the other cases,
I am persuaded you will find the proof
No less conclusive than it was in this.
Come, then, with me, and I will tax your patience
With reading of the documents so far
As may convince you that these sorcerers
Are lawfully convicted and attainted.
Like doubting Thomas, you shall lay your hand
Upon these wounds, and you will doubt no more.

Exeunt.

SCENE III. — *A room in* COREY'S *house.* MARTHA *and two
Deacons of the church.*

MARTHA

Be seated. I am glad to see you here.
I know what you are come for. You are come
To question me, and learn from my own lips
If I have any dealings with the Devil;
In short, if I 'm a Witch.

DEACON (*sitting down*)

Such is our purpose.
How could you know beforehand why we came?

MARTHA

'T was only a surmise.

DEACON

We came to ask you,

You being with us in church covenant,
What part you have, if any, in these matters.

MARTHA

And I make answer, No part whatsoever.
I am a farmer's wife, a working woman;
You see my spinning-wheel, you see my loom,
You know the duties of a farmer's wife,
And are not ignorant that my life among you
Has been without reproach until this day.
Is it not true?

DEACON

      So much we 're bound to own;
And say it frankly, and without reserve.

MARTHA

I 've heard the idle tales that are abroad;
I 've heard it whispered that I am a Witch;
I cannot help it. I do not believe
In any Witchcraft. It is a delusion.

DEACON

How can you say that it is a delusion,
When all our learned and good men believe it? —
Our Ministers and worshipful Magistrates?

MARTHA

Their eyes are blinded, and see not the truth.
Perhaps one day they will be open to it.

DEACON

You answer boldly. The Afflicted Children
Say you appeared to them.

MARTHA

And did they say
What clothes I came in?

DEACON

No, they could not tell.
They said that you foresaw our visit here,
And blinded them, so that they could not see
The clothes you wore.

MARTHA

The cunning, crafty girls!
I say to you, in all sincerity,
I never have appeared to any one
In my own person. If the Devil takes
My shape to hurt these children, or afflict them,
I am not guilty of it. And I say
It's all a mere delusion of the senses.

DEACON

I greatly fear that you will find too late
It is not so.

MARTHA (*rising*)

They do accuse me falsely.
It is delusion, or it is deceit.
There is a story in the ancient Scriptures

Which much I wonder comes not to your minds.
Let me repeat it to you.

DEACON

We will hear it.

MARTHA

It came to pass that Naboth had a vineyard
Hard by the palace of the King called Ahab.
And Ahab, King of Israel, spake to Naboth,
And said to him, Give unto me thy vineyard,
That I may have it for a garden of herbs,
And I will give a better vineyard for it,
Or, if it seemeth good to thee, its worth
In money. And then Naboth said to Ahab,
The Lord forbid it me that I should give
The inheritance of my fathers unto thee.
And Ahab came into his house displeased
And heavy at the words which Naboth spake,
And laid him down upon his bed, and turned
His face away; and he would eat no bread.
And Jezebel, the wife of Ahab, came
And said to him, Why is thy spirit sad?
And he said unto her, Because I spake
To Naboth, to the Jezreelite, and said,
Give me thy vineyard; and he answered, saying,
I will not give my vineyard unto thee.
And Jezebel, the wife of Ahab, said,
Dost thou not rule the realm of Israel?
Arise, eat bread, and let thy heart be merry;
I will give Naboth's vineyard unto thee.
So she wrote letters in King Ahab's name,

And sealed them with his seal, and sent the letters
Unto the elders that were in his city
Dwelling with Naboth, and unto the nobles;
And in the letters wrote, Proclaim a fast;
And set this Naboth high among the people,
And set two men, the sons of Belial,
Before him, to bear witness and to say,
Thou didst blaspheme against God and the King;
And carry him out and stone him, that he die!
And the elders and the nobles of the city
Did even as Jezebel, the wife of Ahab,
Had sent to them and written in the letters.
And then it came to pass, when Ahab heard
Naboth was dead, that Ahab rose to go
Down unto Naboth's vineyard, and to take
Possession of it. And the word of God
Came to Elijah, saying to him, Arise,
Go down to meet the King of Israel
In Naboth's vineyard, whither he hath gone
To take possession. Thou shalt speak to him,
Saying, Thus saith the Lord! What! hast thou
            killed
And also taken possession? In the place
Wherein the dogs have licked the blood of Naboth
Shall the dogs lick thy blood, — ay, even thine!

> *Both of the Deacons start from their seats.*

And Ahab then, the King of Israel,
Said, Hast thou found me, O mine enemy?
Elijah the Prophet answered, I have found thee!
So will it be with those who have stirred up
The Sons of Belial here to bear false witness
And swear away the lives of innocent people;

Their enemy will find them out at last,
The Prophet's voice will thunder, I have found thee!

Exeunt.

SCENE IV. — *Meadows on Ipswich River.* COREY *and his
men mowing;* COREY *in advance.*

COREY

Well done, my men. You see, I lead the field!
I'm an old man, but I can swing a scythe
Better than most of you, though you be younger.

Hangs his scythe upon a tree.

GLOYD (*aside to the others*)

How strong he is! It's supernatural.
No man so old as he is has such strength.
The Devil helps him!

COREY (*wiping his forehead*)

Now we'll rest awhile,
And take our nooning. What's the matter with you?
You are not angry with me, — are you, Gloyd?
Come, come, we will not quarrel. Let's be friends.
It's an old story, that the Raven said,
" Read the Third of Colossians and fifteenth."

GLOYD

You're handier at the scythe, but I can beat you
At wrestling.

COREY

Well, perhaps so. I don't know.

493

I never wrestled with you. Why, you 're vexed!
Come, come, don't bear a grudge.

GLOYD

You are afraid.

COREY

What should I be afraid of? All bear witness
The challenge comes from him. Now, then, my
man.

They wrestle, and GLOYD *is thrown.*

ONE OF THE MEN

That 's a fair fall.

ANOTHER

'T was nothing but a foil!

OTHERS

You 've hurt him!

COREY (*helping* GLOYD *rise*)

No; this meadow-land is soft.
You 're not hurt, — are you, Gloyd?

GLOYD (*rising*)

No, not much hurt.

COREY

Well, then, shake hands; and there 's an end of it.
How do you like that Cornish hug, my lad?
And now we 'll see what 's in our basket here.

GLOYD (*aside*)

The Devil and all his imps are in that man!
The clutch of his ten fingers burns like fire!

COREY (*reverentially taking off his hat*)

God bless the food He hath provided for us,
And make us thankful for it, for Christ's sake!

He lifts up a keg of cider, and drinks from it.

GLOYD

Do you see that? Don't tell me it 's not Witchcraft.
Two of us could not lift that cask as he does!

COREY *puts down the keg, and opens a basket. A
voice is heard calling.*

VOICE

Ho! Corey, Corey!

COREY

What is that? I surely
Heard some one calling me by name!

VOICE

Giles Corey!

Enter a boy, running, and out of breath.

BOY

Is Master Corey here?

COREY

Yes, here I am.

495

BOY

O Master Corey!

COREY

Well?

BOY

Your wife — your wife —

COREY

What's happened to my wife?

BOY

She's sent to prison!

COREY

The dream! the dream! O God, be merciful!

BOY

She sent me here to tell you.

COREY (*putting on his jacket*)

Where's my horse?
Don't stand there staring, fellows. Where's my
horse?   *Exit* COREY.

GLOYD

Under the trees there. Run, old man, run, run!
You've got some one to wrestle with you now
Who'll trip your heels up, with your Cornish hug.
If there's a Devil, he has got you now.
Ah, there he goes! His horse is snorting fire!

496

THE NEW ENGLAND TRAGEDIES

ONE OF THE MEN

John Gloyd, don't talk so ! It's a shame to talk so !
He's a good master, though you quarrel with him.

GLOYD

If hard work and low wages make good masters,
Then he is one. But I think otherwise.
Come, let us have our dinner and be merry,
And talk about the old man and the Witches.
I know some stories that will make you laugh.
They sit down on the grass, and eat.
Now there are Goody Cloyse and Goody Good,
Who have not got a decent tooth between them,
And yet these children — the Afflicted Children —
Say that they bite them, and show marks of teeth
Upon their arms !

ONE OF THE MEN

That makes the wonder greater.
That's Witchcraft. Why, if they had teeth like yours,
'T would be no wonder if the girls were bitten !

GLOYD

And then those ghosts that come out of their graves
And cry, " You murdered us ! you murdered us ! "

ONE OF THE MEN

And all those Apparitions that stick pins
Into the flesh of the Afflicted Children !

GLOYD

Oh those Afflicted Children ! They know well

Where the pins come from. I can tell you that.
And there's old Corey, he has got a horseshoe
Nailed on his doorstep to keep off the Witches,
And all the same his wife has gone to prison.

ONE OF THE MEN

Oh, she's no Witch. I'll swear that Goodwife Corey
Never did harm to any living creature.
She's a good woman, if there ever was one.

GLOYD

Well, we shall see. As for that Bridget Bishop,
She has been tried before; some years ago
A negro testified he saw her shape
Sitting upon the rafters in a barn,
And holding in its hand an egg; and while
He went to fetch his pitchfork, she had vanished.
And now be quiet, will you? I am tired,
And want to sleep here on the grass a little.

They stretch themselves on the grass.

ONE OF THE MEN

There may be Witches riding through the air
Over our heads on broomsticks at this moment,
Bound for some Satan's Sabbath in the woods
To be baptized.

GLOYD

I wish they'd take you with them, ·
And hold you under water, head and ears,
Till you were drowned; and that would stop your
    talking,
If nothing else will. Let me sleep, I say.

ACT IV

SCENE I. — *The Green in front of the village Meeting-house. An excited crowd gathering. Enter* JOHN GLOYD.

A FARMER

Who will be tried to-day ?

A SECOND

      I do not know.
Here is John Gloyd. Ask him ; he knows.

FARMER

         John Gloyd,
Whose turn is it to-day ?

GLOYD

      It 's Goodwife Corey's.

FARMER

Giles Corey's wife ?

GLOYD

     The same. She is not mine.
It will go hard with her with all her praying.
The hypocrite ! She 's always on her knees ;
But she prays to the Devil when she prays.
Let us go in.

          A trumpet blows.

FARMER

Here come the Magistrates.

SECOND FARMER

Who 's the tall man in front?

GLOYD

                    Oh, that is Hathorne,
A Justice of the Court, and Quartermaster
In the Three County Troop. He 'll sift the matter.
That 's Corwin with him; and the man in black
Is Cotton Mather, Minister of Boston.

Enter HATHORNE *and other Magistrates on horseback, followed by the Sheriff, constables, and attendants on foot. The
Magistrates dismount, and enter the Meeting-house, with
the rest*

FARMER

The Meeting-house is full. I never saw
So great a crowd before.

GLOYD

               No matter. Come.
We shall find room enough by elbowing
Our way among them. Put your shoulder to it.

FARMER

There were not half so many at the trial
Of Goodwife Bishop.

GLOYD

            Keep close after me.
500

I'll find a place for you. They'll want me there.
I am a friend of Corey's, as you know,
And he can't do without me just at present.

Exeunt.

SCENE II. — *Interior of the Meeting-house.* MATHER *and the Magistrates seated in front of the pulpit. Before them a raised platform.* MARTHA *in chains.* COREY *near her.* MARY WALCOT *in a chair. A crowd of spectators, among them* GLOYD. *Confusion and murmurs during the scene.*

HATHORNE

Call Martha Corey.

MARTHA

I am here.

HATHORNE

Come forward.
She ascends the platform.
The Jurors of our Sovereign Lord and Lady
The King and Queen, here present, do accuse you
Of having on the tenth of June last past,
And divers other times before and after,
Wickedly used and practised certain arts
Called Witchcrafts, Sorceries, and Incantations,
Against one Mary Walcot, single woman,
Of Salem Village; by which wicked arts
The aforesaid Mary Walcot was tormented,
Tortured, afflicted, pined, consumed, and wasted,
Against the peace of our Sovereign Lord and Lady
The King and Queen, as well as of the Statute
Made and provided in that case. What say you?

501

CHRISTUS: A MYSTERY

MARTHA

Before I answer, give me leave to pray.

HATHORNE

We have not sent for you, nor are we here,
To hear you pray, but to examine you
In whatsoever is alleged against you.
Why do you hurt this person?

MARTHA

                    I do not.
I am not guilty of the charge against me.

MARY

Avoid, she-devil! You torment me now!
Avoid, avoid, Witch!

MARTHA

                  I am innocent.
I never had to do with any Witchcraft
Since I was born. I am a gospel woman.

MARY

You are a gospel Witch!

MARTHA (*clasping her hands*)

                Ah me! ah me!
Oh, give me leave to pray!

MARY (*stretching out her hands*)

              She hurts me now.
See, she has pinched my hands!

HATHORNE

> > Who made these marks

Upon her hands?

MARTHA

> I do not know. I stand

Apart from her. I did not touch her hands.

HATHORNE

Who hurt her then?

MARTHA

> I know not.

HATHORNE

> > Do you think

She is bewitched?

MARTHA

> Indeed I do not think so.

I am no Witch, and have no faith in Witches.

HATHORNE

Then answer me: When certain persons came
To see you yesterday, how did you know
Beforehand why they came?

MARTHA

> I had had speech;

The children said I hurt them, and I thought
These people came to question me about it.

HATHORNE

How did you know the children had been told
To note the clothes you wore?

MARTHA

My husband told me
What others said about it.

HATHORNE

Goodman Corey,
Say, did you tell her?

COREY

I must speak the truth;
I did not tell her. It was some one else.

HATHORNE

Did you not say your husband told you so?
How dare you tell a lie in this assembly?
Who told you of the clothes? Confess the truth.
(MARTHA *bites her lips, and is silent*)
You bite your lips, but do not answer me!

MARY

Ah, she is biting me! Avoid, avoid!

HATHORNE

You said your husband told you.

MARTHA

Yes, he told me
The children said I troubled them.

THE NEW ENGLAND TRAGEDIES

HATHORNE

Then tell me,
Why do you trouble them ?

MARTHA

I have denied it.

MARY

She threatened me ; stabbed at me with her spindle ;
And, when my brother thrust her with his sword,
He tore her gown, and cut a piece away.
Here are they both, the spindle and the cloth.

Shows them.

HATHORNE

And there are persons here who know the truth
Of what has now been said. What answer make you ?

MARTHA

I make no answer. Give me leave to pray.

HATHORNE

Whom would you pray to ?

MARTHA

To my God and Father.

HATHORNE

Who is your God and Father ?

MARTHA

The Almighty !

505

CHRISTUS: A MYSTERY

HATHORNE

Doth he you pray to say that he is God?
It is the Prince of Darkness, and not God.

MARY

There is a dark shape whispering in her ear.

HATHORNE

What does it say to you?

MARTHA

          I see no shape.

HATHORNE

Did you not hear it whisper?

MARTHA

          I heard nothing.

MARY

What torture! Ah, what agony I suffer!
Falls into a swoon.

HATHORNE

You see this woman cannot stand before you.
If you would look for mercy, you must look
In God's way, by confession of your guilt.
Why does your spectre haunt and hurt this person?

MARTHA

I do not know. He who appeared of old
In Samuel's shape, a saint and glorified,

May come in whatsoever shape he chooses.
I cannot help it. I am sick at heart!

COREY

O Martha, Martha! let me hold your hand.

HATHORNE

No; stand aside, old man.

MARY (*starting up*)

Look there! Look there!
I see a little bird, a yellow bird,
Perched on her finger; and it pecks at me.
Ah, it will tear mine eyes out!

MARTHA

I see nothing.

HATHORNE

'T is the Familiar Spirit that attends her.

MARY

Now it has flown away. It sits up there
Upon the rafters. It is gone; is vanished.

MARTHA

Giles, wipe these tears of anger from mine eyes.
Wipe the sweat from my forehead. I am faint.
                    She leans against the railing.

MARY

Oh, she is crushing me with all her weight!

507

CHRISTUS: A MYSTERY

HATHORNE

Did you not carry once the Devil's Book
To this young woman?

MARTHA

Never.

HATHORNE

Have you signed it,
Or touched it?

MARTHA

No; I never saw it.

HATHORNE

Did you not scourge her with an iron rod?

MARTHA

No, I did not. If any Evil Spirit
Has taken my shape to do these evil deeds,
I cannot help it. I am innocent.

HATHORNE

Did you not say the Magistrates were blind?
That you would open their eyes?

MARTHA (*with a scornful laugh*)

Yes, I said that;
If you call me a sorceress, you are blind!
If you accuse the innocent, you are blind!
Can the innocent be guilty?

THE NEW ENGLAND TRAGEDIES

HATHORNE

Did you not
On one occasion hide your husband's saddle
To hinder him from coming to the Sessions?

MARTHA

I thought it was a folly in a farmer
To waste his time pursuing such illusions.

HATHORNE

What was the bird that this young woman saw
Just now upon your hand?

MARTHA

I know no bird.

HATHORNE

Have you not dealt with a Familiar Spirit?

MARTHA

No, never, never!

HATHORNE

What then was the Book
You showed to this young woman, and besought her
To write in it?

MARTHA

Where should I have a book?
I showed her none, nor have none.

MARY

The next Sabbath

Is the Communion Day, but Martha Corey
Will not be there !

MARTHA

                    Ah, you are all against me.
What can I do or say ?

HATHORNE

                    You can confess.

MARTHA

No, I cannot, for I am innocent.

HATHORNE

We have the proof of many witnesses
That you are guilty.

MARTHA

                    Give me leave to speak.
Will you condemn me on such evidence, —
You who have known me for so many years ?
Will you condemn me in this house of God,
Where I so long have worshipped with you all ?
Where I have eaten the bread and drunk the wine
So many times at our Lord's Table with you ?
Bear witness, you that hear me ; you all know
That I have led a blameless life among you,
That never any whisper of suspicion
Was breathed against me till this accusation.
And shall this count for nothing ? Will you take
My life away from me, because this girl,
Who is distraught, and not in her right mind,
Accuses me of things I blush to name ?

THE NEW ENGLAND TRAGEDIES

HATHORNE

What! is it not enough? Would you hear more?
Giles Corey!

COREY

I am here.

HATHORNE

Come forward, then.
(COREY *ascends the platform*)
Is it not true, that on a certain night
You were impeded strangely in your prayers?
That something hindered you? and that you left
This woman here, your wife, kneeling alone
Upon the hearth?

COREY

Yes; I cannot deny it.

HATHORNE

Did you not say the Devil hindered you?

COREY

I think I said some words to that effect.

HATHORNE

Is it not true, that fourteen head of cattle,
To you belonging, broke from their enclosure
And leaped into the river, and were drowned?

COREY

It is most true.

511

HATHORNE

And did you not then say
That they were overlooked?

COREY

So much I said.
I see; they're drawing round me closer, closer,
A net I cannot break, cannot escape from! (*Aside*)

HATHORNE

Who did these things?

COREY

I do not know who did them.

HATHORNE

Then I will tell you. It is some one near you;
You see her now; this woman, your own wife.

COREY

I call the heavens to witness, it is false!
She never harmed me, never hindered me
In anything but what I should not do.
And I bear witness in the sight of heaven,
And in God's house here, that I never knew her
As otherwise than patient, brave, and true,
Faithful, forgiving, full of charity,
A virtuous and industrious and good wife!

HATHORNE

Tut, tut, man; do not rant so in your speech;
You are a witness, not an advocate!
Here, Sheriff, take this woman back to prison.

512

THE NEW ENGLAND TRAGEDIES

MARTHA

O Giles, this day you 've sworn away my life!

MARY

Go, go and join the Witches at the door.
Do you not hear the drum? Do you not see them?
Go quick. They 're waiting for you. You are late.

Exit MARTHA; COREY *following.*

COREY

The dream! the dream! the dream!

HATHORNE

                  What does he say?
Giles Corey, go not hence. You are yourself
Accused of Witchcraft and of Sorcery
By many witnesses. Say, are you guilty?

COREY

I know my death is foreordained by you, —
Mine and my wife's. Therefore I will not answer.

During the rest of the scene he remains silent.

HATHORNE

Do you refuse to plead? — 'T were better for you
To make confession, or to plead Not Guilty. —
Do you not hear me? — Answer, are you guilty?
Do you not know a heavier doom awaits you,
If you refuse to plead, than if found guilty?
Where is John Gloyd?

GLOYD (*coming forward*)
Here am I.

HATHORNE

Tell the Court;
Have you not seen the supernatural power
Of this old man? Have you not seen him do
Strange feats of strength?

GLOYD

I 've seen him lead the field,
On a hot day, in mowing, and against
Us younger men; and I have wrestled with him.
He threw me like a feather. I have seen him
Lift up a barrel with his single hands,
Which two strong men could hardly lift together,
And, holding it above his head, drink from it.

HATHORNE

That is enough; we need not question further.
What answer do you make to this, Giles Corey?

MARY

See there! See there!

HATHORNE

What is it? I see nothing.

MARY

Look! Look! It is the ghost of Robert Goodell,
Whom fifteen years ago this man did murder

514

By stamping on his body! In his shroud
He comes here to bear witness to the crime!

The crowd shrinks back from COREY *in horror.*

HATHORNE

Ghosts of the dead and voices of the living
Bear witness to your guilt, and you must die!
It might have been an easier death. Your doom
Will be on your own head, and not on ours.
Twice more will you be questioned of these things;
Twice more have room to plead or to confess.
If you are contumacious to the Court,
And if, when questioned, you refuse to answer,
Then by the Statute you will be condemned
To the *peine forte et dure!* To have your body
Pressed by great weights until you shall be dead!
And may the Lord have mercy on your soul!

ACT V

SCENE I. — COREY'S *farm as in Act II., Scene I. Enter*
RICHARD GARDNER, *looking round him.*

GARDNER

Here stands the house as I remember it,
The four tall poplar-trees before the door;
The house, the barn, the orchard, and the well,
With its moss-covered bucket and its trough;
The garden, with its hedge of currant-bushes;
The woods, the harvest-fields; and, far beyond,

The pleasant landscape stretching to the sea.
But everything is silent and deserted!
No bleat of flocks, no bellowing of herds,
No sound of flails, that should be beating now;
Nor man nor beast astir. What can this mean?

Knocks at the door.

What ho! Giles Corey! Hillo-ho! Giles Corey! —
No answer but the echo from the barn,
And the ill-omened cawing of the crow,
That yonder wings his flight across the fields,
As if he scented carrion in the air.

(*Enter* TITUBA *with a basket*)

What woman's this, that, like an apparition,
Haunts this deserted homestead in broad day?
Woman, who are you?

TITUBA

I am Tituba.
I am John Indian's wife. I am a Witch.

GARDNER

What are you doing here?

TITUBA

I'm gathering herbs, —
Cinquefoil, and saxifrage, and pennyroyal.

GARDNER (*looking at the herbs*)

This is not cinquefoil, it is deadly night-shade!
This is not saxifrage, but hellebore!
This is not pennyroyal, it is henbane!
Do you come here to poison these good people?

TITUBA

I get these for the Doctor in the Village.
Beware of Tituba. I pinch the children;
Make little poppets and stick pins in them,
And then the children cry out they are pricked.
The Black Dog came to me, and said, "Serve me!"
I was afraid. He made me hurt the children.

GARDNER

Poor soul! She's crazed, with all these Devil's
    doings.

TITUBA

Will you, sir, sign the Book?

GARDNER

                No, I'll not sign it.
Where is Giles Corey? Do you know Giles Corey?

TITUBA

He's safe enough. He's down there in the prison.

GARDNER

Corey in prison? What is he accused of?

TITUBA

Giles Corey and Martha Corey are in prison
Down there in Salem Village. Both are Witches.
She came to me and whispered, "Kill the chil-
    dren!"
Both signed the Book!

CHRISTUS: A MYSTERY

GARDNER

Begone, you imp of darkness !
You Devil's dam !

TITUBA

Beware of Tituba !

Exit.

GARDNER

How often out at sea on stormy nights,
When the waves thundered round me, and the wind
Bellowed, and beat the canvas, and my ship
Clove through the solid darkness, like a wedge,
I 've thought of him, upon his pleasant farm,
Living in quiet with his thrifty housewife,
And envied him, and wished his fate were mine !
And now I find him shipwrecked utterly,
Drifting upon this sea of sorceries,
And lost, perhaps, beyond all aid of man !

Exit.

SCENE II. — *The prison.* GILES COREY *at a table on which
are some papers.*

COREY

Now I have done with earth and all its cares ;
I give my worldly goods to my dear children ;
My body I bequeath to my tormentors,
And my immortal soul to Him who made it.
O God ! who in thy wisdom dost afflict me
With an affliction greater than most men
Have ever yet endured or shall endure,

Suffer me not in this last bitter hour
For any pains of death to fall from thee!

MARTHA *is heard singing*

Arise, O righteous Lord!
And disappoint my foes;
They are but thine avenging sword,
Whose wounds are swift to close.

COREY

Hark, hark! it is her voice! She is not dead!
She lives! I am not utterly forsaken!

MARTHA (*singing*)

By thine abounding grace,
And mercies multiplied,
I shall awake, and see thy face;
I shall be satisfied.

COREY *hides his face in his hands. Enter the*
JAILER, *followed by* RICHARD GARDNER.

JAILER

Here's a seafaring man, one Richard Gardner,
A friend of yours, who asks to speak with you.
COREY *rises. They embrace.*

COREY

I'm glad to see you, ay, right glad to see you.

GARDNER

And I most sorely grieved to see you thus.

519

CHRISTUS: A MYSTERY

COREY

Of all the friends I had in happier days,
You are the first, ay, and the only one,
That comes to seek me out in my disgrace!
And you but come in time to say farewell.
They 've dug my grave already in the field.
I thank you. There is something in your presence,
I know not what it is, that gives me strength.
Perhaps it is the bearing of a man
Familiar with all dangers of the deep,
Familiar with the cries of drowning men,
With fire, and wreck, and foundering ships at sea!

GARDNER

Ah, I have never known a wreck like yours!
Would I could save you!

COREY

            Do not speak of that.
It is too late. I am resolved to die.

GARDNER

Why would you die who have so much to live
    for ? —
Your daughters, and —

COREY

          You cannot say the word.
My daughters have gone from me. They are mar-
    ried;
They have their homes, their thoughts, apart from
    me;

I will not say their hearts, — that were too cruel.
What would you have me do?

GARDNER

               Confess and live.

COREY

That's what they said who came here yesterday
To lay a heavy weight upon my conscience
By telling me that I was driven forth
As an unworthy member of their church.

GARDNER

It is an awful death.

COREY

          'T is but to drown,
And have the weight of all the seas upon you.

GARDNER

Say something; say enough to fend off death
Till this tornado of fanaticism
Blows itself out. Let me come in between you
And your severer self, with my plain sense;
Do not be obstinate.

COREY

          I will not plead.
If I deny, I am condemned already,
In courts where ghosts appear as witnesses,
And swear men's lives away. If I confess,
Then I confess a lie, to buy a life

Which is not life, but only death in life.
I will not bear false witness against any,
Not even against myself, whom I count least.

GARDNER (*aside*)

Ah, what a noble character is this!

COREY

I pray you, do not urge me to do that
You would not do yourself. I have already
The bitter taste of death upon my lips;
I feel the pressure of the heavy weight
That will crush out my life within this hour;
But if a word could save me, and that word
Were not the Truth; nay, if it did but swerve
A hair's-breadth from the Truth, I would not
  say it!

GARDNER (*aside*)

How mean I seem beside a man like this!

COREY

As for my wife, my Martha and my Mar-
  tyr, —
Whose virtues, like the stars, unseen by day,
Though numberless, do but await the dark
To manifest themselves unto all eyes, —
She who first won me from my evil ways,
And taught me how to live by her example,
By her example teaches me to die,
And leads me onward to the better life!

SHERIFF (*without*)

Giles Corey! Come! The hour has struck!

COREY

I come!

Here is my body ; ye may torture it,
But the immortal soul ye cannot crush!   *Exeunt.*

SCENE III. — *A street in the Village. Enter* GLOYD *and
others.*

GLOYD

Quick, or we shall be late!

A MAN

That 's not the way.
Come here ; come up this lane.

GLOYD

I wonder now
If the old man will die, and will not speak?
He 's obstinate enough and tough enough
For anything on earth.   *A bell tolls.*
Hark! What is that?

A MAN

The passing bell. He 's dead!

GLOYD

We are too late.
Exeunt in haste.

523

CHRISTUS: A MYSTERY

Scene IV. — *A field near the graveyard.* Giles Corey *lying dead, with a great stone on his breast. The Sheriff at his head,* Richard Gardner *at his feet. A crowd behind. The bell tolling. Enter* Hathorne *and* Mather.

HATHORNE

This is the Potter's Field. Behold the fate
Of those who deal in Witchcrafts, and, when questioned,
Refuse to plead their guilt or innocence,
And stubbornly drag death upon themselves.

MATHER

O sight most horrible! In a land like this,
Spangled with Churches Evangelical,
Inwrapped in our salvations, must we seek
In mouldering statute-books of English Courts
Some old forgotten Law, to do such deeds?
Those who lie buried in the Potter's Field
Will rise again, as surely as ourselves
That sleep in honored graves with epitaphs;
And this poor man, whom we have made a victim,
Hereafter will be counted as a martyr!

FINALE

SAINT JOHN

SAINT JOHN *wandering over the face of the Earth.*

SAINT JOHN

THE Ages come and go,
The Centuries pass as Years;
My hair is white as the snow,
My feet are weary and slow,
The earth is wet with my tears!
The kingdoms crumble, and fall
Apart, like a ruined wall,
Or a bank that is undermined
By a river's ceaseless flow,
And leave no trace behind!
The world itself is old;
The portals of Time unfold
On hinges of iron, that grate
And groan with the rust and the weight,
Like the hinges of a gate
That hath fallen to decay;
But the evil doth not cease;
There is war instead of peace,
Instead of Love there is hate;
And still I must wander and wait,
Still I must watch and pray,
Not forgetting in whose sight,

CHRISTUS: A MYSTERY

A thousand years in their flight
Are as a single day.

The life of man is a gleam
Of light, that comes and goes
Like the course of the Holy Stream,
The cityless river, that flows
From fountains no one knows,
Through the Lake of Galilee,
Through forests and level lands,
Over rocks, and shallows, and sands
Of a wilderness wild and vast,
Till it findeth its rest at last
In the desolate Dead Sea!
But alas! alas for me
Not yet this rest shall be!

What, then! doth Charity fail?
Is Faith of no avail?
Is Hope blown out like a light
By a gust of wind in the night?
The clashing of creeds, and the strife
Of the many beliefs, that in vain
Perplex man's heart and brain,
Are naught but the rustle of leaves,
When the breath of God upheaves
The boughs of the Tree of Life,
And they subside again!
And I remember still
The words, and from whom they came,
Not he that repeateth the name,
But he that doeth the will!

And Him evermore I behold
Walking in Galilee,
Through the cornfield's waving gold,
In hamlet, in wood, and in wold,
By the shores of the Beautiful Sea.
He toucheth the sightless eyes ;
Before him the demons flee ;
To the dead He sayeth : Arise !
To the living : Follow me !
And that voice still soundeth on
From the centuries that are gone,
To the centuries that shall be !

From all vain pomps and shows,
From the pride that overflows,
And the false conceits of men ;
From all the narrow rules
And subtleties of Schools,
And the craft of tongue and pen ;
Bewildered in its search,
Bewildered with the cry :
Lo, here ! lo, there, the Church !
Poor, sad Humanity
Through all the dust and heat
Turns back with bleeding feet,
By the weary road it came,
Unto the simple thought
By the great Master taught,
And that remaineth still :
Not he that repeateth the name,
But he that doeth the will !

NOTES

NOTES

Page 107. Simon Magus and Helen of Tyre.

[See the poem "Helen of Tyre," in the third volume of the poetical works in this edition, with its head-note.]

Page 114. *Blind Bartimeus at the gates.*

[Mr. Longfellow inserts here a poem which he had already published, and which will be found with head-note in the first volume of the poetical works, in this edition.]

Page 167. The Golden Legend.

The old "Legenda Aurea," or Golden Legend, was originally written in Latin, in the thirteenth century, by Jacobus de Voragine, a Dominican friar, who afterwards became Archbishop of Genoa, and died in 1292.

He called his book simply "Legends of the Saints." The epithet of Golden was given it by his admirers; for, as Wynkin de Worde says, "Like as passeth gold in value all other metals, so this Legend exceedeth all other books." But Edward Leigh, in much distress of mind, calls it "a book written by a man of a leaden heart for the basenesse of the errours, that are without wit or reason, and of a brazen forehead, for his impudent boldnesse in reporting things so fabulous and incredible."

This work, the great text-book of the legendary lore of the Middle Ages, was translated into French in the fourteenth century by Jean de Vignay, and in the fifteenth into English by William Caxton. It has lately been made more accessible by a new French translation: "La Légende Dorée, traduite du Latin." Par M. G. B. Paris, 1850. There is a copy of the original, with the "Gesta Longobardorum" appended, in the Harvard College Library, Cambridge, printed at Stras-

531

burg, 1496. The title-page is wanting; and the volume begins with the "Tabula Legendorum."

I have called this poem the "Golden Legend," because
the story upon which it is founded seems to me to surpass all
other legends in beauty and significance. It exhibits, amid
the corruptions of the Middle Ages, the virtue of disinterest-
edness and self-sacrifice, and the power of Faith, Hope, and
Charity, sufficient for all the exigencies of life and death. The
story is told, and perhaps invented, by Hartmann von der
Aue, a Minnesinger of the twelfth century. The original
may be found in Mailáth's "Altdeutsche Gedichte," with a
modern German version. There is another in Marbach's
"Volksbücher," No. 32.

[Mr. S. Arthur Bent has annotated "The Golden Legend" with fulness and care, and the reader is referred to his
volume for more extended notes than are here expedient. In
a few instances, his work is drawn upon below.]

Page 170.

> *For these bells have been anointed,*
> *And baptized with holy water!*

The consecration and baptism of bells is one of the most
curious ceremonies of the Church in the Middle Ages. The
Council of Cologne ordained as follows:

"Let the bells be blessed, as the trumpets of the Church
militant, by which the people are assembled to hear the word
of God; the clergy to announce his mercy by day, and his
truth in their nocturnal vigils: that by their sound the faithful may be invited to prayers, and that the spirit of devotion
in them may be increased. The fathers have also maintained
that demons, affrighted by the sound of bells calling Christians to prayers, would flee away; and when they fled, the
persons of the faithful would be secure : that the destruction
of lightnings and whirlwinds would be averted, and the spirits
of the storm defeated." — Edinburgh Encyclopædia, art.
"Bells."

NOTES

See also Scheible's "Kloster," vi. 776.

Page 177. *Which a kind of leprosy drinks and drains.*

[In Hartmann von der Aue's poem, Henry suffers from actual leprosy. Mr. Longfellow avoided the repulsiveness which this disease would have caused in the reader's mind, and used it suggestively.]

Page 185. *Is thy great Palingenesis.*

[See Mr. Longfellow's poem "Palingenesis," with its head-note, in the third volume of the poetical works in this edition.]

Page 197.

> *And had not seemed so long*
> *As a single hour.*

[Archbishop Trench rendered this legend in his poem "The Monk and the Bird."]

Page 202. EVENING SONG.

[Mr. Bent, in his annotated edition of "The Golden Legend," remarks that this is modelled upon the choral songs which the Reformed Church of Germany adapted from existing popular chorals, which had long been in use in the social and public observances of the German people.]

Page 207. *Who would think her but fifteen?*

[In "Der Arme Heinrich," Elsie is but eight years of age.]

Page 211. *It is the malediction of Eve!*

"Nec esses plus quam femina, quae nunc etiam viros transcendis, et quae maledictionem Evae in benedictionem vertisti Mariae." — Epistola Abaelardi Heloissae.

Page 240. *To come back to my text!*

In giving this sermon of Friar Cuthbert as a specimen of the *Risus Paschales*, or street preaching of the monks at Easter, I have exaggerated nothing. This very anecdote, offensive as it is, comes from a discourse of Father Barletta, a Dominican friar of the fifteenth century, whose fame as a popular preacher was so great that it gave rise to the proverb,

NOTES

Nescit predicare
Qui nescit Barlettare.

" Among the abuses introduced in this century," says Tiraboschi, " was that of exciting from the pulpit the laughter of the hearers ; as if that were the same thing as converting them. We have examples of this, not only in Italy, but also in France, where the sermons of Menot and Maillard, and of others, who would make a better appearance on the stage than in the pulpit, are still celebrated for such follies."

If the reader is curious to see how far the freedom of speech was carried in these popular sermons, he is referred to Scheible's " Kloster," vol. i., where he will find extracts from Abraham a Sancta Clara, Sebastian Frank, and others ; and in particular an anonymous discourse called " Der Gräue der Verwüstung," The Abomination of Desolation, preached at Ottakring, a village west of Vienna, November 25, 1782, in which the license of language is carried to its utmost limit.

See also " Prédicatoriana, ou Révélations singulières et amusantes sur les Prédicateurs; " par G. P. Philomneste. (Menin.) This work contains extracts from the popular sermons of St. Vincent, Ferrier, Barletta, Menot, Maillard, Marini, Raulin, Valladier, De Besse, Camus, Père André, Bening, and the most eloquent of all, Jacques Brydaine.

My authority for the spiritual interpretation of bell-ringing, which follows, is Durandus, Ration. Divin. Offic., lib. i. cap. 4.

Page 245. THE NATIVITY: a Miracle-Play.

A singular chapter in the history of the Middle Ages is that which gives account of the early Christian Drama, the Mysteries, Moralities, and Miracle-Plays, which were at first performed in churches, and afterwards in the streets, on fixed or movable stages. For the most part, the Mysteries were founded on the historic portions of the Old and New Testaments, and the Miracle-Plays on the lives of saints; a distinction not always observed, however, for in Mr. Wright's " Early Mysteries and other Latin Poems of the Twelfth and Thirteenth Centuries," the Resurrection of Lazarus is called a Miracle, and not a Mystery. The Moralities were plays in which the Virtues and Vices were personified.

The earliest religious play which has been preserved is the "Christos Paschon" of Gregory Nazianzen, written in Greek, in the fourth century. Next to this come the remarkable Latin plays of Roswitha, the Nun of Gandersheim, in the tenth century, which, though crude and wanting in artistic construction, are marked by a good deal of dramatic power and interest. A handsome edition of these plays, with a French translation, has been lately published, entitled "Théâtre de Rotsvitha, Religieuse allemande du Xe Siècle." Par Charles Magnin. Paris, 1845.

The most important collections of English Mysteries and Miracle-Plays are those known as the Townley, the Chester, and the Coventry Plays. The first of these collections has been published by the Surtees Society, and the other two by the Shakespeare Society. In his Introduction to the Coventry Mysteries, the editor, Mr. Halliwell, quotes the following passage from Dugdale's "Antiquities of Warwickshire:"

" Before the suppression of the monasteries, this city was very famous for the pageants, that were played therein, upon Corpus-Christi day; which, occasioning very great confluence of people thither, from far and near, was of no small benefit thereto; which pageants being acted with mighty state and reverence by the friars of this house, had theaters for the severall scenes, very large and high, placed upon wheels, and drawn to all the eminent parts of the city, for the better advantage of spectators : and contain'd the story of the New Testament, composed into old English Rithme, as appeareth by an ancient MS. intituled *Ludus Corporis Christi*, or *Ludus*

Conventriae. I have been told by some old people, who in their younger years were eyewitnesses of these pageants so acted, that the yearly confluence of people to see that shew was extraordinary great, and yielded no small advantage to this city.''

The representation of religious plays has not yet been wholly discontinued by the Roman Church. At Ober-Ammergau, in the Tyrol, a grand spectacle of this kind is exhibited once in ten years. A very graphic description of that which took place in the year 1850 is given by Miss Anna Mary Howitt, in her " Art-Student in Munich,'' vol. i. chap. 4. She says :

" We had come expecting to feel our souls revolt at so material a representation of Christ, as any representation of him we naturally imagined must be in a peasant's Miracle-Play. Yet so far, strange to confess, neither horror, disgust, nor contempt was excited in our minds. Such an earnest solemnity and simplicity breathed throughout the whole of the performance, that to me, at least, anything like anger, or a perception of the ludicrous, would have seemed more irreverent on my part than was this simple, childlike rendering of the sublime Christian tragedy. We felt at times as though the figures of Cimabue's, Giotto's, and Perugino's pictures had become animated, and were moving before us ; there was the same simple arrangement and brilliant color of drapery, — the same earnest, quiet dignity about the heads, whilst the entire absence of all theatrical effect wonderfully increased the illusion. There were scenes and groups so extraordinarily like the early Italian pictures, that you could have declared they were the works of Giotto and Perugino, and not living men and women, had not the figures moved and spoken, and the breeze stirred their richly colored drapery, and the sun cast long, moving shadows behind them on the stage. These effects of sunshine and shadow, and of drapery fluttered by the wind, were very striking and beautiful ; one could im-

agine how the Greeks must have availed themselves of such
striking effects in their theatres open to the sky.''

Mr. Bayard Taylor, in his "Eldorado," gives a description of a Mystery he saw performed at San Lionel, in Mex-
ico. See vol. ii. chap. 11.

"Against the wing-wall of the Hacienda del Mayo,
which occupied one end of the plaza, was raised a platform,
on which stood a table covered with scarlet cloth. A rude
bower of cane-leaves on one end of the platform represented
the manger of Bethlehem ; while a cord, stretched from its
top across the plaza to a hole in the front of the church, bore
a large tinsel star, suspended by a hole in its centre. There
was quite a crowd in the plaza, and very soon a procession
appeared, coming up from the lower part of the village. The
three kings took the lead; the Virgin, mounted on an ass
that gloried in a gilded saddle and rose-besprinkled mane and
tail, followed them, led by the angel; and several women,
with curious masks of paper, brought up the rear. Two characters of the Harlequin sort — one with a dog's head on his
shoulders, and the other a bald-headed friar, with a huge hat
hanging on his back — played all sorts of antics for the diver-
sion of the crowd. After making the circuit of the plaza, the
Virgin was taken to the platform, and entered the manger.
King Herod took his seat at the scarlet table, with an attendant in blue coat and red sash, whom I took to be his Prime
Minister. The three kings remained on their horses in front
of the church; but between them and the platform, under
the string on which the star was to slide, walked two men in
long white robes and blue hoods, with parchment folios in
their hands. These were the Wise Men of the East, as one
might readily know from their solemn air and the mysterious
glances which they cast towards all quarters of the heavens.

"In a little while, a company of women on the platform,
concealed behind a curtain, sang an angelic chorus to the
tune of ' O pescator dell' onda.' At the proper moment, the

Magi turned towards the platform, followed by the star, to which a string was conveniently attached, that it might be slid along the line. The three kings followed the star till it reached the manger, when they dismounted, and inquired for the sovereign whom it had led them to visit. They were invited upon the platform, and introduced to Herod, as the only king ; this did not seem to satisfy them, and, after some conversation, they retired. By this time the star had receded to the other end of the line, and commenced moving forward again, they following. The angel called them into the manger, where, upon their knees, they were shown a small wooden box, supposed to contain the sacred infant ; they then retired, and the star brought them back no more. After this departure, King Herod declared himself greatly confused by what he had witnessed, and was very much afraid this newly found king would weaken his power. Upon consultation with his Prime Minister, the Massacre of the Innocents was decided upon, as the only means of security.

" The angel, on hearing this, gave warning to the Virgin, who quickly got down from the platform, mounted her bespangled donkey, and hurried off. Herod's Prime Minister directed all the children to be handed up for execution. A boy, in a ragged sarape, was caught and thrust forward ; the Minister took him by the heels in spite of his kicking, and held his head on the table. The little brother and sister of the boy, thinking he was really to be decapitated, yelled at the top of their voices, in an agony of terror, which threw the crowd into a roar of laughter. King Herod brought down his sword with a whack on the table, and the Prime Minister, dipping his brush into a pot of white paint which stood before him, made a flaring cross on the boy's face. Several other boys were caught and served likewise ; and finally the two harlequins, whose kicks and struggles nearly shook down the platform. The procession then went off up the hill, followed by the whole population of the village.

All the evening there were fandangoes in the méson, bonfires and rockets on the plaza, ringing of bells, and high mass in the church, with the accompaniment of two guitars, tinkling to lively polkas.''

In 1852 there was a representation of this kind by Germans in Boston: and I have now before me the copy of a play-bill, announcing the performance, on June 10, 1852, in Cincinnati, of the " Great Biblico-Historical Drama, the Life of Jesus Christ," with the characters and the names of the performers.

Page 247. *Here the Angel Gabriel shall leave Paradise.*

[A stage of three stories was often erected, the topmost representing Paradise (hence in Germany this word is used for the upper gallery of a theatre, *anglicè*, " the Gods ") ; on the middle stage was the Earth ; below were the " Jaws of Hell," sometimes represented by the opening and shutting of the mouth of an enormous dragon. Goethe introduces the Jaws of Hell into the stage machinery of " Faust " (V. 6). — S. A. Bent.]

Page 266. *The Convent cellar.*

[One of the most important officials of a convent, under the abbot, called *obedientiarii*, was the cellarer, who was the steward of the house. He had the care of everything relating to the provision of the food and vessels of the convent, was exempt from the observance of some of the services in church, had the use of horses and servants for the performance of his duties, and sometimes separate apartments. — S. A. Bent.]

Page 268. *The old rhyme keeps running in my brain.*

[This first appeared in the " Musikalische Kurzweil," of Nuremberg, 1623:

Zu Klingenberg am Main,
Zu Würzburg an dem Stein,
Zu Bacharach am Rhein,
Hab' ich in meinen Tagen

539

NOTES

Gar oftmals hören sagen,
Soll'n sein die besten Wein'.

S. A. Bent.]

Page 271. The Scriptorium.

A most interesting volume might be written on the Calligraphers and Chrysographers, the transcribers and illuminators of manuscripts in the Middle Ages. These men were for the most part monks, who labored, sometimes for pleasure and sometimes for penance, in multiplying copies of the classics and the Scriptures.

" Of all bodily labors which are proper for us," says Cassiodorus, the old Calabrian monk, "that of copying books has always been more to my taste than any other. The more so, as in this exercise the mind is instructed by the reading of the Holy Scriptures, and it is a kind of homily to the others, whom these books may reach. It is preaching with the hand, by converting the fingers into tongues ; it is publishing to men in silence the words of salvation ; in fine, it is fighting against the demon with pen and ink. As many words as a transcriber writes, so many wounds the demon receives. In a word, a recluse, seated in his chair to copy books, travels into different provinces without moving from the spot, and the labor of his hands is felt even where he is not."

Nearly every monastery was provided with its Scriptorium. Nicolas de Clairvaux, St. Bernard's secretary, in one of his letters describes his cell, which he calls Scriptoriolum, where he copied books. And Mabillon, in his "Etudes Monastiques," says that in his time were still to be seen at Citeaux "many of those little cells, where the transcribers and bookbinders worked."

Silvestre's "Paléographie Universelle" contains a vast number of fac-similes of the most beautiful illuminated manuscripts of all ages and all countries ; and Montfaucon, in his "Palaeographia Graeca," gives the names of over three hundred calligraphers. He also gives an account of the books they copied, and the colophons with which, as with a satisfactory flourish of the pen, they closed their long-continued labors. Many of these are very curious ; expressing joy, humility, remorse ; entreating the reader's prayers and pardon for the writer's sins ; and sometimes pronouncing a malediction on any one who should steal the book. A few of these I subjoin :

" As pilgrims rejoice, beholding their native land, so are transcribers made glad, beholding the end of a book."

" Sweet is it to write the end of any book."

" Ye who read, pray for me, who have written this book, the humble and sinful Theodulus."

" As many therefore as shall read this book, pardon me, I beseech you, if aught I have erred in accent acute and grave, in apostrophe, in breathing soft or aspirate ; and may God save you all ! Amen."

" If anything is well, praise the transcriber ; if ill, pardon his unskilfulness."

" Ye who read, pray for me, the most sinful of all men, for the Lord's sake."

" The hand that has written this book shall decay, alas ! and become dust, and go down to the grave, the corrupter of all bodies. But all ye who are of the portion of Christ, pray that I may obtain the pardon of my sins. Again and again I beseech you with tears, brothers and fathers, accept my miserable supplication, O holy choir ! I am called John, woe is me ! I am called Hiereus, or Sacerdos, in name only, not in unction."

" Whoever shall carry away this book, without permission of the Pope, may he incur the malediction of the Holy Trinity, of the Holy Mother of God, of Saint John the Baptist, of the one hundred and eighteen holy Nicene Fathers, and of all the Saints ; the fate of Sodom and Gomorrah ; and the halter of Judas ! Anathema, amen."

NOTES

"Keep safe, O Trinity, Father, Son, and Holy Ghost, my three fingers, with which I have written this book."

"Mathusalas Machir transcribed this divinest book in toil, infirmity, and dangers many."

"Bacchius Barbardorius and Michael Sophianus wrote this book in sport and laughter, being the guests of their noble and common friend Vincentius Pinellus, and Petrus Nunnius, a most learned man."

This last colophon Montfaucon does not suffer to pass without reproof. "Other calligraphers," he remarks, "demand only the prayers of their readers, and the pardon of their sins ; but these glory in their wantonness."

Page 283. FRIAR CUTHBERT.

[In the first edition there is a variation in this scene, which is best shown by a full reproduction, as follows : —

FRIAR CUTHBERT

None of your pale-faced girls for me !

Kisses the girl at his side.

FRIAR JOHN

Come, old fellow, drink down to your peg !
But do not drink any farther, I beg !

FRIAR PAUL (*sings*)

In the days of gold,
The days of old,
Cross of wood
And bishop of gold !

FRIAR CUTHBERT (*to the girl*)

What an infernal racket and din !
You need not blush so, that's no sin.
You look very holy in this disguise,
Though there's something wicked in your eyes !

FRIAR PAUL (*continues*)

Now we have changed
That law so good,

To cross of gold
And bishop of wood !

FRIAR CUTHBERT

I like your sweet face under a hood.
Sinner ! how came you into this way ?

GIRL

It was you, Friar Cuthbert, who led me astray.
Have you forgotten that day in June,
When the church was so cool in the afternoon,
And I came in to confess my sins ?
That is where my ruin begins.

FRIAR JOHN

What is the name of yonder friar,
With an eye that glows like a coal of fire,
And such a black mass of tangled hair ?

The scene then continues as in the text until near the close, when there is another slight variation, as follows :

THE MONKS (*in confusion*)

The Abbot ! the Abbot !

FRIAR CUTHBERT (*to the girl*)

Put on your disguise !

FRIAR FRANCIS

Hide the great flagon
From the eyes of the dragon !

FRIAR CUTHBERT

Pull the brown hood over your face,
Lest you bring me into disgrace !]

Page 283. *Drink down to your peg !*
One of the canons of Archbishop Anselm, promulgated at the beginning of the twelfth century, ordains " that priests go not to drinking-bouts, nor drink to pegs." In the times of the hard-drinking Danes, King Edgar ordained that " pins or

nails should be fastened into the drinking-cups or horns at stated distances, and whosoever should drink beyond those marks at one draught should be obnoxious to a severe punishment.''

Sharpe, in his '' History of the Kings of England,'' says: '' Our ancestors were formerly famous for compotation ; their liquor was ale, and one method of amusing themselves in this way was with the peg-tankard. I had lately one of them in my hand. It had on the inside a row of eight pins, one above another, from top to bottom. It held two quarts, and was a noble piece of plate, so that there was a gill of ale, half a pint Wincester measure, between each peg. The law was, that every person that drank was to empty the space between pin and pin, so that the pins were so many measures to make the company all drink alike, and to swallow the same quantity of liquor. This was a pretty sure method of making all the company drunk, especially if it be considered that the rule was, that whoever drank short of his pin, or beyond it, was obliged to drink again, and even as deep as to the next pin.''

Page 285. *The convent of St. Gildas de Rhuys.*

Abelard, in a letter to his friend Philintus, gives a sad picture of this monastery. '' I live,'' he says, '' in a barbarous country, the language of which I do not understand ; I have no conversation but with the rudest people. my walks are on the inaccessible shore of a sea, which is perpetually stormy. my monks are only known by their dissoluteness, and living without any rule or order. could you see the abby, Philintus, you would not call it one. the doors and walls are without any ornament, except the heads of wild boars and hinds feet, which are nailed up against them, and the hides of frightful animals. the cells are hung with the skins of deer. the monks have not so much as a bell to wake them, the cocks and dogs supply that defect. in short, they pass their whole days in hunting ; would to heaven that were their greatest fault! or that their pleasure terminated there! I endeavor in vain to recall them to their duty; they all combine against me, and I only expose myself to continued vexations and dangers. I imagine I see every moment a naked sword hang over my head. sometimes they surround me, and load me with infinite abuses ; sometimes they abandon me, and I am left alone to my own tormenting thoughts. I make it my endeavor to merit by my sufferings, and to appease an angry God. sometimes I grieve for the loss of the house of the Paraclete, and wish to see it again. ah Philintus, does not the love of Heloise still burn in my heart ? I have not yet triumphed over that unhappy passion. in the midst of my retirement I sigh, I weep, I pine, I speak the dear name Heloise, and am pleased to hear the sound." — " Letters of the Celebrated Abelard and Heloise." Translated by Mr. John Hughes. Glasgow, 1751.

Page 313. *Were it not for my magic garters and staff.*

The method of making the Magic Garters and the Magic Staff is thus laid down in " Les Secrets Merveilleux du Petit Albert," a French translation of " Alberti Parvi Lucii Libellus de Mirabilibus Naturae Arcanis " :

" Gather some of the herb called motherwort, when the sun is entering the first degree of the sign of Capricorn ; let it dry a little in the shade, and make some garters of the skin of a young hare ; that is to say, having cut the skin of the hare into strips two inches wide, double them, sew the before-mentioned herb between, and wear them on your legs. No horse can long keep up with a man on foot, who is furnished with these garters." (Page 128.)

" Gather, on the morrow of All-Saints, a strong branch of willow, of which you will make a staff, fashioned to your liking. Hollow it out, by removing the pith from within, after having furnished the lower end with an iron ferule. Put into the bottom of the staff the two eyes of a young wolf, the tongue and heart of a dog, three green lizards, and the hearts of three swallows. These must all be dried in the sun, between two papers, having been first sprinkled with finely pulverized saltpetre. Besides all these, put into the staff seven leaves of vervain, gathered on the eve of St. John the Baptist, with a stone of divers colors, which you will find in the nest of the lapwing, and stop the end of the staff with a pomel of box, or of any other material you please, and be assured that this staff will guarantee you from the perils and mishaps which too often befall travellers, either from robbers, wild beasts, mad dogs, or venomous animals. It will also procure you the good-will of those with whom you lodge." (Page 130.)

Page 321. *Saint Elmo's stars.*

So the Italian sailors call the phosphorescent gleams that sometimes play about the masts and rigging of ships.

Page 322. THE SCHOOL OF SALERNO.

For a history of the celebrated schools of Salerno and Monte-Cassino, the reader is referred to Sir Alexander Croke's Introduction to the " Regimen Sanitatis Salernitanum ; " and to Kurt Sprengel's " Geschichte der Arzneikunde," i. 463, or Jourdan's French translation of it, " Histoire de la Médecine," ii. 354.

Page 329. *On the horns of the Dumb Ox of Cologne.*

["The dumb ox of Cologne " was Thomas Aquinas, who was called by his companions in the Monastery of Cologne "the dumb Sicilian Ox." See Robertson's " Church History," bk. vii. ch. 8.]

Page 471. *He must spell Baker.*

A local expression for doing anything difficult. In the old spelling-books, baker was the first word of two syllables, and when a child came to it he thought he had a hard task before him.

www.ingramcontent.com/pod-product-compliance
Lightning Source LLC
Chambersburg PA
CBHW032254020726
47495CB00001B/100